OCCULTIST

SAGA ONLINE

OLIVER MAYES

CONTENTS

With deepest thanks (and sympathy) to the Portal Books Team, without whom this would not have been possible.

This book is dedicated to my English Teacher, Mr. Lowry, who predicted it would be written one day. I'm not sure if this is what you were expecting, but I hope you enjoy it all the same.

1

CHARACTER BUILDING

Damien withdrew from the once cultist infested cave, only to find his fate was sealed. Through a gap in the trees he could see the sun lazily blending with the peaks of the far distant mountains. If he failed to warn Concoret before darkness fell, the consequences would be dire.

He shouldered his pack and set off into the forest at a run, the dull thud of his plated boots punctuating the otherwise eerie calm. He had completed his quest, locating one of the many cultist hideouts in the region and culling their numbers, only to discover a missive among the effects of the fallen: orders from their dark master to infiltrate the nearby town from within and harvest the souls of the innocent while they slept.

The orders would be carried out that very evening.

Damien picked up the pace still further, his breathing quickening to match his step. If this were the sum total of his problems, he might be able to handle it. Unfortunately, he'd agreed with his mom that he was going to complete his assignments before he started playing Saga Online, and she was expecting him at dinner in fifteen minutes.

While it would be terrible if Concoret fell to cultists, it would be far worse if his mother came in to find him, on his bed, wearing nothing but the VR headset and a pair of underpants. If she got to him before he could get to Concoret, she was going to be absolutely furious.

Damien slowed down just a little as he opened his stat window to inspect the day's progress.

Account Name: Damien Arkwright
Character: Scorpius
Class: Warrior
Level: 28
Health: 854/1200
Stamina: 536/950
Stats:
Strength 116 - Agility 72 - Intelligence 37
Constitution 120 - Endurance 95 - Wisdom 37
Stat Points: 5
Experience: 1893/29000

He'd leveled up during combat, granting him five new stat points. He resisted the urge to put them into agility for the minor speed boost and dropped them into strength instead, where they'd be more useful. His stats defined everything Damien could or could not do in Saga Online, so he needed to take their allocation seriously.

It was certainly a more interesting set of criteria to judge him by than his Central Union footprint: male, Caucasian, sixteen, only child, single-parent custody, Online Tuition Bracket B, Household Income Threshold D, Health Insurance Policy D. Getting into Tuition Bracket B had been hard work, but the rest of it said very little about Damien at all. Rather, it was all focused on the circumstances of his birth. He much preferred his character's stat sheet to his own, not least of all because he had some say in what it looked like. While he couldn't customize his own settings, at least he could control how his character would grow.

Damien was no stranger to character building. He knew a character building exercise would quickly turn into a character destroying one if you didn't choose carefully. So, he was all too aware that in failing to complete his assignments, he had not chosen well.

Damien closed the Stat window and willed himself to run faster. That last quest had taken far longer than it had any right to. The cultists were practitioners of dark magic, but they hadn't been the real problem. With nothing but cloth vestments to protect them and very poor physical stats, they barely got halfway through casting before Damien employed his own special brand of magic – sticking his sword through their windpipe. Perma-silenced. No, the cultists had been easy. The problem was what they'd summoned.

Damien hoped never to see another imp again. In all his years of gaming he had never encountered such an absurdly unpredictable enemy.

Knee-high, ferocious and single-minded, imps were the personification of anger following an extensive lobotomy. When under cultist control, they behaved more or less the way you'd expect; clawing and biting, leaping and snarling. Unfortunately, when Damien killed their masters it was as if a cruel, mentally disturbed god had rolled a million-sided die to decide what they'd do next.

One of them had swiped Damien's torch, set itself on fire and clung onto his leg like a limpet, digging its claws in and screaming unintelligibly until it expired. That had caused significant damage, both to him and his equipped gear, as well as forcing him back to the dungeon entrance to find a new torch. Another had fled into the cave, where it maliciously leapt out from every other rock to kick Damien in the shin.

Oddly enough, the least time-consuming of these diversions had also been the worst by some margin; a particularly tenacious imp had clawed its way onto the ceiling and attempted to... relieve itself on him. In that moment, when something had plopped in front of Damien's feet and prompted him to cast his eyes upward, any doubts he'd had about the realism of Saga Online were totally eradicated.

Damien shuddered at the memory. Probably served him right for lying about his age. Blurred out or not, imp ass was not what he'd hoped for when he declared he was eighteen or over. On the plus side, the stunt had backfired spectacularly when the shin-kicking imp slipped in the mess.

Thanks to the imp resistance, the quest had taken an entire hour – a good twenty minutes longer than Damien had budgeted for. Then, just when he thought it was over, Saga Online had thrown this timed event at him.

Damien groaned as he ran, considering his options. Stop his own mother from being a bit mad in real life, or prevent several hundred from being murdered in virtual reality? Somehow, he didn't think explaining the situation would end favorably.

"Sorry, Mom, I know I said this wouldn't happen again but it was really important because I needed to save a bunch of make-believe people's lives and if I hadn't finished I'd have been nearly pooped on by an imp for nothing."

No, that would probably cause more problems than solutions.

He glanced at the clock in the corner of his HUD, confirming that time was still going in one direction and it wasn't the one he wanted.

Suddenly, he stopped running, coming to a halt just before a clearing. This was stupid. He wasn't going to make it, he may as well log off and try to fix it after dinner.

Besides, he thought with a grimace, *it's a virtual town but a very real mother*. He sighed and brought up the in-game menu. It over-laid his vision in transparent blue, the only hint of advanced technology in the game's otherwise rigorously fantasy setting. Concoret would still be there when he got back. Probably.

His anxiety waning, Damien flicked through the menu options, his Neural Overlay Optics Booster headset reading his in-game movements and intentions in equal parts to create the desired effect. He was heading for the logout button when the menu suddenly went out of focus and a window popped up over it:

Voice Chat Invitation: Mobius46, Gamer ID 000046, A/D

Damien screamed internally. It was his handler from Mobius Enterprises. He glanced urgently at the time and decided he had just enough left to take this call. Then he would DEFINITELY log off. He gave a curt nod and heard a ping. They were now connected.

"Heeeeeeeeey! What's going, what's going on, errr," Damien heard papers rustling on the other end, "Damien! Yeah, how are ya, buddy?"

Damien briefly considered providing constructive feedback about his imp experience but decided against it. He could give a more detailed report later.

"I'm doing fine thanks, Kevin, how ab—"

"Greeaaaaaaat, great, that's great. Um, listen, how would you like to run against a mob we need to beta test? You'll be the first person to fight it, ever! Isn't that cool? I'm uploading the file to you now."

Damien resisted the urge to drop the call and log out. This was a much more serious issue than his quest; he could not afford to upset this guy. It was only thanks to Kevin that he could play the game at all.

Kevin had been assigned to him a month ago, when Damien had signed up for beta testing Saga Online. Sure, it was on a private server with no other players and he could only play two zones, but that was still a lot of content. Kevin had set him up with the game, even going so far as to provide him with an aptly named NOOB headset when he heard Damien didn't have one.

It was low-end tech compared to the rest of the stuff Mobius Enterprises was putting out, but still far beyond the means of a family with a Household Income Threshold D rating. The headset was the most advanced piece of gaming equipment Damien had ever owned, quite possibly the most advanced gaming equipment he would ever own. In exchange for such luxuries, Damien was required to test elements of upcoming game content.

As stressed out as Damien was, he had to admit that Kevin deserved his respect. Even if he couldn't remember Damien's name.

"I'm really sorry, Kevin, but my mom's waiting for me, I ha—"

"No... Nonono! Please, don't do this to me!"

Damien faltered. He'd never heard Kevin so upset. His breathing had become labored and it sounded like he was having a panic attack.

"Kevin? What's going on?"

Kevin heaved in a deep breath before expelling it in a garbled wave of hysteria.

"All right, all right, I'm sorry, I haven't been totally straight with you, I've got a live company broadcast at six thirty, and I had a guy, a streamer, who said he was going to do it for me - but he bailed out just a few minutes ago. There are loads of people coming to watch the channel and I've got no one to fill the gap. You two are the only contacts I have left online right now, Damien; if you don't help me, I'm screwed. All the advertising, the preparation, the work I've done on this mob – it'll all be wasted. They'll take it out of my hands and give it to someone else. I'll be passed over, I'll never get high profile projects again. Please!"

Damien froze, catching sight of the clock in his peripheral vision. 18:27. Not that it mattered; if the broadcast started at 18:30 then helping Kevin would make him late to dinner either way.

"I've got to check with my mom. I'll log off and come back before—"

"There's no time, Damien. I have to start uploading the data to your headset now and I need you online. Please stay!"

Damien glanced at the clock again - 18:28. This man had given him the opportunity to test a game beyond his wildest dreams. Now he was relying on Damien for his career. Oh, boy. He didn't know who was going to regret this more.

"OK. Talk me through it, Kevin."

He heard the clacking of keys over his headset and moments later, a download icon appeared in the menu:

File received: spin2win.

Download? Yes/No

Damien focused on the choice box and nodded, prompting a download icon to appear in the top right corner. A terabyte in three minutes.

User Mobius46 would like to teleport you to 'Test Zone'.
Do you accept? Yes/No

With a single nod of his head, the game world disappeared around him and a loading animation appeared. Seconds later, Damien was dropped onto his feet. Without time to brace himself for a landing he collapsed onto his backside. Off to a good start, then.

Cursing under his breath, he stood and took in his surroundings. He was in the center of an enormous underground arena, lit by a multitude of glowing white orbs floating lazily across the enclosed space. Densely packed golden sand underfoot would provide sure footing, but Damien could not see any exits. The most striking features the arena held were four vast stone columns, each the width of several men, that stretched to the ceiling high overhead.

Kevin interrupted his analysis. "I've got you on-screen, Damien. We're live in one minute. Are you ready?"

Damien opened his menu and checked the download progress. Two minutes to go.

"The download isn't ready yet."

"Relax, I'll introduce you first and then we'll get started. Once the download is complete, all you have to do is activate it from your menu and the mob will appear."

Damien gritted his teeth. He thought he'd made it clear they didn't have time to waste.

"You better make it fast. When I don't show up for dinner my mom will cut the power."

Kevin sputtered as Damien's problem suddenly and forcefully became his. "But—but she can't do that. You're supposed to ease yourself out. Turning the software off while it's still running could cause negative side effe—"

"Why are you telling me? I told you I needed to check with her before we started. Now you know why."

Damien wandered over to one of the columns and removed his bag, dropping it carelessly on the floor. He set his back to the column and folded his arms.

"Just set it all up and hope for the best. We've got a few minutes, tops."

Kevin let out a mournful wail. Damien couldn't see him, but he envisaged copious amounts of hand-wringing.

"The feed is supposed to last for half an hour!"

Damien shrugged. There was nothing he could do about that.

"Better get on with it, then."

There was a long pause on the other end of the line.

"Okay, I have an idea. I think…." There was more paper rustling. "Yeah, I think we can make it work. I'm sending you the live feed request now. This is the one that allows everyone to watch what you're doing. They'll see everything through your eyes, so behave yourself!"

A new window appeared on Damien's screen, considerably longer than those that had preceded it. It was a terms and conditions package.

"It's an agreement to do a live stream. Just scroll to the bottom and accept. Nobody reads these things, anyway… and don't tell anyone I said that."

Suppressing a laugh, Damien flicked through several pages before he came to the familiar Accept/Decline box at the end. With a nod, the window disappeared. It was promptly replaced with a chat box.

Kevin let out a long sigh of relief. "Well done, Damien, we're just in time."

The clock ticked over to 18:30 and the chat box suddenly came alive with activity:

TwinkyWinky2047: first!
CactusLover: Hi!

Vargus: wuttup noobs
Naughtylus: second!
Robodozer: first!
Robodozer: oh gaddammit lol
OccumsAxe: lol fail
Enlsdkfislde: Hey guys come watch <u>Sagarama</u> every day at 8pm
EvilAye: Piss off bot
Showtaymuuuu: third!

As more users poured into the chat box, the messages came and went so fast Damien didn't even have time to read one before the next swept in, a stream of useless information that would never be read. In the span of a few seconds, three thousand five hundred and sixty-two people had joined the channel, and it was still rising. Damien was stunned. This was not what he had been expecting.

"Good evening," announced Kevin in a voice that suddenly brimmed with confidence, "and welcome to today's episode of 'The Saga Continues'."

Damien's jaw dropped. He loved that show. This show. *Oh my god*, he thought, hands dropping to his sides, *I'm the highlight of the official Saga Online channel. They're all watching me. Oh, crap.*

"Today we are joined by Damien, AKA Scorpius, a beta tester who has been playing the warrior class on a private test server of Saga Online for a month. Give everyone a wave, Damien. You're live on camera!"

Damien nervously raised a hand before pausing. If it was the same as the episodes he'd seen, they were watching from his perspective. He turned his hand around and waved at himself awkwardly. There was a flurry of activity in the chat box that Damien couldn't follow, although he did catch a few 'hi's and a smattering of 'wuttup noobs'.

"Scorpius has joined us at extremely short notice today to fill in for Aetherius, who decided to pull out at the last minute."

As the chat expressed its dissatisfaction with this turn of events, Damien's shock intensified.

I'm filling in for Aetherius? He's top of the leaderboard in the Streamer Competition!

The Streamer Competition encouraged players to record their gameplay and upload it to their Saga Online profile pages to garner votes from fans. The winner would get 100,000 real-world credits.

A sudden thought interrupted his moment of glory. *Wait, if this was originally tuned for Aetherius then what the hell am I going to be fighting?*

"Today, Damien fights a new boss monster that will eventually be introduced to the core game."

Oh, crap.

"Now, in all honesty, Aetherius would have struggled against this thing."

Nonononononononononono—

"In fact, after a brief description of what he would be fighting, Aetherius was so scared he decided to pull out of the show. I guess when you have a reputation to uphold, you don't fight enemies you're not sure you can beat."

If Saga Online enabled wetting yourself as a method of communication, Damien would have communicated liberally. As things were, he remained silent.

"I didn't invite Damien here today in the hopes that he would win. I only hoped he would have the courage to put on a show. Even when," Kevin cleared his throat, "even *if* he fails, he'll be making gaming history."

Kevin's tone changed to one of sincerity as he addressed Damien directly.

"Damien, I'm sorry I didn't have more time to prepare you for this. You probably can't beat this monster, but somebody has to fight him so we can see him in action and you're the only one we've got. I was worried that if I told you earlier, you'd say no, and I'd have to let down all our viewers. Please, Damien, will you do this for me? For everyone? I'll owe you, big time."

Damien's mind was reeling. Being on this show was a dream come true, but he wasn't ready. Never mind that he was low level and knew next to nothing about his opponent, the power to his unit might be cut at any moment. With so many variables at play, he couldn't focus. In the brief seconds following Kevin's plea, the viewers had swamped the chat with pleas of their own, encouragement and... well, there's always going to be a 'that guy':

5ubzer0: You can do it Damien, stab his freaking eyes out!
BootyliciousBarb: Go on Damien, for the warriors!
Naughtylus: A NEW CHALLENGER APPROACHES!
CactusLover: I shaved my balls for this x_x
Polymorpheus: lol, Aetherius noob, Damien op, get it dun son
Vargus: lol he gonna die... 'opens popcorn'... dis gonna be gud

Damien opened his menu and scrolled to his newly acquired downloads tab. The spin2win file sat there. It was like staring down the barrel of a gun. A quick glance at the header of the chat box informed him that over ten thousand people were now waiting to see what he would do.

The pressure was enormous, but Damien was committed. He had already agreed to help Kevin before being told there was no chance of winning. The only reason to back out now would be because he was afraid. He pondered, briefly, whether that was a good enough reason to leave Kevin hanging. The answer couldn't have been clearer. With a focused glance and a nod, spin2win was activated. A low rumble started under his feet as the chat box squealed in delight.

Kevin's voice cut through the vibration. "I knew you wouldn't let me down! Okay, you keep him busy, I'm going to buy us some time."

The low rumble had become a deafening roar and the entire arena shook as if in the throes of an earthquake. Damien staggered and threw his hands out for balance, trying his hardest not to fall over. He bent his knees and drew his sword, glancing around nervously. Where was the enemy? The rumbling stopped. In that moment of silence, Damien processed what Kevin had just said.

"Kevin? What do you mean, 'buy—'"

Before Damien could finish his question, the ceiling exploded. A thousand fragments of rock, some bigger than Damien himself, were propelled across the arena. Many of the glowing orbs that had been the only light source were snuffed out by flying debris. A chunk the size of a fist whizzed over Damien's head, embedding itself in the column behind him.

The rest of the roof caved in rapidly, unable to support itself in the wake of the apocalyptic force at play. A gaping exit wound in the center of the ceiling marked the cause of the explosion. Something had hit it hard enough to pass straight through with no resistance, a shell of fire surrounding it in the fashion of a meteorite smashing through the earth's atmosphere. It wasn't a meteorite, though. Meteorites didn't have health bars.

One and a half seconds after the initial explosion, the real highlight of the show crashed into the ground, vaporizing everything in a ten-meter radius. The shockwave threw Damien back against the column and pinned him two feet off the ground, spread-eagled and helpless. As his limbs connected with the column, there was a grotesque pop. His sword arm had snapped below the elbow. Unable to grip his weapon, the blade clanged off the stone and span away out of sight.

Stunned, Damien dropped to the floor in a heap. A third of his health bar had been depleted, and that was the good news; his ears were ringing, he'd been disarmed, and he still didn't know what he was fighting. He looked up to find out and immediately wished he hadn't.

In the middle of a smoldering crater, surrounded by shards of glass where the sand had been superheated, was the most powerful enemy Damien had ever seen in this game or any other. Resting on one knee, with an obscenely large serrated blade thrust into the ground in front of him, was Toutatis: The Mad Tyrant.

He was adorned in silver plate mail that still glowed red, except for his midriff which lay bare. The musculature of his abdomen implied that armor was not strictly necessary. Toutatis rose to his full height, dragging his sword out of the ground with one hand, before setting his sights on Damien. The god's face may have been obscured by his helm, but Damien knew full well he was being observed.

A red icon in the shape of a menacing eye had joined the debuffs he already recognized as Fear and Crippled Limb in his battle HUD. He focused on the eye briefly and was rewarded with the debuff's name and description: In the Sight of the Gods - All stats reduced by 20%. Even Toutatis's gaze held power.

It was hard to tell from his position eating sand on the floor, but Damien reckoned Toutatis was about eight feet tall. The sword was two feet longer than that.

Damien frantically reached behind himself with his unbroken arm, searching blindly for his backpack. As he did so, Toutatis produced a roar so unimaginably terrible that its outer edge possessed discernible form. It picked Damien up and threw him against the column he'd recently become so well acquainted with. Sand and shards of glass forced him to turn his face away.

On the plus side, the pack he'd been searching for was now firmly wedged against his lower back. On the negative, he was at half health and the fight hadn't even begun.

The chat box weighed in on Damien's prospects:

CactusLover: yep he gonna die
Vargus: I told you so
Dedpewl: SUPERHERO LANDING!!!!
Naughtylus: @_@ glhf
BootyliciousBarb: Hope you're wearing your brown pants.
Polymorpheus: pwned
Akejfnioegnne: Hey guys come watch Sagarama every day at 8pm
5ubzer0: You can do i- wait, never mind

Damien was now in contact with the pack, granting him access to his inventory. He willed his only health potion into his waiting left hand and uncorked it with his teeth, pouring the bitter liquid down his throat as fast as he was able. A warmth burned in his belly before spreading to every extremity. His right arm snapped back into place and sealed. His health shot up to full. The Crippled Limb debuff disappeared, but Fear and In the Sight of the Gods remained. They were persistent effects and it would take more than a potion to be rid of them.

The ringing in his ears stopped, only to be replaced by ringing of a more conventional kind. Kevin had decided to make a phone call and must have had it on loudspeaker for the entire stream to hear. Damien was too distracted to figure out what was happening, but a nagging voice in the back of his head insisted it was not good news. His suspicion was confirmed when the call was answered.

"Hello?"

"Hi, this is Kevin Bants from Mobius Enterprises. Am I speaking to Cassandra Arkwright?"

There was a terse silence before Cassandra responded coldly, "It's actually Cassandra Brades, but yes, that's me."

Damien's eyes widened. Kevin, you complete idiot. Damien was opening his mouth to convey that exact sentiment when motion from the center of the arena brought him back to virtual reality. Toutatis was spinning rapidly on the spot, his sword outstretched.

As his speed increased, a miniature cyclone formed around him, picking up stray pebbles and sand until Toutatis was surrounded by a dense wall of twisting matter. Lightning arced impossibly from the clear sky above, striking the ground in his vicinity and throwing more sand in the air, which in turn was picked up by the whirlwind.

When it reached full power, Toutatis flung himself toward Damien, carrying the localized tornado with him. Damien scrabbled to his feet and flung himself away as a dull clang behind him signaled Toutatis's impact with the column.

"I wanted to have a quick word with you about Damien, if that's all right?"

"Oh, well, he's coming for dinner now. In fact, he should already be here. Would you like me to fetch him for you?"

Damien was holding his hands over his head, waiting for the killing blow to strike him. But it never came. After a few seconds, he turned around to see why he wasn't dead yet.

Toutatis had sliced deep into the stone pillar, but now his sword was stuck.

"No! No, that's quite all right, Mrs. Brades. It's actually you I was hoping to speak to."

Toutatis growled at Damien before turning his attention to the column, both hands grasping the hilt of his sword as he braced himself to pull it free. The red eye disappeared from Damien's debuff list. If Damien was going to do something, this was the moment.

"All right, so why are you calling me? Has Damien done something wrong?"

"Not at all! Damien has been incredibly helpful, and I just wanted to let you know that you have a wonderful son."

"Thank you. That's very kind of you to say, but I still don't understand why you're calling me. Is there something I should know?"

Damien's priority was to retrieve his pack. He glanced down at the column where he'd left it and his heart sank. Toutatis's left foot was planted firmly on top of it. He might as well try to pick up a mountain. Without his pack, and with his sword flown off to who knew where, Damien would have to try and make some sort of mark on this fight unarmed.

Toutatis heaved and his serrated blade grated against the stone as the first few feet of it came free. Whatever Damien was going to do, he didn't have long. Damien hurriedly circled behind him. Surely there must be some kind of weakness he could explo—

That's when he saw it. Toutatis's extremities were all encased in armor. Every extremity, that is, except one. His greaves ended at the top of his thighs, and in between those thighs there was a prominent bulge showing through soft leather. It wasn't particularly well detailed and Damien imagined that Toutatis was about as well endowed as an action figure, but there was only one thing it could be.

Damien had spent years analyzing enemies for weak points. He knew an opportunity when he saw one. Without hesitation he lined himself up, took three measured paces forward and put all his weight behind his heavily armored right foot.

Toutatis inhaled sharply and rose ever so slightly off his feet. A tiny sliver of his health bar disappeared to mark Damien's achievement.

Time stood still.

Inevitably, Toutatis glared at the person responsible. The red eye debuff appeared in Damien's status bar again.

"Hello? Kevin?" Cassandra said. "Are you still there? Hello?"

Damien pursed his lips. He'd done what he could, but it seemed like it was all downhill from here. If he was going to die horribly, he might as well make the most of it.

"E-excuse me," Damien said pointedly, struggling not to stammer, "but you're standing on my pack. Do you mind?" Toutatis turned to look at his foot and the pack that lay under it, then back again, the red eye debuff disappearing and reappearing in Damien's HUD.

Damien would have laughed if not for the circumstances. He grinned up at Toutatis apologetically, the sides of his lips twitching.

"My mom is waiting for me to come and have dinner, you see, but I'd quite like to have my pa—"

Toutatis's left arm blurred around in a circle, catching Damien in the side with the backhand to end all backhands. First Damien's arm snapped. Then his ribs broke and his chest caved in. His body wrapped itself around Toutatis's forearm as though he were made of putty. At the end of the swing, Damien's limp body was propelled through the air.

He was still accelerating at twenty-five meters, reached terminal velocity at fifty meters and came to an abrupt stop when he hit the wall on the other side of the arena some seventy-five meters away.

"Kevin? Is that my son I just heard? What's going on?"

Kevin collected himself. "Er, yes, that was Damien. He's actually helping me with something at the moment, and I was hopi—"

"Oh. Oh! I see what this is. He's playing that damn game

again, isn't he? I told him not to play until after he finished his assignments, but does he listen to me? Of course not. And now I know why he's late for dinner. Unbelievable!"

"Mrs. Brades, I'm very sorry, it's entirely my fault. Please don't blame Damien for this, he was only—"

"It's *Miss* Brades, thank you very much, and I'll blame whoever I please. Goodbye, Kevin. Please don't contact my son again."

Existence was pain. Damien's status bar was a collection of ominous symbols. From his position encased in the arena wall, he performed a quick check and decided that at least one of them denoted internal bleeding. That would explain why his health bar, already so precariously low, was still dropping.

He tried to free himself from the wall and stopped when his limbs screamed in protest. If he'd known how this fight was going to pan out, he'd have turned off the pain settings in the menu. They were currently set at half, which was considerably more than he felt like dealing with.

He looked up at Toutatis just in time to watch him kick down the enormous column and retrieve his sword. The red eye appeared at the top of Damien's status bar for the final time. The Fear debuff disappeared as Damien rolled his own eyes at the irate god.

"Fine, don't give me my pack back." He paused to cough up blood, the crimson liquid spattering over the sand below him. "You didn't have to be a dick about it."

"Damien, this is Kevin. I'm sorry, I called your mother but it... it didn't go as well as I'd hoped."

Toutatis had started spinning again, preparing to end the epic mismatch. Despite everything, Damien laughed.

"Yeah, numbnuts, I heard the call. You haven't done me any favors. Pull me out. I'm done. Good game well played and all that sh—"

Beeeeeeep!

"You're still broadcasting live, Damien, please don't swear. I can't get you out. When the combat is over the Test Zone will reset and you'll instantly be brought back to life, but you or Toutatis have to die first."

Lightning had started striking the ground around Toutatis again. Any moment now he would charge toward Damien and end the battle. Damien felt he had suffered quite enough for one day. He did the only thing he could do.

"Menu."

Using his eyes to scroll and blinking to click since he couldn't even move his fingers, he set the pain settings to zero. His entire body went blissfully numb.

"You better make this up to me, Kevin. This is not how I wanted to spend my Monday night."

"I will, Damien, I promise. You've done a terrific job. I'm in your debt."

Toutatis lurched forward. It would all be over soon. What a relief. The edge of the blade scythed through the air, coming closer and closer with each rotation. With seconds to spare, Toutatis froze on the spot.

A searing headache burned its way into the core of Damien's mind and he screamed in very real pain. The edges and colors of the Test Zone blurred like a wet painting. Then it all went dark.

Damien grabbed his head in both hands – his real, unbroken hands – and opened his eyes, still screaming. His mother was glaring down at him, one hand on her hip and the other holding his NOOB headset by her side. In his confused state, Damien wondered why the red eye wasn't appearing in his status bar.

It was time for a real boss battle.

2

CHARACTER DESTROYING

Dinner was a quiet affair. Mother and son sat at opposite ends of the table in their modest kitchen.

Cassandra wasn't eating. Her bowl sat in front of her untouched as she stared Damien down, arms folded. The NOOB headset rested in the center of the table between them, the very opposite of a conversation piece.

Damien jammed the last of his pasta into his mouth, being careful to suppress his gag reflex lest it draw comment, and made his play.

"Thank you for dinner."

He stood up and carried his bowl and spoon over to the bio-wash unit, carefully placing them within before making a beeline for his room.

"Sit."

Damien caught her eye and winced. Cassandra stared at him levelly before tilting her head slightly, motioning toward the seat Damien had just vacated. The only sound was the gentle tinkle of cutlery as the bio-wash unit turned over Damien's eating utensils, analyzing how best to render them clean.

Damien gave in. With a long sigh, he trudged back over to his seat and fell into it heavily. Unable to return his mother's gaze, he opted to stare at her shoulder instead. Cassandra unfolded her arms and rested a hand on the NOOB headset.

"Have you finished your assignments?"

Damien kept staring listlessly at her shoulder as if it were the most interesting shoulder in the world. Eventually the silence became too uncomfortable and he was compelled to fill it.

"Not yet, but there's only one assignment left so I have plenty of ti—"

Cassandra slammed her other hand onto the table and Damien flinched, his poorly chosen words fading to nothingness. Cassandra quickly removed her hand from the table and rubbed it on her knee. Damien's guilt dialed itself up another notch. She was too frail to make such dramatic gestures.

Right on cue, her hospital-issue guardian wristband started beeping. It had detected her accelerated heart rate. Her hands withdrew into her pockets with practiced ease. One of them returned holding her pills, the other a small injection capsule.

She used the capsule first, sticking it in her left forearm below the wristband. Then she turned her attention to the pill bottle, unscrewing the top and tipping three of them into her open hand before unceremoniously palming them into her mouth.

Three pills now, noted Damien unhappily. The dose was still increasing.

The two of them observed the ritual, one of three intervals each day, in total silence. They did not talk about Cassandra's heart condition unless it was absolutely necessary. Detecting the medicine in her bloodstream, the guardian wristband fell silent as well. Only a low hiss cut the tension as the bio-washer sprayed its chosen mix of cleaning fluid over Damien's bowl and spoon.

Guilt washed over him in waves.

Cassandra replaced the cap and left the container and injection capsule on the table's edge before extending her hand to lightly touch the NOOB headset again.

"We had a deal, Damien. You finish your assignments first and play games afterward. Remember? You agreed. You said you understood."

Damien initially had no response. She was right. He should

have started his assignment as soon as he was done with his lectures, finished it after dinner, and then started playing. But he'd been watching lectures online since 9am. His boredom had led him to front-load his pleasure, knowing full well it would leave him little time to complete his studies.

Damien had options. He could have apologized. He could have admitted he was tired from studying for eight hours but knew what he had done was wrong. Concessions could have been made.

But he did none of those things. Some dumb animal instinct compelled him to fight against the perceived injustice of his situation. He'd been studying non-stop since that morning. He deserved a break.

Damien fixed his eyes back on his mother's shoulder and doomed himself.

"I was going to do my assignment first, but Kevin called and begged me for help with an online presentation. I wanted to sign out and ask you for permission, but he said there was no time. I knew you'd come in and pull the headset off anyway. Thanks for that, by the way." Damien rubbed the top of his head where a dull pain still throbbed with every heartbeat. "I'll have a headache for the rest of the night, which is going to make completing my assignment that much more interesting."

Cassandra simply stared at him. Damien dragged his line of sight four inches to the right and managed to meet her piercing blue eyes. They were so tired and yet so very, very angry. They saw straight through him and seemed to read his every thought.

It wasn't just her anger that made her hard to look at; her skin was drawn tightly across her face. She was still losing weight and couldn't put it back on. Dark bags scoured the skin under her eyes. Her black hair, once so thick and sheer, had now degraded until it was patchy and thin. Damien found himself wishing this argument would end, if for no other reason than to allow her to eat.

Still she stared at him. Damien stared back defiantly.

"So you were already playing the game when Kevin called you?"

Damien's eyes wavered and his resolve shattered. He looked away. Before, his silence had signified resistance. Now it only signified his crushing defeat.

"That's what I thought."

The bio-washer punctuated the silence once more, commencing drying the cutlery with a low hum.

"Damien, please look at me."

He reluctantly met her eyes again. To his surprise, they had softened. She was biting her lower lip, as she always did when she was forced to make a difficult decision.

"This is hard for me, Damien. You're not an adult, but you're not a child either. I want to treat you with respect, to show you that you're a young man now and not just my little boy."

Her eyes filled with tears and despite her plea for Damien to look at her, he found he no longer could. He stared down at the floor between his feet, struggling not to cry himself. He wanted to forget all of this. He wanted to go and play his game, to go and pretend everything was fine, that his mother was happy and healthy and his life was perfect. Of course he did. That's how this whole mess had begun.

Though her eyes were wet, Cassandra did not allow a single tear to spill down her cheeks, nor did her voice crack and break as it should have. Even ravaged by illness, she was strong.

"The placement exams start just three weeks from now. If you're going to get into a good apprenticeship without paying for it, you have to qualify for Online Tuition Bracket A before then. Then you have to pass the exams. That's a lot of work to do and not much time to do it in. It will give you the chance for a good life, a better life than the one I can provide. I'm sorry, Damien, I really am." She clasped the NOOB headset and gently pulled it over to her side of the table, leaving it to sit next to her prescription medicine. "But I have to do everything in my power to make sure you succeed. Tomorrow, I will send this back to Kevin—"

Damien's lips parted, his eyes widened, his gaze shifting longingly between the headset and his mother.

"Mom, please—"

"—and I'll tell him that you can't help him—"

"—I'm sorry, you're right, I made a mistake—"

"—until after the placement exams are complete."

The words were spoken and it was done. There was nothing that could change the outcome. Damien couldn't help himself. He knew it was hopeless, but the words tumbled out of his mouth anyway.

"The testing I've been doing for Mobius finishes in a week anyway. I can study after!"

"The placement exams are more important. Kevin should get help from someone whose future isn't at stake. Don't argue with me about this. I've made my decision."

Damien stared at her, his lips working but no sound coming out. Now it was Cassandra's turn to look at her feet. There was a rattle and a ping as the bio-washer deposited the newly cleaned implements into their places. Damien was caught between emotions.

He hadn't even known it was possible to feel shame and rage at the same time. He stood up and strode toward his room, attempting to get there before his anger took over. He was too slow. He grasped the door's handle but thought of something hurtful to say before he could open it.

"You know how lucky I was to get accepted for that beta. It will never happen again. This is the first and last time I'll get to use Mobius tech and you've taken it away from me."

Cassandra did not look up. She was hunched over with her hands in her lap, one massaging the other. She looked so small. After a long pause she took a deep breath, most of it escaping her in a ragged sigh. With what was left, she uttered two words that came out as little more than a whisper.

"I know."

Having said his piece, Damien wanted nothing more than to take it back. *But what's done is done.* He lingered a few moments longer, failing to find the word he needed, before entering his room and leaving his mother to sit in the kitchen alone.

It took monumental effort not to slam the door, but at least he managed that much. He stood on the other side of it, fists clenched and eyes screwed shut. He knew everything she said was right. It didn't help. Saga Online had been the one thing he could look forward to every day and now it was gone.

His anger warped into self-pity. He took two steps forward and threw himself onto his bed, burying his face in the pillow. The worst part of it was that Damien had never needed the game more than he did now. The irony was lost on him, the hubris was not. He rolled over and contemplated the ceiling.

Even if everything went well and he found a decent apprenticeship, it would be at least a few years before he started earning enough to support himself. Saga Online had been well and truly confined to his past. Fighting and dying against Toutatis would be his final act.

Damien's body jerked upright. The live broadcast would be over by now, but he could still watch the rerun. He jumped up from his bed and placed himself in front of his desk, swiping right on the monitor to preserve his notes on early twenty-first century politics before clicking the home button.

The Mobius Enterprises front page rendered itself instantly. Saga Online's tab was close to the top, second only to the tab listing VR hardware. Damien pressed his finger to it and Toutatis's form filled the screen in its place. His heart skipped a beat before his brain assured him that it was a picture and he could relax. It was a still image of Toutatis just after his impact, kneeling in the crater with his sword piercing the ground.

Damien was hit by a gut-wrenching wave of déjà vu: the image had been taken from his perspective, when he'd been lying on the sand with his arm broken. There were gold letters in a jagged font directly underneath it:

TOUTATIS, WARRIOR CHAMPION OF THE HEAVENS, HAS ARRIVED. **CLICK HERE** TO SEE HIS FIRST APPEARANCE IN FULL.

Damien obediently clicked the link and the stream loaded. It was twenty-five minutes on a constant loop and he'd been deposited twenty-two minutes in. Without warning, Kevin's voice blared out of the monitor and Damien's hand darted forward to grab the volume dial, twisting it violently to cut the sound. He turned it back up gently until Kevin's voice was audible rather than deafening.

The camera panned in on Damien sheepishly looking up at Toutatis as he politely asked for his bag. The Test Zone had saved the entire combat, allowing Kevin to retrospectively analyze it from every angle in minute detail.

"—main attack is the Whirlwind but there are various other offensive options coded into his AI, as we can see here."

Damien's lips parted as he watched himself fly across the arena and smash into the wall. It was a difficult feeling to describe. While most people only had the opportunity to recreate moments of trauma in their mind, he was getting it in full color, UHD graphics and surround sound. He put a hand on his chest, checking to make sure nothing was broken. As he confirmed he was still in one piece, Kevin's voice was joined by another that Damien did not immediately recognize.

"Fine, don't give me my pack back. You didn't have to be a dick about it."

Damien stared at the screen incredulously. Did he really sound like that? More importantly, is that really what he'd said? It had come naturally at the time but watching himself say it now, from the comfort of his chair, he felt like he was watching a different person. Holy crap, he was a badass. The corners of his mouth stretched across his cheeks into an uncontrollable smirk.

"Well, there are still a few minutes to go but we've reviewed the footage so many times I don't think there's anything I can add. I'd just like to take this opportunity to thank Damien for making this show possible. He put himself on the line, both in the game and in real life, so that we could enjoy this update in full. If you're watching, Damien, thank you. This has been Kevin Bants, hosting what I think you'll agree was a very special episode of 'The Saga Continues'."

Damien actually felt better. Even if he was never going to play Saga Online again, he had been immortalized on the internet. By name! He took a moment to privately bask in the glory. The stream looped around and started again from the beginning.

"Good evening, and welcome to today's episode of 'The Saga Continues'."

Damien quickly paused it. He didn't feel like reliving the experience any more than he already had. He pinched the screen between thumb and forefinger to minimize the video, intending to look at the comments below. He caught sight of the view count first. An involuntary high-pitched whine squeaked its way through his vocal cords.

Current Viewers: 58,973
Total Views: 873,422

He wasn't just famous. He was viral. It had only been forty-five minutes since his mom pulled off his headset and the video already had more traffic than Sim Cities 2074. Damien stared at the numbers, struggling to process what he was seeing. The 'Current Viewers' count was oscillating between fifty-five and sixty-thousand, but the 'Total Views' was rising in leaps and bounds.

As Damien sat there vegetating, it broke through 900,000 views, continuing onward toward the fabled million without any sign of stopping. He shook himself and tore his eyes away from the numbers, fixing them on the comments instead. They were listed from top to bottom in order of popularity.

Ignatius: HE KICKED HIM IN THE NUTS! ARE YOU KIDDING ME? XD
BlackKnight: That was AWESOME! Toutatis totally rocks! Respect to Damien for fighting something so terrifying.
CactusLover: I want a rematch! Damien vs Toutatis round two in a month's time. Aetherius fights the winner! Upvote if you agree!
VintageMintage: It's a shame we didn't get to see Aetherius fight Toutatis, but I can see why he wouldn't want to get stuck in a room with THAT. Kudos to Damien. RIP xoxo
ArmsWavingWildlyWithWildlyWavingArms: Roll over David, there's a new kid in town: #Damien vs Goliath

Damien's head was swimming. This changed everything. Maybe his days of Saga Online weren't behind him after all. He'd have to ask Kevin if he could have the headset back after his exams, but with this much exposure he couldn't imagine him saying no.

Besides, Kevin had thanked him personally AND said he owed him a favor. It seemed like enabling Damien to play would be good news not just for him, but for everyone involved. Maybe he could even start his own channel!

He quickly upvoted the top five comments and sat back, beaming. He'd tell his mom about this development later, but for now there was only one thing he could do to make amends. He closed the Saga Online page and went back to his assignment's source material. He still had an assignment to complete that evening.

His eyes ran over the dense lines of text, scanning them automatically without absorbing any of the information. It was no mystery why he'd decided to log in without completing his last assignment beforehand; it was duller than bio-washer water. The formation of CU was far from his favorite subject. Every time he thought he had a handle on it, the reading material shifted to a new but equally mind-numbing chapter in the Central Union's history.

This particular excerpt detailed the circumstances necessitating the borderless Pan-American alliance: national security scares, leading to divisive politics, justifying an inefficient distribution of public resources, concluding in the rapid deterioration of accountability for those in positions of power, aided by woefully outdated education systems and unregulated information distribution platforms.

The latter two factors further exacerbated an unhealthy obsession with the cult of the individual, flowing into a disproportionate emphasis on beating others rather than winning collectively that itself stemmed from lazy, greedy, unimaginative problem solving techniques in the face of what, to everyone in that era, must have looked like an utterly unfathomable tangle of interlocking, self-aggrandizing, unassailable societal norms.

Or so the textbooks said.

Hindsight is 20/20.

Damien got all the way to the end of the page, which had been signed off with a quote stating: 'Compound interest is the most powerful force in the universe, CU will realign it for the benefit of mankind,' before he realized he'd retained about 25% of what he'd read. He shook his head and returned to the start. It would be a while before he could settle down and concentrate.

So when his mother's guardian wristband started beeping, it penetrated his consciousness instantly. His brow furrowed. She'd just taken her medicine; it was too early for another dose.

A crash came from the kitchen and the innocent beeping melded into an urgent alarm.

Damien shot up, his chair clattering onto the floor. Wrenching his door open, he emerged to find his worst nightmare unfolding in front of him. Cassandra was lying on her back halfway between the table and the bio-wash unit. Her bowl had smashed to pieces, the uneaten chicken pasta lumped in a miserable splat on the floor. She was staring at the ceiling with unblinking eyes, her chest heaving up and down as her hands frantically searched her pockets.

Damien's eyes darted to the table. The pills and the injection capsule were still there. He grabbed them before kneeling by his mother's side. He'd been told what to do in this situation, but shock numbed his senses.

Grabbing his mother's arm, he drove in the injector below her wrist as he'd seen her do a thousand times before. Nothing happened. Damien turned it to face him and realized it was still empty. She hadn't reloaded it since she last used it.

"Damien, look at me."

He made eye contact and his panic grew. Although her breathing was still labored, Cassandra had stopped struggling. She was smiling now, which only scared him even more. She feebly took his hand in her own and squeezed it.

"It's not your fault. I love you very much."

Damien clenched his teeth so hard he felt they might shatter in his head. She had decided she was going to die on the kitchen floor and was too busy worrying about him to worry about herself.

"Don't say that," he said, voice trembling as he fumbled with the clasp on the injector. "You're not going to die." The clasp clicked and the empty cartridge popped out, hitting the floor and rolling away. Under the crippling pressure, Damien had failed to think ahead.

"Mom, where are the cartridges? MOM!" There was no response. Her eyes flickered and her head lolled to one side as she lost consciousness. The screech of the wristband increased in volume and pitch.

Damien was on his own.

The first responders would be there soon, drawn by the emergency signal Cassandra's bracelet was broadcasting, but without immediate treatment they might be too late. Damien bolted to his mother's bedroom, tearing open her bedside cabinet; the drawer crashed onto the floor before he threw the contents out in a frenzy. Where was it? The screech had followed him into the room, cutting into his mind and drowning out rational thought.

From the corner of his eye, he saw it. The little metal box was sitting inconspicuously on Cassandra's dresser. He'd passed the damned thing on his way to the cabinet. He snatched it up and ran back into the kitchen, his shaking hands fumbling to open the box as his vision blurred with tears.

He'd only been gone a few seconds, but it felt like hours. The lid snapped open and most of the capsules spilled out, scattering across the floor. He wailed in frustration and wasted a precious second to look at his mother.

Cassandra was unconscious but alive, her breathing coming in agonizing gasps that were painful even to look at. Her eyes were twitching rapidly, only opening enough to show a glimpse of the whites underneath. Her brain was losing oxygen.

Damien snatched up a capsule and inserted it into the injector. He held it in a closed fist and slowly raised it above her prone body, trying to prepare himself for what he was about to do. It was far too late to deliver the dose to her arm, it wouldn't reach her heart in time. After uttering a single frightened sob, Damien drove the injector through her shirt and into her chest.

Cassandra's body heaved upward, her back arching off the ground. Her fingernails grated against the kitchen tiles as her hands clenched into fists. It was all Damien could do just to hold on. The metallic whine of the bracelet subsided, reverting to intermittent beeping as Cassandra collapsed back to the floor. She was breathing, and her eyes no longer flickered. But they did not open.

Damien pulled the injector out and threw it away, wondering if after all his efforts he'd only managed to kill her himself rather than letting it happen on its own. He cradled her head on his lap, just in time for the terror to finally consume him.

Before he even knew what he was doing, Damien found himself wailing with shock and fear. Each time he stopped, the cold electronic tone would fill the void and he would try to drown it out with his own wretched cries. In the span of a few minutes, he became a child again.

That was how the paramedics found him. That was how they left him when they took his mother away, leaving him to wonder how things might have been different if only he'd been as strong as she was.

3

PLAYING THE HAND YOU'RE DEALT

D amien opened his eyes, briefly worrying that he'd overslept. He sat up in bed and the phone he'd been clutching to his chest all night clattered to the floor. He stared at it dully, trying to remember why it was with him. As he reached down to pick it up, the events of the night before wormed their way back to him.

The paramedics had seen Damien as a liability and elected that he was too young to go without a guardian, opting instead to leave him in the relative safety of his home. They had left him with a hospital calling card attached to his mother's case number. Damien, still not fully back in control of his own mind, had called the number almost immediately after they were gone. A politely detached voice had informed him that there had been no change in his mother's condition, that the ambulance was still on its way to the hospital and that it would arrive in approximately six minutes.

He'd spent most of the night repeating this cycle, calling every few minutes just to make sure there was still no change in her condition. At last, a slightly concerned voice informed Damien that he had called forty-six times in the last two hours and that if there was any change in Cassandra's condition they would call him immediately. A few calls after that, the card stopped working.

Damien curled up underneath the blanket, though it was poor insulation from reality. What was he supposed to do now? Even if he could have brought himself to attend his online lectures and even if he was able to concentrate, his exams suddenly seemed incredibly unimportant.

He thought about finding the NOOB headset, just for a moment, and his lip trembled. If not for Saga Online, maybe this would never have happened. He tightened his body still further until he could wrap his hands around his knees.

It would be better just to wait. If he waited long enough, someone would come and tell him what to do. He wasn't ready for this.

The intercom rang. Damien sat bolt upright. She was back! He jumped out of bed and almost fell through the doorway in his eagerness to welcome his mother home. He flung open the door and directed his eager grin at... a startled looking delivery man.

"Delivery to Mr. Arkwright?"

Damien nodded sullenly, as if everything was somehow the delivery man's fault. He signed his name on the tablet provided and a box was picked up off the floor before being thrust into his hands. Damien turned it over. It had the Mobius Enterprises logo on it. He hadn't ordered anything from Mobius.

Frowning, Damien closed the door and went back inside, only to be met with a deeply unpleasant scene. The kitchen was as he'd left it last night; the chicken pasta was a sad splat on the floor and there were shards of broken plate and injection capsules scattered everywhere. Only Cassandra was conspicuously absent.

He placed the box on the table before purposefully striding around the mess to grab the dustpan and brush. The apartment was not going to look like this when his mother came home. Cleaning up didn't take that long and he found himself once again with nothing but his spiraling thoughts.

Well, whatever happens today, it might as well happen on a full stomach.

He walked over to the food processor and checked the tank. It looked like it still had just enough for one portion of bacon and eggs. Unwilling to dedicate any more thought to the exercise than necessary, Damien thumbed in his order and the machine started to whir. He filled the kettle and switched it on before finally directing his attention to the Mobius package.

Cutting through the tape and cardboard he was met with white chunks of styrofoam. He reached in, grabbed what was inside and pulled, undoing his cleaning by spilling styrofoam onto the floor. Seeing what he now held, he couldn't have been less interested in the mess he'd just made.

It was a sleek, black headset, emblazoned with the Mobius Enterprises logo. It was unlike any headset he'd ever seen. Most headsets were a simple visor with some nodes that attached to the temples. This one would encase his entire head.

He reverentially placed it on the table before rummaging in the box for some clue as to why it was in his house. He found the charger first, examining it briefly before depositing it alongside the headset. As he scraped the bottom of the box, his hands seized upon an envelope with his name printed on it in shaky block capitals. He opened it and found that the message inside was handwritten as well.

Dear Damien,

Sorry for the handwriting, an electronic message would show up in our database and we don't want to draw attention to this bad boy just yet. If you're reading this, you're the proud owner of our prototype headset, the IMBA.

This should allow for greater control while you play Saga Online. After all the excitement of fighting Toutatis, you've drawn a lot of attention to the game. I'll cut to the chase; Mobius Enterprises wants to capitalize on the publicity. They approached me and I decided we could kill two birds with one stone: if you test this headset for us and give us feedback, we'll let you keep it.

Just a thought: now you'll be playing the real game, maybe you should join the 2072 Streamer Competition. You never know!

See you online!
Kevin

P.S. Please pass on my apologies to Cassandra. I was just so rushed to come up with a solution yesterday that things went badly. I hope this gift shows her how grateful we are at Mobius Enterprises for your contribution.

P.P.S. Consider my debt to you repaid!

Damien brayed a harsh dry laugh at the last sentence. He didn't feel like Kevin had repaid his debt at all. No sooner had the thought crossed his mind than he realized it was incredibly unfair. Kevin had no way of knowing what happened last night. The headset was just his way of doing his job and saying sorry at the same time. It certainly looked like a great piece of kit. It was light years ahead of the NOOB headset, at least going by how it looked. Looking at it only made Damien sadder. He was in no position to appreciate it anymore.

He suddenly remembered his breakfast, getting cold in the food processor. After making an instant coffee he sat down and began tearing into his meal, pausing between bites to contemplate the new headset on the table in front of him.

He'd have been all too happy to test it for Kevin if he'd been asked a few days ago, but a lot had changed since then. His mom was now in hospital and after she got out there would be medical bills to pay. Maybe he could sell the headset somewhere for cash? No, that didn't seem like a good idea. It wasn't his property to sell.

Damien paused halfway through a mouthful of bacon and eggs. There was the Streamer Competition. Kevin had given him access. There was an obscene amount of money up for grabs, enough to pay his mom's medical bills and then some. This latest incident would probably push their insurance to the edge, maybe forcing them to lower it to bracket E. It would require drastic measures to keep them afloat. As the insane idea hatched in his brain, he looked at the IMBA headset and discovered a gaping flaw in his plan.

He wasn't sure he could bring himself to play Saga Online.

The prospect of using the IMBA headset filled him with guilt. He had arguably put his mother in hospital by playing Saga

Online, and now he was supposed to help her out of it by doing the same thing? It seemed ridiculous. And yet... it wasn't as if there was anything else he could do. His only other option was to sit at home, twiddling his thumbs while he waited for the phone to ring.

The popularity of his fight against Toutatis was another factor. The stream had shown every sign of breaking a million views when he saw it the day before. Who knew how far it had gone by now? The 2072 Streamer Competition was, in essence, a popularity contest, so the huge amount of views could only work in his favor. Perhaps this was a smart move after all.

He picked up the headset and the charger before going back to his room. So strong was his resolve that he only felt the tiniest nagging sense of misgiving as he removed the NOOB headset charger from the wall and tucked it away in his cupboard, out of sight but not quite out of mind. He grabbed the house phone from where it had clattered to the floor earlier that morning and dropped it in his pajama pocket. He didn't know if that would be enough to alert him when it rang but he was too invested to turn back now.

With the new and improved headset plugged in and the red-lit power icon indicating it was active, Damien carefully eased it onto his head. It was well cushioned, although when he concentrated he could feel a multitude of small hard nodules pressing through the fabric against his skull. At least there were enough of them that the weight was distributed evenly. He lay back until he was completely horizontal and closed his eyes.

He waited for the headset to start counting down, warning him that it was about to take control of his senses. The headset remained eerily silent. Now that he thought about it, the IMBA had seemed a little uncomfortable when he was standing up, but laying down it felt like he wasn't wearing it at all.

Welcome to Saga Online

Damien opened his eyes to find himself standing in a plain white room, wearing a plain gray jogging outfit and sneakers. He shook his head and blinked. That was weird. With the NOOB set there had always been at least a small delay and a gradual immersion into the virtual space. This had been almost instantaneous.

'Before you start playing you must calibrate your headset. Using your eyes only, please follow the red dot around the room.'

The red dot appeared on the wall in front of him and Damien obediently followed it with his eyes. The program ran through for a few minutes, having him point, rotate, jump and generally make as many motions as the headset felt necessary. When it was over, he was invited to review specific body parts. He did some stretches and decided everything was fine the way it was. The first time he'd calibrated his NOOB headset he'd manually set his height to eight feet tall, thinking he'd breeze through the game as a giant. Instead he'd been spawned as a freakish gangly spider creature, lost control of all his limbs simultaneously and fallen flat on his face before sullenly setting it back to the default.

'Scanning. Please stand by.'

Damien had the briefest sensation of his face tingling before the camera panned out of his body. He was suddenly looking at himself in the third person. It should have felt strange, but it was actually like looking at an extremely compliant mirror. Even if most mirrors wouldn't let you look at the back of your own head. His face had been rendered perfectly.

He looked himself over, watching his own hands rotate in a circle in perfect time with the camera circling around him. He dragged it in close and pulled a few faces to see if everything was functioning correctly. Kevin hadn't been kidding – this headset was amazing. He'd been stuck in this room for a few hours with the NOOB set, trying to make his face resemble himself and not some moon-faced uncanny valley copy. Satisfied, he clapped his hands and the camera's perspective panned back into his face.

'Are you eighteen or over?'

Damien put on his best poker face and nodded vigorously. If he told the truth, the game would place a hard cap on his gore, pain and mature scenes settings.

'Calibration complete.'

A keyboard appeared at chest height in front of him.

'If you would like to make and receive phone calls or e-mails while in game, the headset can be linked to your home network. Would you like to link your new device?'

Excellent. Now he wouldn't have to worry about missing a phone call while he was playing. As he keyed in the details, Damien found himself hoping that Mobius really would let him keep the headset. He shook his head roughly before continuing to type. *Focus, idiot. You're here to help your mother.* He finished syncing the headset and the keyboard vanished.

'Please select your character's race.'

That's when it hit him. He should have realized before, but he'd been too awed with the IMBA-set to notice. He was making a new account. His hopes of playing the already well-leveled, well-recognized Scorpius were dashed.

Damien thought about it and decided it was no surprise. On the beta server he'd gone through several updates that were not currently live in the main game. If any of those were related to warrior skills, Scorpius might not play properly. On top of that, Mobius probably wanted him to start afresh so he could test the headset through and through.

Damien scratched the back of his head. This was a serious blow. It had taken a month to get Scorpius to level 28. Valuable time would be wasted repeating boring early game quests when he needed to be building himself a profile and capitalizing on his fifteen minutes of fame. He'd have to talk to Kevin and try to persuade him to transfer Scorpius onto this new online account. Sure, there might be some issues with his gameplay since he was on the test server, but they could patch him so he had the same abilities as regular warriors, right? Kevin had said that Mobius wanted to capitalize on the publicity, so it shouldn't be too much trouble. At the very least, it wouldn't hurt to ask.

Damien brought his attention back to the selection bar. The four core choices were human, orc, elf or dwarf. Kevin had instructed him to play as a human when he was beta testing, but there had been no such instruction this time. He could use one of the other classes instead, taking advantage of one of their combat based racial traits.

Elves had 'Alacrity', granting them 10% increased attack, casting and movement speeds. Dwarves were blessed with 'Stone Skin', reducing all elemental damage by 20%. Last but by no means least, the Orcish trait 'Magic Blood' boosted their health, stamina and mana regeneration by 25%.

Damien was gleefully rubbing his hands together when he realized there was actually no choice at all. There was no guarantee he'd be able to transfer Scorpius over. He needed to take his character creation seriously. As much as he'd like to try something new, that would mean moving into unexplored territory. This was not the time; he needed to stick to what he knew. If he couldn't get his hands on Scorpius, he'd have to recreate him in order to use the Toutatis fight to his advantage. He needed his new character to look as similar to the original Scorpius as possible.

What was more, he needed the human bonus trait, Adaptable, for the 15% increased experience gain. The other three races would be great for making a character shine at higher levels, but Damien needed to develop a character quickly above all else. 'Adaptable' was a better choice for the problem at hand. Reluctantly, he thumbed toward the human silhouette and then nodded to confirm his decision. His excitement was getting the better of him: he'd almost lost himself in the game before it had even started, but at least he'd made the right choice.

'Please select your starting zone.'

A map of Arcadia appeared on the floor underneath his feet. All around it spanned hundreds of miles of varied terrain, from dense vibrant forests to lifeless volcanic wastelands. The capital cities of the playable races were each placed on the corners of the map, far away from each other. Damien immediately walked toward the starting area he'd previously played while on the private test server, directly outside the human capital city: Camelot. He knew the area well, and he'd also be able to join his old faction; The Empire.

The Empire was the vanilla faction for Camelot. You could sign up with them almost immediately after logging in. They provided basic training to get the first couple of levels under your belt, a full set of novice gear to match your chosen class and an endless, steady stream of quests. Almost everyone signed up with them for the early perks, even if they planned on joining a different faction later on. It would be much less troublesome than choosing a different starting zone and trying to deal with NPC's – Non-Player Characters – who looked down on humans. It was an easy choice.

As Damien stopped over Camelot on the map, a blue circle expanded under his feet until it was large enough to encompass him completely.

'Starting area selected: Camelot. Are you ready to enter the game?'

Damien folded his arms and set his feet a little further apart, bracing himself for what came next. He nodded. The walls of the white room suddenly expanded away into the distance at incredible speed. The map under his feet stretched to become life-size as the modest white room warped by degrees into the world he would be playing in.

The cities and environs furthest away from Camelot were the first to leave his range of vision, both traveling and expanding at an even rate. Then they dipped over the horizon that formed as the map started to curve.

The only thing that remained static relative to Damien was the blue circle he stood in. He was fairly sure he wouldn't come to harm by stepping outside it, but he hadn't felt like trying it the first time he played and he certainly didn't feel like trying it now.

Even Camelot itself was moving away, albeit more slowly than everything else. The starting zone was about a kilometer outside of the city limits, which meant its doppelgänger depicted on the map had a kilometer to go before the loading sequence was complete.

'Further settings are available by saying 'Menu'. It is highly recommended you review your settings, read the in-game manual and familiarize yourself with the game before leaving the safe zone. Once again, welcome to Saga Online.'

The map finally stopped expanding. Damien found himself standing on a 1:1 ratio representation of Arcadia, in the middle of a military encampment consisting of a top-down view of tents and training pits. The loading animation was almost complete. There was only one way the map could become more accurate now.

Arcadia rose out of the floor. The first features to appear were mountain peaks in the distance. They were soon joined by the tallest spires of Camelot's castle. The rest of the world followed not far behind. Tiny shrubs became towering trees, puddles plummeted to unfathomable depths and entire cities were born out of the dirt. Well, at least that's how it was supposed to look. Damien knew he was just being inserted into the game world, that this was simply a demonstration of what Saga Online was capable of.

His surroundings were some of the last features to be filled in. As it came to an end, Damien was enveloped by a tent that rose directly out of the blue circle and penned him in, folding itself closed above him and concealing the world that had only just taken form. He felt fur under his feet and looked down before sighing. The tracksuit had been replaced while he was distracted by the loading animation. Again. Damien had thought he'd catch it the second time round, but the switch was too subtle and the distraction too effective. In any case, he was now the proud owner of a set of soiled rags, less comfortable but more in keeping with his new environment.

A moment later, Damien could hear voices and footsteps. He blinked against the light as he stepped outside, his bare feet tickled by the blades of grass that poked in between his toes. A gust of wind brushed his cheek and rustled the branches of a nearby tree, signaling that the physics engine was running smoothly.

The encampment had become populated with knights, rangers, priests and all manner of classes. Another player stepped out of a tent alongside his own, his jaw ever so slightly agape as he took in his surroundings.

Damien smiled. He was back.

4

ALL IN

"Menu."

The world took on a blue haze as the in-game menu hovered before Damien, a series of rectangular boxes stacked on top of each other. Pausing the game simply wasn't possible with other players occupying the same virtual space, so the various characters in the encampment were still moving around in the background. A pair of rangers having a heated debate walked straight into his line of sight before harmlessly passing through the menu.

Despite the loading screen's suggestion, Damien wasn't too interested in re-reading the in-game manual. It was designed for people who had never played any role-playing games before and gave instructions about such things as how to gain experience and level up.

Right at the top of the menu, highlighted in shining silver, was the 'Stats' bar. He focused on it and nodded.

Account Name: Damien Arkwright
Character: ????
Level: 1
Health: 100/100
Stamina: 100/100
Mana: 100/100

Stats:
Strength 10 - Agility 10 - Intelligence 10
Constitution 10 - Endurance 10 - Wisdom 10
Experience: 0/500

Ouch. That was hard to look at. He knew the numbers would all be back to base level, but there was a final insult he hadn't seen coming: his character wasn't even named yet. At least that was something he could fix. Damien dismissed the menu and headed for the conscription stand. It wasn't far.

At the end of the row of tents he came out in front of a jousting arena flanked by a long line of tables, each with a non-player character representative. They were all arguing about which class was best, each of them adamant that their own class was the pinnacle of achievement.

"There's no question, mages are by far the most powerful of all our forces. Without us, you'd all be left stumbling around in the dark."

"Stumbling around in the dark, you say? Gee, that's funny, I thought it was us rangers who scouted out unknown terrain! That way, you wizened old geezers don't have to get your manicured hands dirty!"

"You think you know anything about getting your hands dirty? You're just half-baked assassins. If you weren't such cowards, you'd throw your bow and arrows away and focus entirely on your knife-fighting skills, like we do."

"Such unbecoming malevolence. Mayhap if you had a shred of dignity, you'd be more inclined to preserve life rather than destroy it. That is why priests are superior."

"Oh yeah? And who do you lot cower behind whenever something dangerous shows up? Us! That's who! Fat lot of good you are when you all go down in one or two hits! No warriors, no war! It's as simple as that!"

Damien tracked the sound of the last voice until he found a grumpy-looking veteran with a beard, an eyepatch and a bad attitude. Damien tried to get his attention, which proved difficult since a paladin the next table over had just slated warriors for being "all brawn and no brains."

"Excuse me, I'd like to sign up for warrior training."

The grizzled warrior's remaining eye lingered on the paladin a few moments longer before he grumbled and turned to find the rag-clad boy in front of him. A victorious smirk crept up one side of his battle-worn face and he greeted Damien with a voice that was perfectly calculated to be heard by the entire street.

"Look what we have here! Another clever soul who knows exactly how great warriors are. That makes two hundred and eighty-six just this morning!" He leered over at the paladin's table, his elbow propped on one knee as he stroked his beard in mock rumination. "How are you doing so far, you sanctimonious holier-than-thou numpty?"

"If you were any more evil, I would Smite you myself."

The warrior laughed uproariously. Despite his rush to get on with things, Damien couldn't help but be impressed. The inter-actions between AI characters were incredible. If he hadn't heard a variation on this conversation during his first play-through, he'd have been hard pushed to tell the difference between the recruiters and actual human beings.

The warrior settled and roughly pushed a parchment and quill over the tabletop toward him.

"Just tell us your name, young one, and I'll register you for training at the fighting pits."

Damien picked up the quill. The parchment became overlaid with a keyboard in the same blue hue as the menu screen. Above the blank space on the parchment floated the words 'Please select your character's name'. He tapped 'Scorpius' into it and the letters filled the space, immediately followed by a red cross and small red writing that stated - 'Name unavailable'.

Damien's eyes widened. Why had he not seen this coming? Because the beta server had prepared him poorly for sharing Arcadia with the rest of the world, that's why. Oh well, he could still run with a substitute. 'Scorpius56'. 'Name unavailable'. 'Scorpius16'. 'Name unavailable'. 'XscorpiusX'. 'Name unavailable'.

With each failed attempt, Damien read between the lines of the warrior's exchange with the paladin a little more clearly. A large number of players who'd seen his fight with Toutatis had rushed to claim his character's name. Faltering, Damien had just found out that 'DamienxScorpius' was also unavailable when someone tapped him on the shoulder.

"You gonna be long, mate?"

Damien turned around to apologize and got the shock of his life. There was a clone of himself looking him right in the eye. Behind that one stood two more doppelgängers, each looking more irritated than the one in front of him. Damien dropped the quill, accidentally canceling his registration process. He looked back to the inactive parchment and then at the impatient fanboy who hadn't even recognized the very person he was imitating.

"N-no, that's okay, you go ahead."

"Thanks, buddy."

Damien stepped out of the way, his mind still reeling as the doppelgänger confidently strode in to take his place. He picked up the quill and deftly tapped the parchment several times. The warrior registrar looked up and nodded at him.

"Welcome to the warrior caste, Scorepious Six Hundred and Sixty-Six. You'll find the fighting pits just down the path, on the right."

Scorepious666 did a little fist pump before turning to leave, only to find Damien gawping at him.

"Hey, that's a pretty good likeness," Scorepious666 declared. "You put a hyper-realistic slant on it, that's neat. You don't look much like the real thing but it's definitely original! What face editor are you using?"

When Damien replied with nothing but a long drawn-out moan, Scorepious666 gave him a perturbed look and hurried away down the path, leaving Damien to his own private hell.

This was a complete disaster. His plan was unraveling in front of him. He moved to one side and opened his menu, searching frantically for the connections tab. He had to see if Kevin could help him.

Unless he could secure his character's real name, he'd have

to try and stand out in a sea of human warriors who would all be racing him to level up. Worse still, they'd all have a version of his name that was closer to the real thing than he could get for himself!

He found the connections tab and jabbed his finger at it, breathing a sigh of relief when he found 'Mobius46' in his list of contacts. In his haste he clicked it before realizing the name was grayed out. Kevin was not currently online.

He was trying to think of another way to reach out when he realized his eyes had scrolled past another name. A name that, by any measure, should not have belonged in his friends list. Damien stared at it, trying to figure out if he was reading it right. It simply read 'Aetherius'.

The shock was so great that his previous encounter was briefly erased from his mind.

Why was Aetherius, the current leader of the Saga Online Streamer Competition, on his friends list? Curiosity overwhelmed him. He clicked the name and was invited via the in-game icons to call, message or invite Aetherius to a party. The message icon was highlighted. Aetherius had left him a message. Damien numbly clicked the icon and a message window popped up.

'Hello Damien. Our mutual friend, Kevin, gave me your contact details and asked me to lend you a hand. Send me a message when you see this and I'll give you a boost. It'll be great for your ratings!'

Of course! Aetherius was another of Kevin's testers. After the rude shock of finding out his uniqueness had been stolen from him, this message was like mana from heaven.

Kevin, Damien thought to himself, *NOW you can consider your debt repaid*.

He brought his hands up to chest height and a keyboard appeared at his fingertips. He frantically started typing.

'Aetherius! It's awesome to meet you! I'd be very happy if you could boost me, thank you! Can you come and meet me?'

He sat back and held his breath. Aetherius's name was all in blue, so he was online. If Damien was given a boost through a dungeon with high-level enemies by the most famous Saga Online player, it would solve all his problems at once. He'd quickly rise to level 10, overtaking all the people who were imitating him.

The hard cap on XP gain was one and a half levels. Even if you were being boosted, you could only ever rise by a maximum of one and a half levels per unique experience granting event. That was still a lot: If a level 1 player with 0/500 EXP was set up to achieve the killing blow against a high level dungeon boss, they would effortlessly rise to level 2 and get an additional 250/750 EXP towards level 3.

If a different level 1 player challenged Toutatis in single combat, defeating him with nothing but a rusty spoon and a week of perfect dodging while they waited for him to succumb to tetanus, they would also rise to level 2 and receive an additional 250/750 EXP towards level 3. If they'd had a quest to kill Toutatis as well, they'd receive another 1125 EXP for handing it in, bringing them to level 3 and gaining a total of 625/1000 EXP towards level 4. Even with the quest EXP factored in, it wouldn't really be worthy of the effort. This 1.5 level EXP cap was hard coded, so even the human 'Adaptable' trait would not raise it.

After you hit level 10 the amount of experience required per level increased dramatically. Boosting would only be efficient up to that point, but even if the benefit was short lived it was well worth it. Getting to level 10 would ordinarily take at least a day. A sensibly planned, well administered boost could reduce that to less than an hour. More importantly, Damien would get a huge amount of exposure, not only on his own channel but on Aetherius's channel as well. He could take any name he liked and it would hardly matter – everyone would know exactly who he was. His joy peaked when Aetherius replied.

'Sure thing, I'll be coming all the way back to the Tintagel zone for you. Just make sure you get to the dungeon I've marked on the **map** in half an hour. Don't be late!'

Damien clicked the link and his map opened. A black skull signifying a dungeon entrance appeared near the bottom left-hand corner of the zone's map. Damien didn't know which dungeon it might be, but he didn't need to know anything about it to see that it was far away. Aetherius must have assumed Damien already completed basic training and was combat ready, but he hadn't even managed that yet. Damien shook his head as his hands tentatively typed out a reply.

'Haven't completed basic training yet. Can you give me a little more time?'

Anxious, he bit at his fingernails. It turned out that fingernail biting was not an activity that Saga Online endorsed: as his teeth clacked together, his health bar dropped by a single point.

Damien stared at it incredulously. He had just crossed a minor gaming milestone in the most ridiculous way possible. The first enemy to have caused him damage in this play-through of Saga Online was himself. He considered the events that had put him there and found it unsettlingly appropriate.

Aetherius replied and Damien was forced to shelve his lingering self-pity. He had a more immediate problem.

'Sorry man, got guild business afterwards. If you can't make it, we'll have to do it later, and I don't know when I'll next have an opening. Don't worry, you don't need to do basic training. I'll be there to look after you. See you in twenty-nine minutes!'

Damien groaned. How was he supposed to travel across the zone with a level 1 character? If he was going to acquire some skills beforehand, he'd have to start by permanently branding himself with some terrible variation of his name.

The possibility of '5k0rp1ou5' briefly ran through Damien's

head, making his hair stand on end. Even if he found a name that wouldn't take a non-player character half an hour to say out loud ('Five-Kay-Zero-Erp-One-Uwe-Five'; Damien shuddered at the thought of it), he'd still have to finish basic training before they equipped him with skills and gear. It would already be too late by then.

He'd have to head straight there as he was. If Aetherius said it was ok, it would probably be fine.

He pulled his map into the top right corner of his field of vision and extended his finger to tap the newly acquired location. An opaque blue line appeared on the map, with a red arrow indicating his character at one end of it and his destination at the other.

Damien turned and ran past the fighting pit toward the encampment exit, threading his way through the ambling masses without attracting so much as a second glance. The gates were wide open and he attempted to pass through without stopping, only to find himself running in place on the threshold. A pop-up appeared in the middle of his screen and he paused to read it.

'You have not yet selected a class. If you leave the safe zone you will be vulnerable to attacks from player and non-player characters. The respawn time is 24 hours. Any experience you gain towards the next level will be lost upon death. It is highly advised you select a class before continuing further. Are you sure you wish to leave?'

Damien nodded irritably. He already knew leaving the safe zone without a class was a bad idea but losing this opportunity was a worse one. He'd just have to be very careful. The pop-up disappeared.

Across the threshold of the gate, he broke into a jog. His stamina bar depleted quickly down to 75/100, then it balanced out and started to reduce more slowly.

The well-trodden dirt path of the encampment merged into a sturdy sandstone highway. At least Tintagel should be reasonably safe. It was unlikely there would be player-killing activity so close to a capital city. Players would face severe repercussions from Empire guards if they were caught murdering a fellow citizen in Empire controlled space. They'd end up losing reputation, forfeiting the items and gold they'd looted and wasting valuable game time in a cell, meaning that for all intents and purposes they might as well log out until their sentence was served. Depending on the severity of the crime, that could take longer than death.

Damien's best defense against players was that he was worthless. You didn't gain any experience for killing other players. All the risk and reward circled around the potential to steal some quality loot from them. As it stood, Damien had no equipment, no items, no coin, nothing worth having whatsoever. Somehow this did not provide him with much comfort.

His real worry was the in-game mobs that wouldn't bother to check his level and gear before they tore his defenseless body limb from limb. Damien passed a pair of patrolling knights on horseback heading in the opposite direction and felt a bit safer. If he stuck to the road, he should be just fine.

Camelot was far behind him when a phone icon appeared on the edge of his vision, blinking urgently. There was no indication who it might be. Damien frowned. If it had been Aetherius or Kevin, their player ID would have shown up.

He took the opportunity to replenish his stamina to full, slowing to a walk before focusing on the screen and tilting his head upward very slightly. He was surprised when the minimal movement resulted in the call being answered.

"Hello?"

"Good morning, I'm Liz from the CU Public Service. Am I speaking to Damien Arkwright?"

Damien stopped dead in the middle of the road. If Central Union was calling, it could only be about his mother.

"Yes, you are."

"Please note that all calls are recorded and any and all information revealed in the call is subject to—"

"I agree. Please tell me that my mom is OK?"

There was a nervous cough before Liz continued.

"There has been no change in your mother's condition. She is stable, but the hospital has elected to keep her in a comatose state until a suitable—"

"A coma? A coma! Since when has she been in a coma?"

"Your mother arrived in hospital at eight twenty-six yesterday evening, already in a comatose state. After conducting several tests, the hospital concluded it would be safer to keep her comatose rather than reviving her and risk straining her heart further."

Damien's own heart plummeted into his stomach. When he did not respond, the woman took the initiative.

"The hospital is attempting to locate a suitable heart for her. They will keep her sedated and treated, but what she really needs is a viable replacement."

Damien swallowed. He knew where this was going. The healthcare system was not kind to those with limited income.

"Under Health Insurance Policy D, your mother was two hundred and eighty-sixth in line for a new heart matching her blood type. Due to the urgency of her situation, her status has been upgraded to HIP B and she is currently thirty-fifth in the queue."

So even if thirty-four good hearts were found, Cassandra's situation would remain unchanged. Damien tried not to think about it and failed spectacularly.

"Sir, I know it's a lot of information to process. Please take your time."

"Why can't she be brought up to HIP A?"

"I'm very sorry, but HIP A is exclusively for bionic replacements which are prohibitively expensive. Is there anyone you can ask for financial assistance?"

Damien hesitated. Cassandra would be furious if she found out, but he preferred her angry and alive.

"You could try my father. He doesn't live with us. His name is Leonard Arkwrig—"

"I have already contacted Mr. Arkwright on your behalf. Unfortunately, he is unable to assist you with this situation financially. You will still need a guardian to look after you while your mother is in hospital. Mr. Arkwright is the obvious choice, but you're old enough that the Central Union will take your preference into consideration."

Damien was caught off guard. His back-up plan had fallen through faster than he could even say the words. On top of that, they were trying to force him to leave his home.

"I want to stay here until my mother comes back. That's my first choice."

For the first time since the call started, the voice on the other end of the line went completely silent. Damien had no desire whatsoever to leave his home. It would feel too much like abandoning his mother.

At last the voice came back, but the officious tone was gone.

"Damien, what's happening to you right now is incredibly hard. I'm very sorry. I've been doing this for a few years and I'm familiar with the process. Please may I give you some advice? Not advice from Central Union but from me to you, as honest as I can be?"

Damien stared ahead. Somehow he didn't think he was going to like what came next.

"Ok. I'm listening."

"The Central Union won't allow you to stay in your home without a guardian. If you don't pick someone for us to approach as your guardian, the system will default to you entering state care. You don't want to be in state care, Damien, believe me. If you have anyone who might take you in, this is the moment where you have to tell me. I promise you I will try my best to put you together with them."

Damien could read the underlying message. There was a good chance his mother was never coming home. CU already knew this. Without that bionic heart she was as good as dead. The voice did not move to rush him this time.

The only indication they were still connected was the low murmur of uninvested voices in the background. The voices of CU, where it had already been decided that his mother's life wasn't worth the cost of a bionic heart. That thought sat like a burning coal in his gut, fueling his anger and frustration.

Damien kept control of his emotions, but only just.

"Listen to me very carefully, Liz. My mother is going to come out of hospital and she's going to be fine. She'll come home, and —and everything will go back to the way it was before. She didn't work with a heart defect for the last five years so I could leave her to die. I'll earn the money myself if I have to, but I'm not giving up on her, unlike CU, and I'm not leaving my home!"

He swept his hand through the air and the call was cut. Despite his stamina being full, Damien found himself gasping for air. He closed his eyes, forcing out tears that streamed down his cheeks as he slowly counted to ten.

He'd never cried while playing the game before. It turned the absurd realism of Saga Online's virtual world into a curse. He used to play this game to escape from his life, welcoming the faithful recreation of his emotions and physical state as a way to fully immerse himself in his character's story. Having fielded this extremely unpleasant call, the thin line separating his character from himself had never been more blurred.

As the adrenaline left him, he looked up to find he was being stared at by Scawpeous69. The level 6 warrior was equipped considerably better than he was.

Damien could feel his anger rising again. He took in his copy's dumb look of surprise and the tears that stained his own face, the face that didn't even seem to belong to him anymore. It felt like the game was mocking him. Something inside him snapped.

"What are you looking at? Isn't it enough that you stole my identity without listening in on a private call? Go! Away!"

Scawpeous69's jaw abruptly snapped shut and his features hardened. It was strange being stared at by your own angry face, but Damien didn't flinch.

The copy kept his weapon sheathed but he walked toward Damien slowly, stopping a few feet away.

"This name wasn't my first choice either, but too many people got in ahead of me. The character isn't about the name anyway, it's about what I do with it. I want to be like Scorpius, who never gives up even when it looks like there's no way he can win. The name is just to remind me of that."

He looked Damien up and down before raising an eyebrow.

"You should head back to the encampment and pick a name and class for yourself, even if it's not your first choice. The real Scorpius would never act the way you're acting."

He took in the look of shock on Damien's face before giving him a satisfied nod and heading off through the crossroads, presumably returning to the encampment to hand in a quest. Damien was confounded. He couldn't stop himself from yelling out to the warrior's retreating back.

"But I AM the real Scorpius!"

Scawpeous69 didn't bother turning around. He simply raised his hand and waved it in the air dismissively as he continued forward.

"Now *that's* a delusion I can't help you with."

Before Damien even knew how to respond, the figure was too far away. Just when Damien thought things couldn't get any worse, he'd been chastised by one of his fans for not being enough like himself.

His map was still in the corner of the screen, the blue line beckoning him onward. Between the call from CU and the unwanted advice, he was now running late. Cursing under his breath, Damien wiped his eyes and set to jogging again.

If there was one thing he was learning that day it was that things could always get worse. He wasn't going to linger at the crossroads and find out how much worse. As long as Aetherius could help him, this could all be fixed.

5

FALLING FOR AETHERIUS

A s it turned out, the dungeon was not connected to the highway. It was in the center of a dense forest, off to one side. Damien would have to go a short distance off-road in order to get there. He looked into the woods, which seemed to devour all light that entered its sinister canopy. A death trap.

He brought up his chat with Aetherius and rattled out a message.

'Outside the forest. Doesn't look safe. Can you come and meet me here?'

He stood there waiting for another minute with no response. Had Aetherius not seen it? What if he was in a chat with someone else and by the time he saw Damien's message it was too late? Damien couldn't afford to wait any longer. He'd have to risk it.

Tentatively, he made his way off the road toward the edge of the forest and peered inside. The darkness seemed impenetrable, even up close. His imagination conjured up images of all the things that could be lurking there. Not that it mattered; just about anything would be capable of killing him at this stage. A hungry caterpillar would probably pose a serious threat.

Damien summoned his courage and trudged into the forest.

As soon as he entered, the darkness was greatly diminished. It was less like shade from the trees overhead and more as if a dark miasma was shielding the forest from the outside, fading away as soon as he passed through it.

Perhaps it was to preserve graphics? Given the incredible displays Damien had seen in the game so far, that seemed unlikely. Whatever the reason, Damien was grateful to be able to see. The forest was considerably less creepy that way.

As he made his way over gnarled roots and grasping branches, his eyes acclimatized further. Despite being dense with trees and undergrowth, the forest was not particularly large and he soon came upon a clearing in the middle, where the trees seemed to pull away as if to uproot themselves and escape from the cavernous hole that lay in the middle.

As Damien approached it, the blue line on his map disappeared. He had reached his destination. Aside from the hole, there was nothing of interest to be seen.

It was about thirty feet across and ringed with a knee-high wall of stone. Was this really the right place? Even if it seemed foreboding and grim, it was just a hole in the ground. Surely it couldn't be the entrance to a dungeon?

Damien carefully edged toward it and peered inside. The outer edge was ringed with a stone staircase the width of three men standing side by side. Each stair ended in a jagged point, granting the hole the likeness of a gargantuan subterranean worm's maw.

He could only see about twenty feet down before the darkness swallowed the staircase whole. It made the forest seem jolly by comparison. He edged away from it and folded his arms. Why had Aetherius brought him to this strange place? Come to think of it, why wasn't he here already?

"You made it!"

Damien whipped around. Standing only a few feet away, wearing his signature smirk that seemed wider than the chasm at Damien's back, was the most famous of all Saga Online's streamers.

Aetherius looked every bit as confident and aloof as he did in the streams that Damien had watched reverentially over the two months since the game had begun.

He looked even more glamorous in person, his red and gold robes flowing around him as though he were immersed in the currents of a riptide only he could feel. His long golden hair sat over his pointed elven ears, flowing down over his shoulders. His facial features were typical for an elf, sharp enough to look as though touching them might cause damage.

He regarded Damien through piercing green eyes, the last thing so many of his enemies had seen. Well, until they respawned a day later, anyway.

"Sorry I'm a bit late. You'd be amazed how many people spot me and want to pose for pictures!"

Damien should have been amazed. But after everything that had happened in the brief span between him leaving the encampment and finally meeting with his savior, the emotion that consumed him was relief. He hadn't realized how exhausted he was until the moment he could finally relax.

With Aetherius on his side, everything was going to be all right. He sat down heavily on the wall encircling the dungeon, bracing himself with both hands as he stared between his feet. It had been an ordeal, but he was safe.

"Hey! What's that face for? Aren't you pleased to see me?"

Damien looked up and realized why Aetherius appeared so much taller than him. Technically he was only about a foot taller, but he was also floating a foot off the ground. He drifted over to Damien with his arms folded.

Damien smiled weakly. "Sorry, Aetherius. It really is great to meet you and I'm very grateful you've come to help me out, especially with everything else you have going on. It's just been a really rough day."

Aetherius unfolded his arms and fanned the palms of his hands downward, descending to the floor softly. The breeze that had been blowing through his clothes subsided.

"Come on, Damien, you fought Toutatis! Remember? Surely a short walk across the zone isn't enough to faze you?"

Damien threw his hands up in the air. Ever since Toutatis had shown up, everything had gone wrong for him and he'd had no one to talk to about it. Finally, he had the ear of someone who might understand.

He wasn't even sure where to begin, but it didn't matter. The feelings he'd been repressing for the last sixteen hours poured out of him like an unstoppable flood.

"My mom's in hospital. She almost died in front of me yesterday after Toutatis, but Kevin gave me a new headset so I could play. I thought if I could play as Scorpius, I'd be able to get enough followers to win the Streamer Competition and pay her hospital bills. When I came online, everybody had already made characters with my name. They even look like me! Then *you* message me and I think everything will be all right, but on the way here I got a call from CU. My mom needs a new heart and CU wants to put me into foster care! I don't know what to do. How can I get enough followers to help my mother if everyone's already playing as me? Aetherius, I know you're the favorite to win but this is a life and death situation. Please, can you help me?"

The moment Damien had finished talking, he was incredibly embarrassed. He'd only just met this guy and he was blurting out his whole life story. His eyes dropped back to his feet, his face turning crimson with shame. Aetherius had his own problems, but he'd been kind enough to take time out of his professional gaming schedule to give Damien a quick boost. Not to dedicate himself to a noob player indefinitely. Now he probably wouldn't want to give the boost at all. Damien stood up without taking his eyes off the floor, his arms straight down by his sides and his hands clenched into fists.

"You know what? Forget I said anything. I'm sorry I dragged you all the way out here just so you could listen to me—"

"It sounds like it's a good thing I got here when I did."

Damien looked up and found that Aetherius's trademark smirk had disappeared. He met Damien's eye and thumbed toward himself.

"I promise you that before I leave, I'll have made you world famous, both in the game and out! You have my word."

Damien could hardly believe his ears. He'd thought Aetherius would be offended, but instead it was like a dream come true. If Aetherius was going to help him save his mother then it was totally possible.

"All right, Damien, that stuff you told me just now was a bit sensitive so I'll have to edit it out. Let's start from scratch. Everybody's going to see this, so try to look your best, ok?"

Damien nodded eagerly. He didn't have to pretend to smile. It finally felt like his bad luck was turning around.

Aetherius made a gesture and a wisp of blue light instantly appeared over his shoulder. With a flick of his wrist, Aetherius sent the Mana Wisp in front of him and held three fingers behind his back so Damien could see it. The fingers counted down and when they were all gone, Aetherius's cocky grin was back and he began talking to the wisp as if it were a video camera.

"Hello there, loyal viewers! Today I have a special treat for you. We are joined by none other than Scorpius, AKA Damien! The brave soul who took on Toutatis yesterday has now joined us in the Streamer Competition. Damien, give the viewers at home a wave."

Damien obediently raised a hand and beamed at the camera. Aetherius turned back to make sure Damien had hit his cue. The elf's smile crept a little higher up one side of his face.

"As you can see, Damien hasn't chosen a class yet and he's still wearing the gear he entered the game in. So, first things first, we're going to fix that. Damien, I've brought you some gear to play through your first dungeon! Let's trade them in for those dirty rags you're wearing, shall we?"

Awesome! Aetherius had clearly thought this through. Damien quickly went into his menu screen and found the trade tab. He looked at his equipped clothes tab. The rags he'd spawned in provided no stat bonuses except for one armor point each. He'd be glad to see them gone. He put them into the trade window and waited for Aetherius to insert his new gear. No items appeared on Aetherius's side, but a green tick indicated he was ready to trade.

Damien glanced up at him, puzzled. "I don't see the gear yet. Did you—"

Aetherius turned his head to face the Mana Wisp and laughed, a finger raised.

"Excuse me for just one moment. I probably should've briefed my partner on what we're doing."

He swiveled, leaving the mana wisp behind him and over his shoulder, his smile faltering as he hissed at Damien between his teeth.

"I need you out of those rags. I've got a short spiel about the items prepared and then when I trade they'll be auto-equipped into your empty slots instantly. It'll look really cool! Come on, man, don't waste time. Let's go!"

Damien looked between Aetherius and the mana wisp behind him, then quickly accepted the trade. He didn't want to look foolish, keeping everyone waiting. The rags were unequipped and transferred over in the blink of an eye. Good riddance! Now he was only wearing the mandatory loincloth that Saga Online wouldn't allow you to remove, but that would soon be fixed.

Aetherius beamed and turned his back on him to look at the mana wisp. There was a pause of a few seconds while Damien smiled awkwardly in the game's equivalent of underpants, wondering what the delay was for. Then Aetherius started to speak again.

"Hello, everyone! I'm here with the mighty Scorpius, AKA Damien, who became so popular after his fight with Toutatis yesterday."

Damien's smile faltered. What was going on? Had his interruption prompted Aetherius to start the stream from the beginning?

"I'm here to give him a boost, as well as sharing a special trick with all of you at home."

While Aetherius kept talking, Damien's mind raced. Why wasn't he talking about the gear yet? Did he want him standing here wearing nothing but the loincloth, looking like a complete moron? Then it hit him. He never needed to trade Aetherius the rags. He could've just unequipped them himself. He'd only traded them because Aetherius was recording—

"You see, this is one of the only dungeons where it's possible to boost someone all the way to the boss floor in just five seconds flat!"

—but now it was obvious that Aetherius could have just started again from the beginning. He didn't understand. Before Damien could advance the thought further, Aetherius had turned around and rested a hand on his shoulder.

"Are you ready?"

Damien recognized the grin that crept up one side of Aetherius's face. The hand on his shoulder that was slightly too tight. Most of all, Damien recognized his eyes.

The sharp, green eyes that were the last thing so many of his enemies had seen. He recognized all these things and the wisp zoomed in on his face to capture that final, aching moment of despair.

"Bye!"

Aetherius planted his foot against Damien's chest and pushed. Damien's legs hit the back of the stone wall surrounding the chasm before he tumbled helplessly over it.

He caught sight of the wisp flickering over the top of the entrance to immortalize his fall from grace before the darkness swallowed him whole. Aetherius's laughter followed him all the way down.

6

THINGS CAN ALWAYS GET WORSE

D amien couldn't believe his bad luck. As the wind rushed around his ears, he gritted his teeth and yelled a single word.

"Menu!"

Even as he cartwheeled through the air in the pitch black, the menu remained illuminated and helpfully centered in his vision. One particular option, usually his least favorite of them all, suddenly seemed incredibly attractive. It was a bit of a stretch, but he didn't see how else he might get out of this situation.

"Log out!"

'It is not possible to log out while your character is falling. Please wait until you have stopped falling and try again.'

Damien's vision flashed red and his health bar plummeted. A sickening crunch was followed by a high-pitched screech that rang in his ears, echoing the scream his mother's guardian wrist-band had made not so long ago.

What little remained of his health faded and the screeching ceased. There was only one reasonable conclusion Damien could come to. He was dead. He had never actually died in the game before but he was pretty certain this is what it looked like.

Through his blurred vision he could make out a tiny pinprick of light in the distance. Probably an animation of his character entering heaven, where it would be stuck for the day. Maybe he'd meet Toutatis and get some pointers about landing properly.

Damien lay there, trying to come to terms with what had just happened to him. His body felt sore all over, but at least it had been a quick death and didn't hurt too much. Maybe his pain settings were set at the default level? That would make sense; he hadn't looked at them since he logged in.

Damien closed his menu so he could watch the death animation without anything being in the way. As soon as it was over, he resolved to contact Kevin and tell him what a douche Aetherius was. With any luck, Kevin might be able to get him around the twenty-four-hour respawn timer so he could keep testing the headset.

But first he'd have to get through the stupid death animation, which seemed to be going incredibly slowly.

His eyes widened, and he realized he'd got it all wrong. The light, far from being a simulated version of heaven's gates, was actually coming from the dungeon entrance far above.

He was alive? Damien focused on his health bar. It was so low there wasn't even a trace of green inside it, but upon closer inspection it turned out he had a whopping 4/100 HP. As he watched, it ticked up another notch to 5/100 and the tiniest sliver of green appeared on the left-hand side of the frame.

How was this possible? The gaping maw of the dungeon entrance was barely even visible from this distance, surely over a hundred feet. Fall damage, much like in real life, was calculated by how hard you hit the ground. Unlike real life, it was calculated on a percentage basis to guarantee death for even the sturdiest of characters: the higher the fall, the faster the drop, the higher the percentage cut from your health points. It only took a few seconds for the percentage to exceed 100%. Armor and damage mitigation abilities helped, but not much. Damien had neither. Fall damage from that high ought to have killed him outright.

As he attempted to push himself upright, something shifted underneath him. He lost his balance and collapsed alongside it.

Damien found himself face to face with a monster. Cold eyes stared at him down a long frothing snout, ending in a vicious pair of teeth. Damien yelped and instinctively pushed it away, expecting the beast to start gnashing and biting at any moment.

The creature did not respond. Unlike him, it was very dead. Damien removed his hands from it in disgust and the creature's corpse rolled back to its original position. He dragged his aching body a few precious inches further away and squinted at it in the darkness. It was a giant rat.

He'd killed his fair share of these things when he was playing as Scorpius. They were a pretty common sight in the dungeons across Arcadia, even if they didn't pose much of a challenge after the first few levels. That didn't explain why it was dead.

An idea dawned on him. It was almost too stupid to contemplate, but he couldn't see any other solution that made sense.

"No. No way. You've got to be kidding me."

Damien opened his stat page. As he'd suspected, he'd gained experience points. The screech he'd heard when he hit the floor had been this unfortunate rat. He must've landed right on top of it, and its body had softened the fall just enough to allow Damien to survive. He stared at it in disbelief.

All of a sudden, the ridiculousness of the situation got the better of him. He was lying on the bottom floor of a dungeon dressed only in a loincloth, he'd survived a hundred-foot fall with no skills whatsoever and his first in-game kill had been carried out accidentally by means of a gravity-assisted body slam. He burst into hysterical laughter.

Damien's high spirits were short lived. He may have just performed the most hardcore kill of all time, but he was still in an extremely bad situation. His health had slowly ticked upward to 7/100.

With a mere ten constitution, he was only going to regenerate one health point every ten seconds outside of combat. Well, he could at least try to use the time wisely.

He went into his menu options, selecting 'Settings' so he could review his pain setting. It was at the default, 10%, as he'd suspected. Much less and he might not even be aware when he was taking damage, much more and he might simply wish he was dead to get it over with. Damien considered the various horrible things that had happened to him recently and decided it could stay there.

Then he went into his friends list to delete Aetherius and discovered the name was already grayed out. Maybe Aetherius had already blocked him or maybe he'd just logged out to upload the video as soon as possible, but either way it wasn't possible to connect with him right now. Damien blocked the link on his own screen, severing ties permanently.

Aetherius had promised to make Damien's life easy but had decided to cripple him and make fun of him instead. At some point Aetherius was going to pay for what he'd done. But that would have to wait.

His mother still came first.

To that end, he'd need video content for the Streamer Competition. He clicked the 'Media' tab and was presented with two options: Record and Review. It was a shame he'd only found it just now, but besides landing on the rat there wasn't anything he felt like sharing from that morning. Aetherius was probably going to post his side of the story before too long anyway.

Damien shook his head. There was no point in thinking about that. He'd have to deal with it after he got out of there. For now, he had to make the best of a bad situation. He clicked 'Record' and the menu automatically closed. A small red dot was blinking at him from the corner of his HUD.

Damien blinked back at it. Like the rest of today's events, he hadn't thought this through. Lying on the floor in almost total darkness, wearing nothing but a loincloth next to a giant dead rat was not an ideal streaming platform, but he'd have to make do.

"So.... hello, everyone. I'm Damien, and this is where I am after Aetherius's generous boost. Thanks, Aetherius, by the way. You psychopath. Anyway, as you can see, I'm still alive."

He looked up at the dungeon entrance overhead to make his point.

"All thanks to this cheeky little fellow. Everybody say hi!"

He turned his head back toward the dead rat. It seemed uglier each time he looked at it.

"So, I landed on this thing when Aetherius kicked me in. Survived the fall with—"

A skittering shriek reverberated off the walls. It sounded like another giant rat. Damien had no way of knowing where it was coming from but it was clearly close by. It must have heard him talking to himself and come to investigate. As usual, he'd somehow managed to make things worse. And since it lived down here, it would probably see him before he saw it.

Damien checked his HP. 17/100. Not enough to try and fight it, especially unarmed. He could hear the pitter-patter of feet and heavy rhythmic breathing getting closer and closer. Even though he wasn't live streaming, the blinking red dot added terrible pressure.

All his potential viewers were about to watch him die. Damien considered his few options and only found one that made any sense. He placed his head on the floor and pretended to be dead. At least with no clothes and very low health he'd look the part.

As soon as he'd made his choice, the dungeon went eerily silent. Damien knew better than to raise his head. He kept his eyes locked on the foaming mouth of the dead rat in front of him and waited. He might have to move very quickly if this plan of his didn't work out.

In that case, he would probably be as good as dead anyway, but he'd rather leave himself the option instead of simply closing his eyes and wishing the evil away.

A shape loomed behind his first kill. Despite Damien's inability to see more than a few feet in front of him, the low rattle in the back of the new arrival's throat confirmed it was another giant rat. It was investigating its fallen comrade. He would be next on its list and his HP wasn't getting much higher. 19/100.

He heard the creature sniff the air, searching for the smallest sign of life. Damien did his best impression of a corpse, slowing his breathing and remaining perfectly still. The slightest movement would give him away. A notification popped up in the corner of his HUD

Sneak Unlocked!

Well, if he died here, at least he'd have something to show for it.

But even with this new ability it wasn't going to take the rat long to find him. He needed a plan, something other than pretending to be dead until the rat removed the 'pretending' bit for him. The red light was still blinking as if to remind him what was at stake. Damien had nothing to offer it. All he had was this dead ra—

Wait.

There was a chance. It was only a small chance, but it was better than nothing.

Trying his absolute best not to make a sound, Damien used the dead rat as cover and moved his hand toward it until he made contact. His heart thumping in his chest, he focused every ounce of his concentration into a single word: 'Loot'. An inventory bar opened in his vision with a little pop. The pop made him flinch, thinking the noise would give away his position. In fact, as he remembered an instant later, it was an auditory cue for his ears only.

It was the flinching itself that gave him away.

All at once, the second rat gave a grunt of surprise and swiveled its misshapen head over its brother's corpse. A steady stream of diseased drool spilled out from the beast's lips. Damien remained absolutely still, his hand still pressed against his unwitting savior's chest, keeping the inventory tab open.

There were four items, each more useless than the last: an eyeball, a toenail, a shattered rib and a patch of fur. Damien had never understood why the drop rates in RPGs were so hilariously inaccurate. Surely this thing had more than one toenail? What happened to the other eyeball?

He did not have time to pore over these deep philosophical questions, because the living rat had hopped up on top of the rat corpse with its front legs and was looming over him, extending its snout toward his prone body.

Damien made his choice. His chosen item appeared directly in his hand and he grasped it firmly.

The creature inhaled deeply—

And Damien thrust the shattered rib upward, directly into its exposed throat.

Sneak Attack Multiplier Added!
Critical Strike Multiplier Added!
Damage: 18

The creature roared with surprise.

Damien cried out in exasperation. That damage was absolutely pitiful for a sneak critical. The enraged rodent lunged at him but was kept at bay by the makeshift dagger lodged in its throat. Damien put both hands together around the improvised weapon as he tried desperately to keep the snapping jaws away.

The rat's claws were scraping his arms, causing damage that ordinarily would have been of no concern to Damien whatsoever. Not now, though. His health was so low he couldn't afford to lose a single point. He pulled his feet around until they were underneath his struggling adversary and kicked.

Had he been playing as Scorpius, this maneuver would have sent the rat flying. With low stats and no skills, it only served to reduce his stamina, remove the rib from the rat's throat and allow it access to his unprotected legs. Greedily, the rat took advantage, twisting its head as it attempted to catch them in its open jaws.

Damien screamed with rage. He hadn't come all this way to be killed by a damn rat. He drew it back on his legs and kicked again, harder, and the rat toppled over the corpse behind it.

Damien used most of his remaining stamina to leap after it, landing directly on top of it and pinning it on its back. With his forearm pressed against its critically wounded throat, he raised the shattered rib and plunged it into the rat's chest. It only did 3 damage.

He threw his arm back high above his head and stabbed it over and over and over again. After seven or eight blows, which to Damien felt like a thousand, damage numbers stopped appearing. The rat gurgled blood and joined its compatriot in death.

Damien fell off sideways and landed on his back between the two dead rats, panting for air. On balance, the first rat had been much easier to kill. Maybe Aetherius had it right and jumping head first into dungeons was the way to go.

Covered from head to toe in filth and rat blood, Damien started shaking with anger. He could have found a decent name by now and started leveling all by himself, but he'd trusted in Aetherius instead. Oh, he was gonna get him all right. One dead enemy at a time.

Notifications popped up, informing Damien that he had learned two new skills.

Sneak Attack Unlocked!
Critical Strike Unlocked!

Still lying on the ground, he opened his menu and navigated to the 'Skills' tab.

Sneak Attack: *Initiating combat before the enemy is aware of your presence is extremely effective. Damage is tripled for daggers and doubled for all other weapons when Sneak Attacking an enemy.*

Critical Strike: *Targeting weak points on an enemy will grant a multiplier effect that varies depending on the vulnerability of the weak point.*

Damien read the names without bothering to read the descriptions. Scorpius had used both these skills before, so Damien was already familiar with how they worked. He was more interested in the experience gain. He looked at his Stats page. The experience bar was at 312/500. More than halfway to level 2.

He closed the menu and the blinking red light caught his

attention once more. The headset was still recording. Damien was about to speak when he remembered that was how he'd attracted the last enemy. Then he remembered how much noise they'd made during the fight and decided that if something else was going to come and kill him, it would have done so already.

"Sorry about that. I'm a little preoccupied at the moment. I might not be able to talk much, but I'll keep recording anyway."

He inspected his health. It was back down to 14/100, but at least he'd avoided being bitten. He knew from experience that even if the bite hadn't killed him outright, the secondary poison effect would have resulted in a slow, lingering and extremely annoying death.

He placed his hand on his latest victim and a new loot tab popped up. This one had an eyeball, a thighbone and even a ruptured spleen. Damien sighed wearily. Still trash. He could kill a dozen rats without getting anything useful. He'd probably have to kill a hundred of them to get all the component parts of one complete rat.

Damien had a little more time to inspect the items than he did previously and noted that, like the shattered rib, the thighbone had a durability stat indicating it could be used. He picked it up in his free hand and opened his inventory to run a comparison.

Thighbone
Durability: 10/10
Damage: 5
Properties: None
Description: A versatile item used in crafting, potion-making or, in a pinch, clubbing things to death (or mild annoyance).

Shattered Rib
Durability: 6/8
Damage: 3
Properties: None
Description: A versatile item used in crafting, potion-making or, in a pinch, stabbing things to death (or mild annoyance).

A stabbing weapon and a blunt weapon.

Look at that, Damien thought to himself, *I'm not even level 2 and I'm already dual wielding. So pro.*

He snorted and sat upright, placing a hand on each rat to take all the items into his inventory. Even if it was trash, he couldn't afford to be picky. The items did not budge. Damien frowned before realizing the problem. He didn't have an inventory. In addition to being unclothed, he'd never picked up a backpack.

Sighing, he looked at his health. It had risen to 21/100, the highest it had been since he started this hellish dungeon crawl.

Damien stood up. He was going to get out of here. The novelty of wearing nothing but a loincloth was starting to wear thin, and he still had a streaming contest to win and a mother to save. It wasn't going to be easy, though. Even if he did have weapons now (sort of) he was still almost completely blind.

He looked up at the opening for reference. There had been a staircase running around the outside of it. If the pattern held, he'd probably find the bottom of the staircase connected to the outer wall. With something resembling a plan in mind, Damien crouched down and slowly moved to the edge of the cavern, searching for the stairs.

7

DUNGEON CRAWLER

D amien placed his foot onto the smooth stone tiles with incredible care. He did not want to give away his position to anything that might be lurking nearby. He also needed to stay as quiet as possible so that he'd hear anything coming for him. Just because nothing had attacked him, that didn't mean something hadn't seen him yet.

In the distance ahead he thought he heard a faint scraping sound. He immediately came to a complete stop, scanning the darkness for any sign of life. He was reluctant to move closer without ensuring he kept the element of surprise, but his tools were extremely limited.

Maybe the trash items could come in useful after all. Very slowly, he retraced his steps to the fallen rats and looted the ruptured spleen. Drawing his arm back, he took aim and threw it ahead of him into the darkness.

He waited, his ears pricked, as it landed out of sight with a satisfying splat.

A moment later something clattered across the stone tiles, moving across his non-existent field of vision from left to right as it followed the noise. Now Damien knew where his quarry was. Using the sound of his enemy's footsteps to mask his own movements, Damien followed in a low crouch.

A silhouette loomed out of the darkness a few feet in front of him. He could make out shoulders and a head, tilted down toward the floor. Whatever the enemy was, it was humanoid.

Nerves on edge, Damien lunged forward, driving the shattered rib into the thing's neck and simultaneously smashing the thighbone across its head in the opposite direction. The last fight had been a mess; he wanted this enemy mob dead with as little fuss as possible.

Sneak Attack Multiplier Added!
Damage: 0
Sneak Attack Multiplier Added!
Critical Strike Multiplier Added!
Damage: 20

The attack with the shattered rib had done no damage. Had he missed? The enemy spun round, clacking its teeth menacingly as its empty eye sockets turned on him. Damien realized his mistake. It was humanoid, all right, it just wasn't technically alive. The rags it was wearing had concealed its lack of flesh. No wonder the stabbing attack hadn't done anything.

A bony arm swung at his head and Damien leapt back. The skeleton advanced on him with wild sweeps of its limbs, its teeth rattling all the while. Damien had the reach advantage.

He stepped backward, narrowly avoiding another swipe, and swung the thighbone round in a wide arc. There was a crack as bone connected with bone.

The skeleton fell to its knees, still clicking its teeth. Damien didn't wait for it to get up. He brought the thighbone down on its head, exploding the skeleton's skull into fragments. There was a low rattle and the dungeon fell silent once more.

Level Up!

Damien smiled. Now he was getting somewhere. He knelt and put a hand on the skeleton, hoping for a better weapon. Maybe by the time he got out of here he'd have a whole host of bone-based weaponry. Perhaps he could appropriate this thing's spinal column and swing it around his head like a mace? Unless the game decided the skeleton didn't have any bones to give him. He wouldn't be surprised.

Looting the skeleton, he found something even better. Clothes!

They were only rags, no better than what he'd given Aetherius, but it was a whole lot better than continuing in a loincloth. At least now he could have a little dignity while he murdered rats and skeletons in this cold dank dungeon using nothing but bones and spleens.

He selected the rags and they were automatically equipped on him, leaving the skeleton's body bare. As expected, the skeleton somehow had no bones to offer him.

Damien opened his Stat page.

Account Name: Damien Arkwright
Character: ????
Level: 2
Health: 110/110
Stamina: 110/110
Mana: 110/110
Stats:
Strength 11 - Agility 11 - Intelligence 11
Constitution 11 - Endurance 11 - Wisdom 11
Stat points: 5
Experience: 26/750

The level up had restored him to full health. Finally! He also had five stat points to allocate. Strength, agility and intelligence would increase his damage with specific skills and weapons. Constitution, endurance and wisdom would increase his health, stamina and mana by ten per point, respectively. How he allocated his stat points would affect what gear he could use and how his character would progress.

Heavy armor required decent constitution and high strength, but mage robes would need high intelligence and wisdom to unlock their power. On top of that, he needed to put the points into something useful to stand any chance of getting out of this dungeon alive.

It was an important decision, so Damien was far too focused on the numbers to pay any attention to the light draft that blew into his ear. Until it came again. And again. With the same steady rhythm as one might expect from breathing.

"That was extremely impressive."

Damien didn't hesitate. Even as fear gripped him, his elbow shot backward toward the voice. It connected with something, but didn't budge. He twisted his head and found himself face to face with something far worse than rats or skeletons.

It was humanoid, but it was most certainly not human. A clawed hand had effortlessly caught his elbow before it reached the creature's face. Pale skin was drawn tightly over it, more akin to wearing it like a mask than actually belonging there. And the eyes...the eyes were black orbs with no apparent pupils.

Damien could see his face reflected in them in duplicate, offering a bizarre warped insight into his own terror. It smiled at him, revealing row upon row of shiny white teeth, extending back into its mouth like a shark's. Two fangs stood out in particular, protruding to cover its colorless bottom lip.

The vampire continued to speak as if nothing had happened.

"Although, if you don't mind my saying so, it was also quite pathetic."

Damien moved to pull his elbow away. The vampire's grip was not painful, but he couldn't move his arm so much as an inch. It might as well have been encased in concrete.

But he wasn't going to go down without a fight. He swung his free arm around, still holding the shattered rib. Another clawed hand intercepted it at the wrist and the weapon fell to the floor with an impotent hollow clatter.

"Are you quite finished?"

Damien tried to think of a sensible plan. Nothing came to mind.

"Look, I can see we've got off to a bad start," the vampire said. "I'd like for us to get along. But I really am very hungry, and if you keep trying to kill me I'm going to have to eat you."

He let go of Damien's wrists.

Damien paused. The vampire's own arms retreated underneath a black cloak. Even from just a foot away, the cloak meant Damien had to concentrate in order to perceive the creature's outline. It blended into the darkness perfectly and would have given the illusion of the vampire being nothing but a floating head, if not for a few wrinkles in the fabric. It was probably enchanted for stealth.

"If I was going to kill you, I'd have done it already." The vampire drawled. "Do me a favor. Ask me why I haven't killed you yet."

Damien looked it up and down, trying and failing to inspect it. It was talking and behaving like a player, but none of the cues Damien would have with a player were appearing.

Something else did show up in his HUD, though. A small silver skull flashed above the vampire's head before fading away. This was an elite monster. Probably the dungeon boss. If that was so, Damien could see no reason why it would keep him alive. No reason that meant anything good for him, anyway.

"All right. I'll bite—" The vampire's eye twitched and Damien hurriedly threw up his hands. "Sorry! Bad choice of words. Why haven't you killed me yet?"

The vampire had put the question in Damien's mouth, but Damien had responded by putting his own foot there immediately afterward.

"How *nice* of you to ask. You see, while you would usually serve as a meal, I have a different proposal in mind. One from which we both stand to profit."

Then its maw split into a jagged grin and some of the former light-heartedness returned.

"But I'm getting ahead of myself! Where are my manners? My name is Bartholomew and I am the master of this dungeon. The reason you aren't dead yet is because you have no class."

Damien looked down at himself and frowned. That seemed harsh. He'd only just started playing.

"Okay, look, I know I'm not very well equipped, but that's a bit rude. I don't have any gold yet to buy gear, and I came straight—" He flinched.

Bartholomew was groaning loudly and slowly drawing one of his claw like hands down his face.

"No, you imbecile! No class! No area of expertise! You are yet to choose a discipline. Fortunately for you, I can assist you in that regard."

Damien eyed Bartholomew suspiciously. This seemed like a bid to eat him with extra steps.

"You… want to make me a vampire?"

"HA! Being a vampire isn't a discipline, it's a way of life. One that precious few can accustom themselves to. No, I wish to make you an occultist."

Damien knew all the classes available to human characters. He'd reviewed them extensively before he started playing, and had never heard of an occultist. Despite himself, his interest was piqued.

"What's an occultist?"

Bartholomew's clawed hand whipped out of his cloak and he pointed at the ground at Damien's feet, his fingertip glowing red. Damien yelped and jumped backward, trying to avoid the attack. But Bartholomew's eyes didn't leave the floor.

A red line zig-zagged into the stone tile where Damien had stood, searing a pattern into it. Damien caught his breath and glared at his erratic host. For a moment he'd thought Bartholomew was about to murder him where he stood.

The amused smile the vampire cracked confirmed that scaring Damien out of his wits had been the intention all along. Bartholomew demurely launched into an explanation as the runes continued to form under his extended finger, ignoring Damien's displeasure.

"The occultist is a magic class that can only be taught by a master of the art. There is only one master of Occultism in Tintagel - me. In other words, you are being presented with a unique opportunity."

The glow of the vampire's finger faded away and the completed image on the floor flashed red. While he'd been talking, the rune had completed its long trail. Damien might not have been a master of the art, but he knew a pentagram when he saw one.

As the circle and the star within it flashed, a black portal opened in the air above it with a low hum and a small red body dropped through, landing on the ground with grace and poise. Damien barely had time to register his shock before the creature swiveled to look at him and pulled what appeared to be a well-rehearsed gang sign. Damien recognized it all too well. It was an imp.

"You will gain the ability to summon and control demons, such as this… odious little specimen. Not to worry, though. As your power progresses, you will gain access to more impressive denizens of the underworld, each—"

Damien had stopped listening. He was looking between Bartholomew and the imp. Gears were turning in his head. They clicked into place and Damien realized who he was talking to. The town Scorpius had been trying to save from cultists was in the next zone. The cave where he'd had such a bad time fighting imps could only be half an hour away. Bartholomew wasn't just a class trainer or a dungeon boss. He was the Big Bad Evil Guy of Scorpius's campaign. The cultist leader Rising Tide had defeated just a few days earlier. Aetherius hadn't kicked him into just any old dungeon: this was The Downward Spiral, a place so unspeakable that Rising Tide hadn't shown the footage of what happened there.

Damien stared at Bartholomew slacked jawed. This was more than he could handle.

"You're the leader of the cultists!"

Bartholomew's tutorial ground to an abrupt halt. The moment the word 'cultists' was uttered, the imp stopped throwing gang signs and flinched. Bartholomew very slowly turned his derogatory gaze from the imp to Damien's poorly timed interruption.

"No. I am not the leader of the cultists. There is no such thing. I am the leader of the occultists. Do try to keep that in min—"

"Oh, come on! I've seen plenty of those imp things before, always attached to angry, pale-looking weirdos screaming 'Death to the Empire!' and 'We serve the shadows!" and all that nonsense. I can hardly go anywhere without them popping up and trying to kill me! You can add an 'O' if you want, but a cultist is still a cultist."

The atmosphere changed immediately. The imp glanced between Bartholomew and Damien before scurrying away into the dark. Bartholomew soundlessly closed the all too narrow gap between himself and Damien, the cloak covering his feet so he seemed to float rather than stride. He extended a hand and roughly grabbed Damien by the back of his head, pulling him in close and deeply sniffing his face.

The stench was foul. Damien found himself wondering how the vampire could possibly hope to find anything through his own smell, but the thought was buried somewhere deep down beneath his horror.

Bartholomew seemed to consider for a moment. Then he released him.

"I do not smell the blood of occultists on you. Nor do I smell anything else for that matter, save for the three wretched beasts you slew in my unhallowed halls. This is well, for I can forgive such a minor transgression. Yet you brazenly claim to have fought my brethren before. Are you lying to me? Your life depends upon your answer."

Damien re-evaluated his position. His primary goal was unchanged. While this was definitely an interesting interview, he needed to get out of here and get on with his real objective. That meant not being murdered by a wrathful vampire. Maybe it would be best to try and play along.

"You got me. I've never even seen a cultist, much less been attacked by one. Sorry, I shouldn't have lied to you."

Bartholomew narrowed his eyes. Then his open palm whacked into Damien's shoulder.

"Good man!" he suddenly said, breaking into a toothy grin. "I've always thought being a liar was an indicator of strong character."

Damien rubbed his sore shoulder, trying not to show his relief too openly. For a moment, he'd really thought he was dead. Bartholomew had hit him so hard in his enthusiasm it caused mild damage.

"Err... thanks, I guess. I'm sorry if—"

Bartholomew's face loomed back in uncomfortably close and the stench filled Damien's nostrils once more.

"Even so, your rudeness has sorely tried my patience. I shall ask you some questions. If you answer to my satisfaction, I shall let you live. If not, you might make a better snack than an occultist after all. Do you agree to the terms?"

Damien swallowed the hard ball that had formed in his throat. It didn't seem like he had much of a choice. If he got through this, he might still be able to leave. But something told him he wasn't out of the woods just yet.

"Of course."

Bartholomew smiled again. Even when he'd been in a good mood, Damien found his smile difficult to look at. Now it oozed contempt and savagery. This was the real Bartholomew. Damien liked the previous version much better.

Bartholomew licked his lips. "Let's say you were a budding hero, starting your career in the human capital city of Camelot. Just a short stroll from this very spot. Your first directives would be passed down directly from the highest echelons of society. What do you imagine these directives might entail?"

Damien was in way over his head. He could not leave too long a pause and clearly lying wasn't going to serve him very well. It was clear what Bartholomew wanted him to say.

"I imagine it would involve killing cultists."

Bartholomew raised a warning finger.

"Occultists! But otherwise, good. Yes. Cultist is the name given to us by ignorant fools who do not understand our art. We study the occult. We are occultists. Not cultists. But I'm sure that was merely a slip of the tongue. A slip of the tongue you have committed several times over the course of this conversation and which I generously chose to overlook. Nevertheless—"

Bartholomew waggled his warning finger teasingly.

"—that's strike one. Question two: if you accepted these directives and went about your business for the glory of the Empire, setting out to slay *occultists* left, right and center, do you think it might occur to you to speak with your so-called enemies first? Or would you simply wade in and ritually slaughter them?"

Damien had never considered it that way. He'd only ever played after enrolling in the Empire faction, which had included a warning about 'the cultist threat' and an automatic decrease to his standing with 'cultists'. Everything had seemed simple enough; accept quests, kill listed enemies, accept quest rewards, repeat. He'd never imagined Saga Online might offer a hidden path at such an early stage.

"I suppose there's a good chance people would just follow their orders."

Bartholomew crooned at him, nodding his head as he sarcastically implied Damien was telling him something he didn't already know himself.

"Very good! I commend you for your honesty. However—"

The middle finger of Bartholomew's hand leisurely raised itself up to join the index finger in Damien's countdown to death.

"—I already told you I hold liars in higher regard. Your lack of imagination may yet prove to be your downfall. That's strike two. Last question: let's pretend you came to The Downward Spiral to meet with Aetherius, the widely celebrated occultist murderer."

Damien's eyes widened and Bartholomew caught it, his smile scything even further until it almost reached his ears.

"My dominion may not be what it once was, but I still know everything that transpires within it. It is no secret to me that you were invited here by the leader of Rising Tide, the abhorrent guild that struck me down less than a week ago."

This was bad. Bartholomew was associating him with Rising Tide, Aetherius's Empire-aligned guild. The most prolific occultist killers.

Damien took a step back and Bartholomew took one forward, keeping his face uncomfortably close to Damien's own.

"Let's skip the hypotheticals, shall we? Aetherius betrayed you, casting you down to your certain death. You survived against all odds and showed great determination, if not skill. I watched your progress, hoping to have found a valuable new ally, the first occultist to be recruited from among the heroes normally reserved for the Empire."

The vampire stood back and tapped his chin, considering Damien one last time.

"I am offering you an opportunity to plot revenge against our common enemy. I shall make this offer once, and once only. If you refuse, my patience shall finally wear thin and I will redecorate my dungeon with your intestines. How will you proceed?"

Bartholomew raised a parchment up in front of Damien's face and pressed a quill into his hand. A blue box appeared, just like the one he'd seen when signing up as a warrior back in the Empire's encampment. He knew when he was beaten.

"Where do I sign?"

Bartholomew's smile reached its zenith.

"Good boy. We'll make an occultist out of you yet."

8

THINGS CAN ONLY GET BETTER

Damien squinted at the blue box intently. He wasn't trying to delay his descent into occultism. He already knew it was inevitable.

He just couldn't think of a name that wasn't utterly terrible. He'd already given up on all the names involving Scorpius. They'd be no good to him as an occultist. But everything else he was trying had already been taken.

"Was I unclear about what I'd do with your intestines? I'm sure they'd make a lovely garland at the dungeon entrance. Did you know the human digestive tract is approximately thirty feet long? I could drape it all the way from one side of the opening to the other! Why don't we try it now?"

Ignoring the goading vampire, Damien continued to rack his brain for alternatives. His name was important if he was going to stand out in the Streamer Competition. He could live with it having his year of birth or even being stylized slightly, but every name that was even vaguely presentable and relevant to him was long gone. He tried to calm himself down and focus. There should be a variation of his name that would work for his current situation.

Something collided with his shin and Damien glanced down. It took him right back to his first time fighting occultists. The imp had returned from the darkness and was kicking him repeatedly. Its four-fingered hands pivoted to maintain balance as it struck over and over again, gleefully cackling the whole while.

Damien followed the pattern and moved his leg at the last second. The imp had been going for a particularly vicious kick, so its leg sailed into the empty air before it landed on its back with a thud. It immediately leapt up and started screaming at him in daemonic tongues, which would have been terrifying if it wasn't so high pitched and adorable. It balled a fist at him, shaking it angrily as it continued its tirade. Watching it gave Damien an idea.

He'd had what could only be described as an epiphany. A name that made sense, sounded cool and wouldn't make him look like one of his own fanboys.

He entered: 'Daemien.'

A little green tick appeared next to the box and Damien slammed the quill down on the enter key, terrified that someone else would register the name first or the game would realize it had made a mistake. The blue box faded away with the name 'Daemien' still sitting inside it.

Damien forgot where he stood, throwing the quill into the air. He dropped to his knees and pumped his fists above his head, roaring so loudly in triumph that the imp stopped screaming with a strangled yelp and leapt out of his reach.

"Congratulations," Bartholomew sneered, his hand snapping upwards to catch the quill without looking away. "You remembered how to write your own name. I'm beginning to have second thoughts about this arrangement."

Still, the vampire nodded in approval and regarded his new recruit down the place where his nose should have been.

Damien quickly stood back up, handing back the parchment and dusting off his knees.

"Sorry. I fell a long way to get here. Must have banged my head."

Bartholomew nodded, the quill and parchment vanishing into his cloak.

"Mmm. Quite. Well, that won't be the only head trauma

you'll suffer today, I'm afraid. Now that you're officially an occultist, Daemien, I have some knowledge to pass on to you."

Bartholomew placed his open palm on Damien's forehead. Damien didn't move, but that first comment had been more than a little foreboding.

"Uh, what are you doing?"

"Ahem. What are you doing, *master?*"

"I asked you first."

Bartholomew's claws dug in, but he smirked and continued speaking evenly.

"I'm imbuing you with some basic abilities available to occultists. Your mind is not yet mature enough to deal with the more complex spells and incantations, as you have just made abundantly clear with your impudence. Hold still."

Bartholomew's palm became hot where the skin made contact and pop-ups started appearing in Damien's HUD one after the other.

Class Unlocked: Occultist
Skill Tree Unlocked: Maleficium
Skill Tree Unlocked: Demonology
Chaotic Bolt Unlocked!
Corruption Unlocked!
Summon Imp Unlocked!
Class Trait Unlocked: Soul Harvest
Class Augmentation: Sneak upgraded to Shadow Walker

As the 'Shadow Walker' notification snapped into place, Damien's vision flashed a brilliant white. He closed his eyes against it, making no difference whatsoever. It was so bright it felt as though he must be emitting high-powered beams through his eyelids. Before he could open his mouth to complain, the feeling passed.

He scrunched his eyes open and shut a few times. He'd expected the light to make his vision even worse, so he was surprised to discover he could see clearly. Bartholomew floated in front of him, his form slightly translucent due to his innate stealth. Damien could see all the way through him to the back wall.

"What the hell was that?"

Bartholomew removed his hand from Damien's head. The heat immediately subsided, but Damien hardly noticed. He was too busy scanning the notifications, trying to get a sense of his new-found abilities. As much as Bartholomew insisted that occultists weren't necessarily evil, he could see why their assorted skills might raise an eyebrow or two. They all sounded more than a little malevolent. Damien's new master flashed his fangs.

"Night vision. Just one of the many gifts I grant my followers."

Damien had to admit that was a pretty useful perk of being an occultist. Then he ran his eyes back over the list and found a more urgent notification at the end that had been obscured by the flash of light. It didn't seem like much of a 'gift'.

Class Trait Unlocked: Enemy of the Realm

Reputation Status with Empire has been reduced to 'Loathed'

'Caution! Empire-aligned NPCs will now attack you on sight. Empire-aligned traders and shop owners will no longer do business with you. You will be denied entry to Empire settlements and outposts. Complete tasks that benefit the Empire or defeat enemies of the Empire to increase your faction status.'

A new resource counter had popped up on his HUD as well. It was a translucent teardrop, but the top had the shape of flames. 0/5 sat in the center of it. He assumed it was something to do with the unique trait, Soul Harvest.

Bartholomew stood by silently, reluctantly waiting for him to settle. Damien caught his eye and closed the notifications. He could inspect them later.

"Wow, I've got a lot to learn. OK. So, what's next?"

Bartholomew grabbed him by the shoulder.

"I see you are eager. Excellent. After everything else you have been subjected to today, I think it's time to let you flex your new-found power a little. I have some ideas in mind."

A yellow exclamation mark appeared above Bartholomew's head. Damien was going on his first quest!

"OK, lay it on me. What are you thinking of?"

"There is a task that requires my attention…but quite frankly, it's too boring for me to demean myself with. There are a number of vermin who have seen fit to make this dungeon their home. Unsightly, overgrown rodents such as those you dispatched upon your arrival here. I would have you scour my dungeon and root them out."

A quest notification appeared in Damien's vision. It was entitled 'Infestation in the Occultist Nation'. The objective appeared next to it – 'Kill ten (0/10) lesser vermin inhabiting The Downward Spiral.'

"Ok. Got it. Anything else, *master?*"

Bartholomew nodded, either not noticing or totally ignoring the sarcasm. "I am going to lend you a modest backpack."

His hand disappeared into his robes and returned holding a ragged sackcloth bag with some straps affixed to it. Damien gratefully accepted it before swinging it around his arms. Without an inventory, managing items was almost impossible.

"Thanks. I really needed that."

Bartholomew shrugged.

"It's a poor receptacle. I can provide far better with the correct materials. Go and fetch me five rat furs. I shall use them to construct you a bag you can use on a more permanent basis."

A second quest notification appeared in Damien's display.

'**Fur is all the Rage** – Bring Bartholomew five (0/5) rat furs.'

"Finally, I wish to see if you are able to use the abilities I have granted you. Become well versed in them before you return. If you can do so, I will recognize your aptitude."

'**You Want Skills? I'll Show You Skills!** – Use all new abilities once.'

Damien looked them over. He could do all three quests simultaneously. This would be ideal to get some quick leveling done.

"Oh! And this special minion is now your own. Do not let Noigel's appearance deceive you. He is more useful than he seems."

The imp Bartholomew had summoned during his explanation of occultists, which now seemed like so long ago, came and stood by Damien's side. A new miniaturized health bar appeared near Damien's own along with a final notification.

Special Summon – 'Noigel' Unlocked!

The name had sounded exotic when Bartholomew said it, but written down it appeared to be a corruption of 'Nigel'. Not a name that screamed damnation.

"What kind of a name is that for an imp?"

Bartholomew smirked but did not offer a direct reply.

"I feel that is more than enough for you to be getting on with. Do not worry about finding me. I shall find you. Good hunting!"

The vampire pulled the cloak over his head and abruptly vanished from view. Damien wasted no time in opening his Stat page.

Account Name: Damien Arkwright
Character: Daemien
Class: Occultist
Level: 2
Health: 110/110
Stamina: 110/110
Mana: 110/110
Stats:
Strength 11 - Agility 11 - Intelligence 11

Constitution 11 - Endurance 11 - Wisdom 11
Stat points: 5
Experience: 26/750
Soul Summon Limit: 1/3 - **Soul Reserve:** 0/5

Damien smiled. Seeing his name listed made it all the more real. It finally felt like he was getting somewhere. Maybe this occultist thing wouldn't be so bad. It was interesting to him; maybe it would be interesting to others as well.

Anything to pick up some extra votes would be essential. It sure beat running around with a bunch of players who had the same name and class as him, anyway. He closed the Stat page and navigated to his Skills tab.

Maleficium

Chaotic Bolt: Mana: 30 **Damage:** 15 + (Int x 0.2) – You channel a pulse of rift energy in your closed hand. After 3 seconds the energy can be launched, dealing damage to the first thing it hits. After 5 seconds of holding the prepared spell the rift energy explodes, regardless of its current location. At higher intelligence thresholds this ability can be upgraded, dealing more damage but costing more mana.

Corruption: Mana: 20 **Damage:** 2 + (Int x 0.1) per second – With a directed thought and a flick of the wrist, a target within 30 yards is afflicted with black flames that cannot be extinguished by conventional means, dealing damage over 15 seconds. At higher intelligence thresholds this ability can be upgraded, dealing more damage but costing more mana.

Demonology

Summon Imp: Mana: 100, Souls: 1 – You point at the ground, searing it with runes to open a portal to the demon world. After channeling for 10 seconds, the portal is opened and an imp arrives on the mortal plane. The imp will serve you until it dies or is dismissed. Imp stats improve every five levels.

Special Summon – Noigel: Noigel is smarter than your average imp, but only in the company of his peers. If Noigel is not already on the mortal plane, he will be the first imp summoned when using 'Summon Imp'.

Class Unique Traits

Soul Harvest: Defeating worthy enemies has a chance to drop souls or half souls. These are drawn toward you. Upon contact, they are absorbed and can be expended to cast specific spells. Your Soul Reserve is your maximum number of stored souls. Your Soul Summon Limit is the maximum total soul cost of all minions under your command. Both are increased by wisdom. In addition, when you contribute to a player-kill, you absorb their experience points towards the next level that were forfeited upon death. A kill will result in all experience points being absorbed, an assist will yield EXP proportionate to how many other parties assisted. This ability does not function on creatures or players five or more levels below you.

Shadow Walker: Darkness is your ally. In addition to night vision, your body blends with the shadows when you sneak (translucence 50%). At close range or when moving carelessly, the benefit will rapidly diminish.

Enemy of the Realm: You are a harbinger of chaos, and your existence defies order all across Arcadia. Your reputation with all factions representing the forces of order is set to Loathed.

Damien's eyes flickered over the page, trying to absorb as much information as possible. Years of homework assignments should have made it a very simple task, but there was a lot to process. His character had undergone a complete transformation. He just couldn't figure out whether or not it was an improvement.

He lingered longest on 'Enemy of the Realm'. That explained why he'd received the notification that he was loathed with the

Empire. Bartholomew had given him his freedom and simultaneously taken it away. There was no way back now.

At least he understood how his Soul Summon Limit worked. Noigel had a soul cost of 1, which was why he'd taken up 1 out of Damien's three slots. That meant Damien could still summon two more imps. A sensible side objective for him to fulfill, especially considering Noigel's description in his skill page.

He was just reconsidering the cryptic message regarding Noigel when the imp in question kicked him in the shin again.

The skill description hadn't said much. One of the many things it hadn't mentioned was that Noigel didn't like being ignored.

"Hey, take it easy. I'm almost done."

Noigel stamped his feet petulantly before sitting down in a huff. Damien inspected the imp and a new stat page came up.

Noigel
Stats:
Strength 5 - Agility 10 - Intelligence 5
Constitution 5 - Endurance 10 - Wisdom 5
Abilities: We Are Many, Leap, Bite, Claw.

So, he was agility based. Very nice. 'We Are Many' stood out among the other more conventional abilities. It was probably what made Noigel different from regular imps. However, no more information was offered. Damien closed the page and took the opportunity to examine his new partner.

Noigel's body wasn't bulky, but he still looked surprisingly tough: what little of the imp there was appeared to be all muscle. The torso was lean and sinewy, forming a base for the proportionately thicker legs and arms that ended in sharp claws on both hands and feet.

Two pointed bumps poked out of a hairless head, presumably horns that lay just under the dark red skin.

Feeling himself observed, Noigel rose up to his full, rather unimposing height and twisted his head to look back, sticking his clawed hands on his hips and puffing his chest out. A long slender tail ending in a barbed tip whipped around lazily behind him. He grinned from pointed ear to pointed ear, revealing rows of sharp white teeth that slotted neatly into each other.

It was like looking at what would've evolved if the first fish to crawl out of the ocean had been a piranha. The teeth were menacing, but it was the eyes that held Damien's attention.

They were large black orbs similar to Bartholomew's, each protruding out of its skull in a perfect round bump. They were wide set, providing excellent peripheral vision while making it almost impossible to tell what it was looking at unless it faced you directly. It would be very hard to sneak up on one of these things.

Damien scratched his head. The imp looked very cool and would be a welcome boost to his damage in the early stages of the game, but he'd been hoping for something a little more powerful. Still, he wouldn't know for sure until he'd tested 'We Are Many'. It was time to find Noigel some friends.

Damien turned around to squint into the darkness and stopped. He'd been so focused on Noigel that he'd forgotten. He could see. For the first time since he'd been kicked into the dungeon by Aetherius, Damien was able to get a sense of his surroundings.

The dungeon was much wider down here than it was at the entrance, maybe even wider than the test area Kevin had teleported Scorpius to. Despite that, he could still just about make out the far wall. The bodies of the two rats he'd already dealt with were lying in plain sight, twenty feet or so away. It had felt a lot further when he was sneaking away from them in the pitch black.

A sharp kick in the back of his leg brought him back to the present.

"All right, I get it. We're moving out."

Damien moved toward the two prone rats. He had a bag now; he could loot their items and figure out what he needed later. Noigel predicted his destination, skittering across the floor in front of him on all fours and standing on one of the bodies to do a little dance, waving Damien over.

As much as Damien was grateful to be able to see, it seemed a shame his gift was wasted on watching an imp dance on a dead rat. He needed to make Noigel a little more co-operative. He reached the rats and crouched between them, gathering the items up and nodding in satisfaction as the rat fur he'd left behind earlier was noted by his quest UI. One down, four to go. Then he would have a lovely, fashionable rat-fur bag to go with his babbling demonic chihuahua.

Noigel was chilling out on the floor on his back, his arms behind his head as he stared up at the entrance to The Downward Spiral.

"All right, we're done here. Let's go find some more rats!"

Noigel glanced over at him before blowing a raspberry and turning back to contemplate the sky. Damien hadn't expected this much resistance from one of his own minions.

"What are you doing? I want to get on with the quests."

Noigel didn't even bother looking at him. Damien marched over and stuck his head over Noigel's face.

"We're leaving. Stand up!"

Noigel jumped to his feet. No one was more surprised than Damien himself. He thought about it for a moment and realized what was going on. He stared directly at the rogue imp and pointed to the ground by his side.

"Stand next to me."

Noigel came and stood next to him sullenly, confirming Damien's suspicion: Noigel might not understand him, but he was bound to follow any orders. Maybe he could only understand direct orders? It was worth checking.

"So, uh, do you understand me? I mean, the words that are coming out of my mouth?"

Noigel stopped dancing and stared at him blankly. Then, much to Damien's shock, he opened his own mouth and parroted the noises back at him.

"Ho yoo umersham miiii? Hamim, fuh wormshatta kumin owtta mai moof? Skreeeeeeeeeeeeeeeeeeeeeeee-katakatakatakatakata!"

Noigel fell over laughing, his arms holding his sides as he

rolled around on the ground. Damien sighed. He wasn't certain, but that answer probably meant no. It would have to be direct orders, then.

"Stop laughing. Stand up straight. Follow me."

Satisfied he'd asserted himself, Damien scanned the dungeon floor for any signs of movement. His night vision was vastly better than nothing, but it wasn't perfect. He couldn't see any enemies from where he was standing but there had to be more nearby.

Crouching, he started sneaking toward an unexplored section of the dungeon, hoping to catch an enemy unaware. Noigel stamped alongside him, his feet pounding the tiles as loudly as possible while the faintest glimmer of a smirk stretched the corners of his mouth. Damien stopped and covered his face with his hands as the most unhelpful starting minion of all time sniggered openly.

"When I sneak, you sneak. That's an order."

Damien started sneaking again and had gotten all of five feet before he realized Noigel was no longer by his side. The imp was about half a step ahead of where Damien had left him and was moving with ridiculous care. He raised his leg and theatrically touched the ground in front of him with one toe before dramatically lowering the rest of his body onto it. He followed it up by looking up at his 'master' and urgently pressing a finger to his lips. Noigel was shushing him. Damien finally had enough.

"All right, you want to do it like that?"

He pointed out into the unexplored territory ahead.

"Walk that way until you see an enemy, then run toward it while screaming. That's an order."

Noigel's smile disappeared remarkably quickly. His feet carried him forward, even though all his body language said it was the very last thing he wanted to do. He hissed at Damien as he passed, dropping into a crouch and moving stealthily. Apparently, the little git could remember how to sneak when his life was on the line.

Damien slipped behind him, hanging back a few feet. If

Noigel didn't want to co-operate, he'd make good bait. Damien flexed his fingers, preparing himself for the encounter.

Chaotic Bolt had a three-second charge time, but he couldn't just hold it at the ready or else after five seconds it would explode in his hand. The skill description had been perfectly clear on that account. So, Damien would start charging as soon as Noigel started screaming. It wasn't going to take long.

Noigel had already stopped and was looking over his shoulder at Damien forlornly. He pointed off to the left and Damien caught sight of a large black silhouette at the very edge of his range of vision. He took another step forward and the silhouette spouted a health bar.

The imp released a high-pitched battle cry. Then he sprinted toward the dark figure exactly to Damien's specifications.

The silhouette twisted violently at the same time as Damien closed his hand and concentrated. His clenched fist was forced open by something inside. He looked at his hand, where a ball of twisting purple energy had formed and was expanding rapidly. Damien was so surprised he almost forgot to count.

Meanwhile, having approached the monster exactly as instructed, Noigel chose to act on his own initiative. With ten feet still to cover, his legs pistoned off the ground and launched him across the distance directly into his enemy. The two shadows merged into one as his momentum knocked it even further back, blending them into a furious tumbling ball of fur and claws.

Damien moved closer so he could see well enough to take aim, but he'd only taken a few steps when the pulsing orb in his fist started to whine ominously. It was going to explode soon. He didn't want to be holding it when that happened, and as much as Noigel annoyed him, he didn't want to risk hitting him.

Damien threw the screaming ball into the air over his head. It skyrocketed to the level above before bursting in mid-air a brilliant purple explosion.

Noigel and the rat were still locked in combat. Damien abandoned stealth and ran at full tilt toward the pair, grasping his makeshift thighbone weapon firmly in one hand.

Their health bars were both dropping as they fought tooth and nail. Completely entwined, Damien couldn't tell which health bar belonged to which combatant.

Noigel was in trouble. He'd been pinned on his back by the significantly larger enemy, his arm caught in the rat's jagged teeth. Sensing it had the upper hand, the irate rodent clamped its jaws down before shaking its head, trying to tear the arm off.

"Noigel, hold it still!"

Noigel screamed in pain, but he still managed to do as Damien commanded. Bracing his shoulders against the floor, he dug the hooked claws of his feet into the rat's neck and pushed upward, leaving it standing on its hind legs. Damien had a perfect shot. He took it. The bone connected with the back of the rat's head.

Even without a Sneak Attack bonus, it hit hard enough to knock the rat onto its side. Its jaws loosened enough for Noigel to tear his arm free.

That would be the last mistake it made.

Noigel leapt onto it and clawed out its throat with his uninjured hand. An instant later, Damien swung the thighbone a second time. The fight was over. The rat breathed its last and a stream of silvery vapor poured out of its mouth, pooling on the floor like smoke.

Damien was intrigued. None of the enemies he'd killed until now had done this. After a few moments, the vapor collected itself into a small round ball and floated toward him. It made contact with his torso and was promptly absorbed.

The soul counter on Damien's HUD rose by one point. Mystery solved. Damien nodded in satisfaction, glad another of his character mechanics had been revealed.

Then again, he wasn't too pleased with his spell. Chaotic Bolt had proven itself extremely unreliable in combat. In addition to the wind-up time being too long, the price of failure was too great. In his experience, combat situations often required split-second decisions. If he was forced to make too many, he'd lose an arm to his own spell sooner or later.

At least Noigel had shown himself to be more than an irritation. The little imp had held his own – not that he looked very happy about it. He was still sitting on top of the felled rat, nursing his bitten arm with his other hand. His health was down to a mere ten out of his maximum of fifty.

Damien felt a little guilty about ordering him to take the lead. He was considering apologizing when Noigel looked over at him, his face a subtle blend of contempt and self-pity, and started babbling angrily. He probably wasn't congratulating Damien on a job well done.

"That's not how I wanted to do it either. Next time, follow my instructions the first time round."

Noigel scowled at him, but the babbling ceased. He turned his head away from Damien in an unmistakable sulk. Damien made an exasperated sigh of his own before looting the rat. No fur on this one, somewhat amazingly. It was doubly annoying being told the rat had no fur when he literally had to hold a handful of it in order to check the rat's inventory in the first place.

Oh well. He'd still need to deal with another nine of them before he completed the quest. It wouldn't matter as long as he got four more rat furs by then.

He looted the rest of the garbage for later examination and looked back at Noigel, who was still resolutely ignoring him. Damien bit his bottom lip. He wasn't sure he could blame Noigel for being so angry. If he had to do everything he was told, even when it put him at risk, he'd be pretty angry too.

Noigel might not have done himself any favors by being unhelpful, but what Damien had done in response was undeniably worse. He checked Noigel's health bar. It had already risen back to 15/50. It seemed that despite his constitution being quite low, the imp's health regeneration was a little more potent than Damien's own. Thankfully, he'd also avoided being poisoned. Perhaps he was immune? They'd be ready to go again in a few minutes.

Damien took the opportunity to try and build a bridge.

"If you try to be more helpful, I won't boss you around. Deal?"

Noigel tilted his head up and sideways, apparently considering the proposal. He must have liked it, because a few moments later he faced Damien and stuck his hand out. It looked like he wanted to shake on it. Damien quickly took the imp's hand and grabbed it in his own before giving it a firm shake. His face erupted into a wolfish grin.

"And I *knew* you could understand what I was saying, you little git!"

The imp's jaw dropped. Damien released his grip on Noigel's hand and the imp immediately made use of it, smacking himself in the head and moaning softly.

Noigel lowered his hand and regarded Damien. For the first time since they'd met, it felt like Noigel was looking at him with something other than contempt. Damien wouldn't go so far as to call it respect, but it was a start. He pressed his advantage.

"I should be able to summon another imp now. That would make your life a bit easier, wouldn't it?"

Noigel grinned and nodded eagerly. Damien remembered Bartholomew's demonstration and copied the motion, pointing at the ground with a single outstretched finger and thinking 'summon imp'. The ground at his fingertip glowed red, melting into a tiny ball of molten flame barely larger than the head of a pin. It started tracing out the sigil, but the process was painstakingly slow compared to Bartholomew's display.

Nevertheless, it did not take very long for a portal to open above it. A new imp fell through and Damien's party of two became three.

The two imps looked at each other before throwing gang signs followed by a crisp high four. Damien groaned. He couldn't believe he'd ended up in control of these things.

Damien checked Noigel's health bar again. It was already at 31/50. The wounds Noigel had sustained in combat were still visible, but rapidly closing and fading away.

"That last fight was messy. I think we can do better. You ready to try again?"

Noigel stood up and tensed his healed bicep before grabbing it with his other hand. He was good to go.

"You, new guy – follow me and move quietly."

The new imp pinched its thumb and forefinger together. Without another word, Damien crouched down and started sneaking forward. Noigel and the new imp followed on tiptoes close behind.

9

GROWING PAINS

The next rat they faced fell far more easily.

It was still reeling from Damien's stab in the back when Noigel crashed into it from behind, latching onto its rump with his teeth before slashing and tearing indiscriminately with all four limbs. Damien jumped back as the rat spun in circles, trying to catch Noigel in its jaws.

It was no use. Noigel dug his claws in until the rat stopped spinning and then eviscerated it from the waist down. Damien sent the second imp in and, mercifully, the rodent did not survive much longer. After the thrashing subsided, Noigel cupped a hand to his ear, beckoning Damien with the other.

"Yeah, all right, that was good. Nice improvisation."

Noigel bowed and blew kisses to an imaginary adoring crowd. He obviously thought he'd done a bit better than 'good'.

A cloud of silver vapor left the rat's body, gathering into a ball before drifting toward Damien as though pulled by gravity. The soul orb made contact with his skin and the soul counter rose by a half point. Hmm. So the drop rate wasn't stable. That was a shame, but at least the fight had been easy.

While the two imps chattered at each other contentedly, Damien took the chance to open his menu and go to the HUD adjustment options. He rearranged his resource bars along the bottom of the screen. Health went in the bottom left, mana in the bottom right and stamina in the middle. That way he'd have a vague sense of how they were without directing too much attention toward them in battle.

He tidied up a little more until he was satisfied everything was the right size and in the right place. Then he closed his menu to find a new, unexpected problem. Having taken his eyes off his minions, he had no way of telling them apart. They looked exactly alike.

"Noigel, can you…"

The two imps shared a look and sniggered. Great, so they were messing him around on purpose. Well, they'd have to do better than that. He inspected the one on the right. Instead of saying 'Noigel' it simply said 'Imp'.

The little devils had swapped places while he was occupied. He pointed straight at the other imp. If he hadn't been certain before, the rapidly concealed flicker of surprise in Noigel's eyes made him certain now.

"You. Noigel. Do you want me to send you into combat first? Are you sure pretending to be your friend is a good idea?"

Noigel took one look at his companion and broke rank, running to Damien's side. The new imp didn't seem to understand what had just happened. He stood there, picking his nose and eating it, acting far too complacent considering Noigel's betrayal.

"That's better. New guy, you walk in front of us. Noigel, you're supporting him. I'm staying in the back and testing a spell. All good?"

The imp immediately moved into position ahead of Damien and started to check its surroundings. So Noigel required detailed instructions but could be reasoned with, while other imps always followed orders.

Noigel flapped his hand in the air, gesturing for Damien to lower himself to his height. Bemused, Damien complied, lowering himself until they were face to face with his elbow on one knee. Noigel extended a hand and patted him on the head.

Damien cleared his throat.

"You're doing well, Noigel. But I swear, if you ever do that again, I'll order you into the largest group of enemies I can find."

Noigel grinned but he quickly retracted his hand and turned away, his shoulders shuddering with the effort of not laughing. Damien stood up and brushed off the top of his head. He felt like it might never be clean again. He focused on the less annoying of his two minions and spoke with forced softness.

"Move forward quietly and stop when you see an enemy."

It wasn't long before they encountered the next oversized vermin. With two imps and Damien himself, the fight should have gone well. It might have done, too, had Damien not set himself on fire trying out his new Corruption spell. That left Noigel to fend off the enemy alone, while the other imp stood by gormlessly. After wasting five seconds trying and failing to extinguish the flames, Damien finally had the presence of mind to order it into battle.

There were some muffled screeches as they finished off the rat and then it went blissfully silent.

Damien closed his eyes and shook his head. What a mess. He ordered the two imps to return to him. One of them looked perfectly happy. The other was scratched, bruised, and looked extremely frustrated. Damien didn't need to inspect either of them to know which was which.

"Okay. So, I think we're going to have to set up some ground rules."

The other imp clapped his hands gleefully. Noigel folded his arms and spat on the ground.

"Yeah, I know, Noigel. I messed up. You don't need to rub it in. We just have to make sure it never happens again."

Noigel narrowed his eyes at Damien and stared at him for a long time. When Damien refused to look away, the imp grunted and parked himself on the floor. He lifted a leg high over his head and licked a wound on his inner thigh meticulously.

Damien wasn't sure if this was a reaction to Noigel's injury or if it was simply a commentary on his leadership skills. Probably both.

He directed his attention to the uninjured minion, who was still listening attentively.

"If we haven't been spotted by an enemy, you must try to avoid being detected. If we're attacked, you can defend yourselves. If I'm attacked, you must defend me. You got it?"

The little minion chirped happily and made a mock salute. Noigel paused briefly to shake his head before licking his wounds.

"Noigel, those instructions were just for the new guy. You did a great job and don't need orders. I trust your judgment."

Without looking to see how this would be received, Damien opened his menu and navigated to the Skills tab. He needed to know why Corruption had backfired so spectacularly. He read the description, mouthing the words as he went.

"With a directed gaze and a flick of the wrist, a target within thirty—"

Damien looked at his hand, replaying the moment in his mind. He'd been staring at his own hand when he'd flicked his wrist. He'd targeted himself. Great. Well, at least he knew now.

The half soul of the new rat had already been absorbed, giving Damien just enough to summon another imp and reach his Soul Summon Limit. When the third demon emerged, they all exchanged secret handshakes while Damien went about looting the rat.

Noigel's health was nearly full, but Damien was still only at about two thirds. He didn't plan on waiting; they'd already wasted enough time.

"We're changing tactics. The two new guys stay by me. When we find an enemy, I'll send Noigel to bait it into coming toward us and we'll gang up on it. That OK with you, Noigel?"

Noigel blew another raspberry but moved to take the lead.

It turned out Noigel was a master of rat-baiting. An imp might have had a hard time defeating a rat in combat, but three of them together made it light work.

Noigel would occasionally hang back and let the other two imps do the dangerous part on their own. Damien took advantage of Shadow Walker, Sneak Attack and Critical Strike, finishing fights with head blows. He wasn't interested in Chaotic Bolt or Corruption. His experiences with them had been worrying, to say the least.

With the new strategy in place, the last seven rats fell without incident. Damien hadn't even handed in the quests yet but he'd reached level 3 and was already most of the way to level 4, with a full roster of demons and three spare souls in his Soul Reserve. He held his hand over the last rat and found exactly what he needed: the final piece of rat fur. He'd completed all his quests. All he had to do now was find—

"Loooseer."

Damien turned his head, fully expecting Bartholomew to have reappeared from the darkness, but there was no sign of him. The only living things in his range of vision were the three imps. Apparently, none of them had heard it since they were staring straight at him rather than looking around.

Damien shook himself. All this time at the bottom of the dungeon was taking its toll. He turned back to the rat and found Bartholomew's less than congenial face half an inch away from his own.

"Good afternoon."

Damien screamed and fell backward, his cry turning from fear to annoyance before he'd even hit the ground. Bartholomew chuckled dryly.

"So, how was your hunt?"

"You just happened to show up as soon as it was finished. You tell me."

"I was being polite, but if you want a review I'm more than happy to oblige. You seem to have a propensity for making things as difficult as possible. I particularly enjoyed the part where you set yourself on fire."

"I thought Chaotic Bolt and Corruption would work the same way."

"Next time, I suggest you think a little harder. Aside from that, you did well! I see you've taken a liking to the imps—"

"Looooseeeer."

Damien turned again, just too late to catch the source of the voice. Noigel was absent-mindedly inspecting his claws and didn't seem to have heard anything. The other two imps were huddled together, playing Patty Cake to pass the time.

"—although your relationship with Noigel leaves something to be desired."

Damien's eyes flitted over the imps. The voice had come from close by both times, so why hadn't they heard it? Why hadn't Bartholomew heard it either, for that matter? He readjusted his position so he could talk to Bartholomew while facing the imps directly.

"Yeah, well, it's still early. Noigel might be difficult but he knows what he's doing. I'm glad to have him."

Bartholomew grinned at him approvingly.

"This is good to hear. You may still have a thing or two to learn. That's enough idle chit-chat. Turn over your assignments."

Damien went into his inventory and pulled out the rat fur.

"I've gathered the rat furs to make a new bag."

Bartholomew clasped his hand around it and the "Fur is all the Rage" quest icon in Damien's HUD glowed gold before fading away.

"Excellent. I shall create a new bag for you in due course. You can keep the one you're using until my work is complete. Is there anything else?"

"I've killed ten rats in your dungeon, as you asked."

The text of "Infestation in the Occultist Nation" glowed gold and faded away. His reward, 1150 experience, was easily enough for him to push deep into level 4.

"Well done. I believe I gave you one last assignment?"

"I have tested all the abilities you gave me."

The text of "You Want Skills? I'll Show You Skills!" lit up gold, but it did not yet fade away as the others had done.

"Your choice of tactics was… interesting. I'd have expected you to use Maleficium spells from afar, with imps for defense and Shadow Walker to escape from danger. Instead, you relied on imps for attack and defense and used Shadow Walker to engage your opponents in melee. You're aware that you have magic at your disposal now, yes? You don't have to use rat bones anymore."

"The spells attracted too much attention. They were dangerous to me and they were dangerous to the imps as well if I missed. This way was much—"

Bartholomew waved a hand in front of Damien's face, imploring him to stop talking.

"Yes, yes, I'm sure you comprehend how to use your abilities far better than I do. After all, I'm only the leader of the occultists and you're the prodigy who thinks looking at his hand while he casts spells is a good idea. Still, you have fulfilled the terms of our arrangement." Damien received 1875 EXP, the maximum the hard 1.5 level cap on experience gain would allow. It was enough for him to push straight through level 5 all the way to level 6, with 375 EXP to spare. He was ecstatic. Even by the standards of early leveling, this was fast progress.

"I shall retire to tailor your new bag. In the meantime, there are other important tasks that require your attention."

A new gold exclamation mark appeared above Bartholomew's head. Damien smiled. At this rate he'd get to level 10 in no time. First, however, he had another matter to attend to.

"Can I just take a few minutes to catch my breath? I'll start the next task very soon, I promise!"

Bartholomew inclined his head ever so slightly.

"Very well, I shall grant you a temporary reprieve. Come and find me when you're ready."

Bartholomew floated backward until he faded into the shadows. Damien brought up his Stat page.

He had twenty-five stat points that needed to be allocated. He gave it some thought. There was only one skill he gave a damn about that could scale off his stat points: Soul Harvest. He could hold more souls and have a larger number of imps at his command if he increased his wisdom. It would also increase his mana and his mana regeneration, so he'd have a hard time running out of mana to summon more.

He decided. He'd put these points into wisdom and see how

it went. Maybe there would be more skills that scaled with wisdom in the future.

As they dropped in, his mana pool increased to 400. He quickly checked his Soul Harvest skill. Sure enough, the utility of Soul Harvest had improved greatly.

Account Name: Damien Arkwright
Character: Daemien
Class: Occultist
Level: 6
Health: 140/140
Stamina: 140/140
Mana: 400/400
Stats:
Strength 14 - Agility 14 - Intelligence 14
Constitution 14 - Endurance 14 - Wisdom 40
Stat Points: 0
Experience: 26/2000
Soul Summon Limit: 3/6 - **Soul Reserve:** 3/7

He could now have up to six imps at a time. His Soul Reserve had gone up more modestly, only increasing by two points compared to his Soul Limit's three, but the real prize was being able to use so many summons at once.

"Looooo—"

Damien closed his menu and turned his head in the blink of an eye. Noigel had entered a coughing fit and the voice had vanished. But Damien knew.

"Bartholomew? Where are you?"

A faint clicking from behind Damien prompted him to turn and find Bartholomew occupying the previously empty space. The rat furs were floating in the air beside his head as his fingers manipulated a pair of knitting needles with uncanny dexterity. Damien was taken aback.

He hadn't thought Bartholomew would literally, personally craft him a bag. He'd figured the game would pop a bag into existence with a line of code and Bartholomew would hand it over, along with some prefabricated moan of how much effort it had taken. But no, a vampire occultist faction leader was knitting him a bag out of rat skins.

"I have some questions," started Damien, being careful to put Noigel back in his sights as he spoke.

"Really? Well, I suppose we should all stop what we're doing so we don't risk forcing you to repeat yourself."

"Thanks, uh, that would be great. So, for starters, why is Noigel talking?"

Bartholomew stumbled in his knitting but quickly recovered, retracing the steps before settling back into his rhythm. He spoke to Damien out of the corner of his mouth.

"That's a shame, I was hoping we'd have some fun before you figured it out. Noigel becomes more intelligent the more imps you have in your party. That's his 'We Are Many' ability."

Damien was careful not to look directly at Noigel, but he could still see him in his peripheral vision. He slyly brought up Noigel's stat bar without using any physical gestures. Noigel's intelligence was already at 15. It had tripled, multiplied by the number of imps in play.

Since Daemien had hit level five, some of Noigel's other stats had increased as well: his constitution and endurance had risen by a point each, bringing his health and stamina bars up to 60. His agility stat had risen by a full three points. Not bad. Five pre-assigned stat points for the imps every five levels. It was much less than players received, but at least it was a measurable improvement.

Damien closed Noigel's Stat page and pondered the imp's behavior. Instead of telling Damien he had the ability to speak, Noigel had decided to hide this information and use it to mock him. This did not, to Damien's mind, seem very co-operative.

"Any other questions?"

The bag was already starting to take shape. Bartholomew was weaving the top of it into a plushie rat head, a cute yet somehow macabre tribute to the fur from which it was made. Damien tore his eyes away from it and remembered his question about the mechanics of soul gathering.

"When I started fighting rats I was getting good souls early on, but later some of them weren't dropping souls at all. Was I doing something wrong?"

Bartholomew slowed down slightly as he considered this, then the knitting needles whirled back into action as he lazily intoned his reply.

"It is a question of quality, Daemien, not quantity. Rats lack the inclination to cultivate their souls. As for why the volume of souls decreased, that is simple. You have become considerably more powerful and the rats no longer constitute a worthy offering. Your only recourse is to find stronger enemies."

Damien translated it into gamer speak. He wouldn't be able to collect souls from enemies that were much weaker than himself. He'd have to find higher level enemies to keep his soul count flowing.

"All right, I got it. Thanks for your help. So, what's this quest you want me to do?"

"First things first: your aptitude as an occultist has increased significantly, even if your maturity has not. As such, I have two new spells to bestow upon you as a reward for your dedication."

Bartholomew tapped Damien on the head with a white-hot finger and two new notifications came up.

Summon Wraith Unlocked!
Possession Unlocked!

"The first is a summoning ability. The wraith will only function effectively in the dark, but is extremely dangerous if it maintains the element of surprise. The second allows you to take direct control of your minions. You are left vulnerable while Possession is active, so ensure you conceal yourself somewhere safe. You will test these two abilities in tandem."

'**Slither a Mile in My...Shoes?** – Kill five enemies while in possession of a wraith.'

"And since you need to test the wraith in a dark place, you're going to take the opportunity to build your own lair."

'**Home is Where the Sacrificial Organ is** – Establish an occultist base in a secret, preferably cave-like location.'

"Off you go. By the time you return I'll have finished your bag."

Bartholomew did not fade away into the shadows as he had done before, but he removed his attention from Damien completely and buried himself in his knitting. He had found a couple of spare buttons and was giving them a new purpose as rat eyes for Damien's plushie bag. Damien set aside his complaints about the extremely cute yet disturbing item and focused on the serious issue.

"You want me to build a base…somewhere?"

Bartholomew did not raise his head. He seemed to be trying very hard to ignore Damien completely.

"Yes. Very important. You're an occultist now! You have to learn to make sacrifices, literally and metaphorically, and the first sacrifice you're going to make is moving out of here and finding your own place to live."

Damien hadn't built a base when he'd been playing Scorpius. He'd never received a quest instructing him to do so and had more than enough to keep him occupied without it.

Even so, from what he'd seen on Saga Online's various streaming channels, he was pretty sure most players didn't build their bases in dank caves. They set them up in occupied towns to integrate themselves with society, offering a variety of services ranging from blacksmithing to enchanting to practice their skills, improve their stats and make extra gold. It appeared occultists were not quite so sociable.

"I've only just started playing—I mean, learning how to be an occultist. You can't kick me out into the world yet!"

Bartholomew stopped knitting and the rat furs fell to the floor in a heap. Bartholomew pointed at him with a slender finger, punctuating the most important words by jabbing the finger into Damien's stomach.

"I am not kicking you out. I am guiding you on your journey of happiness, self-improvement and, ideally, revenge. Establishing your own domain is crucial to this process. Also, you're smelly and stupid and having you here is an affront to my senses. Begone! And return when you have completed the tasks I've assigned you!"

Bartholomew raised his hands and the furs levitated themselves back off the floor into their flight formation. The knitting resumed at pace. Damien wasn't too happy, but he decided he was going to milk Bartholomew for information before he committed to a course of action.

"What do I need to build a base?"

"Build? You don't build anything, boy! Just find a place you like and call it home. When you've done that, you can come back and I'll have actual construction tasks for you."

Now Damien was annoyed. This was a waste of time he couldn't afford. When he'd played as Scorpius, he set an inn as his home base and could quickly find his class trainer and gather as many quests as he wanted from people in town. What Bartholomew was proposing was totally unacceptable.

Damien would have a home base in the middle of a cave somewhere, totally removed from anything useful. Then, just for the privilege of talking to his class trainer and primary quest giver, he'd have to come back to The Downward Spiral. All the way down the steps. Then all the way back up again. Every single time he needed something from Bartholomew.

Damien wasn't having it.

Bartholomew had made it obvious that Damien wasn't welcome, but he'd fallen just short of telling him not to build his base here directly. Damien looked at a section of The Downward Spiral and defiantly thought 'home'. A patch of ground up against the wall flashed green and a much larger red circle highlighted an area around it, stretching to cover almost the entire dungeon floor. A notification showed up underneath Bartholomew's quest.

'Congratulations! You have chosen a home base. In order to start building you will either need to clear the surrounding area of hostile forces or, if they are capable of diplomacy, come to an agreement with them.'

There was a clatter and a thud as Bartholomew's concentration lapsed. The materials for Damien's bag fell to the floor again, forgotten. Damien turned and found Bartholomew looking decidedly hostile: his arms were at his sides and his fingers were curling hypnotically, closing then opening again. He was aware Damien had claimed a chunk of his territory.

"What do you think you're doing?"

"I'm working on my assignment. I've selected an area, in a secret, dark, cave-like location to turn into my base. Just as you instructed. Next, I'll negotiate with the current resident so he'll allow me to build here. That's you, right? So this should be easy!"

Damien's world blurred. He had the briefest impression he was spinning before his back ended up against the wall. Bartholomew was holding him there by the scruff of his shirt.

"Don't be snide. I made it perfectly clear I don't want you here. What inspired you to go against my wishes?"

Damien's hands were clasped around Bartholomew's arm, but they weren't capable of doing anything. Bartholomew had the situation firmly under control. Even so, Damien could see his gamble was on the verge of paying off; despite the speed and strength used to move him so quickly, Bartholomew had dealt no damage. Even the way he was holding him – by his rags rather than his throat – showed that Bartholomew didn't want to risk injuring him. He was just trying to scare him.

It was just as well they weren't technically in combat, since the imps had gathered behind Bartholomew and were hesitating. Even Noigel wasn't sure what to do. Damien shook his head at them in case they got any ideas and tapped Bartholomew on the arm.

"I'll tell you why I want to build my base here, and if you don't agree, I'll leave."

Bartholomew lowered him down, scraping Damien's back on the wall as he did so, before dropping him. Damien landed on his feet, once again defying Bartholomew's intent. The vampire grumbled and stuck his hand on Damien's shoulder, pressing down until he was on his knees.

"I am the leader of a group that once pitted itself against the entire Empire. I have subjugated scores of powerful demons, laid waste to hundreds of settlements and cultivated the loyalty of thousands of subjects before the Empire even existed. I do not share living space. If you still wish to waste your words, by all means go ahead."

Bartholomew removed his hand and leered down at him, but Damien knew for all Bartholomew's power he had something to lose. His speech, designed to intimidate, only revealed how badly he longed for his former glory.

Damien rested his hands in his lap but did not stand up. That would've been a step too far. What he did do was stare Bartholomew directly in the eye.

"Ever since I got here, you've done nothing but talk about how great and powerful you are. And you are! Great and powerful, I mean. But if I'm to believe what you just told me, you're nothing compared to what you used to be."

Bartholomew's eye twitched and he brought his face in very close.

"This is not going well for you so far."

"Then it's not going well for either of us," Damien snapped back. "If you force me to leave, you're not just making my life difficult, you're risking the most valuable thing you have. Me."

Bartholomew's head recoiled as if Damien had swatted him in the face. Then he howled with laughter. It was even more sinister than Damien had anticipated, a booming, echoing cackle, fading into a rasp that lingered in the mind long after it had actually expired. Bartholomew had clearly mastered the evil laugh during his reign. Damien patiently waited without looking away. His apathy only annoyed Bartholomew even more.

"And what makes you so certain you have any value to me at all?"

"Aside from me, how many 'aspiring heroes' have come down here and signed up to be occultists?"

Any trace of amusement disappeared from what was left of Bartholomew's features.

"Yeah, that's what I thought. I was at the Empire's recruitment area this morning. Don't give me that look!" The mock horror on Bartholomew's face was immediately replaced with a sour pout. "You knew damn well where I came from when you blackmailed me into becoming an occultist. But did you know how many warriors joined the Empire's ranks today? Nearly three hundred. That was just this morning. It's probably more by now. And that's just the warriors! How many new soldiers of the Empire will be recruited by the end of the day? A thousand? More?"

Bartholomew's nasal cavity flared.

"I don't see what the Empire's lackadaisical recruitment tactics—"

Now it was Damien's turn to laugh. It may have lacked Bartholomew's timbre, but it got his sentiment across.

"You want me to find a spot in another location? What if even a fraction of those new recruits wander into the area where I set up my base? I'll die, that's what. I don't see how that helps either of us. So, you can wallow here by yourself and wait for someone else to land on a rat while I get ganked outside, or you can offer me protection until I take revenge on Aetherius."

Bartholomew drew a finger across his distended lips. He was considering the proposal but still didn't seem to like it very much. Damien gave him one last push.

"Imagine how famous you'll be when one of your disciples kills such a well-known hero of the Empire. You'll have people fighting each other to become occultists!"

This did provoke a response. Bartholomew's eyes gleamed before they fell upon Damien and narrowed once more. Despite all the correct boxes being ticked, he wasn't going to let Damien have what he wanted that easily.

"Your enthusiasm is undeniable. But you're a weakling. Aetherius is one of the strongest heroes in Arcadia. How long do you suppose it will take to exact your vengeance? What if you fail? I will not allow you to stay here indefinitely."

Damien thought quickly. The Streamer Competition was going to end in six days' time and the prize money would go along with it. If he didn't win the competition it would hardly matter if he had to find a new base. Nothing in Saga Online would matter. He'd have to find the money for his mother's bionic heart by some other means.

Killing Aetherius was the ideal solution. Now that his plans to revive Scorpius had been crushed, he couldn't think of any other way of gaining the publicity he needed in such a short time while also presenting Bartholomew with a concrete goal. It was perfect! The fact that killing Aetherius would bring him immense pleasure was just the icing on the cake.

"Give me a week. If I haven't killed Aetherius by then, I'll leave your dungeon either way."

Bartholomew regarded him evenly.

"Seven days, starting from now. Whether or not you've killed Aetherius, you will leave. Do we have a deal?"

Damien stood up and grabbed Bartholomew by the wrist, shaking it vigorously. He didn't bother hiding his joy. Bartholomew didn't bother hiding his disgust.

"Deal!"

Bartholomew pulled him in closer. "But I won't have you cluttering up my killing floor. Come with me. We'll find a more suitable corner for you to skulk in."

10

VICTORY LOVES PREPARATION?

artholomew led Damien and his imps to the back of The Downward Spiral. The vampire placed the palm of his hand against a seemingly innocuous section of cavern wall and muttered under his breath. Bright white light seared across the crevices and a couple of seconds later the wall collapsed inward, forming a perfect alcove where the rock had given way.

Bartholomew picked his way through the rubble without missing a step and gestured for Damien to follow.

"This should meet your requirements, I believe. Tell me what you think, so I can tell you how little I care."

Damien clumsily clambered through the debris and whistled. It wasn't much to look at, but it was certainly spacious. If Damien were to stand on Bartholomew's shoulders (although he was pretty sure he'd die in the attempt), he'd still only be a third of the way to touching the top of the domed ceiling.

"Yes, I can already sense that you're about to recommence your incessant whining: 'But master, it's so small, why aren't there any furnishings, where's the latrine, etcetera, etcetera. But this is far more than you—"

"It's great! Thank you for letting me stay here, Bartholomew!"

Bartholomew looked a little put out that he'd inadvertently made Damien so happy.

"Curses. I knew I should have made it smaller. Consider yourself lucky. Well? What are you waiting for?"

Damien stared at him, nonplussed, before realizing what was missing. He focused on the center of the room and thought 'home'. The translucent green circle reappeared before expanding to fill the space, climbing up the walls and spreading over the ceiling until the whole room was bathed in it. It seemed this room was much more suitable for his purposes than the patch of ground he'd flippantly designated as his base outside.

"Remember, this is only temporary. If you refuse to honor our agreement I won't waste my energy throwing you out. I'll simply seal this door, and I won't bother checking if you're inside when I do so. Have I made myself clear?"

Damien fluttered his eyelashes.

"Oh, Bartholomew, you don't have to pretend to be so mean. You're actually really nice."

"Ugh. Don't make me regret this more than I already do. Your first base-building assignment is to build a Soul Well. This will be the core of your base, so choose the location wisely."

'**Soul Well That Ends Well** – Construct a Soul Well in your base.'

New menu options available!

Damien opened his menu and found a new option had appeared. It was called 'Base Schematics'. He opened it and was presented with a long list of tabs. Most of them were grayed out, but the Soul Well was sitting pretty right at the top.

Soul Well
Health: 250
Description: The dark heart of an occultist base. Can be filled with souls.
Requirements: twenty stone blocks, one soul.

He nodded and the menu closed unexpectedly. He was about

to bring it back up when he noticed a transparent gray outline in the dark, directly in the center of his vision. He looked to Bartholomew for guidance and was slightly alarmed when the gray outline followed, turning red where it overlapped with Bartholomew's body. Ah. Clever. This was to show how much space the structure was going to occupy so Damien could decide where to put it.

He focused on the center of the room and nodded gently while keeping his eyes trained on the same spot. There was a click in his head and the Soul Well schematic rooted itself to the ground. An empty loading bar appeared above it, probably displaying how close it was to completion. The only problem was that it wasn't moving.

"Loooseeer."

Damien rolled his eyes. It was good to know he was not in fact going crazy. Still, he needed to make an example of Noigel before he got too cocky. It was hard enough controlling him already. Damien pretended he hadn't heard anything and looked to Bartholomew.

"Well? What now?"

"You've chosen where you're going to build? I suggest you start building, then. Although," he grinned mischievously, "you could have your imps do it for you instead."

Damien grinned back. He understood completely.

"Hey, Noigel. Come here."

The imp strutted forward ahead of his posse. Damien looked him up and down. It was hard to tell there'd been any change, not least because Noigel was hiding it. There was at least one sign the imp hadn't thought to cover up: he was standing more upright than when they'd first started working together.

He came to a halt in front of Damien, his face pulled into a calculated mask of stupidity. If he hadn't proven himself to be so wily in combat, Damien would have told Bartholomew to take him back. Since Damien didn't have the luxury of throwing away advantages, no matter how small, he was going to have to punish Noigel for his insolence instead.

Sheesh, thought Damien, *I'm starting to sound like Bartholomew*.

"Noigel, I heard some strange noises when we were outside. They were coming from almost exactly where you were standing, actually. It sounded like someone was calling me a loser. You wouldn't know anything about that, would you, Noigel?"

Noigel pointed at himself, his mouth falling open in a show of surprise that would've been much more convincing if Damien didn't already know the answer to his own question. Noigel made a big show of looking around himself and adamantly shook his head.

"Oh dear. If you couldn't detect it, it must be quite powerful. And it's mocking me! We need to make sure we're safe." Damien pointed at the other two imps. "You two, stand outside the door and tell me if you see any strange enemies."

The two remaining imps looked at each other and shrugged before moving outside and standing guard. Within five seconds they'd started playing Patty Cake again. Since Damien knew there was no danger, he couldn't care less.

"Sorry, Noigel, but that means you're going to have to build the Soul Well by yourself. I'll talk to Bartholomew about how to defeat this mysterious enemy while you work on it. Chop chop!"

Noigel was dumbfounded. He stared at Damien with his mouth open and made several dumb noises that were far more legitimate than when he was simply pretending to be stupid. Then he frantically pointed between the two imps and himself, gesturing that they should swap places.

"No, Noigel, that's very brave of you, but you're my best minion. I won't risk losing you to some unknown enemy. It's much safer for you in here. You'd better get started; that Soul Well won't build itself."

Noigel looked to Bartholomew for help. Somehow the vampire managed to keep a straight face. He simply looked at Noigel and shrugged. Noigel parked himself on the floor and folded his arms. He was refusing to co-operate. Damien was delighted.

"Build the Soul Well. Now."

With a low moan, Noigel rose to his feet and dragged himself over to the rocks that littered the floor. They were almost as big as he was. It looked like hard work. Damien knew time was of the essence, but as far as he was concerned this was time well spent. When Noigel picked up the rock, a timer had appeared above the empty loading bar. An hour until completion. Bartholomew gave the exercise his seal of approval.

"You're going to be a fine occultist."

"Thanks, I'll take that as a compliment, I guess. So, what does the Soul Well do?"

"The Soul Well tethers minions to your lair. You must first collect souls and imbue the Soul Well with them, but the rewards are substantial; minions in your lair will perform assigned tasks and guard against threats in your absence, allowing you to further your own agen—"

A phone icon appeared in the corner of Damien's HUD and Bartholomew's voice was dulled to a distant murmur. It was a call from the outside.

"Bartholomew, I'm really sorry, I…err…I need a moment. Can you give me a couple of minutes?"

Bartholomew looked at him angrily and his mouth started moving faster. Damien managed not to roll his eyes. He could do without being killed for impoliteness.

But he wouldn't be able to hear what Bartholomew was saying without rejecting the call, and since it might have something to do with his mother there was no way he could do such a thing.

"I'm sorry. I'll be right back."

He turned around and wandered to the opposite end of the room, half expecting Bartholomew to stab him in the back. When he made it there intact he decided the danger was past. The in-game danger, anyway. He took a deep breath and tilted his head up.

"Hello?"

"Good afternoon, I'm Sam from the CU TRACK agency. Who am I talking to?"

"This is Damien."

"Hello, Damien. Since this is a landline, can I assume you're at the Brades residence?"

Damien looked around himself and took in the dirty walls, the angry vampire and the small red demon that was constructing his new home base's first feature.

"Kind of?"

"I'm sorry, Damien, can you be more specific? I need you to help me so that I can help you. Are you at home?"

Damien was immediately suspicious. Why did they need to know where he was?

"I'm not at home right now."

Damien wasn't sure if that was technically true or not. Sam shared his lack of conviction.

"Then why did you answer the landline number? Look, Damien, I'm trying to help you. Please don't make this difficult."

"I'm answering the call from a mobile device that's linked to my home phone. Why does it matter?"

"Mr. Arkwright, your location is important because I understand you are currently alone in your residence, which is why I am calling."

"Why don't you start by telling me how my hospitalized mother is?"

"That is your right." Sam's voice was slightly pained.

It was replaced with a series of clicks and clacks as he worked at his keyboard.

"Your mother's condition is unchanged since we contacted you earlier today."

Damien breathed a sigh of relief. All right, well, that was actually some good news for a change.

Sam picked up exactly where he had left off.

"Due to these circumstances, and you being a minor, CU has decided to place you into temporary state care. But don't worry; this is just until your mother's condition improves."

Damien froze. So much for good news.

"Local CU agents are on their way to collect you. Please do not be alarmed. They may look a little scary, but this is for your own safety. If you are not currently at the residence, please return there within thirty minutes. I am obliged to tell you that failure to comply could result in a charge of evading authorities, but I'm sure that won't be a problem. If you have any questions—"

Damien hung up.

He was left staring at the wall, blood rushing to his head as panic scattered all logical thought. He raised his hands and pounded the stone as hard as he could, achieving nothing except inflicting damage on himself.

"I take it you received ill tidings from your realm."

Bartholomew had appeared by his side.

"If you must return, I can reclaim possession of Noigel and supervise his construction of your Soul Well. I'd like you to dismiss the other two imps. You should see for yourself what happens."

Damien nodded as his thoughts started to catch up with him. Bartholomew was right. He did need to return. If the CU agents took him into custody, he'd be left with no chance of winning the streaming contest. For now, he needed to log out and make a plan. His mouth dropped open as his thoughts caught up and he realized that Bartholomew had been in earshot for the entire call.

"How much did you hear? And doesn't it surprise you that I come from… another realm?"

Bartholomew shrugged.

"I heard all of it and understood none of it. I have many talents but deciphering the strange language of your realm is not among them. As for Arcadia not being your original home world…you're talking to a magic practitioner and demon summoner. It is not such a strange concept for me that you come from a different place in time and space. As far as I'm concerned, you're just an annoying demon that summons itself."

Damien knew he'd spoken perfectly clearly. Maybe NPCs were programmed not to understand. He didn't have the time to waste finding out.

"Thank you, Bartholomew. I'll leave Noigel with you."

He strode to the entryway and pointed at the two demons. They quickly stopped playing Patty Cake and locked their eyes ahead as if they'd never even considered straying from their duty.

"Good job, guys. I'm sending you home. You're dismissed!"

The two imps looked relieved, then threw shapes at him as a parting gesture. Portals opened above each of them and they were sucked through, still holding their poses. Two swirling gray orbs dropped through the rapidly shrinking portals before they vanished entirely. His soul count rose to four out of six, a half soul apiece for each imp.

"Provided your minions are in good health," Bartholomew chimed in, "half of their soul cost will be returned to you when your covenant is terminated. If they are wounded, all the soul energy will be lost."

Or in normal person speak, he'd get half the soul cost back for dismissing minions at full health. That might come in handy later. For now, only Noigel remained.

"Bartholomew will look after you," Damien told him. "I expect the Soul Well to be finished before I come back."

With the two imps gone, Noigel couldn't taunt him anymore. He looked at the pile of rocks still strewn across the floor and decided to make his last stand. He threw the rock he'd been oh so slowly lugging on the floor and let out a piercing cry, stamping his feet up and down furiously.

"Fear not," Bartholomew cooed softly. Noigel flinched as the vampire's hand stroked his head. "I'll keep you safe from whatever it is that insulted your new master. If I find the creature responsible, I'll teach it a lesson it won't soon forget."

He lowered his lips to Noigel's ear and breathed a scratchy whisper into it. Noigel's skin broke out in goosebumps at the first syllable.

"So get back to work."

Noigel promptly picked up the rock and ran with it to the construction site as fast as his legs could carry him. The timer reappeared, now cut down to a mere half hour. It appeared Noigel's work ethic depended on whether he was properly motivated. Bartholomew gave Damien a knowing wink while Noigel was occupied.

"You're fortunate I find Noigel even more irritating than you, if only by the narrowest of margins. I'll ensure he completes his assignment in good time, but do not forget: you have assignments to complete as well. I expect you to return as soon as you are able."

Damien was already in his menu and hovering over the Logout button. He spared Bartholomew a bow before he hit it and the ten-second timer to log out began.

"Thank you for everything, Bartholomew. You won't regret it. I'll kill Aetherius, I swear."

Bartholomew inclined his head very slightly and the ghost of a smile twisted the corners of his mouth.

Damien's vision went black and all sound was cut off. He blinked and his eyes opened to the inside of his IMBA set's visor.

He was lying down in bed, back in his room.

11

THE ROAD LESS TRAVELLED BY

D amien tried to rise but had to lie back, his head still spinning from the rapid transition. After a few seconds he got his bearings and raised himself up again, pulling the helmet off his head before setting his feet on the floor. CU agents were on their way to his house and would be there in less than half an hour.

What was he going to do?

He couldn't keep them out. If they wanted to come in they would, one way or another. Damien gritted his teeth. He already had a lot to do and not much time to do it in; he wasn't going to let the same people who refused to help his mother screw up his only chance to help her himself.

He jumped up and started grabbing armfuls of clothing from his wardrobe.

He was leaving.

Damien didn't know where he was going but it hardly mattered. Anywhere was better than here. He thrust a pile of clothing into the bottom of his backpack and reverentially placed the IMBA set on top of them, upside down with the charging cord stored safely inside. Then he got dressed himself, checking his pockets to make sure he had his wallet before slinging the bag over one arm and heading through the kitchen.

At the sight of the leftover bacon and eggs, his stomach

rumbled. That would save him the trouble of buying a meal. He paced over to the table and wolfed down the cold food without bothering to sit. It was only as Damien lost momentum that he realized the insanity of what he was doing.

He didn't have enough money to survive outside, let alone go on the run from CU. It was six days until the competition ended. He might have stayed with friends, but he didn't really have any he trusted enough for this. Even if he did, that was where CU would look first.

Damien shoveled the last of his breakfast into his mouth and looked wistfully at his mother's room, contemplating while he chewed. He was going to have to do this by himself, and as ugly as it was, he could only see one way of doing it.

Hesitantly, he walked into his mother's bedroom. Her handbag was sitting on the dresser. Her card would be inside. Damien had used it himself, when Cassandra was too tired to get groceries, so he knew the pin code and had the relevant permissions.

Even if he was doing it to try and save her, it felt like a huge breach of trust. What would she have to say about this?

Nothing, if she died.

The last thought galvanized him and he guiltily rummaged through the bag until he found what he was looking for. He took the card and placed it carefully into his wallet. He wouldn't use it any more than necessary. Damien turned to leave and froze when there was a knock at the front door followed by muffled words.

"Damien Arkwright? This is CU. Open up."

A second voice bickered with the first, but Damien couldn't hear through the door.

That was fast. He thought he'd have more time. Damien back-tracked into his mother's room and quietly shut the door before moving to the window. He crept up to it and poked his head around the side of the wall. The window shade prevented a clear view of the corridor but he could still make out two people off to the right, standing at his door.

A hulking monstrosity of a man with a shaved head was

doing the knocking. A scruffier, bearded gentleman with tech-specs leaned against the wall with his arms folded, periodically checking the stairs.

Both of them wore black suits, although the big guy's didn't fit properly and the smaller man's shirt was hanging out. If these were CU agents they clearly were not the A team, or even the B team; these guys were way down the alphabet. There was another series of knocks, louder this time, before they turned to each other. Damien strained to hear.

"Looks like he's not home yet."

"Whatever." The bearded man pushed himself off the wall. "The kid's sixteen, it's not like he's going anywhere. He'll come back."

The brains of the outfit touched a finger against his ear, pacing slowly up and down until his call was answered.

"This is Shaw... No, he's not answering... But what if he's inside?... With all due respect, sir, we didn't sign up to be babysitters, we have—Yes, I remember what happened... Yes, I know what a punitive demotion means... Fine, but I really think we would be better utilized—Understood. Understood, *sir*... Goodbye."

He removed his hand from his ear and swore loudly. Then he hissed down the corridor and gestured for his colleague to come over. Damien quickly lowered himself below the window frame as heavy footsteps drew near.

"So?" boomed the deeper bass of his companion. "What did he say?"

"He wants us to wait outside for the brat. It's 'less intimidating'."

Right on cue, the house phone started to ring. There was silence from outside as the two of them listened in, waiting to see if it was answered. Damien remained in place under the window sill, breathing shallowly through his nose. The ringing stopped and he let out an involuntary sigh.

"All right, let's go. We can stand at the front gate."

The heavy footsteps clomped past the window again, but they were not joined by those of his irate co-worker.

"Stuff their rules, we're going in! This division is full of soft-spined pencil pushers. I'm not standing on ceremony all day waiting for this little twerp. He's probably still inside. Break this door down!"

"Are you sure that's a good idea? You know what happened last ti—"

"Don't argue with me, I'm your superior! Break this door down, I said!"

There was a long, labored groan before the heavy footsteps paced their way back to Damien's front door. After a few seconds, there came an almighty crash. Damien's heart thundered in his chest.

A moment later two sets of footsteps clumped against the floor just outside the room.

Damien forced the window open and clambered through it. Without even pausing to cover his tracks he fled down the fire escape, forcing himself not to look back.

When he reached the back gate of his building's complex, Damien allowed himself to slow back down to a walk. There was no sign of anyone waiting for him. Right before he crossed the threshold, a deeply unsettling thought brought him to a halt.

There was a camera directly over the gate. When he walked through it his face would be scanned and he'd be identified automatically. He knew this was true because he'd seen plenty of actual criminals caught on TV in exactly the same way. The facial recognition technology CU utilized had always made him feel safe – until now.

He pulled up his hood and turned away from the camera as he passed through the gate, quickly crossing the road and turning into an alleyway.

If he went far enough through the backstreets without using the main roads they should have a harder time picking up his trail. If he was very lucky, they wouldn't be able to figure out where he'd gone at all. Even so, a single camera catching his face meant they'd immediately pick him up again. He couldn't expect to get lucky forever.

Damien paused in the alleyway. This was going to be impossible. Maybe it would be better to turn himself in right now, before things got any more out of hand. He could even pretend he'd come back from somewhere outside and had never been in the apartment at all. They probably wouldn't even bother checking the footage if he came back quickly. Some victory that would be, but if he couldn't hide his face from the cameras there was no other choice. He hadn't had this in mind when he'd packed his bag, so he hadn't brought any clothes up to the task. Unless…

How hadn't he thought of this before?

Damien looked around to check he was alone and opened his bag. The IMBA set looked like an ordinary motorcycle helmet to the untrained eye. He might look a bit strange, but it sure as hell beat state care.

Damien dug it out of his bag before taking the thought one step further, taking off the hoodie and changing his shirt to one of a completely different color. He hadn't thought far enough ahead to bring another pair of trousers or shoes. It would have to do. He stuck the IMBA set on his head, making sure it was switched off, before tilting the visor up slightly so he could see through the crack.

He closed the bag and continued down the alleyway. He needed somewhere with a lot of people, somewhere he could blend in. More than that, he needed somewhere cheap he could stay without being hassled. He knew just the place.

Even in the middle of the day the outdoor market was in full flow, with people jostling for position at vendors selling every conceivable thing. A loud man at a stall was hollering down the road trying to sell computer parts, while a jolly-looking lady on the opposite side of the street was selling what she optimistically described as fresh fish.

Damien wondered how she hadn't been called out for false advertising and staggered through the stench, struggling to find his footing with his vision so constricted. Everybody was too busy bargain hunting to give the boy with the black helmet any attention. Still, it wasn't a cold day and Damien was starting to become very uncomfortable in the heavy headgear.

He blinked sweat out of his eyes and stopped at the side of the road, tilting his head to get a better view of the storefronts. One in particular caught his eye. He'd found what he'd been looking for – a pod hotel, offering hourly rates. He could hole up there while he planned his next move.

Damien edged his way between a jeans vendor and a stall full of action figurines before pushing his way through the door. He had to adjust to the low lighting as he stepped out of the sunshine and into the gaming den. It was only slightly brighter in there than it had been in Bartholomew's dungeon, ideal for people who spent their lives staring at screens.

There was a section in the front reserved for people who wanted unrestricted internet browsing, a mix of screens and mini-projectors occupying each alcove in sets of desks with dividers put up between them. There was another section further back where the much larger pods sat in rows, crammed together in bunches to fit more of them in. It looked remarkably unsafe; if one fell over, they'd all go. Damien had no doubt it was in direct contravention of several CU regulations. Perfect.

"It's a bit hot for that helmet, ain't it?"

Damien hurriedly took the IMBA set off, wiping the sweat off on his jeans before looking at the counter. There was an old man standing behind it, swiping through an ancient touch-screen phone.

"Hi!" said Damien, carefully avoiding the question. "I'd like to use a pod, please."

The phone gave off an electronic blip before it was set down. The man who'd been operating it brought his eyes into focus on Damien, staring at him appraisingly over a pair of thick-rimmed spectacles. He looked old enough to have seen the turn of the millennium.

"Sure thing, I'll need to see some ID."

Damien was crestfallen. He'd never used a pod hotel before and hadn't realized he'd need his identity card. He couldn't use it in his current situation, CU would know where he was immediately. This exercise was becoming harder all the time.

"I don't have my ID on me. I didn't realize I'd need it. Sorry, I'll come back later."

He turned around and was just putting his helmet back on when the millennial called out to him.

"Hey, little man, no need for that. This one's on me."

He held up his own ID card and waved it at him.

"Just bring yer own next time, ya'hear? Now, how long you stayin' for?"

Damien beamed at him. He'd be crazy not to make the most of this.

"I want to stay the night, head out tomorrow at noon. Is that all right?"

"Wait, what? The whole night?"

Damien started to worry, but the old man laughed and he relaxed.

"You sure know how to enjoy yourself! Just slap your money on the counter and I'll put you in for the day."

Damien fished through his wallet, being careful to hold it against the counter to hide his ID as he removed Cassandra's cash-card. He didn't have enough on him to pay for a whole day's stay and wanted to save what little he had for emergencies. He'd just have to pay his mom back later.

The card was read successfully and Damien punched in the pin.

"Awesome! Here's your key card, good for any unoccupied pod until noon tomorrow. I'll show you through."

The old timer hobbled out from behind his desk, touch-screen phone still in hand, and led him past the divider desks. Damien caught sight of a couple of people playing games or watching videos, but the place was mostly empty. The pods were all unoccupied, each of them open and waiting. Despite everything that had happened, Damien was thrilled. He'd never used a pod before.

"Alrighty, there's a compartment just here on the outside where you can put your bag, unlocks with the key card. Same card unlocks the shower round back. No towels, you just blast the air dryer when you're done, but no more than fifteen minutes per visit, ya'hear? If you just need toilet stuff, that room over there will do the trick. Don't think you'll want to spend more than fifteen minutes in there, though."

The man pointed at an open toilet stall across the way, whose missing door had been replaced with a makeshift curtain.

"You've got heat lamps in the pod too, just don't turn'em on while you're doing your fancy VR whachamaggigit or you'll come out with a tan. The Wi-Fi password is on the inside of the door. Anything else you can't figure out yourself, give me a holler. Oh, and my name's Gian. Have yourself a good time!"

Damien gave him a grin and a thumbs up which Gian returned in kind before wandering back to his desk, his nose already buried in his phone again. Damien climbed into the pod and looked over the buttons. His host had been very helpful, but everything was clearly labeled. It wasn't hard to figure out how to use it.

After a few seconds, Damien found the button he was looking for and the door closed with a hiss. He selected another and the entire pod swiveled to horizontal. Damien grabbed the charging cord out of his bag before sticking it into one of the sockets by his waist, plugging the helmet in and switching it on. He needed to check something. He used the IMBA set to browse the Wi-Fi instead of going into the game, navigating to Aetherius's page with a series of blinks and subtle rolls of the head.

The front page of Aetherius's online channel confirmed Damien's worst fears. It was an image of him, his online face absurdly similar to the real thing, naked except for a loincloth and a big friendly grin. The video was entitled:

"Damien (aka Scorpius) gets a five-second boost. Let's see how he does!"

With forced calmness, Damien hovered over the video and activated it. Sure enough, Aetherius hadn't included the bit where Damien gushed out his fear of losing his mother and begged for help. Or how Aetherius had promised to make him famous. This is what the two-faced, lying, treacherous narcissist had meant. Damien was very famous now.

It didn't have as many views as the "Damien vs Toutatis" fight had before, but this video had only been put up a few hours ago. Damien's one big advantage had been people thinking he was cool for fighting Toutatis. Now that had been taken away. He was famous for being kicked down a hole, naked. Aetherius had turned him into a sideshow for his own benefit.

Damien clenched his fists. He was already committed to winning the competition to get the money; he didn't have the means to pay for his mother's operation any other way. But Aetherius had made this difficult. The only way he was going to win back people's respect and get votes would be to humiliate Aetherius in kind. Damien looked at the comments:

Shmushypoopookins: Welcome to the meat grinder, kiddo XD
ODLHODLHODLHODLH: Hole in the ground 1 : 0 Damien
L3g0la5s: Lots of people feeling pretty stupid for making characters called 'Scorpius' today, hurhurhur.

No sympathy whatsoever. Just one user after another waiting to take a cheap kick at Aetherius's leftovers. Scavenger trolls. Still, at least Damien had one advantage going for him. Everyone thought he was dead. As long as they thought that, he could level up in private and start attacking Aetherius's guild with a twenty-four-hour head start.

His character was still too weak now, but it wouldn't be long. Once he got to level 10 he could start trying to pick off the weaker members. He had to get to level 10 as soon as possible.

Damien closed the page and loaded up Saga Online. It was time to get back to work.

12

NO REST FOR THE WICKED

"Ah, Daemien! As expected, if slightly later than I'd hoped. So, did you vanquish your enemies?"

Damien blinked, waiting for his night vision to kick in. The entire dungeon was nearly pitch black. The dim light barely made it past the entrance, let alone reaching into Damien's lair. After a few moments, Bartholomew's aesthetically challenging face blurred into view. "No, but I've held them off for now. I should be all right for the next few hours. Is the Soul Well ready?"

Bartholomew dramatically stepped out of the way, flourishing his arms for effect. The structure he revealed was underwhelming to say the least: it was a hodgepodge pile of rocks. It had the appearance of an igloo that had been dropped from a great height. The layer of rocks on the ground were set firmly and squarely, but after that it looked like someone had simply stacked boulders on top until no more would fit.

Damien stared at Bartholomew angrily before deciding his wrath was better directed at something weaker than himself. He looked around for Noigel instead and found the imp dozing against the wall. He was lying on one side, his claws kicking feebly in the air. He was dreaming of doggy paddling…or maybe disemboweling rats. Damien knew where he'd have put his money.

Too sensible to shout at Bartholomew and too kind to shout at his sleeping minion, Damien opted for sarcasm instead.

"Wow, I'm so glad I put my faith in you two. I've never seen such a pretty pile of rocks before."

"No need to take that tone. All that's required for its completion is soul energy. Go add the final ingredient to your structure and then tell me if your customary impudence was fitting."

Damien obediently walked up to the 'structure' and placed his hand on it. A prompt appeared.

'Embed one soul? Yes/No'

He nodded and silvery wisps flowed out of his open palm, pouring into the cracks in the rock. The cracks glowed and the rocks rearranged themselves in front of his eyes, twisting and grinding against each other until they fitted together as perfectly as the pieces of a jigsaw puzzle. The translucent blueprint faded as its dimensions were filled. The result was a rounded, sealed dome.

Damien could feel it thrumming against his hand as though the soul within were bouncing off the sides, struggling to free itself. It felt like the vibrations of an engine, or at least that's how he imagined an engine might feel.

He removed his hand and inspected it, surprising himself when a Stat page came up in much the same manner as when he inspected Noigel.

Daemien's Soul Well
Health: 250
Souls: 1/10

In addition to the brief summary, there was a red cross in the top right corner of the window. When Damien focused on it and nodded, it was quickly overlapped by a text notification:

'Destroy the Soul Well? Yes/No'

"Ah. That brings back memories. I remember when I constructed my first Soul Well. You are so incredibly, remarkably weak."

Damien declined the option to destroy what he'd just finished building and turned his attention to Noigel, grumbling in his throat. A notification came up stating that the 'Soul Well That Ends Well' quest was complete, although Bartholomew had spoiled it a little with his rudeness.

Damien hunkered down so he could address his stirring imp at eye level.

"Hello, Noigel. Did the mysterious voice come back while I was gone?"

Noigel narrowed his eyes before sullenly shaking his head.

"That's good. Whatever it was must have moved on. If it comes back I'll have to keep you here as a builder, for your protection. Let's hope the voice doesn't come back. Don't you agree?"

Noigel stared at him, his big black eyes examining Damien's expression as he tried to discern whether Damien was stupid enough to believe what he'd said or if he was being played. Damien kept his face quite blank. At last, Noigel replied with a single curt nod.

"Great! I'm glad we're on the same page. You have a rest while I make the preparations for the next quest."

He stood up and went into his quest list. The 'Slither a Mile in My.... Shoes?' quest was sitting at the top. So, he had a new summon to play with, as well as this spell 'Possession'. He went into his Skills tab to examine them in detail.

Summon Wraith: Mana: 250, Souls: 3 – You point at the ground, searing it with runes to open a portal to the demon world. After channeling for 10 seconds, the portal is opened and a wraith arrives on the mortal plane. The wraith will serve you until it dies or is dismissed. Wraith stats improve every five levels.

Aside from the mana cost and soul cost increase, the text was identical to that of the 'Summon Imp' skill. This thing cost three souls, so judging from the description of Soul Harvest it should also take up three slots of his Soul Summon Limit. That was a lot more expensive than the imps. He hoped it would be worth it. He scrolled down and found the second of his new abilities.

Possession: Mana: 150 – You point at a summoned minion and take control of it, seeing through its eyes and acting in its place. Your body is left vacant for the duration of the spell. The spell will end when the minion is destroyed or you choose to cancel the possession, returning to your own body.

Whoa. That's a cool ability right there. He wouldn't have to put himself on the front line anymore; instead, he'd be able to assume control of one of his own demons.

Excitement gripped him and he checked his soul count. He had three souls exactly. Perfect. He pointed at the ground and eagerly thought 'wraith'.

The customary red flares appeared under his watchful eye, but they were not tracing out a simple pentagram as they had done with the imps. This was something slightly more complicated, something Damien did not immediately recognize. It was only as the runes finished tracing that Damien made out the scythe etched within the circle's confines. The lines glowed and a portal opened from above as it had before.

Where the imps had dropped through and landed on the ground with a low splat, the wraith demonstrated itself to be markedly different right from the start. It did not drop; it descended. A tail of shadows unfolded through the dimensional rift, latching to the ground on contact. The rest of the body followed. Long curved blades protruded from under each arm, both of which were crossed over an incorporeal, skeletal torso. Its head was lowered as if in prayer, yet Damien could not recall having ever seen a creature that would so offend God with its mere existence.

The portal closed as the summoning was completed, yet the wraith did not stir. Damien took the chance to inspect it.

Wraith
Stats:
Strength 5 - Agility 30 - Intelligence 5
Constitution 10 - Stamina 15 - Wisdom 5
Abilities: Shadow Beast, Impale, Slash.

The wraith had a hefty chunk of agility, but the rest of the stats were quite low. Not that it mattered; if what Bartholomew had told him was to be believed, this thing would be fulfilling the role of an assassin. It certainly looked the part. Even as Damien stared at it from a short distance away it was phasing in and out of his vision, the body blending with the dark background at the edges. It was at once insubstantial and fearsome.

Damien mustered up his courage and stood directly in front of it. This thing belonged to him. It shouldn't be able to harm him.

"Hello, wraith. Can you hear me?"

The wraith's head snapped upward, allowing Damien to look it over properly for the first time since it was summoned. The eyes were all black with no apparent pupils, just like Bartholomew's and those of the imps. The rest of its face was all but featureless; where the mouth and nose should have been there was only empty shadow.

The imps were functional but had personality, silly though it may have been. This thing was a creature of actions rather than words. Not wasting any time, Damien pointed at it and thought 'Possession'.

His vision swam and blackened. When he opened his eyes, he was staring at himself. Only they weren't his eyes, and he was most definitely not himself.

As if in a bad dream, he watched his own body buckle and collapse, his eyes milky white and unseeing. Instinctively he dashed forward and caught it, surprising himself with his own speed. It was only as he stretched out his arms that he remembered what was going on. The curved blades extended from under each of his forearms and he hadn't taken a single step to cover the ground between them. He'd simply glided. He was inside the wraith.

He looked himself over, glad not to have stabbed himself with the vicious arm-blades by mistake, and lowered his unconscious body to the ground.

That done, he started to check out his new form. It was a very strange sensation. The strangest part of it was that he had no legs. How was he supposed to move like this? He'd moved instinctively when he went to catch himself, but it seemed much more difficult when he had to think about it. Tentatively, he leaned backward. His body followed his movement and reversed gently. Ah, so all he had to do was lean in the direction he wanted to go. It was kind of like walking, just without having to catch yourself with your feet before you fell.

He spun his torso each way and found with delight that he could turn on the spot. A total range of movement. His tail twisted behind him as he rotated, merging with the shadows and clinging to the floor to keep him balanced and upright.

The 'Shadow Beast' skill was probably a variant of his own 'Shadow Walker'. That much was clear from the name and the wraith's appearance. Since the tail could cling so tightly to the featureless stone floor, he had an inkling of another way in which it might be applied.

He came to a stop facing the cavern wall. An opportunity for fun had presented itself, and Damien was never one to miss an opportunity.

Damien tilted forward, not stopping before making contact with the wall itself. As he drew next to it, his lower body latched onto the wall and he found himself scaling the side, defying all sense of gravity.

Elated, he drifted all the way to the top of the domed ceiling, hovering upside down over his Soul Well. He spotted Noigel flipping him the finger and would have ordered the little cretin to drop and do fifty pushups were he not lacking a mouth and functioning throat in possessing the wraith. He compromised, flipping a finger back. Inability to speak aside, this demon had some unique advantages. Damien doubted its damage would be close to that of a true assassin, but no assassin could walk up walls so easily, so far as he knew at least.

Returning to ground level, Damien thought, 'cancel Possession'.

He opened his eyes – his actual eyes.

His vision was entirely red. Noigel was squatting on his chest, jabbing him painfully with a clawed finger.

"What on earth is it?"

Noigel pointed at himself, then the wraith and finally at the ceiling. He concluded his bid with an attempt at puppy eyes that was far more grotesque than cute.

"You can't possess the wraith yourself."

Noigel brought his hands together in a beggar's grasp, exaggerating a trembling lower lip.

Damien had an idea. "All right. But you might be sorry. You, wraith," he ordered. "Pick up Noigel, climb to the top of the ceiling and then run down the wall."

Noigel whooped, cackling with glee, and danced off toward the wraith, fists punching the air.

The wraith considered Noigel in silent menace before dragging him toward the wall. Noigel's face was a picture of anticipation, as though on a rollercoaster winding slowly to the peak of the tracks.

Damien watched as the wraith climbed slowly, then descended at pace as ordered. Noigel screamed in delight.

Damien couldn't help but laugh. After the day he'd been having, it felt good to be laughing about something.

"Again," he said, sending the pair off once more.

Bartholomew appeared like a ghost by his side, putting the wraith's stealth to shame.

"You don't have time for childish games."

And the moment was over.

"I'm collecting myself."

"I set you a task. Kill five enemies using your new minion. Not giving Noigel a treat."

"He's just having some fun," Damien said. "He did build the Soul Well quick enough. He's okay reall—"

Noigel's joyful cheering was cut short by a retch, followed by a loud wet splat. The wraith returned a few seconds later, still holding Noigel by the arm. The imp's face had gone a vibrant shade of green. The wraith let go and Noigel collapsed on the ground, mewling pathetically.

Damien cleared his throat.

"Fine, I'll get going. I'll just wait until my mana replenishes. These rats roaming around should go down fast enou—"

Bartholomew interrupted him with a loud tut and a waggling finger.

"That will not do. The rats no longer constitute a threat to you. I do not recognize them as enemies, nor will they grant you soul energy."

The vampire pointed upward.

"You're going to take this outside. And having precipitated your minion… sullying my generously donated living space with the contents of its stomach, you're going to leave immediately. Otherwise I shall grab you by the back of your head and use your face to mop it up. Get out of my dungeon, and if you have any common sense you'll bring something to clean up with when you return."

"Ooh, is that a new quest? What's the reward?"

"Your life. Now get out."

13

GOBLINS!

Damien reached the top of the stairs and stretched. He'd only been in The Downward Spiral for a few hours in total, but it felt like days. Even the miserable clearing, complete with the creepy trees casting ominous shadows in every direction, seemed pleasant after what he'd been through.

It might have been dark in that forbidden copse but it was nothing compared to the evil that lay beneath. If Damien had thought the bottom floor of Bartholomew's dungeon was bad, the floors above it had been only a little better.

It was a long way from the bottom to the top, and the entire pathway was riddled with traps. He'd skipped them all on his first entry by taking the faster, less advisable route. Courtesy of his alliance with Bartholomew the traps had all been helpfully highlighted red, but there had still been a few close calls. Noigel had screamed more than once to prevent Damien from putting his foot somewhere he might not get it back.

Still, he was out now. It felt good to be back in the overworld; he'd had his fill of dungeons for the time being.

Damien took a long-awaited breath of fresh air and smiled, just before his eyes fell on the place where Aetherius had tried to kill him that morning. The smile wavered. Despite the long walk through Bartholomew's gauntlet of death, he suddenly didn't feel like hanging around. He turned and beckoned toward

Noigel, who'd stopped following him to peer over the small stone wall surrounding the entrance.

"Come on, Noigel, don't be a chicken."

The imp gave his surroundings a last furtive glance before scurrying behind Damien's legs, still apprehensively scanning the trees. He didn't look very comfortable being outside. The wraith glided into position behind them both, as reticent and emotionless as ever. Damien picked his way through the undergrowth, not really knowing which way he was going. Once he got out of the forest he'd know where he was. He found the edge of the trees and stepped out into the afternoon light.

There was the road off to his right, just around the bend. He could follow it back down to his early leveling spot, Drum Lake, and start his quest there. He was about to set off when he realized neither of his demons had followed him out of the forest.

He squinted and saw Noigel's head poking out from behind a tree. As for the wraith, it was standing directly on the threshold of the forest. Now that Damien looked closer, he could see the same cloak of darkness he'd observed earlier surrounding the trees. He wondered if it was purely aesthetic, or if it had a gaming function. He'd have to ask Bartholomew later.

"What's the matter with you two? Get out here. We still have a lot of traveling to do!"

The wraith immediately complied, floating through the translucent black curtain. The moment it did so, the shadows enveloping it were stripped away and its body started to degrade. It stood there without complaining as the sunlight sizzled against its skin, the blades on its forearms shortening and the muscles wasting away.

"What the – inspect!"

Wraith
Stats:
Strength 5 - Agility 15 - Intelligence 5
Constitution 5 - Endurance 10 - Wisdom 5
Abilities: Shadow Beast, Impale, Slash.
Status effects: Exposed.

Damien panicked. He'd spent his last three souls on this thing and now it was weaker than Noigel. What the hell was going on? Then he caught sight of the status effect: 'Exposed'.

"Go back into the forest."

The wraith leaned back and floated through the curtain again, just a touch faster than it had come out. Damien stuck his head through and breathed a sigh of relief. The sizzling had stopped.

Within a few seconds the shadows pooled around the wraith and it was back to its menacing self. At least he now knew one practical application of the shady veil engulfing the trees. It wasn't much of a consolation: Bartholomew had given Damien a quest, requiring the use of a minion that couldn't handle sunlight, right in the middle of the day.

Great teaching skills, Bart. Way to go.

As Damien waited for the wraith's health to return to full, he eyed up the 'Shadow Beast' ability in the still open window. This was probably the culprit, but without any information beyond the name he himself was still in the dark. His own skills all had detailed descriptions, why wasn't it the same for his minions? It was exactly as he made this observation that a glowing '+' sign appeared directly behind the ability in question. A nod of his head later and he got exactly what he wanted, although it only served to confirm his suspicions:

Shadow Beast: While occultists have merely adopted the darkness as their ally, others were born into it. Users of this ability will enjoy drastically increased movement speed (100%), the ability to cling to shadows with ease and advanced stealth capabilities (translucence 75%) in poorly lit places. However, upon contact with light sources they are 'Exposed', reducing their stats by up to 50% and inflicting damage over time to a minimum of 10% of their total hit points. The speed of the damage over time and extent of the stat reduction are calculated based on the intensity of the light source.

Well, that was a bit of a mouthful. Damien could see why the developers hadn't included the full list of abilities in the Stat window, although he'd have preferred it if they'd made finding detailed information a little more obvious. It was something he'd have reported to Kevin, if he didn't have more pressing issues at hand.

At least he hadn't discovered this flaw in combat. That would've been a real problem. He opened the menu and checked the time. It was four in the afternoon. Still two hours to go until dusk started and another half an hour until it fell. Well, he wasn't going back down without anything to show for it, and he wasn't going to sit there waiting for two and a half hours either.

Change of plan. He'd have to find some enemies in a dark place. He opened his map, looking for a cave he remembered from his time as Scorpius, but there were no markers. As far as the game was concerned, Daemien had never been there before and thus didn't know there was anything to find. Damien knew better. It was about five minutes due west, at the foot of a hill.

"Follow me."

Without waiting for Noigel to start complaining, Damien set out across the open plains at a jog. The sound of his footsteps were soon accompanied by a low hiss and crackle that reminded him of the food processor making his bacon and eggs that morning.

Noigel ran straight past the simmering wraith to be by Damien's side, his head swiveling round in every direction, eyes wide with fear. Damien took note and started going a little faster. It wasn't just the wraith that was exposed out here.

The opening in the hill appeared exactly where he'd remembered, and he smiled before realizing the sizzling had stopped.

He turned and was surprised to find his wraith was no longer cooking but had become little more than a stick figure. On top of that, it was struggling to keep up the pace, lagging behind and then sputtering forward in short bursts. The only thing Damien could do for it was reach the cave as fast as possible.

They arrived without incident and Noigel immediately ran straight inside while Damien waited for his wraith to catch up. As he was standing there, he saw a sign posted to one side that hadn't been there in his last play-through. He approached it, his brow furrowing. There were words printed entirely in white block capitals, sandwiched between a skull and crossbones at the top and Aetherius's guild symbol, a swirling red vortex, at the bottom. As he read it, his jaw dropped.

THIS CAVE IS RESERVED FOR MEMBERS OF RISING TIDE. IF YOU ARE FOUND USING THIS CAVE WITHOUT PERMISSION YOU WILL BE KILLED, YOUR CORPSE WILL BE LOOTED AND YOUR DEATH WILL BE POSTED ONLINE. K THNX BYE
    – RISING TIDE

Damien knew vaguely that Rising Tide had started to appropriate large areas of the game world as their own, but he'd never imagined it would affect him directly and thus had never given it much thought. Like so many injustices in life, the appalling unfairness of it only became apparent when it happened to him personally. Having been kicked down a pit by their guild leader that morning, Damien took this very personally indeed.

Tintagel wasn't a heavily contested zone. This cave was only a short walk away from Camelot itself, a place designed to allow people to safely level up. Yet Rising Tide had not only decided the world wasn't big enough to share, but were also threatening to kill anyone who used it 'without permission'?

He finished seething and turned to find the wraith had caught up. It looked terrible. He could either search for another place, which would mean another long march through the countryside with a scared imp and a floating trash bag in tow, or he could risk being discovered by the very people he wanted to destroy.

He'd just go in, do the quest and leave. He wouldn't be there long enough to get caught. Besides, the really dangerous members of Rising Tide would have better things to do than killing goblins in a cave. Glancing around to make sure no one was looking, Damien ushered the wraith ahead of him.

As soon as the wraith stepped across the threshold and into the shade it began restoring itself. The damage was extensive, so it took longer than the first time round, but Damien brought up the wraith's Stat bar after it was finished and confirmed it was good as new.

Noigel looked considerably more comfortable as well. He either hadn't seen Rising Tide's sign, couldn't read, or both. Damien's gamble to drag the wraith through sunshine had paid off; now he needed to make it count.

He quickly pointed Noigel in front of them and the imp led the trio down the passageway into the depths of the hill.

Damien couldn't remember the layout, but he knew what to expect. It was a series of tunnels that occasionally opened up into wider spaces, like a rabbit warren but bigger. The main difference was the inhabitants. Unlike rabbits, brown gobbos were coordinated, vicious and fiercely territorial.

Some goblins were smart and capable of complex thought, but not the brown ones. Their defining characteristic was hunger, and not for carrots either.

As a warrior who'd come here when he was good and ready, Damien had simply stood at the entrance of a narrow passageway and bellowed down it so all the enemies would come running at once. Then he'd slaughtered them one by one in the enclosed space, where their numbers counted for nothing. It had also meant he didn't need to worry about being attacked from behind.

As a fledgling occultist who'd come here out of necessity, still wearing rags and more worried about a possible attack from behind than the certain one in front, Damien would require a different approach. He wasn't strong enough yet to attack or be attacked by a party of players. Being stealthy usually took time, but this needed to be done with speed. First things first, he needed Noigel on board.

"Noigel, you're going to watch the entrance. If you see anyone coming, you'll run here and... tell me so... crap. Hang on."

Damien was going to have to possess the wraith to complete the quest, and his real body would be quite unoccupied. Time for more tests.

He sat down with his back against the cave wall, pointed at the wraith and thought 'Possession'.

Now controlling the wraith, he gently leaned forward and poked his unconscious body in the head. He immediately felt pressure in the middle of his – well, the wraith's – forehead. He'd become his own voodoo doll. Canceling the possession, he turned to talk to Noigel.

"If you see or hear anyone coming, start poking me in the head. That should make you happy, you little sadist. Don't do it unless it's an emergency, otherwise we're going to be here for a while. Those are your orders."

Damien possessed the wraith again and lined himself up with the passageway. The movement was quite easy to control if he wasn't moving too fast, but he had yet to test it in combat. If he didn't get it right the first time, he wouldn't have the souls to summon another one. That would put him in a very bad position indeed.

Well, he thought in the silence, *better get it right first time*.

He leaned forward carefully and glided down the passageway until he arrived at the first doorway, peering around the corner discreetly. There was a lantern hanging from the ceiling, but otherwise it was poorly lit. Good. A modest, earthen chamber with three passageways leading out of it, not including the one he'd entered by.

He poked his head into the passageway on the left. It was a small room, the only feature of note a dirty stack of hay in the corner with a pillow and empty sleeping sack. Probably a guard kept watch here at night, since this seemed to be some form of crossroads.

And if it wasn't here, it was probably patrolling, as many mobs do.

Damien floated inside the chamber, avoiding the lantern light. He had reached the passageway on the far side when he heard something grating against the floor ahead of him. A few moments later a brown gobbo plodded lazily into view, dragging an axe behind it and picking its bulbous nose.

Damien drew back behind the doorway. It was level 7. Not

too much higher than he was, thankfully. Still, he'd rather have the element of surprise than a fair fight.

He quickly rotated and forced himself to lean a little further than he was comfortable with, speeding back toward the empty room with the hay. He cut straight through the torchlight and felt his skin burn, but the sensation was gone as fast as it had come and he was safely concealed by the time the brown goblin entered.

Damien watched it traipse into the middle of the chamber. It lingered a little longer before turning around and going back the way it had come, still dragging the axe.

As soon as it turned, Damien was soundlessly creeping along the side of the chamber toward it. It hadn't even managed to leave the room before he drew back the wraith's arm and drove the attached blade straight through the goblin's back.

Sneak Attack Multiplier Added!
Damage: 90

No critical, Damien thought. *That's strange. It looks pretty critical to me.*

The axe dropped out of the goblin's fingers as it fell to its knees with a groan, looking down to find a blade growing out of its chest. It started to cry out, but Damien was faster. He brought his free arm across his body and sliced straight through the neck, the blade passing through it faster than coffee through a finals student.

Sneak Attack Multiplier Added!
Critical Strike Multiplier Added!
Damage: 180

Damien didn't know exactly how much health the goblin had, nor did he need to. Unless brown goblins stored their brains somewhere besides their heads, this one was a goner.

He stopped for a moment, listening for any signs he'd been discovered. When the tunnels remained deathly silent, he withdrew his blade and allowed the goblin's body to slump to the floor. The soul energy twisted out of the goblin's newly vacated neck cavity and formed an orb, which floated into the wraith's hand before being absorbed. So Damien could gather souls this way as well. Very useful.

Inside, Damien was elated. Wraith combat handled like a dream embodied in a nightmare. For the first time since he'd started playing as an occultist, he felt powerful. It was all he could do to prevent himself from rocketing down the passageway to find his next target.

So giddy with pleasure at the wraith's effectiveness, he forgot about its aversion to light and backed up under the lantern, his skin immediately hissing and boiling. He recoiled and stared up at it angrily. This was something he could do without. Sweeping forward, he swung at the rope holding the lantern in place before propelling himself back to his safe haven, the empty sleeping quarters. The wraith was incredibly quick when he needed it to be. He was already through the door when he heard the glass shatter behind him, followed by the whoosh of igniting oil.

From the remaining unchecked tunnel on the opposite side, a pair of surprised squawks sounded, alarmed by the sudden conflagration.

Cursing his hasty decision, Damien ducked out of sight just as the gargling voices filled the chamber. If the mysterious fire wasn't cause enough for concern, the sight of their enflamed, decapitated friend probably would be.

So much for stealth.

As soon as he took in the scene Damien realized he was in luck. The two new arrivals were far too busy putting out the fire to be concerned with their surroundings. They were extinguishing it with the only suitable tools they had available: their bare feet.

It was remarkably effective. They were disproportionately large compared to the rest of their bodies and must have also been incredibly tough; the two goblins tirelessly jumped up and down on the fire for a good twenty seconds before it was well and truly out.

The moment they finished, the entire chamber was plunged into darkness. Of course, Damien's wraith had Shadow Beast, so Damien could see perfectly fine. If the wraith also had a mouth, he would've smiled. This was turning out well.

All he had to do was wait for the goblins to split up and then pick them off.

The goblins jabbered at each other urgently, a level 8 and another level 7. Damien prepared himself. He'd seen this scenario play out plenty of times. One of them was going to stay here and keep watch while the other ran for reinforcements. He'd have to kill the remaining guard quickly and chase the other down, before he could sound the alarm.

The two goblins nodded at each other and against all Damien's expectations did the worst possible thing. They ran at full pace in completely opposite directions, each of them screaming at the top of their lungs.

The level 7 ran deeper into the warren, exactly as Damien had predicted. The level 8 was running down the passageway to the outside, right toward Damien's unprotected body. He'd been caught off guard. He was so surprised that he hesitated, losing precious seconds.

The higher level goblin was getting closer to stumbling upon his hollow shell with every step and Damien had no doubts about what it would do when it found a human having a nap. He had no choice. The low level goblin might alert the rest of the warren to his presence, but the other would snuff it out first. He put the level 7 out of mind and lurched into the room, struggling to align himself with the doorway leading to the passage outside.

The screaming in front of him abruptly stopped. It had found him. Damien stretched his body forward as far as it would go and the room blurred as he shot forward. A startling view of the level 8 goblin raising its axe above his human head rushed to greet him and he threw his hands out in front to brace for impact.

He smashed into it at full tilt, hard enough for his tail to lose its grip. The two of them bounced down the corridor, giving Damien a taste of life inside a washing machine.

Damien blinked and held his aching head before checking his health. He was down to 37/100. Not good.

His mind rebooted slowly. *Where is the goblin?*

Then he noticed his blade arm was sticking into something brown and oozing. Through some luck he'd run the goblin straight through; impact damage had likely taken care of the rest.

Damien withdrew the blade and rose on his smoky tail.

He'd only just gathered himself when Noigel came bounding forward, waving his arms around frantically, mewling, jabbering and pointing back the way he'd come.

Damien had no way of communicating with him. Probably the worst thing about possessing the wraith was not having a mouth.

When Damien responded only by staring dumbly, Noigel ran over to his human body and started furiously tapping it on the forehead. He was doing it so hard it hurt, and Damien irritably moved forward to make him stop when he realized what it meant.

Someone was coming.

Members of Rising Tide were here. And there were likely goblin reinforcements coming from behind. He was trapped on both sides.

Damien didn't feel so powerful anymore.

He canceled the possession, brushing away Noigel's incessant pokes as he reacclimatized himself to his regular body. Carefree voices were already echoing down the corridor from outside, players happily going about their questing or grinding without a care in the world.

Damien staggered to his feet, one hand braced against the wall to stop himself from falling over as Noigel clutched his head in despair and the wraith looked on with annoying calmness.

"Back inside!"

After a few more steps Damien regained his sense of self and hurried back into the chamber. There were already screams coming from the bowels of the cave. The goblin had found allies. It didn't sound like they were taking the threat lightly, either.

Damien was sandwiched between higher level enemies on one side and unknown members of Rising Tide on the other. They'd all converge on him at any moment.

He reached the side chamber with the hay. It was the only option he had left.

"In here, quick!"

He sprinted inside, Noigel and the wraith following close on his heels. A few seconds later the stamping feet of the goblin horde reached their peak and the glow of burning torches shone from the chamber into their hiding place.

The wraith shrank into the darkest corner of the room while Noigel and Damien each cowered on either side of the doorway.

It sounded like half the cave had been called to arms. The stampede passed straight through the room, running toward the exit. Damien's eyes widened as he realized what was about to happen.

A warbling shriek of outrage came from afar and was immediately echoed by the rest of the goblin tribe. Moments later, the clang of metal striking metal reverberated through the cavern. The goblins and the guild were fighting it out.

Damien pointed at the wraith.

"Possession!"

The wraith hadn't fully recovered yet, but that didn't matter. The player characters would be keeping the goblins nicely distracted. He could get this quest finished off before anyone knew what was happening.

Damien followed the screams. Goblins were spaced out down the narrow corridor, jostling for position and waiting to jump into the fray. Not a single one of them was facing in his direction.

Standing against them was an aggravated level 12 paladin, swinging his war hammer in wide arcs to keep them at a distance. The rest of his party were arrayed behind him, providing support as needed.

Damien couldn't hope to kill the paladin. He had plenty of time to kill a few of the things facing away from him, though.

He spotted the runt of the litter, a level 6, and slashed it straight through the neck. It died without so much as a whimper. There were two more goblins only a couple of paces ahead, but they were far too busy fighting for position to notice him. Damien scissored his arm blades through the two of them horizontally at their throats, each blade passing through each goblin's neck for a double decapitation.

After finishing these two, a ping and a gold glow in Damien's peripheral vision confirmed that he'd killed five enemies and the quest was complete. All he had to do now was get back to Bartholomew, which was easier said than done.

Rising Tide players blocked the only exit, and they were going to win this battle. It was only a matter of time before they pushed the goblins back and searched for the cause of the disturbance.

He turned and propelled himself back to the side room before canceling the possession.

"Noigel, I need you to go outside and lure the enemy party through the room as fast as possible so we can escape. Don't worry—" he quickly blurted out as Noigel's eyes started to water, "I won't let them kill you."

Noigel had other ideas that didn't involve acting as bait. He stood behind the wraith and started trying to shunt it out into the chamber, failing to move it even an inch. Damien realized it had gone quiet. The battle had ended much faster than he'd expected.

"No, Noigel, I need the wraith in case someone checks in here. We're not discussing this! Get in po—"

"Helloooo? Anybody home?"

The sound had come from right outside the chamber. It was too late for Noigel to go now. Resisting the urge to punch the imp in the face, Damien pressed a finger to his lips, motioning for him to be silent.

"Somebody bring a torch, I can't see a damn thing... That's better. All right everybody, stick together. There's definitely something funny going on in here. Might be players. We can have ourselves a good old-fashioned lynching. Wunderra, check the rooms as we go along. I don't want to get ambushed."

Damien blanched. He had to hide. The wraith had already withdrawn to the back of the room and was blending in with the corner, but Damien's Shadow Walker skill wasn't nearly as advanced as the wraith's Shadow Beast. It was only a small room; if they entered, they'd spot him for sure.

He did the only thing he could, joining the wraith at the back wall and crouching down to blend in. Noigel, however, had no affinity for the shadows. He'd be spotted instantly.

Light bobbed into the chamber and Wunderra appeared in the doorway, his torch held high. Noigel was standing just in front of them, trembling with fear. The light swept over him and Damien panicked. This was it. The moment Wunderra called out to the rest of the party, they'd be trapped like rats in a cage. Noigel had failed to follow his instructions, and now it had got them all killed. Damien hadn't wanted Noigel to leave once Rising Tide entered the chamber beyond; it would have drawn as much attention to the room as it took away from it. Now there was no choice. He needed Noigel out of there, and fast. Only he couldn't give him any instructions, or else Wunderra would hear.

The blood pulsing in his ears, Damien stared at the back of Noigel's illuminated head and silently vented at him:

This is all your fault, you disobedient little git. If you'd listened to me, I'd have dismissed you before they caught you and we'd all still be alive. Why are you just standing there? Do something! If you just stand there, we're all going to die. Run! Run awa—

For once, it seemed that Damien and Noigel were in agreement. The imp abruptly screeched in abject terror and darted out of the room between Wunderra's legs, his hands flailing in the air as he made a beeline toward the passageway on the opposite side. Wunderra yelped in surprise and leapt upwards as Noigel passed underneath him, turning his back on Damien's hiding place to trace the imp's movement with his torch.

Noigel paused in the far doorway and bent over, waving his little red rump at the players while they looked on open-mouthed. He started running down the corridor again, still screaming, as an arrow whizzed over his head. The players gave chase, stampeding after him.

Damien hurried out, keeping an eye on Noigel's health bar. He'd taken no damage but would surely be caught soon, and the sound of the chase had traveled far enough away for Damien to be safe.

He dismissed Noigel, imagining the looks on the players' faces as he got sucked back into a portal. Cries of dismay echoed down the tunnel but Damien didn't hang around to find out what they thought of it all.

Running for the exit, he could barely hear anything besides his own heartbeat. Once out in the sunlight, he dismissed the wraith too so it wouldn't slow him down or draw unwanted attention.

He wouldn't feel safe until he got back to The Downward Spiral.

14

THE HIGH ROAD OR THE LOW ROAD

"Ah, there you are. Did you bring something to mop up Noigel's vomit?"

Damien had forgotten about Bartholomew's threat. He paused and shook his head. Bartholomew sneered at him for a moment, then shrugged.

"No matter. The rats ate it while you were gone. It appears they serve some purpose after all. Did you complete your quest?"

"I did, and it almost got me killed. Everything that could go wrong did. You didn't even warn me the wraith can't go in sunlight!"

The quest text glowed gold and Damien advanced to level 7. He'd have been much happier if not for the condescension Bart followed it up with.

"In fact, I did. I told you the moment I bestowed the wraith upon you. It's hardly my fault you summoned it so hastily upon your return. Yet despite your inability to heed your betters, here you stand. Wiser, more experienced and quite alive. Still as whiny as usual, I might add, so at least you still possess enough energy to complain. You may as well put it to good use. Tell me what happened, and why Noigel isn't with you."

Damien was not pleased, but as Bartholomew drawled on he

realized it was true. He *had* been warned about the wraith's aversion to light, approximately ten minutes before CU called and made him homeless. Of course he hadn't remembered in the midst of all that! Not to mention, the ordeal could have been avoided had Bart simply allowed him to kill five rats instead. At the very least, a small, gentle reminder before he set off on his ill-fated trip would've spared him the shock of finding out first hand. Still, explaining this to Bartholomew would only invite more snide feedback. Damien didn't have the time or the energy. With some difficulty, he collected himself and gave his Machiavellian master the rundown.

There were three things he really wanted to address, so he made them the focus: the black curtain surrounding Bartholomew's cursed wood, the claiming of the cave by Rising Tide and his near escape thanks to Noigel. Bartholomew listened without a single interruption until he was completely finished.

"I am pleased that Noigel did his part, but I believe you may have played a larger role in your salvation than you realize. Tell me; when Noigel fled and drew your enemies away, what did you have in mind?"

"I was thinking if he didn't run out of the room right then and there, he wouldn't have had to worry about Rising Tide anymore. I'd have strangled the little turd myself."

The comment was half made in jest, but Bartholomew extended a clawed hand to rub his chin as if he'd been entirely serious. Damien was about to take it back before Bart posed him a second question;

"And from what you told me, Noigel was out of sight when you dismissed him. I take it you didn't yell down the corridor, past the arrayed Rising Tide forces, that he was dismissed?"

Damien hadn't thought about that. He'd been so intent on saving Noigel that he hadn't realized it shouldn't have been possible. He was still trying to figure it out when Bartholomew solved it for him.

"I knew I wasn't mistaken when I recruited you. Those were mental commands. I was planning on teaching you this a little later, but it appears you've already happened upon it yourself: your minions are bound not to your orders, but to your will. If you will them to do something with sufficient conviction and clarity, you can give them orders without the need for speech."

Whoa! Having demons to draw upon was already a sweet ability, now he could control them with his mind? It was a superb application of the headset technology. Mobius had outdone themselves when they created this class.

He thought about it some more and realized Aetherius had been controlling his Mana Wisp without vocal instructions as well. The wisps were only useful for lighting dark areas or using their viewpoint for streaming, and only one could be summoned per player at a time. With combat troops under his command, Damien felt he could get a lot more use out of this little gimmick.

"It will require some time to successfully issue more complex orders without saying them out loud," Bartholomew continued in the ensuing silence, "so I suggest you practice when you are able. The dark wall of energy surrounding the forest is a far simpler matter. It's the border of my territory. I once had many safe havens like this spread far and wide, but the combined efforts of the Empire in general and Rising Tide in particular have diminished it to what you see now."

"Rising Tide is a problem for me as well. I need somewhere safe to level... to become stronger, but Aetherius's guild is running quests right next to my home base."

Bartholomew's eyes widened warningly and Damien hesitated.

"Uh, our home base. Fine, your home base. How am I supposed to improve if they're constantly hovering over me?"

Bartholomew reached forward and patted Damien on the head.

"I have just the quest to answer that question. I will only say it once, so if you wish to resummon Noigel so you don't have to inform him yourself afterward, now is the time to do so."

Damien pointed at the ground and the sigils started to

revolve. Noigel dropped in and was striking a pose until he caught Damien's eye. The imp lowered his gaze and started fidgeting with his fingers awkwardly.

"You did well, Noigel," Damien said. "I'm still here, aren't I?"

Noigel stood taller and grinned.

Bartholomew interrupted their reunion.

"Now we're all here, I have a new set of assignments for you." He paused for effect, hands clasped behind his back. "I have a choice of two quests. One is easy, one is hard, both have rewards worthy of the effort invested in them. The first is simple: kill ten hostile enemies outside of this dungeon. As long as they are worthy adversaries, any ten enemies will do."

'You Take the High Road - Kill ten enemies (0/10)'

Bartholomew continued. "The second quest only requires you to kill three enemies. Already much easier, is it not? However, the three enemies must be members of Rising Tide."

Damien was surprised an NPC would give him a quest that targeted other players. Bartholomew had made no secret of his hatred for Rising Tide during Damien's conscription, not to mention the subsequent deal to provide early game protection in exchange for Damien's pledge to kill Aetherius. Even so, for the "loathed" status between their factions to translate into quest rewards for killing Rising Tide members was extremely strange. As far as Damien knew, player killing was quite separate from questing in Saga Online. An activity pursued for loot, guild territorial rights and glory, rather than EXP. This quest removed the separation between player-killing and questing completely.

Regardless, this was clearly the harder quest. Mobs were significantly easier to kill than players; they followed predictable patterns and had set moves. Players, on the other hand, could think for themselves and choose their own abilities, making them almost as difficult as an AI-controlled boss monster.

"How can you expect me to take on a whole guild at level seven?"

Bartholomew looked at Damien quizzically. He answered in a lilting, almost comedic tone, yet his words were patient and honeyed.

"I'm sure I don't know what you mean. Level seven? Is that some means of measuring power in your own home world? And I'm only asking you to dispose of three, one after the other if you like. You could always pursue the simpler quest instead. But while that quest is simpler, this one comes with material rewards."

Bartholomew produced folded garments of deepest, darkest blue, overlaid with leather bindings and bronze plates that were equal parts decorative and protective. On top of them sat a curved and serrated blade, bound to varnished wood with two perfect rings of silver. Damien immediately started to salivate. Bartholomew stowed the items before he could finish gorging his eyes.

"I crafted these while you were gone. One of the perks of being a lonely vampire is having an inordinate amount of time to hone my crafting skills. The silver rings were a real annoyance for me, I hope you appreciate that. You didn't really think it would take me the entire day just to finish your bag, did you?"

Damien was taken aback. It was true; Bartholomew would have finished crafting the bag long ago, but Damien had forgotten all about it following the difficult events of that morning.

"It's quite all right. I know that whatever was going on in your home world made you most troubled of mind. The bag has been ready for you since you returned and now I have made you something to replace your wretched rags and bones as well. However, rewards under my tutelage are earned, not given freely. Make your choice."

He procured the rat-fur bag and tossed it underhand to Damien, who caught it squarely and looked up to find Bartholomew had disappeared. End of discussion. The second quest had appeared in his HUD when Bartholomew vanished.

'**And I'll Take the Low Road** - Kill three members of player guild Rising Tide (0/3)
Rewards: Occultist Apprentice Robes (set), Sacrificial Dagger (unique).'

Damien swapped packs, transferring his scarce items to his new inventory one by one as he weighed up his options. He needed that gear. Since he had no access to shops, he wouldn't be able to buy equipment like normal players. He looked down and pinched the rags he'd looted off the skeleton that morning between a thumb and forefinger.

He needed those robes badly. But was he ready? Level 10 seemed a more appropriate level to start targeting Aetherius's guild directly, and even then only barely.

However, there was another factor to consider as well.

The item transferral finished, Damien left the empty bag on the ground for Bartholomew to collect at his leisure. Then he opened his skill tab and scrolled through until he found what he was looking for: the section of his Soul Harvest ability related to player killing:

'....In addition, when you contribute to a player-kill, you absorb their experience points towards the next level that were forfeited upon death. A kill will result in all experience points being absorbed, an assist will yield EXP proportionate to how many other parties assisted. This ability does not function on creatures or players five or more levels below you.'

Damien read it through. Then he stared. Then he read it through again, his eyes widening as the revelation hit him. When he'd first become an occultist, it had all been a little over-whelming. He'd been so busy getting to grips with his new spells and his status as an 'Enemy of the Realm' that he'd sorely underestimated this ability. He'd mistaken it for a little extra perk on top of his new resource, soul energy, set at the bottom of the skill description as a footnote. In fact, it might be the most important asset he had. The foundation of his entire class.

He checked his experience bar for reference. He currently had 258/2000 experience points. Usually, upon death, all this exp would be lost. If he'd understood correctly, if an occultist killed him, they'd absorb the 258 exp instead. That was a fairly modest amount, but it could've been as high as 1999. An occultist could potentially get a vast amount of experience by killing a single player on the verge of hitting the next level. That wasn't all: since he was a human with the 'Adaptable' trait, the experience he stole would be increased by a further 15%! An exceptional combination of passive abilities!

The inference was clear; the Occultist faction were dedicated player killers. It shouldn't have come as a surprise, given the role of occultists in Arcadia's quest plotlines. The earlier quests had been warm up exercises, allowing Damien to familiarize himself with his abilities and hone his playstyle. This one was forcing him to decide whether or not to play the class the way it was designed to be played.

With a very limited amount of time to kill a very high-level character, abusing the player-killing mechanic of his Soul Harvest ability would be the fastest way to bridge the level gap.

A smile began to form on Damien's face. This could work.

At the very least, he could try the 'Low Road' quest and move on to the 'High Road' quest if things didn't work out. He was going to give it his best shot, though.

Damien finished fantasizing and looked down to find the empty bag he'd left at his feet was already gone. If only his stealth was as advanced as Bart's, player-killing would be easy. Then he turned to Noigel, who was looking up at him expectantly.

"We're doing the Low Road quest. We're going to kill three members of Rising Tide, the people chasing you down that tunnel earlier. Up for some revenge?"

Noigel only had to think about it for a moment before he nodded in agreement. Damien hoped he was up to the task. He needed Noigel to keep watch while he completed the quest. He was going to have that gear, and he had a pretty good idea how he was going to do it.

It started with him making his way up to the entrance of The Downward Spiral and logging out. The waiting time was extended from ten seconds when he was safe in his base to thirty in potentially hostile territory, a feature designed to prevent players from escaping combat. He wouldn't be able to log out at all in dungeons, and the process would be cancelled if he took damage or moved.

The extra twenty seconds spent standing around were a small price to pay in exchange for getting the traps out of the way. Damien shifted his weight from one foot to the other, trying not to think about his rumbling stomach, until the timer finally hit zero.

He opened his eyes on the inside of his pod and cast his eyes towards the digital time display. It was 17:00 on the dot. There was no point starting the quest while there was still daylight in Saga Online, so it was a good time to deal with some of his real world problems instead.

The old man was still on duty in the pod hotel but Damien took the bag and IMBA set with him. As long as he wasn't there, the pod would be available for use by anyone. He put them back on and went hunting for food down the street, eventually finding a hot dog stand had come to replace the fish vendor from earlier that day.

Not a moment too soon.

While he waited, he also found some cheap disposable face masks. They were intended to help with pollution, but Damien saw they had potential as disguises. All he'd need now was a pair of dark glasses so he wouldn't have to put this hot helmet on whenever there were cameras around.

He got his hot dog, attracting only a couple of bemused glances, and made his way back into the pod hotel where he could eat in relative privacy.

Before logging back in he decided to look up Rising Tide online. Sure enough, the guild with the most famous player in the game was doing well enough to have its own website.

It was really quite professional looking, and could easily have been mistaken for a company website – especially considering the tabs were labeled with terms such as 'Recruitment', 'Technical Support' and 'Human Resources'.

Damien navigated his way to recruitment and was rewarded with a page showing off the guild's in-game benefits to new recruits: namely several settlements spotted around the starting zone with like minded players and useful features.

He found the one nearest the Goblin Warren and clicked on it. 'Rising Tide - Tintagel 1.3 headquarters'. It sounded like a military facility. It also sounded like they took themselves way too seriously. Damien checked the stats.

Level 1 Guild Outpost
Capacity: 17/20
Services: Inn, Vendor, Blacksmith, Tailor, Portal Stone, Guild Hall (Guild Quests).
Defenses: Guard Towers, Wooden Barricade, Fortified Gate.

Damien was impressed. He hadn't been sure what to expect from a guild settlement, but it sounded more like a small village. He'd got at least one piece of useful information out of this: seventeen current lodgers. So those would be the people currently using this settlement as their home base, huh? A lot of them would be logged off, and then quite a few more would be out questing later that evening.

A plan started to form in his head. If he attacked the players while they were questing, they'd be in groups and combat-ready. But if he attacked them while they were idle in the outpost, waiting to join a group or perform guild duties, they'd be off-guard. That could work.

He took a screenshot of the outpost layout for later use and checked the time. It was 18:30. Dusk would have settled over Arcadia. He was ready.

He logged back in and blinked as he looked around. As expected, he was still at the top of The Downward Spiral, in the center of Bartholomew's private forest. As he got his bearings, a portal opened next to him and Noigel dropped out of it. Damien hadn't been sure if Noigel would still be bound to him after he logged out, so it was a relief to know that minions bound to himself would come back into the world as soon as he did. Damien assigned his new stat points before comprehensively checking all his stats and spells, except for the Maleficium branch of magic, which he wasn't using.

Account Name: Damien Arkwright
Character: Daemien
Class: Occultist
Level: 7
Health: 160/160
Stamina: 160/160
Mana: 460/460
Stats:
Strength 16 - Agility 16 - Intelligence 16
Constitution 16 - Endurance 16 - Wisdom 46
Stat points: 0
Experience: 258/2500
Soul Summon Limit: 1/7 - **Soul Reserve:** 6/7

He'd improved a lot since he'd started. Of the skills he'd accumulated, he thought he knew which ones would be best for this particular mission. He was going to use Possession and Summon Wraith, as they posed the least risk to him personally.

It was already dark even outside of the forest, so Damien had no reason not to put his demonic task force together. He summoned the wraith first, then, one by one, summoned as many imps as he could. He'd managed to fill his Soul Reserve after wading through corpses to leave the Goblin Warren, so in addition to the wraith he could still summon three more imps to join Noigel.

All assembled, four imps and a wraith wasn't much of a force to be attacking an encampment with. He'd have to plan his moves carefully. At least the Rising Tide website had been helpful enough to provide him with a map of the facilities.

"All right, we're moving to a Rising Tide outpost. Stay out of sight whenever possible. If I tell you to stop, everybody stops what they're doing and drop down. We need to get to the encampment without being seen. Follow my lead."

15

THE LION'S DEN

Damien picked his way through the undergrowth and his retinue followed. He checked through the miasma to make sure it was suitably dark. As always, the dusk period had come right on time at 6:30pm. The only light left was a warm orange shimmer on the horizon. By 8pm it would be pitch black, save for moonlight.

He took one last look around and set out at a jog. Looking behind to make sure everyone was following, he sighed with relief when the wraith looked perfectly normal. It wasn't translucent, but it could travel at dusk with no adverse effects. The imps were flanking it on all four sides, the five of them moving in perfect unison. Even Noigel was taking it seriously.

After twenty minutes of traveling, Damien finally got his first glimpse of the outpost. It was every bit like the pictures had shown.

It had been placed in a sensible strategic position, at the center of an open plain so that large groups would be clearly visible from the walls. These were thick and tall, fashioned from wooden poles that stretched two stories high. Most of the encampment was made of wood, as was attested by those buildings that were tall enough to be spotted over the parapets.

The central Guild Hall was the tallest of them, complete with a bell spire and a matching 500-pound bell. The copper to craft it was mined from the dungeons surrounding the outpost shortly after it was first settled. *Thanks, Rising Tide website.*

The site had also informed Damien that the bell was primarily used to announce emergencies. Damien hoped he wouldn't hear it ring tonight.

He couldn't see the gate from his position around the back, but that was only part of what he needed. He was searching for some kind of cover he could use to close in.

Occasional stumps dotting the landscape showed where Rising Tide had acquired the wood from. This had once been a forest, and they'd picked it clean to house their members. Not quite all of it, though. Further around the side toward the gate, Damien spied a cluster of trees that had either avoided the purge or grown back and not been cut down since. That would get him as close as he needed to be. It would be a safe vantage point from which to watch people enter and exit until night truly fell.

Damien circled round the edge until he had put the trees between himself and the outer wall, then he crouched down and moved toward them, not stopping until he was safely behind the largest tree. He turned to find the demons had all followed in his footsteps without making a sound.

That was no surprise as far as the wraith was concerned, but Damien had expected at least two of the imps to break into a game of rock-paper-scissors by now.

Instead, they were all watching him intently, occasionally glancing at their surroundings but otherwise entirely focused. Damien was very grateful for this. He needed them for protection, but had been worried they'd actually end up drawing attention to him. It was one of those rare occasions where he was entirely glad to be proven wrong.

He checked the time in his menu. 18:55. Still just over an hour until true nightfall. That would give him plenty of time to watch their movements as he planned his own.

But there were no movements to be seen. No one patrolling the ramparts, or any other such defensive measures. It figured. This outpost was in the middle of the Empire's safest zone.

With nothing to see, Damien brought up the screenshot he'd

taken of the outpost layout to memorize the buildings. His plan was starting to look pretty good. At least, that's how he felt until 19:46, when nine people arrived at the settlement.

He knew from their usernames that a good many of them were the players who'd nearly caught him using the Goblin Warren. They'd obviously been playing all evening, because they were all much higher level than Damien by now.

The lowest level among them was a level 9 priest. The rest were anywhere between level 10 and 12, with the paladin towering above them all at level 14. He'd been level 12 when Damien last saw him.

Busy night.

Ten minutes passed, and Damien was beginning to think he might have to call the attack off.

But then a party of four set off from the gates, much to his relief. Even better, the paladin was among them. That meant a dangerous threat was leaving, and more likely than not most of the other players would have gone offline, leaving a skeleton crew in the outpost itself. That was what Damien needed.

At 20:00 precisely, the laboriously long sunset faded into a blanket of pure shadow, sweeping over everything.

Showtime.

Damien turned around and one of the imps stood up and saluted. He didn't have to ask if it was Noigel.

"I'm going in with the wraith. You and the other three imps watch over my body while I'm gone. Stay hidden, but if anything detects us and tries to run away or attack, kill them by any means necessary. Got it?"

Noigel gave a thumbs up and the other imps each gave a sharp nod. Everything was in place. There was no reason to delay. Damien lay down on the ground at the foot of the tree and looked over at the wraith.

"Possession."

He opened the wraith's eyes on the world and immediately twisted toward the wall. The biggest problem with infiltrating a structure like this would normally be getting past the gate, but Damien had solved that problem during his earlier test run. He leaned forward and shimmered out of the trees, scanning the top of the wall for any movement as he covered the open ground swiftly and silently.

Damien reached the wall and his lower body clung to the wood, pulling him upward. He committed, leaning directly into the wall. The shadows latched on and dragged him until he was horizontal and climbing straight up the side.

When he reached the top, he peered from the outer wall into the compound. It was deserted. There were torches scattered around the camp, but aside from those at the gate none had been lit yet. Damien had arrived in his perfect window of opportunity. He needed to act before it closed.

Quickly leaning forward, he hurtled down the wall into the encampment, drawing to a stop behind an inactive merchant's stall. Then he circled round the inside of the wall, keeping a watchful eye on all the doorways as he moved beside the Guild Hall. From here he could watch the whole square and be ready to make his move.

For a while there was no movement at all. Perhaps all five people had logged off for the night. But if there was an admin allocated to the hall at all times, someone should be out there to light the torches before too long. Sure enough, the Guild Hall doors clunked open and the bend ahead of Damien was illuminated with flickering fire.

A level 10 assassin was lighting torches along a predictable path. Each time the player stopped to light a new one, she'd stand still for three seconds, completely focused on the task at hand. She was less aware than the rats had been in The Downward Spiral, and easier to read.

Of all players, Damien would have thought an assassin would know to be watchful. But players always feel safe in their home base.

With her back still turned, Damien glided up to her and looked for the best place to strike, doing his best to stay just out of her torchlight. She was well armored for her level, but the leather guarding her neck was not especially thick.

His first sweep cut through the thin layer of clothing and

sliced into the assassin's throat. It was a confirmed sneak critical, but the blade had lost some of its force from the debuff he
suffered entering light. He swung an identical strike from the
opposite direction, enabling him to get the kill quickly enough.

A level 10 player might have a lot of health depending on
where they put their stats, but assassins had little interest in
more health. They relied on evasion for defense, which was –
ironically – why they were quite easy to kill when you sneaked
up on them.

The assassin's body collapsed, her torch extinguishing as it
hit the ground. It was one of the easiest kills Damien had made
since he started playing and also one of the most rewarding, the
majority of his XP bar filling up immediately. The experience
points were closely followed by a stream of silver vapor which
flowed into the wraith, granting two full souls' worth of energy.

Damien had made his first player kill.

He turned and made his way back to the Guild Hall, going
around the outside to avoid the few torches that had been lit.
The body had fallen outside the light, so Damien wasn't too
worried about it being found.

He was more worried the player he'd just killed would
contact a guild mate offline and sound the alarm. There was
nothing he could do about that except act as quickly as possible.

Opening the Guild Hall doors by a crack, Damien peered
inside. Reminiscent of a Viking feasting hall, a long table led to a
raised platform with a staircase leading up to it on either side.
Only one side of the hall had been lit. There was still plenty of
space for Damien to conceal himself if he moved quickly.

He slipped in and closed the door behind him, darting out of
the fires' glow before his skin started to crackle. Despite his
efforts, someone heard him enter.

"Spanish, is that you?"

A figure leaned over the half-lit balcony, torch in hand. This
one was level 13. A mage, by the look of his robes.

"It's no use sneaking, I heard the door close when you came
in. You know I hate it when you sneak up on me!"

Damien looked around for any other signs of movement, but it appeared he and the mage were alone. He slid up the dark side of the room toward the stairs and poised himself at the bottom to wait.

"Fine. But if you jump me from the shadows I'm hitting you back."

Damien considered this. His opponent was 6 levels higher than him. The wraith would get blasted if he got spotted before he could engage, and thanks to his bad luck the mage was now alert to someone concealing themselves.

Footsteps thumped angrily down the stairs and the light of their torch spilled out ahead. Damien decided he'd rather not attack from the front. He'd have to go around and get behind the mage.

Damien turned and shot for the stairs on the opposite side. He put on a burst of speed when he had to pass through torch-light and turned up and around sharply. Luckily, there was only the barest hint of a hiss as he flitted in and out of the light.

His control was improving. He was around the corner and on the raised level before the mage had reached the lower floor. The mage called out again, his voice reverberating off the walls, loud and stern.

"SpanishInquisition? This isn't funny. If I find you're in here and messing with me, I'm gonna blow you away."

Damien didn't like the sound of that. He dashed toward the flight of stairs the mage had just descended, but something caught his eye.

There was a table with a noticeboard behind it. Both of them were covered with plans and timetables. He made a note to take a closer look after he'd dealt with the mage.

Said mage was heading toward the front door slowly and carefully, checking his surroundings with the torch raised over his head and the other hand draped in fire. The spell he was holding cast yet more light. Worse still, he was keeping his back to the wall.

Sneaking up on him was going to be impossible, and he'd

already inadvertently cut off Damien's route to him by lighting up the other side of the room.

Damien searched for another path to the front door that hadn't been illuminated and found one, down the middle of the ceiling where torchlight from the floor couldn't quite burn the shadows away.

Without hesitating, Damien moved up the wall and further, until he was upside down, then picked his way down the middle of the ceiling. He returned to the floor directly next to the front door and watched the mage make his slow, careful advance down the hallway.

The mage suddenly stopped and glanced up to the right, distracted. He nodded slightly and spoke to the open air, apparently communicating through his headset.

"This isn't funny. Come out now!"

There was a pause and Damien couldn't hear anything, but the mage's expression changed to one of relief and the flames went out in his hand. He stopped looking around himself and lowered his torch. This was what Damien had been waiting for. Slowly, he moved into position and waited for the right moment.

"Oh man, I was certain it... No, I thought I heard you come in and you were going to make me the star of one of your stupid videos—Wait...you got killed by what?"

Damien pounced. Rather than using slashes which might be turned away by fabrics or defensive magics, this time he opted for maximum armor penetration. He struck the mage in the back with a flurry of impalements, running him through the torso five times. It happened too fast for the mage to know he was dead, so the first three strikes had Sneak Attack damage modifiers. Two of them also found vital organs, earning them a Critical Strike damage modifier as well. What little of the mage was left slumped to the floor.

The mage had been almost twice Damien's level, his experience bar larger by several orders of magnitude. From the EXP explosion that followed, it was clear why he'd been so concerned about dying.

Damien hit level 8 and passed straight through to level 9. There was more work to be done before he could pat himself on the back. The assassin had called the mage through the headset and now both of them would be calling other people. Damien's window of opportunity was closing and he still needed one more kill for Bartholomew's quest.

He turned for the door but then remembered the table he'd seen at the far back corner of the room. It had looked important.

Damien shot down the hallway and up the stairs, ignoring the burn as he swept past the arrayed torches. He slowed to a halt directly in front of the table, far away enough not to be burned by the torchlight but close enough to see.

There was a raid schedule on the noticeboard. A list of all the elite dungeons Rising Tide would be visiting each week, with times, places and the current party compositions.

Damien double-checked that his headset was still recording so he could go over the schedule in detail later. He panned backward to get a final overview of the whole schedule. Perfect. All he had to do now was find a third victim so he could dismiss the wraith and get out of here.

He'd left the Guild Hall and was moving across the courtyard towards the inn when the Portal Stone at the courtyard's center was lit up by four glowing blue spheres. Players were teleporting in. Damien changed direction and increased his speed, making it to the outer wall as the glow faded and the players arrived.

It was the party of four that had left earlier, led by the level 14 paladin. They immediately drew their weapons, looking around themselves warily. One of them pointed at an immobile lump resting below an unlit torch; the assassin's body. The four of them ran towards her as a group, the paladin picking her up as the others flanked him, before running into the Guild Hall.

Moments later the bell at the top started ringing.

Alarm clanging, the paladin came back out, meticulously checking the darkness around himself with his war hammer in hand. Then he yelled loud enough to be heard by the whole encampment.

"Level two breach! Players have been killed! Meeting at the Guild Hall, now!"

Damien considered this. He didn't like his odds against the heavily armored paladin, but a few other Rising Tide members were leaving the Inn and running across the courtyard to safety. He'd have to move fast, but he might be able to pick off a straggler.

He circled the outer wall to stay concealed and was moving up the other side of the Inn to position himself near the door when there came a rhythmic tapping in the center of his forehead. Noigel was signaling him to come back. Damien didn't need Noigel's help to know things were not going according to plan, but he still needed one more player-kill to complete Bart's quest.

He ignored the irritating sensation and paused around the corner from the door, waiting for another player to exit. He'd been in position for all of five seconds when the tapping on his forehead lost rhythm, becoming urgent and sporadic.

Perhaps there was another problem.

Damien turned to the outer wall and rocketed up the side of it. He looked out towards his hiding place from the top and immediately saw why Noigel was so agitated; there was a level 12 ranger approaching the trees where his body and the four imps were concealed. The trees weren't thick; the ranger was going to spot them with ease.

There was a shout from below and Damien turned to see the paladin pointing up at his outline on the wall, with several recruits gathering around him and raising their weapons. The element of surprise was completely gone.

Damien retreated over the wall, hurtling down it before setting his sights on the ranger. This would be the last chance he got to kill a member of Rising Tide tonight. He certainly wouldn't be going back to the outpost again while they were all on high alert.

The ranger reached the first tree and braced his back against it, his crossbow held at the ready to ambush Damien's prone body. Before Damien could reach him, he jumped from around the tree and pulled the trigger.

A crossbow bolt ejected at high speed, only to fall short when one of Damien's imps threw themselves into its way.

Noigel's tapping became a thumping fist.

The remaining two imps leapt toward the ranger before he could reload his weapon, claws extended and teeth bared. He knocked one back with a blow from the butt of his crossbow and caught the other in an outstretched hand before throwing it back. The crossbow disappeared as he swapped it for a pair of short swords that materialized in his grasp.

So focused was he on the two imps, he hadn't noticed the shadowy figure hurtling towards him across the open plain. Damien punched an armblade straight through his side, his armor penetration aided by momentum and his damage enhanced by Sneak Attack. The two imps leapt in while the ranger staggered sideways and Damien continued his assault. It was not a drawn out engagement.

Damien advanced almost to level 10. He canceled Possession and pushed himself onto his feet. Once he'd collected himself, he signaled for his minions to follow him and ran out from under the trees, directly away from the outpost.

They needed to get far away as fast as possible, especially since the player they'd just taken down would soon give the others their location.

Once they were moving, Damien took stock. He still had the wraith and three imps. Having already collected souls through possessing the wraith, Damien's soul count was full, 7/7. Not only did players grant him excellent exp, they dropped far more soul energy as well. Most important of all, the quest was complete. He was going to get to level 10, he was finally going to get some great gear and he'd done it all in less than a single day.

Even better, he'd found and recorded Rising Tide's raid schedule. When Damien first told Bartholomew he was going to kill Aetherius he'd been completely sincere, but he also hadn't been certain how the hell he could do it.

Between the discovery of his Soul Harvest's true value, his

success assassinating players in the outpost and this new sensitive information, Damien knew he had a chance, even if it was a slim one.

He grinned as the bell at the top of the Guild Hall sounded out over the empty plains around him. His first bid to save his mother and take revenge on Aetherius had been a success.

And this one-man war was just beginning.

16

PURPOSE

D amien picked his way through the traps littered throughout The Downward Spiral. He was so eager to collect his reward that he had a hard time concentrating on minding his feet, even with the traps highlighted.

It was much more dangerous going down than it was going up. After all, the traps were designed to kill people who were entering the dungeon, not leaving.

After an arduous journey, with some close calls that made Noigel squawk in panic, Damien finally reached the boss floor. No sooner had he touched down than Bartholomew appeared a short distance away. The vampire inspected him thoroughly and nodded with approval.

"You have become considerably stronger in a very short time. I am most pleased. It won't be long before you're ready for some new abilities. I take it you completed one of the quests? Which will you hand in, I wonder?"

"I killed three members of Rising Tide. I'd really like to collect the reward, please."

Bartholomew grinned broadly.

"You decided to take the low road? A very sensible choice given your time constraints. Although I suspect the items I showed you earlier had some place in your reasoning?"

"Yeah, maybe just a little. Can I have them? Please?"

Bartholomew relented. He nodded and the quest flashed gold in Damien's HUD, bringing Damien's experience up to level 10. His bag weighed a little heavier on his back as the material rewards were added to his inventory. Without a moment's hesitation he opened his menu to inspect them.

Occultist Apprentice Robes (Set)
Boots, Cloak and hood, Leather Bindings, Leggings, Robe (5/5)
Set Bonus: +5 to Agility, Constitution, Endurance and Wisdom
Description: A powerful set granted to worthy initiates. These garments are designed to bolster an apprentice's mana reserves and survivability while maintaining enough flexibility to engage in light combat. (Each individual piece provides +2 Agility, Constitution, Endurance and Wisdom. Having all five pieces equipped provides an additional +5 to these stats).

Sacrificial Dagger
Durability: 50/50
Damage: 25 + (Agility x 0.5)
Stats: 15 Agility
Description: A dagger crafted with the intent of performing ritual slaughter.
Special Ability: Sacrifice – Soul Reserve (0/1). This weapon has a single soul slot which is filled when it achieves a killing blow against a target that provides experience.

Damien had no sooner finished reading than he excitedly equipped everything at once. The rags dematerialized into his backpack and Damien felt different. Slightly faster on his feet. A little lighter and a bit more robust.

He braced himself and looked down. The quality of the equipment had been obvious even when held in Bartholomew's hands, but now they were equipped Damien could see he was wearing a masterpiece.

The magic robes were held tightly against his upper body by

the leather bindings and bracers, ensuring he did not have any loose fabric hanging around his torso or upper limbs. The robes fanned out below his knees, just high enough not to interfere with sneaking. In fact, they would mask the profile of his legs so long as he was crouched down.

The boots were black leather, already pliable, a snug fit with soft soles that wouldn't tap against the ground. He also had a cloak with a hood, concealing his face and hiding the sacrificial dagger at his waist. The gear perfectly embodied the synthesis of assassin and mage.

Damien looked at his mana bar. The set had granted him an extra 15 wisdom, which manifested as an extra 150 mana points. It had also boosted his summon limit to 8. But what he was really excited about was the sudden increase in his agility stat. The set and the dagger granted 30 agility between them, bringing Damien's total to 49. The dagger was agility-based for damage, so this would make him much more useful in close combat than swinging bones around. The sacrifice ability on the dagger seemed very useful for gathering souls, so he'd waste less time killing trash mobs to summon more imps.

Not to be overlooked was the gear's impact on his health, which had almost doubled from 190 to 340. It was nice to be a little less squishy.

Finally, his stamina had increased exponentially, which would allow him to run faster and further as well as taking more successive swings with his weapon. Since he'd only be swinging a light dagger with decent damage, Damien imagined he'd have a difficult time running out of stamina in combat from now on.

"The robes I would ordinarily craft enhance the mind, but I decided to make these after watching your efforts against the rats this morning. You seemed intent on being involved in close combat. Hopefully this makes it a more viable option. Do you find your rewards suitable?"

"Bartholomew, I can barely even speak to you at the moment because my mind is so blown by how good this gear is."

"I shall take that as a yes. When you are finished marveling at your gear – without a word of thanks, I might add – I shall be waiting to teach you some new skills and to assign you a trait."

Damien snapped out of his reverie and dashed after Bartholomew, realizing as he ran that after eight hours of game time, he was finally wearing shoes.

"Bartholomew – master – this feels, like, the best thing anyone has ever given me. I'll cherish it like a newborn child."

"Yes, indeed. Well, even I wouldn't advise wearing newborn children. They're far too small and it takes far too many of them to craft a garment of reasonable size."

The vampire grinned and lowered his face to Damien's level.

"First, there are new skills that I judge you competent and powerful enough to wield. I grant them to you now."

He tapped Damien on the head and a brief hot glow on his fingertip was followed by three new notifications.

Summon Hell Hound Unlocked!
Implosion Unlocked!
Gateway Unlocked!

Damien went into his Skills tab. He found two of the new skills in the Demonology tree.

Summon Hell Hound: Mana: 250, Souls: 3 - You point at the ground, searing it with runes to open a portal to the demon world. After channeling for 10 seconds, the portal is opened and a hell hound arrives on the mortal plane. The hell hound will serve you until it dies or is dismissed. Hell hound stats improve every five levels.

Implosion: Mana: 100, Cooldown: 30 seconds – You point at a summoned imp and open an unstable portal to its realm. The portal opens instantly, dismissing the imp and pulling all objects within 10 meters sharply toward its location. The force is strongest at the edge of the effect.

Another minion, and then this very strange spell. If Damien was reading it right, it would briefly turn one of his imps into a black hole. Very nice. It seemed designed for crowd control rather than damage. The 30-second cooldown was pretty long too, and it was going to cost him an imp every time he used it as well as the mana. He was sure he'd figure out how to use it in time. There was no sign of the 'Gateway' spell. Maybe it was in his Maleficium skill tree?

There was a phlegmy cough and Damien closed his menu to find Bartholomew staring directly into his face.

"You have a worrying tendency for distraction. As I was saying, you have also become sufficiently powerful for me to grant you a trait. Are you ready?"

Damien remembered traits from Scorpius. He'd got one at level 10 and another at level 20. The traits were specializations that gave each class unique advantages in certain fields. Damien couldn't wait to find out what traits an occultist might have.

"I'm ready. Show me my options."

"I shall grant you one of three traits. Choose wisely, as when you take one you forgo the others. The first trait will make Chaotic Bolt more volatile the longer you wait before casting it. The second trait will cause Corruption to spread to anything that comes into contact with a target affected by Corruption. The third trait will imbue your imps with wings, granting them faster movement speed and the ability to fly. Which do you choose?"

The three choices came up in a window on Damien's HUD. Bartholomew waited patiently in the background rather than continuing to talk, re-enforcing that Saga Online took trait allocations very seriously.

1. **Controlled Chaos**: Chaotic Bolt's damage increases the longer you hold it.
2. **Contagion**: Corruption spreads by touch.
3. **Hell's Angels**: Your summoned imps have wings.

Damien stared at them. It seemed these traits were all related to the starting abilities. All three of them were cool, but he'd given up on Chaotic Bolt and Corruption long ago. They were Intelligence-based and he'd put everything he had into wisdom to maximize his Soul Reserve and Soul Summon Limit.

Even if he were still using either of them, it would be difficult not to pick Hell's Angels. His imps would get into combat faster and he'd have more strategic options with them. Plus, they'd look absolutely epic. He cleared his throat, wanting to make sure there was no room for misunderstanding.

"I've given it careful thought and I'd like to have trait three, Hell's Angels, please."

There were a host of cheers behind him and Damien turned around to see his imps had locked arms and started line dancing, kicking their little legs out with joy as their tails thrashed behind them.

Damien couldn't help but chuckle. He'd be pretty happy if he was getting wings as well. Bartholomew raised his finger and hovered it in the air between Damien's eyes.

"Are you sure?"

"I'm sure."

The finger connected and the imps' cheers of joy turned to surprise. Damien looked at them and saw the trait was already taking effect. Bones grew from their shoulder blades, extending outward and upward with leathery skin stretching over them. Each fully stretched wing was about the same breadth as one of the imps it was attached to.

Noigel didn't wait for an order. He launched into the air and flapped the wings repeatedly to steady himself, hovering above the other two imps as his tail lashed below him for balance. He twisted slightly in mid-air and swept to a stop just above Damien's shoulder, dropping onto it with ease.

"It appears Noigel has reaped the rewards of your combined efforts as well. I hope he did his part in your most recent quest?"

Damien recalled the tapping on his head that Noigel had persisted with, giving him the warning that saved his life.

"Yeah, Noigel did great. I'm very happy with him."

"All that leaves are the base upgrades. Follow me."

As Damien obediently followed in Bart's footsteps, he admired the striking appearance his new trait had granted his imps. The trait was something he'd overlooked. New skills were usually available from class trainers every five levels and traits came, one way or another, every ten. While he had some experience with these two aspects of Saga Online, he had no experience managing a base. He hadn't stopped to consider how it might be improved.

Bartholomew stood by as Damien looked his base over. After seeing the outpost that the guild had collectively built, his room seemed a little…. minimalist. The only feature in it was the Soul Well, which was essentially a dome of rocks. Maybe 'Gateway' wasn't a spell at all.

Damien opened his menu and navigated to 'Base Schematics'. One of the previously grayed-out options had become accessible, confirming his suspicions, and the Soul Well icon was flashing as well. Damien started with the new building.

Gateway
Health: 250
Description: The Gateway allows you to create a portal from your location back to the Gateway.
Resources: 30 stone blocks, 400 mana

It was a Portal Stone! Well, it had a different name, but it did almost exactly the same thing. Once this was built, Damien would be able to teleport back to his home base.

Damien selected the schematic and his vision was filled with the red-shaded area it would occupy. From the outline he could see a flight of stairs leading up to a circle of floating, rune-etched stones. Awesome. He set the Gateway plan against the back wall and looked at his party to set them to the task of building it.

The two remaining imps were taking it in turns to do increasingly large wing-assisted backflips while the wraith stared resolutely ahead. Noigel was still sitting on his shoulder. Damien decided the other three minions should be enough. It had taken a while for Noigel to warm up to him; he didn't want to risk losing the progress he'd made.

"Alright, you lot are collecting resources and building the Gateway. Get to it!"

The imps smartly saluted and ran up to the wall, immediately picking out a rock embedded into the side of it and starting to dig it free. An empty progress bar showed up under the Gateway, stating that construction would take four hours. That was a lot longer than the Soul Well had taken, but Damien supposed Bartholomew had assisted with that one by providing pre-made rubble.

It was getting late, anyway.

He could get some sleep and wake up to a completed building. While the two imps had leapt into action, the wraith stayed exactly where it was. Damien was surprised. It had always been so compliant before. Bartholomew coughed lightly to draw Damien's attention before he could order it to work again.

"Each of your minions serves a specific function in your base. The imps are your builders and can also gather resources, if they are present. The wraith has a scouting and defensive function. You tell it where to stand guard or where to patrol and it will do its best to eliminate threats."

Damien frowned. That might have been vaguely useful if he was making a base somewhere else, but anything that was capable of getting past Bartholomew would make short work of his wraith. He could dismiss it and use the freed space in his summon limit to get more imps to build the Gateway.

He realized with a start that his Soul Well still only had one soul in it, so he'd only be able to bind one soul's worth of demons to it. His Soul Reserve was at 7/7, so at least he could fix that problem right now.

Placing his hand on the well, a command came up on his HUD.

'Tap the Soul Well once for each soul you wish to embed.'

Damien thought about it and tapped the rock twice. Each tap

made his hand shimmer silver before long strands of energy twisted out of his fingertips and into the cracks in the rock. It now had three souls in total.

Next, he dismissed the wraith, which passed through its portal without so much as a word. The soul energy was left behind in a neat orb which flew toward Damien, granting him one and a half soul energy. Damien opened his menu and went back into the Building Schematics tab. The Soul Well icon was still flashing. Damien selected it and found there was an upgrade available.

Soul Well II
Health: 500
Soul Capacity: 20
Requirements: 30 stone blocks, 10/10 Soul Well capacity

Just when you think everything's under control, something else comes up. If it was at all possible for both buildings to be ready by the time Damien woke up, that was what he wanted. But he only had three souls in the Soul Well and six and a half in his own Soul Reserve. He'd have to dismiss one of the imps to hit the quota.

He looked at Noigel and thought about it. He needed everything upgraded as fast as possible, but didn't want to offend the imp by dismissing him. That would send a bit of a mixed message. At last he came to the best compromise he could think of.

"Noigel, you've done a great job today. I wanted to let you chill out for a while, but I need half a soul to upgrade the Soul Well. I've got to dismiss an imp. The other two will have to build all through the night. I can dismiss one of the other imps if you'd rather stay, but I reckon you'd rather I dismissed you and brought you back later. Do you want to build or be dismissed?"

Damien was surprised when the imp responded not with his usual animated array of hand gestures, but with the same throaty whisper he'd employed to tell Damien what a loser he was that morning.

"Damien gave Noigel wings. Noigel will help."

The imp hopped off Damien's shoulder onto the ground and turned to give him a thumbs up. It was all Damien could do to snap his jaw shut before Noigel noticed. Then, without being ordered, Noigel ran up to the imps and started helping them lug the rock they'd found. The timer on the Gateway construction went from four hours to three. Damien singled out an imp that wasn't Noigel before he lost track of which was which.

"Good job today! You're dismissed."

The imp broke off from the group, saluted sharply and leapt through the portal above him, aided by a swift beat of his new wings. The construction time went back to four hours and Damien received the last half soul he needed. He returned to the Soul Well and tapped it seven times, embedding every soul he had. On the last tap he received the notification he'd been hoping for.

'**Upgrade Soul Well?** Yes or No?'

He nodded eagerly, then ordered the imp helping Noigel to get to work on the Soul Well. A building timer appeared. Excellent. Both buildings would now take eight hours to complete, and should be finished by the time he got back. Bartholomew loomed over his shoulder as Damien watched the imps set about their task.

"That's a lot of work for two imps. Will they be all right?" Damien asked.

"Oh my, do I detect concern? They're literally hell-spawn, Damien. You'd be wiser to worry about yourself."

"Well, yeah, they might be, but they're *my* hell-spawn. I need to make sure they're in good shape and don't hate me. Especially Noigel. Will they be good to go tomorrow?"

"They'll be absolutely fine. This is a considerably nicer environment than where they come from. Which do you imagine is worse? Eight hours constructing buildings or eight hours in hell? For all intents and purposes, they're on vacation."

So far as Damien was concerned, the important thing was

that completing the structures wasn't going to wear his minions out or have any other adverse effects.

"Alrighty then, that sounds great. Sorry, Bartholomew, it's very late and I need to get back to my world. I'll see you in the morning for more quests."

"Aren't you forgetting something?"

Bartholomew looked down at him smugly and did not offer any further guidance. Damien knew whatever it was must be important. Then he remembered he hadn't allocated his stats. He went into the Stats tab and dumped all fifteen stat points from his last three levels into wisdom.

With his gear taken into account, his wisdom stat had skyrocketed to 79. His Summon Limit increased by another two points, going up to 10. That gave him a fair bit of flexibility with his minion set-up, especially now he had hell hounds to test. Rather disappointingly, his Soul Reserve only went up by a single point, to 8.

Despite putting all his points into wisdom up to level 10, in all that time Damien's Soul Reserve had only increased by three, compared to his Soul Summon Limit increasing by seven.

"Bartholomew, why does my Soul Reserve increase so much more slowly than my Summon limit?"

"It's completely normal. It requires a great deal of wisdom to contain souls beyond your own and exponentially more with each extra soul you attempt to contain. It does not require quite so much to lead a group of creatures that are bound to your will. I assure you, your current Soul Reserve is abnormally high given your level of expertise."

"Oh. That's good, then, I suppose. Well, thanks very much! I'm heading out, I'll see—"

Bartholomew shook his head and his smugness returned.

"You're still forgetting something. And I can guarantee you're going to be extremely annoyed when you return in the morning if you don't figure out what it is."

Damien sighed and pondered what he might be missing. His stats were all updated, his gear was equipped, he'd handed in all his quests, the imps would be building all through the night... oh.

He checked his Summon limit and saw the imps were still bound to himself. If he logged off without binding them to the Soul Well, they'd disappear at the same time as he did and he'd come back online to find his buildings unfinished, all because of a simple mistake. This base management thing was a pain.

"I bind all my current minions to my Soul Well."

Bartholomew nodded curtly as Damien's Soul Summon Limit was allocated to his base.

"I'll see you tomorrow."

Damien started the ten-second countdown to log off as Bartholomew changed tone. His levity was replaced with sudden seriousness and contemplation.

"Although your progress was excellent today, you'll improve more slowly from now on. At your current rate you still stand no chance of defeating Aetherius six days hence."

With three seconds left until logout, Damien remembered the raid schedule and smiled.

'Don't worry. I have a plan."

Bartholomew had just enough time to curl an eyebrow before Damien's vision faded and he woke up back in his pod.

The IMBA set was finally starting to feel uncomfortable after being worn on and off for an entire day, but Damien wasn't quite ready to take it off just yet. Without logging back in, he scrolled through the interface and found what he was looking for.

Recordings.

The headset had recorded everything following his fall into The Downward Spiral, when he'd first found the option in his menu. They were big chunks, each of them at least a couple of hours long. He had plenty of space to store them, but they'd need tidying up sooner or later. Not right now, though. His priority was to make sure he had the whole raid schedule, intact.

He skipped through the footage until he found what he was looking for. It was even better than he'd hoped.

The quality of the IMBA set recording was incredibly high. The only image he needed was the last one, where he'd stepped back and taken in the schedule in its entirety. The words and symbols stood out crystal clear on his screen. *Sorted.*

As soon as he'd evaluated what he had, Damien realized he was going to go full-time player killer.

The schedule made it possible. He knew where people would be and when. He knew they'd be distracted fighting powerful enemies. And best of all, they'd have no idea he was coming for them.

He took a screenshot of tomorrow's schedule entry before tilting the pod so he could stand upright in it. It had been a long, stressful day and he'd already been running around, either in his city or in his mind, for over twelve hours. Even so, he wanted to have some idea of what was next before he slept. That way, he'd wake up with purpose.

Rising Tide was a large guild and there were an awful lot of activities listed throughout the next day. Damien checked them chronologically, cross-referencing between the schedule and the internet so he could research the different dungeons and sift through player profiles to find suitable targets. Most of the events were far out of his reach. There were either too many players or their levels were simply too damn high. Others were too far, the trip even more dangerous than killing the players due to his negative reputation with the Empire. Empire-aligned players and NPCs would likely kill him on sight.

He'd ruled out all of the morning's events before he found a serious contender.

12:30pm – The Maw – 10-player raid.
Illydin, Roranoa, Azreal59, Jinks, Dryfus, Shankyou, Rhinohide, Metalstorm (two spaces remaining).

The dungeon was close, just a small way into the next territory. It would only take twenty, maybe twenty-five minutes to get there. Off to a good start, then. The mobs were levels 15 to 19, with a nasty-looking level 20 final boss: 'The Boulder'. Sounded like a riot.

He looked up the players via their online profiles. The guild already had the party components that were hardest to get: two tanks and two healers. He kept digging and discovered that Metalstorm was a gunslinger; a hidden damage based class, much like his own, that had been discovered a couple of weeks into Saga Online's grand opening. The two empty slots were probably reserved for more damage-based characters. Fortunately, none of the players currently signed up were over level 20, except one.

The assassin, 'Shankyou', was level 23. Damien would have to be careful not to get seen by that one, or else he'd end up in a very difficult situation. Assassins had good PK'ing move sets without even trying, so one more than double Damien's level could snuff him out with ease.

Still, with a little luck and a lot of caution he could probably find a way to take him out. Especially if he leveled up a little more beforehand.

His main concern was the unknown slots. If Damien logged on tomorrow and some level 30 do-gooder had decided to boost the group, the whole thing would become almost impossible. Well, no good worrying about that now. He'd just have to get to the dungeon, find a safe vantage point to watch the players gather and see who showed up.

Just like that, Damien had a plan.

He gratefully pulled the IMBA set off his head and stored it away, finishing his water before tilting the pod back to horizontal. It was 22:45. What a day. He reached out to turn off the display and the pod went dark, save for the outlines of the various buttons.

His thoughts went back to his mother and he briefly considered pulling out the IMBA set again to see if he could find out anything about her situation online. He managed to stop himself, but only just.

If CU was trying to find him, monitoring internet searches for Cassandra Brades would be a smart way to go about it. It seemed like a low possibility, but it was still a possibility of him being hauled out of his pod half asleep and escorted to a detainment facility. He'd have to find a safe way of checking up on her later.

Damien turned up the heat a little and rolled onto his side. Even though he was so tired, his mind couldn't help but replay the many events of that day. His thoughts lurched uncontrollably between ecstasy and dread, pride and shame until after many fitful attempts he fell into a close approximation of sleep.

17

DAY TWO

D amien soon found that waking up in a pod was even less pleasant than going to sleep in one. Opening his eyes to find a padded wall in front of his nose felt much like waking up in a coffin. Following a brief panic while his brain rebooted, he managed to find the button to display the time. 10:23. He'd overslept, but all things considered that was no surprise. At least it wasn't too late to go and get some breakfast, if he hurried.

Damien slung his bag on his back, scooped up the headset under his arm and paced towards the door.

"Good morning, little man. How was your stay?"

He looked at the counter, behind which stood his wizened host. Gian wasn't actually looking at him; he was too busy tapping madly at his phone screen while various laser sounds blared out of it.

"It was great, thanks. Just getting breakfast and I'll be right back."

"No worries, you've got the pod until noon… unless you want to go again?"

Damien couldn't believe his luck. He'd no sooner started worrying how to extend his stay than it was practically done for him.

"Yeah! I mean, yes, please, that would be perfect. Thanks."

The laser battle ceased and Gian looked up at him knowingly.

"No worries. Heck, I'd feel guilty letting you go. You're better off here than in some unsanctioned dive, which is all you'll get without ID. You pay, I let you use my credentials – we make a good team."

Damien smiled and took his mom's card out to sign up for another night in the pod. That was one more worry off his list. As long as he had this place he could focus on what mattered. Feeling much happier than when he'd woken up, he let Gian get back to his game, jammed the headset on and headed out into the street.

It didn't take long to pick up a couple of sandwiches, but on the way back he spotted a sunglasses stall that hadn't been there the previous day. While the enhanced items were outside of his budget, there was a discount bin full of regular sunglasses off to one side. Damien found a pair of scratched-up aviators with wide, face-covering lenses and quickly paid for them. He wouldn't have to wear the IMBA set when he went outside anymore.

His work done, he returned to the sanctuary of his pod so he could eat in private. He finished the first sandwich and checked the time. 10:47. If he logged on at 11 he'd have enough time to sort himself out before he headed to The Maw. He decided to use the last few minutes to take a much-needed shower while he reviewed his plan.

Damien knew how elite dungeons worked but he'd never actually been to one in Saga Online before. Well, besides The Downward Spiral, but that didn't count.

Elite dungeons posed a much greater challenge than the regular caves and encounters scattered around Arcadia, which is why they had to be done in groups. For the sake of extra immersion and realism, the dungeons weren't disconnected from the world map and replicated for multiple groups at once, like other online RPGs. Everyone in Arcadia had to fight over the limited dungeon spawn rates. They would reset eventually, but their non-instanced nature created competition between players: letting another group complete the dungeon before you would mean a lack of loot until the next reset.

The Downward Spiral was an exception. Defeating Bartholomew had put an end to all cultist...occultist...activity in the region. It had been a one time offer with permanent consequences for the game lore. Rising Tide hadn't posted the footage from that particular fight, letting the various Empire NPC's confirm their victory instead. Aetherius had remained tight lipped regarding why he wouldn't allow the footage to be shared, but eventually the word got out: of the forty players who entered, only a handful survived. Apparently, it had not been an impressive victory.

In the case of The Maw, Damien would be hoping to take advantage of Rising Tide being distracted as they dealt with the harder elite mobs of the dungeon. While they had all their tanks and melee fighters up front, Damien would be free to pick off the healers, spellcasters and ranged units in the back. The players might be higher in levels, but the back line would have the squishiest targets and they'd all be looking the other way.

It was a lovely theory, but there were all sorts of things that could go wrong.

If he didn't make his first strike count, the party would turn around and decimate him. If he didn't know where Shankyou was he wouldn't be able to attack at all. He'd just have to watch carefully and wait for the right moment.

Damien finished his shower, drying himself off with a blast of warm air before getting dressed and hurrying back to his pod. Fed, watered and washed, he was ready to go. He jammed the headset back on and set the pod horizontal to log in.

His eyes hadn't even adjusted to the darkness before a gleeful squawk sounded out some distance in front of him. There was a low whoosh of air and a light weight dropped onto his shoulder.

"Hey, Noigel. All the constructions complete?"

The imp flitted off his shoulder and flew toward the end of the base, landing lightly on a raised stone platform in front of the back wall. Damien's eyes were still adjusting, but for once it wasn't necessary to wait: his newest structure was bathing its surroundings in faint blue light.

It was a flight of stairs leading up to a flat plateau, about the same height as Damien. He strode up the steps, taking in his newest building. Rock-hewn spheres spun lazily in a ring rising into the air, held together by strands of blue mana. Each of the spheres were slightly different sizes and bore different sets of symbols; one was covered with engraved numbers, another was filled with scratchy infernal runes. The whole effect cast a dim glow over one side of Damien's base.

"Admiring your new structure, I see."

Bartholomew was standing on the platform with him. He made a mental note to try and catch him first next time.

"Yeah, it's pretty neat. How do I use it?"

The words had hardly left his lips before Bartholomew tapped him on the head.

'Portal Unlocked!'

Damien went into his Skills tab to check it out.

Portal: Mana cost: 100, Channeling cost: 10 MpS, Casting Time: 10 Seconds – You open a portal back to the nearest allied Gateway. The portal remains open until you cancel the spell, you run out of mana to channel the spell or the Gateway is destroyed. You cannot use this spell while in combat. Upon entering combat, the portal will close within ten seconds. Passing through the portal yourself will automatically cancel the spell.

"Great, now I won't have to waste time traveling back. How about the Soul Well?"

Bartholomew simply pointed toward the center of the room, where there stood a rather different-looking structure than the one Damien had left. The dome was still there, but it had become the foundation of something more. The imps had spent the night piling stones around it in a square before laying a great stone slab on top.

It looked like a makeshift picnic table, but the runes etched into the surface hinted at something a little more sinister. Damien inspected it briefly and found it now had a maximum Soul Capacity of 20. A new side objective for him to fulfill. His second imp was dozing underneath it, in an idle state after finishing its tasks.

It was only then Damien remembered he would need to start his own task, accumulating souls and minions before he got to The Maw. It would be better to start early than late. Besides, he still needed to test the new spells and gear he'd received yesterday.

"All right, Bartholomew, I'm heading out. I'll be back later."

"Hold on. You're leaving very suddenly, without even asking for quests. What are you scheming?"

"I'm heading out to attack a group of Rising Tide players. Sorry, I don't think I'll be doing any quests today."

Damien had expected a lot of pushback, possibly even a tirade, but all he got was a hum of understanding and an approving nod.

"I'm glad to see you're pressing your agenda. Still, there's no reason why you can't perform some errands on the way. Where is your hunt taking you?"

Damien laid out his plan, explaining his discovery of Rising Tide's raid schedule and his decision to attack a party entering The Maw. Bartholomew was stroking his chin and nodding until Damien mentioned the name of the dungeon.

"The Maw? The creatures there are out of your league. The same can likely be said for any group of heroes seriously attempting it. Are you sure this is wise?"

Damien knew Bartholomew had a point. This was much more dangerous than what he'd done yesterday, and catching up on sleep hadn't left him as much time to prepare as he'd wanted. Even so, he'd already spent the night planning it out and wasn't going to let his efforts go to waste.

He was committed.

"I don't know if I can do it, but I'll just have to try my best. I won't be ready to kill Aetherius unless I gain more experience."

Bartholomew scratched his head and shifted uncomfortably, his lower body shimmering below him before fading out of vision again. He looked both concerned and indecisive, a pair of emotions that were decidedly not at home on the vampire's desiccated face. At last, he shrugged and resigned himself to Damien's choice.

"I am against this, but given your lack of time I don't see a more sensible alternative. Just be careful; it would be a shame to lose the fine craftsmanship I put into your robes after I gave them to you only yesterday."

Oh. So that's what he was concerned about, Damien thought. *I should have known.*

"Yeah, sure. Thanks. So, you have anything you want me to do around The Maw?"

Bartholomew snorted.

"I think not. I hadn't planned on sending you in that direction until tomorrow, assuming you lived that long. I won't prevent you from leaving, but nor will I add to your self-inflicted burden.... wait, there is one thing you can do. Gather up any metal you find on your travels. I need it for my own projects, and whatever is left will be very helpful to you in the near future."

The words had no sooner been spoken than a new quest – 'Rock? Heavy Metal!' – flashed up in Damien's peripheral vision. He needed twenty units of iron in order to complete it. That would be more than Damien could hope to find in one trip, unless he abandoned his plans and went spelunking instead.

"What kind of quest is this? One day you're having me kill Rising Tide members, the next you want me to grab a pickaxe and mine iron?"

"Not at all. That would be a waste of even your paltry talents. There should be at least some quantity of metal lying around after you've executed your ambush. If you're successful, anyway."

That single observation changed the quest from a long, boring grind into one that fit his own agenda perfectly.

"Ah... I see. Right. That's actually not a bad idea."

"Naturally, it's one of mine. I've got another one for you as well, at no extra charge: you should get a move on if you don't want to miss your deadline."

Damien checked the time and saw it was already 11:10. Just as always, the closer he got to a deadline the faster the time seemed to pass him by.

He looked back to say a hasty goodbye and found that Bartholomew was hastier. He'd vanished, again, even while standing right in front of him. He was nothing if not consistent.

Without a word, Damien gathered up his two imps and started the long trap-laden trek to the world above.

18

CRY HAVOC

It was only when he reached the edge of the forest that the difficulty of the task ahead really set in. It was broad daylight outside. Damien had always known this would be a problem, yet somehow it seemed considerably worse when it was staring him in the face.

He checked the map once more to confirm he'd made the right choice. The roads might be more convenient, but that was no good since they were also full of NPC patrols. Even if he somehow avoided them, there was an Empire guard post set at the chokepoint between zones. Damien didn't fancy his chances of getting through there.

He'd researched an alternate route that would allow him to avoid trouble: a cavern off to one side that passed through the mountain range at the border and into the next territory, used almost exclusively by players on the Empire's naughty list.

With luck, the cavern would also be an ideal place for him to gather souls and accumulate more minions before he got to The Maw.

It wasn't going to get any better than that.

He picked through the undergrowth on the edge of the wood, exiting on the far side so the forest itself would block his view to the road and vice versa. Noigel quickly flapped onto Damien's shoulder and scouted all around them while they were on the move. The remaining imp followed close behind, whining and nervous but still obedient to a fault. Just over an hour to go until the Rising Tide party were due to start The Maw.

Damien was right to have been worried about traveling during the day. It was only a fifteen-minute trip from his base to the edge of the territory, but they still had to hide on three separate occasions when Noigel spotted travelers.

There was nothing for Damien to do but take shelter behind the nearest cover and wait until they passed by. He pushed on in the gaps, grateful that his raised agility and endurance stats were helping him move faster.

Despite the advantage of his gear, what should have been a quick trip ended up going excruciatingly slowly. Occultists clearly had their drawbacks.

By the time he reached the edge of the mountain range and successfully found the cavern entrance, Damien had barely thirty-five minutes left before the raid was scheduled to start. Time was compressing. He ran straight in without a second thought, relieved to get out of the open yet panicking that he was so far behind schedule.

It was only when he hit the spider's web that he realized there was more to be worried about.

Webbing covered his face and bound his eyes shut. The rest of his body followed and in no time at all Damien was completely ensnared. A piercing multi-toned screech came from the ceiling above.

"Noigel! Cut me loose!"

A pitiful wail from his shoulder indicated this was unlikely to happen. He'd carried Noigel straight into the web with him. As the two of them kicked and struggled, Damien felt the web sag with the weight of an extremely undesirable third occupant. The landlord, depending on how you looked at things. Only this landlord would be extracting a very different kind of revenue.

Damien thrashed in the web again, only succeeding in entrapping himself further. He could feel Noigel on his shoulder kicking against him to try and free himself, but the imp had no more success than Damien. He felt a long stick scrape down his head and against his face, the pointed tip gouging into his cheek. In his desperation he fought to grab it so he could pull himself free. It was only when it recoiled at his motion that the realization hit him. It was one of the spider's legs!

With his eyes sealed shut he could only imagine how big it must be if one of the legs felt like a lance. His mouth had been sealed by his thrashing as well, but fear piqued his focus, resulting in a mental command that could not have been clearer.

'Kill the spider!'

The second imp had been behind them and had not followed them into the trap.

With a piercing scream, the imp beat its wings and pulled into the air before colliding with the spider above them. The battle cry was quickly drowned out by a grating screech from the imp's much larger enemy and the web thrummed violently back and forth from the force of the impact. Damien's eyes were still sealed shut, but he didn't need to see to know the imp wouldn't win by itself.

He had to do something. With his limbs restrained, there was only one thing Damien could think of. He balled his trapped hand into a fist and focused on it, the Chaotic Bolt forcing his fingers open.

The imp let out a second cry as it pressed the attack, Noigel cheering it on from his prison.

But the cry was cut short and Noigel's cheer faded to a whimper. The brief silence was broken by the unmistakable thud of a small body hitting the ground.

The spider's mandibles clicked grotesquely as it scuttled down to reclaim its prize. Damien's hand stopped forcing itself open and started producing a familiar whine. He twisted his hand in the web until his palm was facing directly upward and released. He didn't know if it was going to hit the spider, nor did he care.

With his low intelligence stat, Chaotic Bolt was far too weak to make any sort of mark on this enemy. It was, however, perfect for burning through webs. It exploded above him and the strands around Damien disintegrated.

Webbing lost, the remaining structure could no longer support their combined weight. Damien, Noigel and the spider tumbled to the floor in a disorientated, screeching, flailing heap, the spider landing on its back. Damien might not have been familiar with spell casting in combat, but stabbing an enemy which was in body contact with him was not particularly difficult. He equipped his dagger and stabbed it recklessly and repeatedly, wanting to put a swift end to this unforeseen abomination. Noigel bound forth to aid him.

Aside from Toutatis, it was the most terrifying combat Damien had endured in his entire Saga Online career.

Suffering under the dagger and claws, the spider thankfully died quickly. Damien had nothing to show for his ordeal but 350 XP, half a soul and a brand new phobia.

What a disaster.

Damien dusted residual cobwebs out of his face as fast as he could. Noigel followed suit, finding time to deliver a few furious kicks and a big glob of spit onto the corpse of their would-be embalmer.

Now that Damien's eyes had re-adjusted he could see everything clearly. Some grunt at Mobius Enterprises had obviously thought it would be funny to put a solo player-killing trap right inside the entrance, where players would barely have a chance to light a torch or adjust to the darkness before they blundered right into it.

On the plus side, the dagger's 'Sacrifice' ability was functioning properly. In addition to obtaining half a soul from the dead arachnid, the blade was coated in the same silver smoke that Damien recognized as soul energy. As long as he used the energy in the dagger he could potentially gather souls twice as fast as before, maybe even faster if he could kill enough targets in melee. Which was important right now, since he had a lot of lost time to make up.

He pointed the dagger at the ground and cast Summon Imp. The runes burned into the floor and the mist surrounding the dagger dissipated. The new imp hadn't even finished performing its cheerleader introduction routine before Damien was pacing into the cave, looking around warily for more webs as Noigel and the rather disappointed new arrival formed up behind him.

Damien had somewhat naively expected a simple path through the cave from A to B. This could not have been further from the truth. There were forks in the road that looped back on themselves, passageways leading to exits back into the zone he'd just left and of course, his all-time favorite: good old-fashioned dead ends.

On a normal play-through Damien would have reveled in the chance to map out the whole area. Today, after twenty minutes of aimless, increasingly panicked wandering, he felt like wrapping his hands around the neck of the level designer responsible for this mess. While the spider placement had been poorly thought out and inconsiderate, the floor plan bordered on cruel and unusual punishment.

Had Damien not been so tired yesterday when he planned his route, he might have thought to check an online map. Instead, he'd taken it for granted and was paying a disproportionate price.

There weren't even enough enemies for him to gather a significant force. There were a few lone wolves which were easy enough to kill and occasionally his path would be blocked by a web, which he'd destroy with great prejudice before slaying the spider personally.

Yet none of these enemies were giving him more than half a soul at a time. Worse still, as his rush to find the exit overtook him, he ran his group straight into waiting enemies. For every two imps he summoned, one was slain defending him from the wolves that lay in wait to ambush them. His rush to get out of the cavern was costing him troops, and there was no point in making it to The Maw if he hadn't replenished his forces by then.

The imps were good cannon fodder but Damien was losing them almost as fast as he could summon them. The wraith was a strong attacker but a poor defender, and not much of a team player either. He'd be wasting souls on it too, since the last leg of the trip would be through daylight. Assuming they ever made it outside. That left the hell hounds, which hadn't even been tested. He'd have to cross his fingers.

Damien stopped in an unoccupied corridor and pointed his loaded dagger at the floor, combining the soul within with two he'd scraped up into his soul reserve. A new rune started to take shape. The imp rune bore a simple pentagram, the wraith had a scythe as its demonic symbol, and the newest addition to Damien's sigil collection was the jagged outline of a pair of jaws.

This time the portal was stood up on the ground rather than suspended in the air. The newest addition to Damien's troops padded out of it and the enclosed space was suddenly filled with the smell of brimstone.

The hell hound was about the shape and size of a Doberman, but with a longer snout full of razor-sharp teeth that the runes had denoted as its defining feature. It bore another distinct characteristic that Damien found a little more striking: it was on fire. The portal closed and it came to a stop in front of him, standing at attention with its vivid yellow eyes fixed on Damien's own. This was starting to look quite promising.

"Inspect."

Hell Hound
Stats:
Strength 20 - Agility 25 - Intelligence 5
Constitution 25 - Endurance 25 - Wisdom 5
Abilities: Bite, Dash, Detect, Enflamed.

Interesting. It had slightly less agility than the wraith but was far superior in other respects. It had much more health than his other minions, too: 25 constitution translated into 250 health points, five times more than Noigel had started with. Damien couldn't have called the hell hound a tank, but it was certainly tanky.

The high stamina meant it would deal with prolonged combat better than his other creatures as well. This was a much-needed front line unit. Bite and Dash would be fairly standard attacking and engaging moves. The other two seemed worthy of further investigation. Damien stared at them and focused on his desire for more information. It was much easier to coax the plus symbols into existence now he knew it was possible. He activated them one after the other:

Enflamed: While enflamed, attacks performed by the host have a chance of setting the target on fire, illuminating them and inflicting damage over time. In addition, the bearer of this ability is immune to fire damage.

Detect: Heightened senses allow the user to detect targets up to 50 meters away. The distance is reduced depending on the measures the target has taken to conceal themselves and the user's physical and mental state.

A double whammy of useful abilities. 'Enflamed' looked extremely cool and had excellent combat applications, but the real prize was 'Detect'. An early warning system would prevent him from wandering into ambushes and allow him to maintain the element of surprise. At least it would, if the hound wasn't broadcasting their presence by being on fire.

The ability description said, 'While enflamed'. Did that mean it could be turned off? Damien pointed at the hound and gave it his first order.

"Lose the flames. Now."

The hound gave a quick bark and shook itself as though it were drying off. Flames gone, Damien had to readjust to the darkness for a couple of seconds. When he regained his night vision he saw a feature the flames had been concealing. Rather than fur, this dog was covered in thick black plates. There were gaps in-between which Damien reckoned were weak points, but imprecise attacks with bladed weapons would require a great deal of force to break through.

He was surprised this hadn't been mentioned in the dog's list of abilities and was more surprised still when he checked and found that 'Armored' had replaced 'Enflamed'. So, the dog could swap between being on fire or being more resistant to physical attacks. *Offense and defense. Sweet.*

Damien had expected to trade an advantage for stealthiness but had stumbled upon a completely different advantage instead. The only thing left now was to test it in combat.

"Hound on my right, imps in the back. Let's go."

They all formed up except for Noigel, who disregarded the order and remained on his shoulder. When Damien gave him a pointed stare, the imp folded his arms and haltingly pieced together a sentence, sounding every bit like he was speaking a foreign language.

"Noigel not just imp. Noigel *special* imp."

Of course. Besides Noigel he had three imps out, so Noigel could speak thanks to his 'We Are Many' ability. Damien was surprised the imp hadn't been talking more but decided not to ask about it. His curiosity might be mistaken for encouragement.

He gave Noigel a nod before jogging back down the passage. His minions stayed in position behind him, the hound effortlessly keeping pace by his side. They made quick pace through the already scouted territory and had almost reached the unexplored segment when the hound barked, making Damien jump.

"Hey! What was that for?"

The dog wasn't looking at him. It was staring ahead and growling, its lips peeling back to reveal the disproportionately large teeth. As obvious a tell for the 'Detect' skill as Damien could've hoped for. Since the hound was only matched by the wraith in terms of eloquence, it would be up to him to bridge the communications gap.

"Tap your foot if there's an enemy."

Still growling, the hound deliberately raised its front paw and dragged it against the ground. Detect was functioning as advertised.

The enemy was almost certainly a wolf, given that he'd been running into them constantly. It would be a good chance to see his new summon in action.

"When you attack, I want you to run past and hold their

attention. Be evasive until we arrive from behind, then dash in and engage with us. Do you understand?"

It dragged the same paw against the ground once. Damien pointed ahead. It was testing time.

"Go get 'em."

The hound stopped growling and dashed forward. It wasn't as fast as a wraith, but it was quite a bit faster than Damien expected. He ran forward to catch up but hadn't made it when a yelp echoed off the cavern walls. Using a bit more of his stamina to increase his pace, he came across the skirmish as he rounded the corner.

The hound had tried its best to follow Damien's instructions, but it hadn't gone exactly as planned. Not least of all because the target was a bear.

Damien hadn't thought he could hate this cave any more than he already did, but now it had decided to dump a high-tier enemy on him only when he committed his highest-cost unit. The wolves he'd been running into had about two hundred health each. This bear was endowed with a thousand points of life, with strength and stamina in good measure. It was no stretch to define it as a deadly encounter.

The hound had managed to get past, but not unharmed. Plates covering one side of its body had been shattered to pieces and although it was standing its ground and snarling it had lost a third of its health.

Damien had no intention of risking himself against an enemy this strong, but the hell hound wouldn't last by itself. There was only one thing for it. Damien pointed at the three imps standing behind him then thrust his finger at the bear, willing them to go for the head. The three of them rose without hesitation before flinging themselves into battle on their wings.

They didn't do much damage, but by scratching all around the bear's face they obscured its vision. The bear lashed out around itself with powerful sweeps of its huge paws, but the imps were too nimble and small for the strikes to connect, quickly changing position whenever they saw the bear committing to a new blow.

The bear reared back, allowing the hell hound to jump up and seize it by the throat between its powerful jaws. Then it thrashed violently to inflict as much carnage as possible.

Roaring with pain, the bear lashed out, but the hound immediately released its grip and pushed off, avoiding being caught before it twisted back into position to wait for another opening. A fifth of the bear's health bar was now empty and it was also taking bleeding damage.

This was going well. As long as they stayed in control they could wear it down like this. Damien reinforced his command to the imps, telling them to attack from above in the hopes of providing the hound another opening.

One of them moved too carelessly during the transition and managed to drift straight into a sweeping claw, spiraling away before collapsing in the dirt. The attack had not been targeted and the imp managed just barely to survive, but it was battered, broken and incapable of fighting on.

Damien still had a use for it, though. This was exactly the kind of scenario he'd envisaged using Implosion for when he'd first read the skill's description.

He pointed at the wounded imp and prepared to cast. A bright red circle immediately appeared around it on the floor, showing the range of the spell. The circle was brighter toward the outside than the center, reminding Damien it would pull targets at the edge of its range more powerfully. The problem was, all his own minions were also still in range.

"Hound, back to me, then imps back to me when the hound is clear. Go!"

The hound darted past while the bear was still preoccupied with the last two imps. As soon as the hound made it past under their combined distraction, the imps darted out of its reach behind Damien.

With the minions clear, Damien ordered the injured imp to hold still and be quiet. It stopped trying to get up and froze in place.

The bear looked around and quickly found a human standing directly in front of its attackers. It roared with the depth and volume of a jet engine and dropped to all fours as it charged, the ground trembling under its advance. Damien waited as long as he dared. If the power was strongest toward the outside of the ring, he couldn't afford to get this wrong. A sub-par effort would not be enough to stop a half ton of angry fuzzy wuzzy.

The bear reared up, ready to bring down a paw the size of a small refrigerator onto this new, flimsy adversary.

"IMPLOSION!"

There was a crack like a sonic boom and a jagged tear ripped between dimensions above Damien's fallen imp. While the portals his summons regularly traveled through were perfectly formed and utterly balanced, this one was more unstable than a two-legged chair with low self-esteem.

The crack was followed by a loud bang as reality caved in around it, widening what had been a hairline fracture into a gaping exit wound in the fabric of the universe. The imp was quickly pulled through and the anomaly snapped shut, but not before it had seized upon everything that wasn't nailed down within its vicinity. The force Implosion exerted on objects at optimal distance was phenomenal.

Clumps of dirt were torn from the earth, pebbles and loose rocks in the walls and ceiling formed a deadly maelstrom as they pinged off each other at the imp-losion's center, and the oblivious bear's head, which had been at the very furthest point away, was jerked backward with a sickening snap. It was as if it had reached the end of an invisible, unbreakable chain.

The hell hound's reaction was instant, triggered by instinct rather than waiting for Damien to put it into words. While the bear staggered backward on its hind legs, the power behind its charge utterly nullified, Damien's newest summon demonstrated why it could only be a product of hell. In two short strides and one savage leap it cannoned into the exposed throat, sweeping the huge enemy off its feet. It set upon the bear with such unfathomable violence that Damien was compelled to utter a moan of awe, tempered by pity.

The bear convulsed on the ground under the combined efforts of Damien's forces. It had been a powerful brute of a creature that he had absolutely no business fighting, but he was still surprised when its death heralded an explosion of soul energy and experience. He'd had no idea that his abilities could harmonize with such devastating effect.

His experience rose by almost 2000 points, the same as he might have expected for completing a rudimentary quest. The cavern practically glowed silver with the quantity of soul energy left behind by this worthy foe, all of it gathering up in a cloud that streamed into Damien's free hand in long spiraling lines. It had granted him three souls all by itself. Damien knew exactly what they were good for. He summoned another hell hound, bringing his unit count up to 9/10.

The rest of the cave was considerably easier after that.

19

TWO BIRDS, ONE STONE

After another ten minutes of dodging large encounters and ploughing through small ones, they finally found the way out. Damien suspiciously swept for spider webs before entering zone two of the human race: Brociliande. Or as players preferred to call it, 'Bro's Land'.

While Tintagel consisted of wide open plains with scattered lakes and hills, this zone was a luscious forest. The trees were widely spaced and the foliage was not too thick, but they'd still serve better at hiding his movements than the open plains of Tintagel.

Damien was fully loaded with souls so at least that was one less thing to worry about, even if it had taken twice as long as he'd planned. The raid was about to start and he was still fifteen minutes away. He'd missed the opportunity to scout out his enemies, and the further Rising Tide went into the dungeon the more opportunities he'd miss to ambush them.

He slowed down as he neared the waypoint on his map, not wanting to be spotted having come all this way. The Maw was set at the bottom of a gigantic sinkhole situated at the edge of the zone. Damien had found it on his first play-through when he'd gone sightseeing.

It was no less beautiful than the first time he saw it. Thick green vines ran down the face of steep white cliffs, giving way to a lush mossy cauldron of life below. There was a modest water-fall trickling down the eastern side, feeding a stream that passed through the middle into a rocky opening that dominated the entire west face.

This was the entrance to The Maw. Stalactites of all shapes and sizes hung down from it, granting it the appearance of a monstrous mouth full of sharp, crooked teeth.

The players were gone, but Damien could see the signs they'd passed through: the remnants of a large campfire were gently sizzling by the side of the stream, surrounded by trampled earth. The early arrivals had probably used it to prepare buff-food for everyone while they waited.

The developers of Saga Online had sensibly ensured people would feel their own hunger and thirst while they played in an attempt to prevent them from neglecting their bodies. While in-game refreshments would have no effect on this, it was possible to cook food that provided temporary improvements to your stats.

Damien ordered his demons to his side, gathering his wits. Just getting here had been an ordeal and now the real challenge was about to begin. He needed to focus. He needed to remind himself why he was here. Taking on Rising Tide was only a means to tempt votes in the streaming contest to get a cash prize to save his mother's life. Failure wasn't an option. Success here at The Maw would grant good footage to start uploading.

With grim determination, Damien approached the mouth of the dungeon and gingerly stepped inside.

It wasn't as dark as he'd hoped. Stalactites in the ceiling were embedded with green glowing crystals that cast a pulsing glow over their surroundings. The dungeon layout was surprisingly linear, yet also surprisingly large to make up for it. It was about the width of a highway and from what Damien could make out it was approximately the length of a highway as well.

He considered for a moment before dismissing a hell hound and summoning a wraith in its place. Now he had a hell hound for tanking and detection, a wraith for damage and sneak attacks and four imps for interference and crowd control. A more balanced group for the task ahead of him.

He started by sneaking, not wanting to reveal his presence to any creatures the Rising Tide party might have missed. When he found a horde of dead wolves splayed out under the light of a stalactite he moved in to give them a closer look. They might be able to tell him what he was up against. The causes of death varied, but Damien was quickly able to divide them into two groups: those with heads and those without.

The wolves with their heads intact had died in various ways but had one thing in common: they all had a gemstone, the same shape and size as those casting light from the stalactites, embedded in their foreheads. The only difference was that these gems were gray and inactive, much like the wolves themselves. That was strange enough, but the wolves without heads were stranger still: their heads were nowhere to be found.

The same pattern was repeated over and over, the enemies all wild animals either bearing inert gemstones or with their heads unaccounted for. When Damien found a group of three bears, all of which were headless with singed fur around their necks, he finally opted to start running rather than sneaking.

It felt like he'd been running forever when he caught a glimpse of a green flash far ahead. Then, to his horror, he realized the seemingly infinite passageway was coming to an end. A pulsing green glow, more consistent than the flash he'd just seen, was illuminating an entryway into a much larger space.

It was light at the end of the tunnel, but for Damien it was anything but.

By the time he caught sight of the players he knew it was all over. They'd reached the boss chamber already.

Damien's mind raced. There was only one option left. He'd have to attack them while they were fighting the boss.

He was so tired yesterday that he'd foolishly declined to look up the details of the boss fight. He hadn't planned on the group getting this far before he made his move. He hadn't planned on a lot of things that were happening to him that week. 'Winging it' would be carved upon his gravestone.

The nine-strong raiding party moved to one side of the chamber and gathered around a warrior equipped with a lance and shield. Damien recognized the name from the schedule: Rhinohide, the main tank of the raid group. It appeared he'd taken on the role of party leader as well, pointing at players and briefing them before ushering them into position.

Once they'd all gathered against the wall, the warrior went by himself into the center of the room. Hanging above him was a markedly different stalactite: it was larger than the others and rather than being dotted with tiny green gemstones it contained a single gem, this one the size of a beach ball.

Damien was just wondering where the boss they'd been so diligently preparing for might be when Rhinohide whirled his lance around his head and thrust up to strike the gemstone. Light spilled out of the crack and the warrior leapt back before slamming his shield into the ground, bracing himself behind it.

There was a bright green flash followed by a brilliant pulse of arcane energy.

Opaque, luminescent magic enveloped Rhinohide entirely. The sphere dissipated and he reappeared, his health at less than half and his armor sizzling. One of the priests immediately threw out his hands and the tank was enveloped in white light, his health restored, the fire sputtering out. They'd clearly done this before.

All at once, the remaining stalactites crumbled into fragments. Rather than falling to the ground below, the rocks and boulders rolled across the ceiling into a single giant mass of rubble, drawn and held there as if by a magnet.

The rest of the party had been mere onlookers until that point, but now they started to take fighting stances and ready themselves. It wasn't long before the rubble had collected itself into a huge misshapen ball which fell to the ground, coming to rest in the middle of the charred black circle the arcane explosion had created.

It was the weirdest boss Damien had ever seen. Only when it started to unfold itself did Damien realize its true form. A golem.

It rose to its full height, towering over the assembled players. Damien could just about make out the gemstone Rhinohide had destroyed embedded in its forehead, the green shine gone and replaced with the dull gray he'd seen in those animals whose heads hadn't been blown off down the path behind him. At least now he'd solved the mystery of how they'd died. As soon as the golem stood upright the raid party leapt into action.

The fight had begun.

Damien was starting to have second thoughts. The group was a lot more organized than he'd anticipated and he couldn't see any weak links. On top of that, he was the only one there who didn't know what to expect.

They were swarming the golem, the warrior holding its attention while everyone else looked for an opening. Priests focused on keeping the tank alive, occasionally throwing out smaller, faster heals to party members who'd been hit by flying chunks of rock. Melee characters ran up to its feet and wailed on it until they got its attention, at which point they'd run away and let the tank take over again. The mage and rangers kept their distance, pumping fireballs and explosive projectiles into the thing's face, where the other characters couldn't reach. It all looked very well rehearsed.

It was Shankyou, the assassin Damien had mistakenly thought would be his biggest problem, who made the first mistake.

He sprinted around the edge of the battle, watching his footing rather than his enemy, when the golem swung and launched a handful of small green crystals directly across his path. Each was a direct hit. A series of rapid explosions swallowed up the party's highest-level player. The party leader shouted out a single word of encouragement.

"Idiot!"

Damien cursed under his breath. There was one player he

definitely wouldn't be killing today. Yet as soon as the smoke cleared Shankyou was running again, his body coated in a metallic golden sheen. It was a Holy Barrier. He'd barely taken any damage at all. The lucky player threw their team's second priest a wave of thanks as the shield faded, then circled round the boss and threw himself onto its leg before starting to climb.

Damien had seen it all, but his attention was elsewhere. When the boss had turned around to deliver its payload, he'd been granted a clear view of its back. Set between where the shoulder blades would've been was a glowing green gem, the same shape, size and color as the one Rhinohide destroyed before the battle began. The gem was obviously a weak point, which explained why Shankyou was now trying to scale the thing in order to reach it. If the explosion it would cause was anything like the one Rhinohide had triggered it should be more than enough to wipe him out. Of course, in all likelihood he would jump clear long before it detonated, but Damien had a different idea in mind.

"You, imp. You're up. Wait for my signal."

He turned back to see how much progress Shankyou had made. He was spending more time clinging on for dear life than climbing, making what little progress he could in between the earthshaking blows.

Damien didn't want to send in the imp too early. The longer it was there, the more likely it would be spotted, or simply killed by mistake in the crossfire. It was only when Shankyou reached the golem's waist that Damien sent it forward, keeping his commands short, accurate and careful. The imp was to stick to the outer wall and put the golem between itself and the players.

The party was far too preoccupied to notice the imp's diminutive form as it scurried into the cave. Shankyou had already demonstrated what would happen if the golem noticed you weren't paying attention and no one was eager to get berated by Rhinohide. It was no surprise the tank was stressed out, considering he was trying to dodge and parry a mountain.

Damien realized he'd distracted himself and his eyes darted to the monster's back. Shankyou had already finished his ascent.

Even now he was chipping away at the gem with his dagger. It didn't do as much damage as Rhinohide's charged lance attack, but what he lacked in power was made up for with speed. There was a clink that echoed around the cavern even through the din of battle, informing everyone that the gem had sustained serious damage.

Damien's window of opportunity was rapidly closing. He abandoned all caution and urged the imp to get to the gem as fast as possible. The wings immediately unfolded and it flew toward Shankyou in a straight line. It was almost there when the gem shattered and long lines of green light started to emanate from it.

Shankyou immediately kicked off with both legs, putting his agility to use by backflipping away from the blast zone. The imp flew in underneath him and touched down on the deteriorating gem less than a moment later. Damien already had his finger raised in anticipation.

"Implosion."

The rift appeared directly on top of the gem. While the golem was far too large to be affected, Shankyou was considerably smaller. His graceful dive was rudely interrupted and he was torn out of the air, smashing head first into the very thing he'd just been trying to escape from. The collision damage was calculated first, costing him a relatively modest chunk of health.

The exploding gem in his face did the rest.

Shankyou's last contribution to the raid was a confused scream before he was vaporized. Damien's HUD flashed. Experience from a level 23 player rushed to fill his EXP bar and in the blink of an eye he was level 11. It worked! The boss had dealt the killing blow, but as long as Damien damaged them beforehand he'd still get XP for the assist! He could do this!

Back in the fight, Rhinohide was roaring profanity. He had no view of the golem's back from where he was standing and no idea there was any foul play.

"That's a kill point minus, you imbecile!"

Damien sniggered and quickly motioned for another imp to come to his side.

His strategy seemed sound; now he needed to figure out his target priority. As long as he left the tanks and healers until last they should survive for a good long while, keeping the boss busy and Damien's other targets alive. If he killed the damage dealers, it would slow down the fight and give Damien more time to pick them off.

The golem had entered an enraged state as soon as the gem was destroyed, hitting harder and faster than before, but it was also shrinking. It had started the fight as large as a two-story building; now it was shedding rocks rapidly with each step and swing. Rhinohide was dying faster than his dedicated priest could heal him and soon he had to retreat. The moment he did so the whole party broke rank, running around in all directions as they tried to dodge the walking rockslide. No longer tethered by a tank, the golem stomped after whoever happened to be closest.

The movements of the players were fairly random, but it was obvious they were trying to avoid moving too close to each other.

Damien had a solution to that.

He mobilized his next imp, sending it to fly high above so it would be ready to drop down at a moment's notice. He saw a chance to catch three people in an Implosion at once, but one of the priests was among them and unfortunately Damien needed him alive. For now.

It wasn't long before a much more savory option presented itself: the golem had set its sights on a mage and was chasing after her while the paladin followed off to one side, trying to stay close in case he needed to intervene. Damien decided to help him along.

The imp plummeted out of the sky to drop down between them and Damien cast Implosion. The two hapless players flew across the open ground and smashed into each other before collapsing in a heap. The mage took far more damage than the paladin, but Damien only needed to register a little bit of damage on each so the game would define them as his enemies before they were destroyed. Neither of them managed to get their bearings before the golem raised a craggy foot and smashed them into dust.

The first Implosion had been concealed behind the golem's back, but this one had been executed in plain sight with everyone watching. The party might not have known exactly what was happening, but they knew imps and black holes were not a staple of this boss fight.

Fortunately, they had their hands full. The golem had shrunk to half the size and a large green gem, even bigger than the two that preceded it, had been revealed in the center of its chest.

That wasn't all that had been revealed. Magma was oozing between the cracks in the boss monster's carapace, coating its body in liquid death. When it stood in place the lava pooled around its feet, preventing anyone from standing too near. Damien could tell it was the final phase of the fight.

Rhinohide had resumed his role as tank, leading the creature around in a slow circle to prevent it tracking lava over the entire arena floor. Everyone else was fighting with everything they had. It was time for Damien to do the same. He sent in the rest of his forces.

The hell hound led the charge with the imps following just behind, bursting into the cave before charging straight toward the primary healer. The enemy party hesitated, not knowing whether to keep fighting the monster in front of them or the demons attacking from their flank.

It was the ranger, Jinks, who reacted first, taking the arrow she'd already nocked and firing toward the new threat. She was smart, smarter than Damien would've liked. The arrow sailed over the hell hound and Damien thought she'd missed until it sunk deep into the torso of his second imp.

It was a one-hit kill, the imp disintegrating even as it fell to the ground.

Damien only had Noigel to rely on for Implosions now. This ranged player would have to go. The hound changed directions and dashed toward her. Jinks hastily strung another arrow but couldn't release before the hound barreled into her, knocking the two of them into a fresh pool of lava. In a matter of seconds, the pair had ignited. This was not great for Jinks, but the hell hound was used to being on fire as a matter of course. Now enflamed, it latched itself onto the ranger's arm and held her in place as her health plummeted.

Her dilemma divided the party.

Rhinohide was screaming for everyone to kill the boss as fast as possible, but the party's second warrior, Roranoa, had other ideas. He turned away from the boss and ran past it toward the prone pair, obviously hoping to save his comrade. The reserve priest, Dryfus, desperately cast healing spells on Jinks to buy her time for Roronoa to intervene. As long as the hell hound was both biting her and cooking her alive, any attempt to restore her health was futile.

With the hell hound performing admirably, Damien turned his attention to the wraith. The lava illuminating the center of the room had prevented it from joining the charge, but in the chaos it had skirted the edge of the boss chamber until it was behind Dryfus. In Roronoa's absence, he was quite undefended. It lurched forward, armblades raised, the warm amber glow of the nearest lava pool enough to expose it. It would have to act quickly, before its health and stats dropped too low.

Roranoa had encountered a problem, but he wasn't aware of it yet; he'd failed to learn from Shankyou's mistake. He was too absorbed with Jinks's dilemma to notice the boss swiveling to face him, a heavy, red-hot hand raised. Rhinohide called out, trying to warn him of the danger. Too late. The golem squashed the off-tank flat, searing him inside his armor like a burger patty. White light radiated from his armor as Dryfus abandoned Jinks to cast a new Holy Barrier on the errant warrior instead, but the healing spell he was following it up with sputtered and died as the wraith's first armblade passed through the back of his throat.

The remaining three party members were all busy fighting the boss and could only look on helplessly as Jinks, Dryfus and Roranoa fell one after the other.

All that remained of the once-mighty party was the main tank, the primary healer and the gunslinger, Metalstorm.

While the group might have been brought to its knees, the

three of them together would still be more than enough to handle Damien's disruption if they dealt with the boss first. Metalstorm demonstrated as much when he raised his hands, each holding a preposterously large revolver, and pumped two explosive shells into the golem's exposed chest gem. On the second shot there was a distinct clink of shattering glass and a pained roar.

Damien was running out of time. He sent his wraith and his hell hound straight toward the survivors, hoping to deal some damage and disrupt them so the boss could finish them off. The wraith extracted its arm blades from the priest and went straight for the next one while the hell hound ran down the lava track the boss had left in its wake, sprinting between its legs before lunging at the tank's throat. Yet now the party had appraised their new enemies, Damien's minions posed little threat to the higher-level characters.

The wraith made it halfway before the gunslinger swung his hands around and took aim. The shells he used were designed to kill far stronger enemies and it only took one shot for the exposed wraith to be blasted to bits.

A perfectly timed shield bash saw to the hell hound. It was knocked back, stunned and at low health without having inflicted a single point of damage. To add insult to injury, Rhinohide had used Damien's own strategy against him: the hell hound was knocked straight back into the path of the boss and was swiftly crushed underfoot.

With his wraith and hell hound destroyed, Damien could only look on as the three survivors put everything they had left into their attack. They were visibly worn down, having fought for five minutes with no break. Without a stand-in, the priest's healing was becoming slower and slower. He was almost certainly running out of mana. The tank's health bar would spike up, only to be brought to the very edge of zero by another absurdly overbearing attack.

But the gunslinger still had one final trick up his sleeve.

He dipped a hand into his pocket and leapt off the tank's back, throwing a fistful of gunpowder directly at the boss's head.

It ignited upon contact with the lava oozing from the cracks, with predictable yet impressive consequences. The Boulder cradled what was left of its head in its hands, leaving the crucial chest gem exposed. With barely more than a quarter of his health remaining, Rhinohide committed his remaining stamina to an all-or-nothing final lunge. Despite being swatted around by the house-sized boss, his accuracy had not been diminished. He struck true.

A sound somewhere between the crunch of gravel and the tinkle of broken glass echoed throughout the arena. They had done it.

The boss clutched at its chest as green light spilled out between its fingertips. It was going to blow, but Rhinohide didn't even have enough stamina left to run. The gunslinger and the priest quickly ran to his side and put one of his arms over each of their shoulders, dragging him out of the blast zone.

Had they backpedaled and kept their eyes on the boss, they'd have noticed the small red body clambering up onto its shoulder.

Noigel had been parked on the golem's back, dodging the lava flow as he waited for the gem to be destroyed. Now his moment had come. Damien sent him in.

Noigel swooped down and dropped to the floor at just the right distance, putting the retreating trio at maximum Implosion range. Damien said the magic word, and it wasn't 'please'. The players were caught completely off guard.

They were still clutching each other tightly as they hit the ground at the golem's feet. They only took the most minuscule damage from the fall, but that's all Damien needed. Rhinohide barely had time to sputter one final curse before the boss collapsed on top of them and all four were enveloped in a perfect sphere of opaque green light.

When the dust settled, Damien was quite alone. He blinked, not quite believing what he'd just accomplished. It was only when he tentatively checked his stats that the enormity of what he'd done sank in. Out of the nine players in the raid, he'd only failed to claim experience for one. In addition to the eight players he'd managed to damage before their deaths, he'd also managed to steal experience for the boss. He didn't know whether he'd shared it with the three players who had been killed in the aftermath of the golem's death, but either way the rewards of his labors were clear to see.

He'd entered the dungeon at level 10. Now he was level 17.

20

TO THE VICTOR, THE SPOILS

D amien whistled slowly.

"Wow…"

He'd never heard of anyone leveling up so quickly, aside from players being boosted when they'd just started the game. He'd achieved this all by himself. Seven levels in five minutes was absurd.

Shiny clouds of soul energy hung above his victims and he felt like he'd just woken up on Christmas morning. There was enough soul energy here to fill his Soul Well twice over! Too bad he had no way to store the excess. On top of that, there was still looting to be done. Damien reached out to touch Rhinohide's charred remains while thinking 'loot'.

The warrior's body was immediately replaced with a bountiful brown sack, tied at the top with golden rope. Rather than emptying the bag, Damien repeated the process with all the players' remains, turning the battlefield from a macabre open graveyard to a glorious collection of loot bags, each filled with the promise of unknown rewards for his endeavors. He'd receive a random item of equipped gear from each of them, as well as a small portion of their materials and gold, if they had any.

He quickly checked to make sure his headset had been recording and was delighted to confirm it had caught the entire battle. As soon as he decided to declare against Aetherius, this would get everyone's attention very nicely. For now, though, he had better get a move on. He knew the bags would last for about an hour before they faded away, but he had no idea how long the soul energy might linger.

First things first. He pointed at the ground and re-summoned Noigel. The imp spun through at speed and twisted in mid-air, his wings stabilizing his movement with cat-like reflexes to land him on his feet. He quickly surveyed the scene in front of them to confirm all the targets had been eliminated before standing at ease, throwing Damien a thumbs up. Damien returned the gesture in kind before going into his Stat page.

He had 35 unallocated stat points. Damien thought about it, but not for long. There was only one trait he really needed to grow, and that was his Soul Summon Limit. He dumped all his points into wisdom.

Account Name: Damien Arkwright
Class: Occultist
Level: 17
Health: 410/410
Stamina: 410/410
Mana: 783/1210
Stats:
Strength 26 - Agility 56 - Intelligence 26
Constitution 41 - Endurance 41 - Wisdom 121
Stat points: 0
Experience: 3598/17000
Soul Summon Limit: 1/14 - **Soul Reserve:** 9/10 (0/1)

Damien's grin became a little broader. The increase to his Soul Summon Limit was a touch more than he'd expected. The boost in stats had been high enough to push his Soul Reserve up a whole two points as well, combining with the Soul Slot in the dagger for a maximum total of eleven.

As for the loot, he wanted to make sure he gathered every single resource he could. He took a brief look into his skill tree to double-check how his portal worked. It very specifically stated that if he passed through his own portal it would close. It didn't say anything about demons. The gears turned in his head and it wasn't long before he had a plan.

Filling his empty troop roster with imps still didn't come close to using all the souls available to him right now. Gathering souls, he'd found, could be a slow process, a check on the occultist's power. Yet not everyone could be expected to wipe out a raid group alone. He had to pause to regenerate mana after the ninth imp, but at least his high wisdom had also increased his mana regen.

Imps parading around the chamber, Damien pointed at the floor and activated the gateway. The portal that appeared was just like those he'd seen his minions using so regularly, only this one had his base on the other side.

"All forces, carry the loot bags back to my base for inspection and bind yourselves to my Soul Well. Clear?"

The imp battalion immediately went to work. They followed his instructions perfectly, gathering up the bags and carrying them away into the portal. Damien kept an eye on his minion count, watching it drop as the imps bound themselves to his base.

After ten of them had gone through, the remaining four stopped and looked at Damien. He was halfway through repeating his instruction when he realized what had happened: his Soul Well had hit full capacity. The new one had a maximum capacity of 20 souls, but he hadn't embedded any new souls in it since the upgrade. 10 would have to do. He closed the portal to preserve his mana, waiting a few more minutes for it to regenerate, then summoned a new team to repeat the process. This time he recruited two hell hounds and a wraith, as well as one final imp to bring his Soul Summon Limit back to full. There were still a few souls left behind after his Soul Reserve had refilled, but he'd done as well as he was able.

Damien now had a full count of 14 minions at his back, a team of ten imps attached to the Soul Well in his base and a full Soul Reserve. He took one last look around before ordering his team through a new portal, passing through it himself last. As he set foot on the raised stone platform housing his Gateway, the portal closed behind him with a squeaky pop.

The base was usually quiet and dark, but the enflamed hell hounds were lighting it up and the imps had scattered themselves across the room to dance, sing and fly, sometimes all at once. The wraith Damien had summoned quietly retreated to the darkest corner, immune to the imp revelry. His base had turned into a satanic frat house party.

Bartholomew was standing next to the Soul Well in plain view as he examined the huge pile of loot, his face a mixture of surprise and pride. It was the first time Damien had spotted Bartholomew before Bartholomew spotted him. Another victory!

Damien slipped down the stairs past his minions and lightly tapped Bartholomew on the back of the head.

"So, how did I do?"

Bartholomew turned, his mouth working between a grimace and a smile, but he couldn't even pretend to be angry. A window popped up next to his head, looking uncannily like a speech-bubble:

'Your reputation with the Occultist faction has risen to 'Honored'.

It was about time he got a bit of recognition around here. The window faded and he looked back at Bart to find he'd grown an unsettlingly warm smile. It really was quite disturbing.

"I can see why you had little interest in accepting quests from me this morning. Well done. Don't let me keep you; it looks like you have some base management to attend to. Not to mention examining your spoils of war."

Damien nodded and stood in front of his hoard of treasures, trying to decide which one he would open first. He was grateful for the loot bag system. It made life considerably less gruesome than if he had to rummage for goods in dead people's pockets. *Yeesh. No thanks.*

He went for the bag the boss had dropped first, easily distinguished by its larger size. The cloth unraveled itself to reveal a small pile of gold coins, a block of glowing green ore that Damien would've run away from in real life and a clunky war hammer with excellent stats. Damien sighed. Not only was the war hammer too high level for him, but it was also a strength-based weapon. Too bad. It would've been nice to get a weapon upgrade. While it wasn't quite as useful as new gear, at least it looked big enough to provide the iron for Bart's quest quota all by itself. The glowing rock was a mystery. He'd never seen anything like it.

"That's an interesting item you have there."

Bartholomew had silently followed him to examine his hoard, his voice coming from directly over Damien's shoulder.

"Which? The green rock?"

Bartholomew picked it up in the palm of his hand and brought it up to his nose socket for closer inspection.

"I believe I can turn this into a magical artifact for you."

Whoa, really?

Damien knew some bosses dropped rare items that could be turned into powerful trinkets, but he'd never been able to test it in his offline beta. Even the low-level elite dungeon bosses were too powerful to be taken on alone, and the drop rates for magical crafting materials were very low.

"Great! Go for it!"

Bartholomew turned it over in his hand before eyeing the gold on the other side of it greedily.

"It will, of course, require a small fee. One hundred gold coins should cover the expenses, plus my time."

Damien looked at the pile of gold sitting on his Soul Well and a number appeared over it. It was a hundred and twenty-six gold coins exactly. Had it been two hundred and twenty-six gold coins, he was pretty sure Bartholomew would have asked for two hundred gold. It didn't really matter. The artifact he created would have a unique ability on it and could be worth hundreds of times more.

"All right, Bartholomew. Take the gold and make me the artifact, please."

Bartholomew removed a purple bag, inlaid with golden

summoning sigils matching those on the gateway, and set about clawing the vast majority of Damien's wealth into it. *Oh, well.* It wasn't as though he could have popped into a shop in Camelot and used it himself, anyway. Perhaps having a class trainer who could craft items was supposed to compensate for the occultists' inability to enter towns or trade with local NPCs. Bartholomew picked a last coin off the tabletop and Damien was left with twenty-six gold.

"Oh, and it will take me forty-eight hours to finish crafting the item."

The vampire floated away, leaving Damien to grumble alone. Still, it was something to look forward to. If it was really good, it could be one of the permanent artifacts that some of the players had, with skills so powerful they could be incorporated into their playstyles. That was worth any price.

Damien picked through the rest of the gear and piled up all the useless equipment on one side, taking the additional gold into his inventory and leaving anything he wasn't sure about in a second miscellaneous pile. He was about halfway through when he found something worthy of consideration: a dagger with a vicious curved blade the length of his forearm, sharp on the edge with a cruelly serrated spine. He picked it up for inspection.

Shankyou's Striking Dagger
Level Requirement: 19
Durability: 23/50
Damage: 50 + (Agility x 0.5)
Stats: 30 Agility
Description: A dagger designed to pierce deep with the sharp edge before the serrated spine tears muscles and ruptures organs as it is withdrawn. Business up front, party in the back.
Special Ability: When this dagger is drawn out after a piercing strike, it deals an extra 50% of its damage.

Damien read the description and the special ability several times before depositing the dagger in his backpack. Shankyou had good taste. Until he hit the level requirement, though, it would be slightly less useful in his hands than his trusty shattered rib. It might take a little longer before Damien reached level 19, but it would be worth the wait. Especially since he could use a dagger in each hand.

There were a few other pieces of above-average gear, but nothing Damien could effectively use. With all the bags looted and the metal items piled at his feet, Damien checked Bartholomew's quest to see how close it was to completion.

'**Rock? Heavy Metal!** - Gather twenty (0/20) units of iron ore.'

Damien blinked. There were definitely more than twenty units of iron here. Maybe it needed to be refined? How was he supposed to do that without access to a blacksmith? Setting the quest aside for now, he examined his Soul Well to see if he could upgrade it yet.

Soul Well II
Health: 200
Soul Capacity: 10/20
Upgrade Available! Soul Well III
Requirements: 30 stone blocks, 10 iron bars, full Soul Capacity (20/20)

Great. Now he needed iron even more. He was just about to give up and go to Bartholomew for help when he felt something tugging at his trouser leg. He looked down to find an imp had split from the festivities and was vying for his attention.

"Hey, Noigel. I'm a bit busy right now."

Noigel was undeterred. With one hand he continued pulling at Damien's leg while the other beckoned him to come closer with a twisting finger. Damien sighed and lowered himself to one knee.

"Look, Noigel, you did great today, but I don't have much time and I have t—"

"Open your menu, scroll down to the Structures tab and

construct a Demon Forge. Then you can smelt the equipment into purified bars and collect on Bartholomew's quest."

Damien stared at the creature googly-eyed. He knew Noigel could speak in theory but had gotten so used to watching him communicate in pantomime that the sudden eloquence came as a bit of a shock. The imp's eyes flashed as he noted Damien's surprise before he reached forward to pat him on the head.

"You did a good job today, Daemien, well done. Who's a good boy? It's you! Yes! You are! Good boooooooy!"

The imp finished and quickly wiped his hand on his thigh as if Damien's hair might have contaminated his skin. Damien was still frozen in mid speech, but Noigel wasn't done.

"There, now you know how it feels. I'm a demonic entity, not a domestic animal. Maybe if you'd summoned a few more imps before you talked to me you'd know that by now. Anyway, got to go. There ain't no party without Noigel! You should swing by and chat sometime, you know, when you're not 'busy'."

Noigel patted him twice on the cheek and gave him a thumbs up. The gesture was haunting. It was a perfect mimicry of all the times Damien given Noigel positive feedback before, right down to the childish enthusiasm with which he thrust out his arm and the pure optimism on his face.

The innocence of the gesture was permanently marred when Noigel winked at him, turned on his heel and casually sauntered away to join a pack of his line-dancing brethren.

Damien just about had the presence of mind to inspect him before he was lost in the throng. Noigel's intelligence had risen to 75 points. It appeared that somewhere between 15 and 75, Noigel had actually become worth talking to. This thought was confirmed when Damien opened his menu, went into his Structures tab and found the forge available for construction exactly where Noigel had said it would be.

Demon Forge
Health: 500
Function: Run and maintained by a team of imps, the Demon Forge allows occultists to smelt metal and repair equipment

without having to set foot in civilized society. A must-have
utility for the discerning introvert.

Requirements: 30 stone blocks, 1 soul

The information had come at a price Damien hadn't known
he'd be willing to pay, but at least Noigel had pointed him in the
right direction. It was doubly interesting that Noigel had
informed him of the structure's existence before Bartholomew
had updated his skills in line with his new level. Damien
couldn't see any reason why he shouldn't start construction then
and there. He selected the building and set it down in an empty
space up against the wall. The ten imps bound to his Soul Well
immediately stopped what they were doing and went to work.
The countdown to completion lowered and lowered as more of
them applied themselves to the task until finally it was at a mere
thirty minutes. Damien dumped his remaining 10 Soul Energy
into the Soul Well before binding the last five imps in his party
to it as well. The building time dropped to twenty-four minutes.
That would do nicely.

It was already coming up to 2pm. He could leave them to it
and get some lunch while he waited. He was very interested in
talking to Noigel, but that would have to wait until he got back.

"I'm heading out. I'll be back in a little while," said Damien
to no one in particular. But Bartholomew gave him a gentle nod
and one of four imps chipping away at the stone walls threw a
hand up in the air with the thumb and forefinger pressed
together.

He logged out.

21

A FREAKY TIME

A few moments later and Damien was pulling the IMBA set off his head while he collected his thoughts. Things were going well! Once he could smelt iron he'd finish off his base and get back to leveling up. Maybe he'd even have enough time to hit another Rising Tide raid before the end of the day. No time to waste, then.

He quickly gathered up the headset and his other things and exited the pod. Gian looked up from his phone to give him a wave, distracted yet sincere. Damien waved back and slipped on his new sunglasses and the pollution mask before stepping out into the heat of the street.

It didn't take long to find decent food. Wearing the sunglasses and pollution mask instead of the IMBA set was a big improvement. Not only was he more comfortable, his range of vision was significantly better, even with his hood up to cover the rest of his face.

So much better, in fact, that he managed to find a noodle bar he'd previously missed, almost directly opposite the pod hotel. Noodles weren't his favorite, but he wanted to get back to Saga Online as soon as possible so he could keep working.

It was quarter-past one in the afternoon and the place was packed. Damien took a seat in the window and slurped down the carbohydrates as he watched the world go by. Today was going pretty well so far, but he couldn't let up.

First he'd have to finish upgrading his base, then he'd have to go back to Bartholomew and see what new skills he'd acquired, assuming Noigel didn't get there first. Not to mention he still needed to analyze the footage from the Maw and plan his next move against Rising Tide. No, today was far from over. If he worked fast enough he might even be able to plan out another ambush for that evening.

Damien was in between mouthfuls, racking his brain for an evening raid scheduled on the Rising Tide timetable, when he saw two men approach the door of his pod hotel. Had they just walked straight in Damien might not have noticed, but they were behaving strangely even by the standards of pod-hotel enthusiasts.

One of them was a big bald dude, wearing a plain white t-shirt and jogging pants. It wasn't his lack of fashion sense that drew Damien's attention. He was behaving oddly, cupping his hands over the window to unashamedly peer inside. The second man was more stylishly attired, sporting a summer jacket and a pair of enhanced glasses. He walked straight past and leaned against the wall on the opposite side of the doorway, slowly turning his head as he meticulously scanned the street.

The two men had arrived together, Damien was sure of it, but now it seemed like they were taking pains not to be connected. It was only when the big man glanced over at his companion and shook his head that Damien was sure he hadn't been imagining things.

His first thought was that they were attempting a robbery, but that made no sense considering it was broad daylight and there were cameras all along the street.

He'd just discarded this theory when the well-dressed man tapped the side of his glasses and started to speak. The motion jogged Damien's memory and there was a jolt in his stomach. It was the two CU agents who'd come to apprehend him from his home, now camouflaged in plain clothes.

Damien was no longer hungry, but he put his head back

down and kept eating. The worst thing he could do right now was move, even though that was what his instincts were screaming for him to do.

His mind was flooded with thoughts, all centered around one extremely important question. How had they found him? He'd never shown his face, he'd only ever gone outside wearing the… IMBA set…. with the Mobius Enterprises packaging left on the kitchen table. Thanks, hindsight.

Damien buried his face in his bowl. He really thought he'd been careful. Now he felt childish and stupid. He raised his head just in time to catch his pursuers entering what had once been his safe haven.

Without a word, Damien left his half-finished noodles on the table and set off down the street. His head was still spinning and he had no idea where he was going, but he needed to get away.

As he put some distance between them, Damien tried to process what had happened. If he'd been inside a pod when they showed up there'd have been no escape. If he'd still been wearing the IMBA set when he went outside, they'd probably have gone straight to the noodle bar to pick him up.

He'd been so comfortable, so confident, and yet he'd only avoided capture by a hair's breadth. Now he'd have to find another place to log in, which was even more annoying when he'd already pai—

Damien stopped in the street as the realization scattered his thoughts into oblivion and the blood thrummed between his ears. He'd paid the old man with his mother's card. He'd allowed Damien to stay without ID; that alone would be enough for CU to shut him down. They'd get the card details off him in no time at all.

The face mask suddenly felt suffocating and clammy as Damien's breathing became panicked. He needed an ATM. His own meager savings wouldn't last a day, let alone pay for another pod hotel. A signpost at the end of the street with a cash symbol on it caught his eye.

Damien paced down the street toward it, stopping just short of breaking into a run. He didn't want to draw attention to himself when he knew the street was being observed. He got stuck behind a group of window shoppers and had to force his way through the middle of them to get by.

Reaching the hole in the wall he shoved the card in, picking out the pin number and going straight to the withdraw option.

The most he could take in one go was five hundred credits. He punched in the figure and waited anxiously as the machine processed the transaction. After ten seconds that seemed like ten minutes, the ATM coughed out the credits and Damien thrust them into his pocket. That wouldn't be enough. He repeated the process and waited for the second installment, glancing nervously down the street back toward the pod hotel.

When he turned to the screen, it had frozen. 'Please Wait' was still showing on the front, but the archaic loading animation of the spinning circle below it had ground to a halt. Damien tapped the button to withdraw the card and got nothing. They had the card details already and had managed to close it down in a matter of minutes, mid-transaction.

Damien started mashing the eject button and looked around for anything else he might usefully press when he noticed the tiny pinhole camera set into the top of the machine. Not only had they taken his card, now they knew where he was and what he was wearing, with people poised to chase him only a couple of minutes away.

His gut twisting, Damien abandoned the transaction and ran the rest of the way to the busy junction at the end of the market. He didn't dare look up, but he could practically feel the cameras watching his every step. His disguise had been rendered completely useless. If he stayed here with his every step being monitored and relayed to his pursuers he wouldn't last five minutes. He had to find a way out of here.

Looking around frantically, he spotted an automated taxi rank off to the left with only a few people in line. He jogged toward it before slowing down again as the folly of his choice struck home. If the cameras saw him get into an unmanned taxi they could track it and restrain him at their leisure, maybe even redirect it to go where it suited them. He might as well walk straight into a holding cell.

Damien paced past the taxis, suppressing the urge to pull off his increasingly humid mask. They might know what he looked like, but as long as he denied the cameras his facial features CU would be forced to track him manually. That would only mean so much if he was still on foot, yet every other available choice invited failure.

He passed a tram stop and was growing increasingly fearful when a nasal toot on the other side of the road attracted his attention. Hidden down a narrow side street was a cluster of rickshaws, complete with ragged-looking drivers who were hungrily beckoning tourists from the main road. Damien had always found them to be a nuisance; now they represented a small miracle.

Turning back to use a crosswalk he'd passed a short while ago, his heart stopped. The big man was stomping down the street toward him, bald head shining like a beacon as he scanned the crowd and pushed his way through the strollers. Summer Suit followed in his wake, peering around from behind his human battering ram whenever he had the opportunity.

This was it. They were going to get him.

Damien was left with only one viable option. He turned toward the highway with his toes overhanging the sidewalk and glanced up-road. There was a tram coming in the outside lane, only a few seconds away. Damien took a deep breath and waited until the last moment before running out past it.

Damien reached the opposite side of the road and made a beeline for the rickshaws, looking over his shoulder to see if he'd been spotted. His pursuers were still single-mindedly advancing down the road. It looked like he was OK.

Right up until Summer Suit stopped and pressed a finger to his ear, his free hand snatching his partner by the back of the shirt, before slowly turning his head to stare across the road. *Damn.* Damien jogged forward and went for the first rickshaw in line. The driver quickly put out his cigarette and gave Damien a nod.

"Take me downtown. Err, Victory Road."

"Fifty credits, boss."

Fifty? But Damien didn't have time to haggle. He nodded and got into the back. The driver looked at him patiently. Out in front of them, the agents were trying and failing to cross the road. The big one was well-built for pushing through people but not quite so well adapted to weaving through traffic.

Damien fished into his pocket and pulled out a bundle of crisp notes, trying not to drop them from his shaking hands. He removed fifty and thrust it toward the driver.

"I'm in a hurry. And I want to go that way, down the road behind us."

The driver took his sweet time counting the money. Clearly he didn't like being told people were in a hurry. Damien bit his tongue and looked at the main road.

Summer Suit had lost his temper and left his companion behind, reaching into his pocket for a badge which he thrust out toward the oncoming vehicles. An automated car stopped for him and he advanced, just as the driver finally finished counting for the third time.

"Sure thing, boss."

The driver twisted the handlebars and the nippy little vehicle turned on the spot, the electric motor whirring under their feet. Damien looked out the window as they sped away. Summer Suit had made it across and was looking all around himself, only a couple of feet away from where Damien's rickshaw had been at rest. He pressed a finger against the rim of his glasses and was yelling at the wall as Damien rounded the corner.

Damien took off his bag and set it beside him, rummaging around for new clothes. It wouldn't take long for CU to review the footage and figure out what happened. He needed to disappear.

The rickshaw had no doors, but the compartment still concealed him from the outside if he sat in the middle. This would be his best chance. He took off his hoodie and changed his shirt first, attracting a bemused look from the driver.

"I paid you fifty credits for a short trip. The least you could do is watch the road."

The driver narrowed his eyes, but obediently set his sights back ahead.

Damien swapped the sunglasses out for his second pair. The face mask was white on the inside but blue on the outside, so he simply swapped it round and put it back on. He considered what to do about his tell-tale backpack and decided to cover it with the hoodie he'd been wearing. He could carry it in one hand rather than on his back. Anything would help.

As soon as he was finished he poised himself on the edge of his seat, waiting for a chance to leave the rickshaw. Ideally, he wanted the driver to continue onward without even knowing his passenger was gone. That way he wouldn't be able to tell CU anything if... when they tracked him down.

A chance came when they stopped at a busy crosswalk and the rickshaw was swarmed with people on all sides, bringing it to a standstill. The driver was steadfastly ignoring him.

Damien slipped out into the crowd and walked away without looking back. He turned on the sidewalk and glimpsed the rickshaw trundling away out of the corner of his eye, the driver apparently none the wiser.

Yet he had no idea where to go next. He wasn't as familiar with this part of town as he was with the area surrounding his home. All he could do was keep walking and cross his fingers. He found an internet café and gratefully stepped out of the heat, happy to be back on track.

Within two minutes flat he was back on the street again, turned away when he couldn't provide any ID. And so it was with the next place. And the next. No matter where he went, without some proof of who he was everyone turned him down.

Even the regular internet cafés without pods wouldn't let him in, explaining to the increasingly distraught teenager that they needed to provide a clear link to all their customers' browsing histories in case CU called them up on it. Some would at least direct him to the next place to be rejected from, but more often than not they'd fold their arms and offer him nothing but an unapologetic smile.

The sun was getting low in the sky and Damien had walked all the way to the outskirts of town by the time he found his next prospect, down a narrow back street. A dirty sign on the top proudly proclaimed it as 'Freaky Freja's Pleasure Palace – all your virtual reality needs catered to'. It looked like an utter dive, but Damien was exhausted. Any place would do.

He stepped inside and removed his sunglasses and face mask, a congenial smile unwillingly plastering itself to his face. There was a lady standing at a counter filing her nails. Damien could only assume it was 'Freaky Freja' herself, judging by her green hair and the multiple piercings and tattoos. Even her eyebrows were dyed green.

"Hi, do you have pods here? I'd like to stay twenty-four hours, please."

The woman looked up at him and immediately went back to what she was doing.

"Sorry, kid, this isn't the kind of establishment you're looking for. Beat it."

Damien held the smile and stepped up to the counter, folding his arms on it and staring straight at her. The lady rolled her eyes and sighed but otherwise showed no signs of acknowledging his presence.

"It's exactly the kind of place I'm looking for. Don't worry, I'm not looking to do anything… freaky. I just want a quiet place to play my game. I've got my own headset and everything."

"Great. Take it somewhere else."

Damien checked the price list behind her. A hundred credits a night for a pod, fifty to rent a headset, two hundred and fifty to rent something called a 'sanitized crotch-scanner'. There were other options, but that was as far down the list as Damien felt like going.

He could see why she wasn't interested in him staying. Besides obviously being a minor, he'd be taking up space that might be used by someone who'd pay more. He reached into his pocket and sorted through his notes before holding out a hundred and fifty. It was a lot, but he was so tired. He had to try.

"I'll pay for a headset as well. You won't even have to give it to me."

Freja stopped filing and looked between him and the money. Then she wordlessly extended her hand to him, palm up. Damien handed it to her and she counted it before giving him a last look and depositing it in her desk.

"All right, but no coming out after 9pm. I don't need my customers getting antsy about some teenager running around. I get any complaints, I'll have to throw you out. Copasetic?"

Damien didn't have a clue what copasetic was, but it sounded good. He nodded eagerly and relaxed. He could finally get off his feet.

"And I'll need some ID."

Damien's face fell. He didn't even need to say anything before Freja was rolling her eyes again.

"Seriously? Come on, man, I've got CU crawling up my a—I mean, CU is not particularly fond of my establishment as it is, I don't need the hassle. Sorry, you'll have to go somewhere else."

She retrieved the money and slid it back over the counter. Damien couldn't believe it. Just when he'd finally caught a break, it had been taken away again. He tried to keep smiling, but he couldn't do it. He didn't have the strength left to pretend he was happy.

The entire day had been wasted and he was no closer to finding somewhere that would have him. He missed his home. He missed feeling safe. More than anything, he missed his mother. His mouth tightened, his throat clenched and to his shame he felt his eyes start to sting.

Crying wouldn't solve this. Cassandra was relying on him. He'd just have to keep trying.

He reached down and put his sunglasses on before slowly drawing the money back into his pocket. He just about managed to murmur out a choked thank you before he turned to the doorway and trudged miserably toward the street.

"Oh, for the love of— what's the matter with you?"

Damien snapped upright and turned to find Freja had stood up and come out from behind her desk. He cast his face down at the floor, not wanting to be examined when he was in such a state but reluctant to start walking again. He was so tired.

Freja stopped in front of him and folded her arms under her considerable bosom.

"It's a pod hotel kid, it's not the end of the world! Just get your ID and then go somewhere nicer than this, huh?"

Damien could hear her tone softening as she spoke. His last chance had arrived. He swallowed, and then he chose his words very carefully.

"It's not that. My mom's in hospital, in a coma, and... and I'm locked out of my house. So I don't even have my ID. Nobody will let me go anywhere without ID. I can't do anything. I–I can't.... I just want—"

It wasn't hard pretending to be sad. In fact, there was no need to pretend at all. His voice trailed off and he clamped his mouth shut as the first tears spilled out from the corners of his eyes.

Freja stomped off to sit behind her counter and regarded him balefully, tapping her long fingernails against the tabletop. Then she let out an exasperated groan, rolled her eyes one last time and held out her hand while still staring up at the ceiling.

"Give."

Damien meekly stepped forward, trying to discreetly wipe his face as he handed Freja the money again. She dumped it in an unseen compartment behind her desk without even bothering to count and then rummaged around with her head ducked down out of sight. There was a jingle and she returned holding a single key-card. He slowly reached out to take it but she held on tightly, forcing him to make eye contact. The severity of her blue-eyed stare made it feel like he wasn't even wearing sunglasses.

"You don't linger. Straight in, straight out. You need to ask for anything, don't come out of the pod. Ring for service. You look out of your pod and someone else is around, you wait until they're gone before you leave. Don't make me regret this."

Damien nodded and after a tense silence Freja loosened her

grip. Worried she might change her mind, Damien quickly murmured his thanks before passing through the curtain.

What lay behind was a pleasant surprise. It was both private and incredibly organized. His last pod hotel had really been an internet café with a few standalone pods chucked in at the back. This was the real deal.

The entire room was lined with pods, rectangular rather than cylindrical and stacked horizontally on top of each other in sets of four. There must have been at least a hundred of them. Each had a tinted window and neon lights decorating their doorway, bathing the room in myriad colors. It was a far cry from the grungy impression it made on the outside.

Damien checked his key and found it was imprinted with the number six, matching a pod right next to him. Freja had put him as close to the exit as possible. He gasped with relief and clambered inside before sealing the door behind him. It was excellent. The other pod had only allowed him to either lie down or stand; this one had just about enough room for him to sit without his head scraping the top. There was even enough space to share with another person...

Damien considered the plastic-coated bedsheets and the conveniently placed box of tissues and realized that was probably exactly what it was designed for. Oh, well, it was a bed and there was Wi-Fi. That was all he needed.

He was working his way through the various features when there was a light tap on the window. He wheeled around wide-eyed, a perfect picture of the CU agents forming in his mind. It was Freja, which wasn't much better. Surely she wasn't going to throw him out after all that?

Damien reluctantly opened the pod and she leaned down until her head filled the frame. She looked uncomfortable and for a moment Damien was afraid he'd been right. His fear was only somewhat lessened when she held out a jug-sized plastic cup full of thick green liquid.

"Sorry about before. I've never been good with kids. Here, have this. On the house."

Damien didn't generally enjoy being referred to as a 'kid' and he wasn't sure how a cup of sludge was going to benefit him, but his mother had raised him well. He took it in both hands, employing a weak smile to hide his skepticism, and placed it in the alcove of his pod with undue reverence. He obviously didn't hide his skepticism well enough, because Freja's rough demeanor made an instant comeback.

"It's nutrient juice, genius. Go slow, there are enough calories and vitamins in that to last you a day. You look like you need it."

She closed the door and left before Damien could utter another word. So much for customer service. But if it really was nutrient juice she'd just done him a huge favor. He'd had it before, when he and his mother had been tight on money. It wasn't the most pleasant sustenance, but it was the most efficient by some margin.

He took a sip and his face tried to crawl back into itself. Oh yeah, that was the real deal all right. At least now he wouldn't have to worry about food.

Damien smiled for the first time since he left Gian's pod hotel, genuinely and without even thinking about it.

His immediate concerns had all been taken care of. Somehow, against all the odds, he was still here. He had to make the most of it. He forced one last slurp of NJ down his throat, fighting the urge to chew, and pulled his IMBA set out of his bag. There was no time to rest. Not yet. He had a guild to destroy.

22

UNTAPPED RESOURCES

S afely inside his new pod for the evening, Damien pulled the SIMBA set on, closed his eyes and opened them again within his base.

A portal appeared on either side of him and the wraith and two hell hounds he'd declined to bind to his Soul Well emerged from two separate portals to greet him. The imps chattered at each other excitedly, glad to see their master had returned.

All except one.

"Where have you been, Mr. 'I'll be back in a little while'? What time do you call this?"

Damien wasn't actually sure. He hadn't been keeping track. He opened his menu and let out a low whistle. 17:43. He'd been on his feet for the better part of five hours.

"Hey! Don't open your menu when I'm talking to you! That's just rude."

Damien closed the menu again and looked down to find Noigel with his arms folded, tapping his foot impatiently. This was the second time Noigel had mentioned the menu. Very interesting.

Still, it could wait until after he'd put his base-building back on track. His Demon forge had been completed and the imps had even dragged the equipment due for smelting next to it. Damien ignored Noigel and pointed instead at the forge.

"Imps, take all the equipment to the forge and smelt it down. Leave the materials next to the forge and tell me when you're done."

Noigel grunted and sullenly stalked away to carry out the command. At least he was still obedient, even if he'd turned into a complete smartass. Damien decided the rest of the imps could manage without him for a minute or two.

"Not you, Noigel. Come with me. We're going to have a little chat."

Damien led Noigel up the stairs of the Gateway. From there, he'd have a good view of the forge. Noigel flew to the top and was once again tapping his foot by the time Damien made it there himself. The imp glanced at his bare wrist before looking up and shaking his head in mock disgust, a smirk on his face and a twinkle in his eye. Damien reached the top and folded his arms, looking down at him.

"So, you wanted to talk. Here's your chance. What do you want to talk about?"

"Why, I want to talk about me, of course! You've been neglecting me over the last couple of days. We should have done this a while ago. Fortunately for you, I'm a very patient imp."

Damien pinched the bridge of his nose. Noigel was even more conceited than he'd imagined. The imp's increased intelligence had made him go from irritating to almost unbearable. It had also inflicted a number of changes on the way he presented himself. Noigel was no longer a knuckle dragger, instead standing fully upright like a human being. The nasal quality of his voice had also diminished almost to nothing, although it was still a bit squeaky around the edges.

"My bad, but if you haven't noticed I've been a little busy lately. You serve me, not the other way around. Try to remember that."

"Oh, but I know very well! And how sad it is you've left me unable to serve you at full capacity for so long. Throwing me into battles, trying to use me as bait – menial tasks that any imp could perform! But that's OK, you got there in the end. I forgive you."

"I don't need your forgiveness. I need to know what supposedly makes you better than other imps. Spill."

Noigel's jaw went slack.

"Did you miss the part where I was talking to you?"

"I already have Bartholomew if I want someone to talk down to me. Your ability to speak is not particularly useful. If that's all, I have a base to run."

Damien turned and made for the steps. He'd only taken a single step before Noigel screeched in protest.

"*Wait!* Ahem. Wait. I'll spell it out for you. I possess Forbidden Knowledge."

That was more like it. Damien turned back and stared at Noigel, tapping his foot and looking at his wrist. The imp scowled at him before relenting.

"Like you, I am not originally of this world. When my intelligence hits a certain threshold, I see things as they are. Stats, levels, skills – everything."

Damien stopped tapping his foot. That did sound useful. It also explained how Noigel had known about the menu. Damien pointed at Noigel and inspected him. The imp's stat window popped up above his head. To Damien's surprise, the imp nonchalantly strolled forward and the stat window remained in place.

Noigel then turned around, his hands clasped behind his back, and started reading his own information. He scanned the window for a few moments before pointing out a new ability Damien hadn't noticed. 'Forbidden Knowledge'.

"There, see? Just like I said."

Damien abandoned all pretense of disinterest. Noigel was self-aware. Well, at least to some degree. He knew game mechanics and could read pop-up windows. Bartholomew had known Damien didn't live in Arcadia and wasn't even surprised by logouts, but had never been able to give direct answers to his questions. The vampire had to skirt around instead, trying to explain gaming mechanics in terms of magic and mysticism. Noigel was several stages beyond that.

"What's the threshold for you gaining Forbidden Knowledge?"

"Fifty points of intelligence. Or nine imps, plus me. That's when information boxes start appearing and your menu functions make themselves known."

That made sense. If Damien had been playing at a more leisurely pace he'd have bound nine imps and Noigel to his Soul Well by now, discovering all this at a much earlier level. While other players might be able to ask various NPCs and guild-mates for guidance, the occultist class was a little more... reclusive. Noigel's Forbidden Knowledge was a clever way of balancing that out.

"This is good to know. Thank you for the information."

Noigel gave him a mock bow, complete with a flourish of his hand.

"My pleasure. Also, your materials have been processed."

Noigel had no sooner finished speaking than an imp landed on the platform next to Damien, saluted smartly and pointed down. Damien followed its finger and was most pleased. The iron bars had been stacked into pyramids at the foot of the forge. A brief inspection gave Damien the exact number: Fifty-two bars. It was more than enough to complete Bartholomew's quest and fuel his own construction needs.

"Master, might I make a suggestion?"

Damien converted his laughter into a choking, whooping cough and looked back to Noigel, his eyes watering. He'd never been called 'master' before.

"Yes, Noigel, what is it?"

"If you tell me what you wish to build or upgrade, you can queue the orders with me and I can issue them on your behalf, leaving you free to do other things."

"So, you're a minion management UI as well?"

"What's a yew eye?"

Okay, so he wasn't entirely self-aware. Damien decided that was a conversation for another day and looked down upon his base. The Soul Well needed upgrading. He needed to hand in his quest and see if there were any new skills for him to learn.

Bartholomew would normally have made an appearance by now. Strange. He could leave the construction to Noigel while he went to seek him out.

"Alright then, Noigel, something simple to start. Go tell the imps to upgrade the Soul Well."

"Sure thing! One augmented Soul Well coming right up!"

He leapt off the side of the Gateway and glided down until he was standing on top of the Soul Well. A harsh bark attracted the attention of the idle minions, who gathered around him in a circle. Noigel switched to his demonic tongue, babbling at them in a measured tone. Then, without warning, he screeched at them at the top of his lungs, stamping his feet and thrusting his claw at the structure below him.

The imps immediately set to work as Noigel chased them around and berated them in a seemingly endless tirade. He was a dictator through and through. It seemed to work, though. Damien watched the timer on the Soul Well get lower and lower as Noigel harassed them until finally it was at a mere five minutes.

The imps were working far faster than they ever had when Damien asked them nicely. He nodded in satisfaction and glanced at the entrance to Bartholomew's boss floor. The vampire still hadn't made an appearance.

Time to pay him a visit for a chang—

"I hope you don't take everything Noigel says too seriously."

Damien groaned and turned around. Bartholomew was standing in the middle of the platform, exactly where Noigel had been until a few moments ago.

"Could you stop doing that? Please? How long have you been here?"

"He's very useful, but he does tend to drivel on about 'levels' and 'experience points' when he gets too full of himself. I think it's an attempt to drive people to insanity, personally. Fortunately, I'm immune to such feeble mind games."

Yeah, I bet you are, thought Damien.

"Don't worry, Bartholomew," he said aloud, "I think I can

handle it. I was just about to come find you. Do you have any new skills for me?"

Bartholomew looked him over and shook his head. Damien's disappointment was quickly cut off by what his mentor said next.

"I acknowledge your ability as an occultist. It is time for me to step down as your master. You are your own master now. I have one final gift for you: my blessing, and with it, the ability to learn the ways of occultism without me."

He reached out and tapped Damien on the head for the last time. A notification popped up.

'Bartholomew has granted you his dark blessing. Congratulations! You are a fully-fledged occultist. From now on, new abilities will become available without returning to your class trainer.'

It seemed now that Noigel's true abilities had awakened and he was there to assist, the game was phasing Bartholomew out. With this, Damien was a fully independent player.

"Thank you, Bartholomew. You taught me well. I'll do my best to bring you Aetherius's head."

The vampire smiled at him before his expression darkened and he waved a warning finger.

"I still want you and your base gone four days hence. It will become quite disturbing in here now that—well—"

Damien was halfway through raising an eyebrow when a fresh screech from Noigel cut Bartholomew short. The vampire groaned and massaged his temple wearily. Damien just managed to contain his laughter. It would be a shame to spoil this moment.

"Don't worry, Bartholomew, I'll be out of here in no time."

His old mentor nodded approvingly.

"You can always come find me if you wish for more tasks, or advice. I look after my own."

That was... oddly touching. It was strange, but Damien felt a little less alone.

"Thank you. Really. I might just take you up on that."

Bartholomew gave him a respectful nod and drifted past him down the steps. Damien remembered the last item on his agenda at the last moment and called out after him.

"Bartholomew! You can pick up the iron you wanted for your quest if you like. It's right over there, by the forge."

Bartholomew paused on the steps and looked over at the forge, where a large portion of the imps were clustered in a frenzy of activity. At some point Noigel must have used the forge to kit them out with hammers and pickaxes and now they were clanging away like there was no tomorrow. Bartholomew winced with every blow. Damien quickly thought better of his suggestion.

"Actually, you know what, I'll just bring—"

Bartholomew demurely raised a hand toward Damien without bothering to look back at him. It was polite, but it demanded silence. He floated the rest of the way down the steps and turned toward the forge. At his approach, Noigel's screeching died in his throat and all the imps came to a total standstill. It went from raucous activity to deathly silence in the blink of an eye. You could have heard a flea fart.

Bartholomew picked his way through the workers, stopping in front of the mountain of iron before withdrawing the small purple bag from his cloak. He held it out in front of himself with one hand and swept iron bars into it with the other, humming to himself cheerfully all the while. The bag appeared to have an endless capacity, allowing Bartholomew to get every single one of the twenty bars into it without so much as a sag in the fabric.

Damien got his notification that the quest was complete and Bartholomew departed without looking back. Damien smirked. What a show-off. The moment Bartholomew crossed the threshold of Damien's base, Noigel screeched with ludicrous intensity and the imps returned to work at twice the pace.

The imps were putting the finishing touches to his Soul Well as Damien headed down the stairs. Two days ago it had been a shoddy pile of rocks. Now it was an obsidian altar set on a plinth of cold iron. A far more fitting centerpiece. Noigel was examining his team's work, flicking imaginary specks of dust from the altar's surface.

Damien looked from the Soul Well to his dwindling pile of iron. Between the construction materials, the tools his imps had been using and Bartholomew's quest, the majority of it was already gone. Damien had no problem with that. There was no point in hoarding materials when he could be using them instead. Even so, considering what he'd had to do in order to get them, Damien had hoped it would last a little longer.

"Noigel, how much iron do we have left?"

"Sixteen bars," Noigel said without looking up from his imaginary dusting. "The party we fought was pretty well equipped. Lucky for us! Do you want me to use five iron bars to make you an item chest? You can store all your stuff in there, ya know, rather than having it lying around outside."

"No, I'd rather save it for now. Is there anything we can use instead?"

Noigel snapped his fingers.

"There are those trees outside The Downward Spiral. We can make an item chest with wood instead. You should go with a team now and bring back some wood for construction."

Damien frowned.

"Why do I need to go?"

"Have you seen your imps? They need adult supervision if they're going to get anything done. Not to mention it's a long way to the top. They'll follow instructions less precisely if you aren't close by."

That sounded like a good reason. Nevertheless, Damien had bigger priorities than keeping his base tidy.

"It'll have to wait until I come back, then. I need to plan our next move. You're in charge while I'm gone. I'll be back as soon as possible."

Damien went into his menu and was hovering over the logout button when Noigel spoke.

"Err, master, if you don't mind my asking, why do you need to leave in order to plan our next move?"

Damien closed the menu and looked back at Noigel,

scratching his chin. How much could Noigel actually understand?

"I need to use the internet to cross-reference information from Rising Tide's raid schedule with online resources pertaining to the dungeons they'll be running tomorrow and the details of their party."

Noigel stared at him blankly.

"I'm sorry, master, that seems awfully strange to me…"

Damien chuckled to himself and opened his menu to log out again. Noigel wasn't as clever as he thought. No surprises there.

"….because there's a perfectly good internet browser you can use right here. It's in your 'Settings' tab. From there go to 'Connections', then 'External Browser'. That way you don't have to waste time logging in and out. Right?"

Damien eyeballed his menu for a good five seconds before wordlessly following Noigel's instructions. The little git was right. Tucked away two sub-menus deep was the option that would allow Damien to go online while he was still in-game. He'd never even heard of it. The menu closed automatically and a browsing window appeared in the top right corner of his screen, closely followed by a glowing keyboard that materialized in front of him at his waist.

"Oh. Thank you, Noigel. That's very helpful."

The imp was still trying his best to keep a blank face, but his eyes were gleaming.

"My pleasure, master. Oh, and since you're staying, you can accompany a team of imps to get that wood while you do your research. If you want to, of course. Master."

Damien had no response. It was definitely better than logging out. It was just annoying that Noigel was being rude in such a polite, helpful way. Damien had liked it better when he was stupid.

"Make sure everything's in order when I come back."

Noigel gave him a salute that dripped with disrespect. Damien had to contain a groan of disgust as he led the minions still attached to him out of his base. After a brief delay he heard Noigel scream again and the clanging of pickaxes on stone began anew. Maybe he was clearing space for new buildings, or gathering rocks for use in later construction. At least he was industrious.

Damien led his team to the top and assigned them to fell a tree as he focused on the browser, pulling the raid schedule from his headset into a separate window on his left. There were a few raids, but the lower-level ones were no good to him: half the people who'd signed up for them had already met their end earlier that day against him and the golem, optimistically thinking they would live to fight again tomorrow.

There was only one anywhere near Damien's level. It was not to his liking. A twenty-man raid on a level 25 dungeon. This was not good. He'd only just about managed to get away with fighting a ten-man raid today, and that had been with a liberal amount of help from the boss.

Even Damien wasn't cocky enough to believe he could take on a group of twenty people, with or without the element of surprise.

Yet he couldn't spend the day doing nothing. He'd lost too much time already, thanks to CU's intervention. Not to mention there was no guarantee Freja would let him stay in his pod another day. He needed to make the most of it now.

With more optimism than he felt, he started checking the players one by one in the vague hope they'd be under-leveled. His hopes were dashed. He checked the profiles of eight players before wringing his hands in frustration. If anything, they were overpowered for the dungeon they were facing. Not a single one of them had been less than level 25 and some were pushing 30, almost twice the level of his own character.

Damien gritted his teeth. Why? Why were so many people playing a dungeon that wouldn't give them good gear for their level? Whatever it was, it was screwing him over. In desperation he looked up the dungeon, 'Twisted Forest', hoping it might provide some sort of explanation. If the monsters were unusually powerful he might be able to use them to his advantage.

A brief search turned up nothing out of the ordinary. There

were a lot of monsters, as you'd expect for a larger raid, but even the boss was only level 25. It made no sense.

He was still mulling it over when he realized it had been quiet for some time.

He looked up to find his minions had finished harvesting the tree and were patiently waiting. Damien led them back down, passing the traps almost automatically after making the journey so many times, still looking for more information as he went. He found a lead in the third result.

JOIN CLAN GODHAMMER TODAY! Home base in Brociliande with raids every day and exclusive control of the extremely lucrative **Twisted Forest**! Recruiting starts at level 20, apply on the clan website.

Damien clicked the link and found himself on Clan Godhammer's front page, complete with a spiel about the benefits of signing up. It seemed Godhammer had put their main base right next to the Twisted Forest and were advertising it as their own dungeon. The site went on at some length about how Twisted Forest had huge amounts of rare herbs and crafting materials. It was obviously a big selling point for them.

Damien's lips parted as the gears turned in his head, grinding out the answer. Rising Tide was running Godhammer's dungeon, right under their noses. That's why they needed higher level players; so they could do it quickly and get out before they were noticed. That didn't help Damien, though. Knowing the reason why didn't make the task ahead of him any more possible. It only meant that the players he'd be fighting would be stronger, his window of opportunity shorter and the trip to the dungeon more dangerous.

The sounds of construction in his base faded. Disheartened by his discovery yet determined to find a solution, Damien walked in to check the fruits of Noigel's labors. He was met with a terrible sight. He should have seen this coming.

"Noigel? What is that?"

The imp was racked with shudders from the effort of

containing his mirth. The minions had already finished creating the item box and even now were dutifully transporting leftover materials to it in a gang line. Next to it stood a monument that defied god, good taste and common sense, all in one go.

Damien wasn't sure what he'd expected Noigel to be doing in his absence, but it wasn't this. There was a statue of an imp standing on its hind legs with regal posture and a fist pumping into the air. It was slightly larger than Damien and the spitting image of the little bastard standing in front of it.

"I-I thought this would be a good design, mah-mmmah-master. For muh-muh-morale."

Damien had a brief but powerful urge to pick up Noigel and drop-kick him like a football. He took a deep breath and calmed himself. This was an easy fix and he had better things to do.

"I'll deal with you shortly, after I've dealt with something more important. If that thing is still there when I'm done, you can kiss your command privileges goodbye."

Damien strode up the stairs to his Gateway, turning his back on the obscenity blighting his base, and sat cross-legged in the middle of the platform to continue his work.

He did some extra research on the dungeon, trying to find some way of turning his fortunes around. After what felt like a long time with no results Damien grew frustrated.

"Hey! How's planning going?" Noigel asked.

"I only have a few days left to defeat Aetherius," Damien sighed. "The only Rising Tide raid tomorrow morning is too high-level, has twenty people and they're attacking a dungeon in another guild's territory."

Noigel kept his mouth shut but moved around to stand next to Damien and read through the browser with him. After a while Damien forgot the imp was even there as he clicked through one player profile after the next.

This was hopeless. There was no way he could do this by himself. Noigel arrived at the same conclusion, piping up for the first time in ten minutes.

"Is there anyone you can ask for help? This is kinda ridiculous for you to attempt alone."

"There's no one, Noigel. It's just me."

The imp scratched his chin.

"If you weren't an occultist, you could tell the other guild Rising Tide was invading their territory. But they're allied to the Empire, so they're naturally hostile to you. They'd attack you on sight."

Damien snapped. Being told there were guilds besides Rising Tide that might also kill him did not qualify as useful information.

"Gee, thanks, Noigel! As if I hadn't thought of that already! It's good to know that if I decide to give up, I can come straight to you for new and exciting ways to die!" He flung a hand out at the Clan Godhammer page as Noigel bristled. "I might as well send their guild leader a message and let them know I'm...."

But of course. That was exactly what he should do. Except he didn't have to do it in-game; he had the guild's website right in front of him. He froze in mid-speech, the realization piercing through his cloud of anger. Noigel filled the gap, unaware of his master's epiphany.

"Hey! It's not my fault you keep choosing such impossible tasks! If anyone has a death wish here—"

"Noigel—"

"—it's you! Going off on your own to attack an out—"

"—Noi—"

"—post while I'm tapping your head for half an hour, wondering if you'd rather die than cancel your possession! Then for an encore we go fight a golem bigger than an—"

"Noigel! Shut up for a second. You did it. Good job. Well done!"

"—incubus, as if fighti...what?"

Damien didn't answer. He was already scrolling through the Clan Godhammer page, looking for somewhere or someone he could post to. After some rummaging around he managed to find a Q&A forum. Excellent. He could post here anonymously and it wouldn't link back to his Saga Online account. Noigel squinted at the page and scratched his head.

"What's with all the squiggly lines? Does this make sense to you? What are you doing?"

So, his knowledge was confined to official Saga Online resources. That was a relief. Noigel was already enough of a troll without having unrestricted access to the internet. Damien steepled his fingers, considering what to say.

If he told Godhammer that Rising Tide was going to attack tomorrow, they might start guarding the entrance to the Twisted Forest and he'd lose his chance entirely. He needed to put them on edge and have them ready to go without preventing the raid from happening.

"I'm trying to start a guild war. If I can pit Rising Tide against Godhammer, it'll make my life much easier."

The imp grinned from ear to ear.

"Perfect! So, how will you get them on your side?"

"I won't. I'll tell them Rising Tide is attacking their dungeon. Then, while they attack each other, I'll attack them both."

Noigel went uncharacteristically quiet. It didn't last long.

"Let me just see if I've got this right. You're going to attack a party of twenty hostile heroes. And to make this easier, you're inviting another twenty hostile heroes?"

"Yes. They'll weaken Rising Tide's party for me and I'll pick up assists while sitting on the outside of the battle. Better yet, I can attack Godhammer's party as well. Half the danger, twice the experience."

"I don't know how to put this gently, Daemien, so I'll just go ahead. Your math is really bad."

Damien snorted. He knew where Noigel was coming from, but this was a far better idea than fighting Rising Tide's raiding party by himself with nothing but lower level mobs to serve as a distraction. In any case, it was the best plan he had, and he didn't have time to think of another one.

Damien set his fingers to the keyboard and began typing.

Guest02439: Is the Godhammer headquarters going to be undefended tomorrow morning? It's important. Pm me. Thnx.

Now he just had to wait. If he got no response he could continue baiting them. He didn't think it would be necessary. If anyone from the clan was watching the forum, that message would be enough to get their attention. In the meantime, he had something else he needed to do. He minimized the external browser menu and examined the notifications that had been highlighted since his discussion with Bartholomew.

Demon Gate Unlocked!

Demon Gate: Mana cost: 300, Cooldown: 30 seconds – You focus on an imp in your line of sight and swap places. Any momentum acting on you is transferred to the imp and vice versa. Use with caution.

Was this…. a teleportation skill? Oh, man. This he had to see. He slyly glanced at a group of minions that had formed a circle around a single breakdancing imp. It was currently doing the worm. He focused on it and muttered the spell under his breath.

He should have heeded the last three words of Demon Gate's description.

In an instant Damien found himself lying on the floor in the exact same position as his imp had been. The momentum was well and truly transferred. His head whacked into the dirt and he took 14 points of damage. The real damage was done to his pride.

Another day, another poorly executed test. Better to find out now than in combat. His imps diplomatically turned their backs on him, whistling as they wandered off to form new recreational groups elsewhere. Noigel sniggered behind him but managed to contain himself for the most part.

Damien dusted himself off and noted the timer that had appeared on his HUD, counting down from thirty. Thirty seconds was a long time in combat. He'd have to be careful with this ability. It might get him into more trouble than it got him out of.

There was a ping and his browser window glowed at the edges. He'd got a response!

Hughbris(Ghmod): That's an oddly specific question. What do you want?

Damien went into his media page and took a still image of the Rising Tide raid schedule. He cropped out 'Twisted Forest' from the top so only the names of the players and the time of the raid would show. If they knew Rising Tide's target was the Twisted Forest, they could assemble a much larger force outside the dungeon entrance and prevent them from entering. Even so, he needed Godhammer's forces gathered somewhere nearby, ready for action. Their base would do nicely.

Guest02439: Rising Tide is attacking your headquarters tomorrow morning. Aetherius loves his publicity stunts. I just quit the guild - surprise surprise, they're jerks. Here's your warning. Hope you get them. You're welcome.

Damien closed his browser before the mod could reply and reviewed his actions. There was a danger that the players Godhammer committed to defense would be even more dangerous than Rising Tide's party, but it was a risk he had to take.

Without advance warning, the likelihood of them forming a party strong enough to take RT's group head on would be slim, especially on a weekday morning. Damien had also diverted them into their base, not too far away from the dungeon. As long as they were ready and waiting, he could summon them with a simple message when the time was right and use them to block the Rising Tide raid group's only exit. Hopefully they'd take the bait.

He clapped his hands and all activity ceased as every minion looked in his direction.

"Five imps, both hell hounds and the wraith on me. That means you too, Noigel. We have drills to run."

23

STOP. HAMMERTIME

D amien yawned and shifted his weight, the branch creaking underneath him. He hadn't had as much sleep as he wanted, but at least there was no chance of him arriving late. He'd risen at the crack of dawn and shown up a full hour before Rising Tide were due for their dungeon run on the Twisted Forest.

He'd done it for the same reason the undercover raid was scheduled so early: gamers are not nature's early risers. For Damien in particular, it was much safer to travel before the sunrise, what with the benefits of the Shadow Walker ability and the menagerie of minions following in his wake.

It had also given him time to scout the terrain and prepare.

After some deliberation, Damien had decided the treetops would be the safest place to hide while awaiting his targets. Having honed his use of Demon Gate the previous night, it was simple enough to position himself in unconventional hiding places.

His first trait, bestowing wings upon his imps, had made for an unexpectedly useful combination with his latest spell. Damien smirked as he thought of all the tricks he'd learned after just a few hours' practice. Why he'd ever decided to play a warrior was beyond him now.

Sure, the extraordinary strength was a rush, but he was much better suited to the tactical combat occultism provided. It was just a shame he was so squishy. *Well, you can't have everything.*

He checked the time on his display. *Not long now.* The sun had already breached the horizon and light was bursting through the forest canopy, speckling the ground below with a shifting mosaic of leafy shadows. The unfortunate venue for his ambush had forced him to swap out the wraith on his way there: while his tests with it in the Downward Spiral had been instructive, there was no application for what he'd learned in this environment.

Damien crept along the branch until he was covered in foliage and squinted down at the canyon that had led him into the Twisted Forest. This dungeon was markedly different from the others he'd heard of. Usually they were linear and predictable, a single path with mobs all along it and a boss at the end, maybe a mini-boss or two if it was a serious undertaking.

The Twisted Forest had an entirely different mechanic. It was an open arena with enemies spaced out across the map, lying in wait to ambush players. Only when all of them were slain would the boss, a corrupted druid elder, appear at the forest's center. Damien had no intention of letting things progress that far. As long as he stayed near the entrance, he wouldn't trigger any patrols.

He was more worried about his forces on the ground. He'd positioned them in a patch of thick undergrowth, as far from the entrance as he dared, and had left Noigel in charge. Well, not exactly in charge. He'd given Noigel very specific instructions on how to engage. If the imp had any lingering reservations about the plan, he'd kept them to himself.

Damien opened his browser to check on the Godhammer website while he waited. It wasn't very helpful. If there had been any discussion about the intel he'd provided, it had happened internally. He decided it couldn't hurt to post another message. Better to keep them on their toes.

Guest02439: Anybody online? I sure hope so...

It was answered almost instantly, in a private chat window no less. Damien took this to be a good sign. When he saw the author, he went from delighted to conflicted in a single breath. They'd taken it more seriously than he'd anticipated.

Hammertime(GhAdmin): This is Godhammer's leader. I hope you're not wasting my time. Who are you?

At least he had their attention.

Damien was still thinking about how he should respond when the sound of footsteps echoing down the canyon raised the hairs on the back of his neck.

They were here.

He moved the browser off to one side and watched as the Rising Tide raid party tentatively filed into the dungeon zone, warily checking their surroundings.

Twenty heroes, all armed to the teeth and all at least eight levels higher than he was. The tree he'd so carefully chosen to perch in suddenly felt considerably less safe. It was too late to move now. He'd just have to hope nobody had the bright idea of looking up.

With the lightest possible movements of his head, Damien navigated into his media tab and took a screenshot of the full party at the dungeon's entrance, complete with a timestamp. Then he sent it to the private chat Hammertime had opened, his fingers poised over the keyboard, waiting.

Hammertime(GhAdmin): I'm not sure what your game is, but if that's where I think it is, you're as good as dead. I'm on my way with my own group. If you leave now, maybe you'll get out alive.

Ordinarily, Damien would have found the posturing quite funny. Being threatened by people online was a regular occurrence. However, his circumstances did not lend themselves to humor. Time spent out of the game wasn't something he could afford.

Nor could he die here. This was his big play, a way to enter the Streaming Competition with a bang.

He hoped Hammertime arrived before the Rising Tide party set out too deep into the forest. A well-tailored message might elicit the desired haste from the guild leader.

Guest00439: Come get some, if you think you're hard enough.

With a shake of his head, he closed the browser window for good. If that didn't provoke a response, nothing would. The party below him had already gathered around a hasty campfire and were preparing their buff food.

There were too many of them for Damien to pick out individual targets. He'd have to do it the old-fashioned way instead: their classes and levels were easy enough to see and would provide a rough indication of how easy they'd be to kill. Assuming he didn't get spotted first.

There was at least one player he did remember well enough, though: the mage, Krackle, who was the highest level at 29 and the designated party leader. He was currently overseeing the distribution of buffs, ensuring everyone was taking the raid seriously.

Thinking themselves alone, the rest of the group had relaxed since entering the forest. As the broth was shared among those gossiping excitedly around the fire, the veterans moved between the trees, harvesting the herbs and flowers Godhammer had touted on their page as precious, privileged resources. They were organized, but even so it was difficult to co-ordinate such a large group of people.

Krackle had called the resource harvesters back to get their food when the chatter of conversation was cut short by the sound of marching feet reverberating down the canyon. Everyone fell silent and looked at each other wide-eyed. Damien had painstakingly constructed their worst-case scenario. With elite dungeon mobs waiting to pounce in the trees ahead of them and a guild on the march behind them, they had nowhere to go.

It was Krackle who responded first, shouting orders and

pointing, ordering his group into a hasty defensive formation. As the footsteps drew close enough to drown out his speech, the rangers and assassins moved into the trees on either side of the clearing while the other players scrambled into position, melee classes forming a wall with gaps allowing the casters behind them line of sight.

They were still scrambling for position when Hammertime arrived at the head of his forces.

Damien bit his lip. Only a few minutes ago he was happy not to be playing a warrior, but Hammertime was giving him second thoughts. He was a beast. Level 38. Plate armor coating his torso and chainmail on his limbs, signed off with a customized helmet in the shape of a lion's head. The most imposing thing about him was his size.

Damien hadn't quite made it to level 30 with Scorpius, but he'd done his research on the class. Hammertime had clearly taken the 'Behemoth' trait. The technical aspect of this trait was that 30% of your natural strength was added to your constitution. The aesthetic accompanying it was that your character ended up being built like an elephant. It wasn't the trait Damien would have gone with; he'd had his eye on something a little more subtle. Still, he couldn't deny it looked awesome.

The second most imposing thing about Hammertime was the size of his weapon. It was, predictably, a war hammer, but it was unlike any Damien had ever seen. The hammerhead was a cylinder of gleaming black metal, about the size and shape of a keg, with spikes covering the face. It was essentially a meat tenderizer, scaled up several hundred times. The strength requirement must have been obscene.

Hammertime strode forward without drawing it, pulling the attention onto himself while his guild raced in behind to make their own battle lines, blocking off the exit. It wasn't a full raid group, but the presence of the guild leader tilted the odds squarely in Godhammer's favor. He came to a stop halfway between the two forces and addressed the trespassers.

"Did you imagine I wouldn't come?" he shook his head

before scanning Rising Tides battle line. "Who's the party leader?"

As one, the members of the Rising Tide group who were out in the open looked at Krackle. Damien had to stifle a laugh.

Pursing his lips, Krackle hesitantly raised his hand.

"I am. We didn't come for a fight. We just wanted to do the raid and leave as quickly—"

Hammertime raised a finger to his lips.

"I didn't tell you to speak. First, you're going to listen. Then, you're going to obey." He turned away from Krackle to address the group at large. "Which one of you posted the messages to our website?"

Damien screamed internally. Why was he being so reasonable? They were supposed to be rabidly attacking each other by now, not having a discussion!

Krackle looked among his party and received only frightened stares and confused shrugs.

"Nobody here sent you any messages. Like I said, we don't want a fight. Why would we message you when we were trying to do this quietly?"

Hammertime stared him down, but Krackle didn't look away. Damien didn't like where this was going. He needed to provoke them into fighting before they figured out they'd been set up. Most of his minions were with Noigel, but he'd hidden two in the trees around him. It wasn't what he'd planned for them, but it looked like it was up to him to get this started.

He picked the closest one and thought of exactly how he wanted it to move. The imp crept to the far side of the trees and then jumped from branch to branch, making its way toward the Godhammer party.

"I don't want a guild war," Hammertime intoned. "We agree on that much. The only reason I'm here is because we received an anonymous tip that Rising Tide would attack our base this morning. So, imagine my irritation when they message again today, along with a picture of you lot entering my dungeon. It's not complicated: someone here thought it would be funny to rub your little unsanctioned raid in my face.

I've already decided who I want. The one who sent the messages."

The imp reached the tree closest to the Godhammer party and started to clamber down it. Damien looked over the players to make sure it hadn't been seen. All eyes were still on Hammertime.

"Since they've ruined your raid, it shouldn't be too much trouble to give them up. I know they're here, because they took a pic... you know what? Hold on a sec, I'll show you."

Nope. That absolutely could not happen.

Damien was out of time.

He changed the imp's orders and it shimmied around the tree before kicking off, gliding on its wings directly over the Godhammer formation. Damien waited until it was suspended in the air over their heads, prompting a couple of the players to look up as he triggered Implosion.

One of the many things Damien had learned during testing yesterday were the benefits of using Implosion while the imp was in the air. Half the party was yanked off their feet and the whip-crack of the rift was quickly followed by the clang of metal on metal and shrieks of surprise. Players collided and spun helplessly before falling back to the earth, disorientated, unguarded and on top of each other.

While it did very little damage, with one carefully placed spell Damien had thrown them into total disarray.

Hammertime's head snapped around, his mouth falling open in dismay as he watched his guild mates struggle against each other to escape the dogpile.

The Rising Tide party stood frozen, stunned by what had just happened. Before Krackle could utter a word, a single ranger in the trees who'd had an arrow nocked and pointed at Hammertime decided that this was the opportune moment to release. The arrow sailed through the air and pinged off the top of Godhammer's guild leader's helmet, ricocheting harmlessly into the trees. Hammertime twisted back round, fury in his eyes, and took his gargantuan war hammer in both hands.

Krackle clapped his hands together to channel mana. There

was only one way his party were getting out of there alive now. His party followed suit, activating their combat buffs and preparing their own spells.

Hammertime was striding slowly and purposefully towards them when Krackle finished casting, unleashing a gigantic fireball. The guild leader knelt and crossed his arms in front of his face, bracing for the hit. But Krackle wasn't targeting him.

The fire streaked past him like a comet and struck the pile of imploded players directly at their center. The five players who hadn't extricated themselves from it fast enough were totally unprepared to shield themselves from the assault. Those who didn't die on impact were incinerated where they lay.

Damien only shared the experience with Krackle, since they were the only two who had inflicted damage. While Damien hadn't dealt the killing blow, he got plenty of experience for the assists. He rose to level 19. But there was no time to check his stats.

Down below, Hammertime charged straight across the open ground toward Rising Tide's party. He'd activated his second trait, Berserker Rage, and was suffused with an incandescent red glow. He did not look happy. Spells and projectiles that would have killed Damien in one shot were pinging off his armor with all the force of BB pellets.

Rising Tide's primary tank ran ahead of his party to try and do his job, his shield raised up on one side in anticipation of where the hammer was positioned to strike.

That's optimistic.

Hammertime was not a level 25 dungeon boss. Hammertime had not carefully tailored his skills to provide enemies with a rewarding combat experience. His hammer connected with the shield, the shield connected with the tank's face and half a second later the tank's face connected with the trunk of the tree Damien was sitting in. Damien felt the tremor even up in his high branch.

Upon watching their hardiest party member get snuffed out in one swing, Rising Tide broke into two groups and made for the trees on either side.

Damien gulped. This fight was on another level. But he hadn't come here to be a spectator, and two levels was not worthy of the effort and planning he'd put into this endeavor.

He had to make it count.

The two parties had both been split and disjointed skirmishes were breaking out all around him. This was his moment. A movement in the trees on the far side of the clearing drew his attention. One of Rising Tide's rangers was standing on a thick bough, using the trunk of the tree for cover and taking potshots at anything with a red name. He was isolated, and Damien's remaining free imp was only two trees away.

After a brief mental command, the imp landed gently on the branches above. The ranger was so focused on his targets that he didn't realize he had a visitor. Damien hurriedly equipped his newly available level 19 Shankyou's Striking Dagger while keeping his Sacrificial Dagger equipped.

Dual wielding, baby.

Taking a final calming breath, he ordered his imp to drop down. The moment it landed on the branch behind the ranger, Damien stabbed forward with his left hand and cast Demon Gate. He must have practiced the motion a hundred times the night before. It paid off.

His arm was half extended when he cast the spell and he'd no sooner swapped places with his imp than the serrated blade sank through the leather jerkin and deep into the unsuspecting ranger's back. In his haste he'd failed to hit a critical spot, but he still did three times more damage for getting a sneak attack with a dagger.

The leather armor offered little resistance against the strike, but Damien was still surprised to see he'd hit for 182 damage. He was even more surprised when the ranger peered over his shoulder, his health bar still 3/5 full.

Damien quickly stabbed him with his Sacrificial Dagger and used it to pin the ranger against the tree as he struck again and again with Shankyou's serrated blade, filling him with holes. The serrated spine did half its damage each time it was withdrawn. The stabs had their damage reduced by armor, but the 50%

damage for withdrawing the blade suffered no such penalty. In this scenario, quantity and quality were one and the same.

The ranger had barely realized what was going on before Damien plunged the blade into the back of his neck instead. The benefit of hitting with a critical strike was the last straw and the ranger became dead weight, falling out of the tree and tumbling lifelessly to the ground below them.

Damien went up another level. Level 20. That was a big milestone, but he couldn't savor it yet.

While he'd dispatched the ranger, Godhammer had rallied. Their leader had provided them with the space to get back into position and they'd reorganized for the task at hand.

Half of them had returned to blocking the entrance while a well-balanced party of five swept through the area, hunting down the divided interlopers as Hammertime relentlessly chased them into the open. While he was still berserking, it was impossible for Rising Tide to form a cohesive group. It was all they could do to stay out of his reach.

At this rate, Damien would be left with an angry guild leader and approximately a dozen enemies to deal with by himself. This required a rebalance. It was time to unleash his secret weapon. He stared at the priest standing in the back of Godhammer's party and reached out to Noigel with a single word. *'Now'*.

Damien was so invested he hadn't realized how exposed he was standing out on the branch, staring straight at the hunting party. It became apparent when a ranger fired an arrow that whipped into his stomach, doubling him over and almost knocking him out of the tree. He stuck his back against the trunk as the second one whizzed past his ear.

He yanked the arrow free from his torso. They weren't the hardest hitting weapon in the game, but Damien was severely under-leveled to take them head on. He'd lost almost a third of his health and it hadn't even been a critical hit. Great. This was exactly what he didn't need. He'd tested the range of his mental commands yesterday precisely to prevent something like this from happening. Where the hell was Noigel?

"Up there," the ranger yelled.

Damien still had ten seconds left before he could use Demon Gate again. He reached out to Noigel with all his will and re-enforced the command as the hunting party rounded the corner.

Damien had no room to maneuver on the branch. He'd trapped himself.

The other four members stood by as their ranger nocked another arrow and held it steady, taking his time to ensure he got the head shot. His focus was interrupted by a scream from behind them as Noigel thundered into the clearing.

Damien had deliberated for some time how he might best use his remaining Soul Summon Limit. Hell hounds were great shock troops, but without imps backing them up they lacked utility. The problem was that even with their wings, the imps were too slow to keep up. The solution was simple: stick the imps on the hell hounds. And thus, the hell riders were born.

Noigel was the first to emerge, yodeling shrilly at the top of his lungs in a bid to draw attention away from Damien and onto himself. It was certainly a sight to behold. He was riding his hell hound like a surfboard, his tail wrapped around his steed's neck and his wings pivoting for balance.

The ranger turned to see what all the fuss was about and found his vision filled with dog teeth.

Noigel's fury knew no bounds. Seamlessly unwinding his tail, he barreled head first into the priest in a blur of flailing claws to prevent her channeling a healing spell. The moment he left the hound's back, it ignited.

The three unaffected Godhammer members were rooted to the spot, frozen to inaction by horror and confusion. Their hesitation was brief, but it cost them dearly. While their attention was divided between the dying ranger and the screaming priest, the other two hell riders caught up.

The imps lifted off and followed Noigel's example, sinking their claws into their enemy's faces and scratching mercilessly. The damage was trivial, but it interrupted channeling and blocked line of sight while the two new hell hounds joined their predecessor to gang up on the hapless ranger. Then they ignited as well, frying him to a crisp.

Damien leveled up to 21. His health was restored. Most of the party were scarcely aware they'd lost one of their number in the chaos. The only unaffected member nearby was the warrior tank, who was totally unequipped to remove the face-hugger imps without inflicting more damage on the players they'd attached themselves to.

While they reeled from the unconventional tactics, Damien found his personal teleportation imp and cast Demon Gate, swapping back to his original position in the safety of the concealed bough while his imp was transported to the branch overlooking the group.

He took control of the hell hounds from Noigel, directing them to sprint out of range as he sent the Demon Gate imp to fly over the group's heads. Then he Imploded it. All four remaining Godhammer members hurtled into the air along with the ragdolling, burning body of their former team mate.

Despite the Implosion, the hell rider imps had not disengaged and were still clinging to their targets, clawing away like maniacs. Damien's hell hounds wheeled around, pounded forward and leapt into the air to rejoin them, ignoring the tank to catch the more vulnerable party members in their jaws.

The tank hit the ground the hardest and was slow to rise, his armor working against him. He staggered to his feet just in time to bear witness to the full extent of his failure. The priest had already fallen, prompting Noigel and his hell hound to assist in ensuring the demise of the other two. Seconds later the mage and assassin joined their healer. Damien rose to level 23.

As soon as they were done, his hounds put out their flames and the imps mounted again before they dashed into the trees. They were unsuited to combat against heavily armored enemies, especially while Damien's Implosion was still on cooldown. Those Rising Tide members who weren't being chased by Hammertime moved in to finish off the isolated player.

Damien didn't feel like putting himself at risk again, at least not until his Demon Gate was available. That didn't mean he was going to sit and do nothing. He lay down flat on the branch and pointed at Noigel's hell hound just before it disappeared from view. Possessing his hell hounds was certainly a strange sensation, but he'd rather that than an imp any day.

He stumbled a little as he transitioned from two-legged and prone to four-legged and galloping but managed to keep himself upright and maintain the pace. Noigel cooed and patted him heavily on the head.

"Whoosa goood booooieeee?"

Damien tried telling him to knock it off, producing nothing but a low growl in the back of his throat. Noigel squeaked out a peal of high-pitched laughter and redoubled his efforts, scratching him behind the ears while they were still on the move. Damien ignited his host body briefly and the unwanted petting was abruptly replaced with a slew of demonic curses. Justice served, Damien led his platoon behind a tree and sniffed to activate his newly acquired Detect skill.

All the players within range were now highlighted in red, even through terrain and cover. It was a wonderful skill for scouting out enemies. Not that there were many of them left. Hammertime was easily distinguishable from everyone else due to his larger profile and tell-tale weapon. He'd split his remaining forces in half again, taking two players with him while the other three continued to watch over the only exit.

On the other side of the clearing, the last seven Rising Tide members were licking their wounds, using the scarce time available to them to prepare for the inevitable onslaught. Damien didn't like to admit it, but he'd need their help to stop Hammertime. While Damien's minions and daggers were very effective against unguarded targets with mid-level armor and low health points, he had very little in his skill set to deal with a level 38 behemoth. That was a task better suited to magic damage, which Krackle had demonstrated he possessed in abundance.

Damien followed the profiles of the three-strong Godhammer party and caught sight of them through the trees. He was relieved to see Hammertime's berserker rage had ended, although his choice of team mates went some way toward compensating for the loss of his special ability.

The guild leader had hand-picked a paladin and a mage, both

standing a short distance behind him on either side. The paladin was likely specced to heal. If something wasn't done about him, Hammertime would be practically impossible to bring down. The Rising Tide party clearly agreed, because one of their number stepped out from behind a tree and loosed a charged arrow straight toward the paladin's chest.

Hammertime casually thrust his arm out to the side and intercepted it, the arrow piercing the chainmail and digging into his forearm. His armor level was now weak enough for projectiles to pierce him. Not that it made much difference when his constitution was so disproportionately high.

The paladin channeled mana to restore the sliver of health the arrow had taken away, while Godhammer's mage moved even faster, sweeping her staff out in front of her to launch a volley of arcane missiles from the tip. The enemy ranger hadn't even finished nocking his second arrow before the projectiles locked on and he exploded in a cluster of blue light.

The rest of Rising Tide ran out to make their last stand and Hammertime stepped between them and his team mates. The mage began buffing him with an anti-magic aura. After Krackle's first fire-bomb, Hammertime had chosen his support very carefully before moving to mop up the survivors.

The healer was bad news, but the anti-magic aura the mage was providing was even worse, countering Hammertime's only weakness.

Damien lurched out of the trees so fast that Noigel almost fell off, the other two hell riders falling in behind him. He needed to take care of that mage if they were going to have any chance. All three players were completely focused on the party in front of them.

Noigel wisely stayed quiet this time as they approached, and Damien got his Sneak Attack in, headbutting the back of the mage's head at full tilt. The collision hurt him as well, but the hound's armored plates negated a fair portion of the damage. He wasn't prepared to use his bite attacks on another player – that was just a little too weird to contemplate – but the rest of his team quickly took advantage of the opening he'd provided and attacked with full force.

Damien left Noigel to guide them and turned to charge the paladin, hoping to interrupt him before the inevitable healing undid their work. The paladin had a different spell in mind. Without a hint of panic, he locked eyes with Damien and raised his forearm up from the elbow before closing his hand into a fist.

Damien burst into the wrong kind of flames.

They flashed white and gold, searing through his armored plates faster than Damien had thought possible for a spell with no casting time. Damien had miscalculated. The paladin had the 'Smite' ability. Demons were little more than fodder against holy power.

Damien's host body may as well have been bathed in acid. The hound was dead before he could even reach the paladin's feet. Damien's possession ended, transporting his perspective back into his human body.

He blinked and fixed his eyes on the battle just in time to see another of his hounds seared with holy fire – dying within seconds before the paladin started channeling to heal the mage. Damien couldn't afford to lose what little he had left. He disengaged his three imps and sent them high into the air, ordering the last hell hound to attempt a last-ditch effort to kill the mage.

It did not go as well as it might have. Hammertime sprinted toward the hound, wrapped a hand around the back of its neck and squeezed, ignoring the flames as it ignited in self-defense. He wrenched it off his team mate and pelted it at the ground behind him before stomping on its head with a massive steel boot.

One of Rising Tide's assassins took advantage of the distraction to close and finish the mage off, making good on all of Damien's hard work.

Damien lost experience for sharing the kill, but the objective had been accomplished. The anti-mana aura surrounding Hammertime sputtered and faded. Right on cue, a fireball pounded into the behemoth's chest and he staggered back, visibly hurt for the first time in the encounter. Hammertime's health dropped by almost a quarter.

Krackle was standing at a distance with a healer by his side, providing fire support as the three remaining front-line combat players closed in on the paladin to make their last stand.

Thinking quickly, Damien took stock of the situation. He had three imps left, all of whom were being completely ignored amid the battle raging below them. His spells were all ready for use. He would use Rising Tide to gamble everything he had on a final attack.

Noigel and another imp soared upward while the remaining imp divebombed, landing on Hammertime's head before he'd regained his balance. Damien Imploded it. Hammertime was barely affected at all, since he was in the eye of the storm.

But it wasn't designed to pull him in. Rather, it pulled the players around him. Since the imp was so close to the ground, the range of the pull was maximized. The paladin, the assassin, the mage's body and all three of Rising Tide's close combat units were caught, flying off their feet and crashing into Hammertime on all sides.

The assassin and the dead mage were lightly armored. The paladin and his three attackers, not so much. They did far more damage to Hammertime as projectiles than they ever could have hoped to achieve as players. They struck him simultaneously on all sides, their assorted armor and weaponry inflicting blow upon blow.

The Behemoth toppled, landing on top of the luckless assassin with an almighty crash.

It was a huge series of hits, and even though it was entirely physical damage it still removed a good chunk of Hammertime's health, bringing him down to just under half. The rest of the players were spread-eagled around and on top of him in varying degrees of trouble, but every single one of them was disorientated and helpless.

Without hesitation, Krackle began charging a fireball to maximum power. Killing four of his own team for the chance to take out a guild leader must have seemed like a good deal. Only he and his priest hadn't been caught in Damien's ability, and both of them were completely absorbed by the scene in front of them.

This was it. Damien could end it, here and now.

Noigel sensed Damien's intention and frantically moved to obey, the other imp following swiftly behind him. They glided over the pair before hurtling downward, each of them landing behind one of the distracted enemies. The priest turned too late and Noigel's partner sprang upward, raking his claws across the player's face. Krackle was too busy concentrating on what he was doing to notice. Noigel touched down behind Krackle just as he launched a miniaturized sun at ally and enemy alike, draining every last drop of his mana. He'd left himself completely defenseless.

Damien cast Demon Gate.

He'd learned from his mistake against the ranger in the tree. This time he made sure he got the critical hit. He thrust his left hand forward and drove Shankyou's dagger straight through Krackle's left shoulder blade, piercing him through the heart. As he withdrew it, scraping the jagged edge back through the wound, he plunged the sacrificial dagger into Krackle's neck until it protruded out the other side. Krackle got a free class change, transcending his status as a fire mage to become a kebab.

It was more than enough. The moment he saw the soul energy flowing into his Sacrificial Dagger's handle, Damien knew he had won. Out ahead of them, there was a deep whoosh as all the air rushed inward to feed the expanding ball of flame.

When it exploded, the flow reversed and Damien's cowl was swept off his face by a scalding-hot blast of air. The terrain in front of them had been transformed into a hellscape. The lower level players were all made equal in the blink of an eye, leaving only Hammertime clinging to life at the heart of the explosion. He fought to push away the burning bodies, what little health he had left dwindling in the inferno.

He even abandoned his hammer in his rush to escape the flames, to no avail. Godhammer's guild leader managed to stumble halfway out of the area of effect before his legs caved in underneath him and he fell face forward onto the ground, deader than the century-old song that had inspired his name.

Krackle had done the most damage and delivered the killing blow, but he was already gone. Damien had seen to that. There was only one living player who had dealt damage to Hammertime and the players scattered around him.

Damien's screen flooded with notifications. In a server first, he had gained five consecutive levels. Three when the fireball hit, another two when Hammertime finally succumbed to his wounds. He was now level 28, around the same average level as the players he had come to destroy.

It was only when the imp next to him screeched that Damien tore his eyes away from the carnage and came to deal with the sole survivor of his plan. The Rising Tide priest had no one to protect him and didn't resist Damien's daggers. His life ended in three swift stabs.

That done, Damien checked all around, hardly believing the fight was really over. The three members of Godhammer who had been watching over the exit were nowhere to be seen. They must have fled when they saw their leader perish.

Some forty players had entered the Twisted Forest that morning. Now only one remained. Damien had overseen the destruction of a raiding party, a defensive team and a guild leader who had been more than twice his level at the start of the encounter. He was nearly level 30. All of his careful planning had granted him the fastest solo leveling in Saga Online's brief history.

He opened his menu and checked the media page. There it was. The whole fight; stored and saved on his headset. He hadn't known when he was going to declare against Aetherius, but now the moment was here it couldn't have been more obvious.

Move over, Hammertime. It's humble-brag time.

24

REACHING YOUR TARGET AUDIENCE

Damien positioned himself in the middle of the scorched earth, directly on top of a glowing mass of soul energy. With souls to hand, he started the long, arduous process of re-summoning his minions. He wanted to look his best for his big entrance into the competition. He minimized the menu and set it to one side, opening his Stat page with one hand while he summoned imps with the other.

Despite the damage he'd taken from the arrow in the gut, he didn't see much point in increasing his constitution. His survivability was based on mobility, not heavy armor, so it wouldn't count for much. His agility was already high enough to kill squishy targets. Intelligence was useless to him, since he wasn't using spells from his Maleficium tree. Strength was even more useless than that. And he could swing his daggers around all day without running out of stamina. That left wisdom. It hadn't failed him so far. Damien plugged his free stat points into it, pushing his wisdom to 187.

Account Name: Damien Arkwright
Class: Occultist
Level: 28
Health: 520/520
Stamina: 520/520

Mana: 1218/1870
Stats:
Strength 37 - Agility 97 - Intelligence 37
Constitution 52 - Endurance 52 - Wisdom 187
Stat points: 0
Experience: 18492/28000
Soul Summon Limit: 9/20 - **Soul Reserve:** 10/10 (+1/1)

His Summon Limit was now 20. Beautiful. But his Soul Reserve hadn't increased at all. That was odd. Maybe a base of 10 was the maximum? He'd have to ask Bar—

"Nice work, master! Didn't know you had it in you!"

Damien couldn't help but smile. More than once during the fight he hadn't been sure he'd had it in him either. He had ten imps now, enough for Noigel to assist him with his Forbidden Knowledge, so he canceled the imp he was summoning and started summoning a hell hound instead.

"Thanks, Noigel. You weren't so bad yourself." He winked. "Get all the imps to start gathering bodies in this crater, and stick Hammertime and Krackle somewhere everyone can see them. I'm calling Aetherius out and declaring war on Rising Tide."

Seeing how scared Noigel had been of Rising Tide before, Damien had expected resistance. Instead, the imp snapped smartly to attention and grinned evilly.

"I'll get it done. Oh, and you should check your notifications, O maleficent one!"

Damien stepped forward out of the crater, smirking as Noigel yelled orders at the rest of the imps. If not for his micro-management of Damien's forces, the outcome might have been entirely different. It was very difficult to co-ordinate so many minions at once, especially in the heat of combat. Queuing orders with Noigel so he could carry out plans on his behalf removed a great deal of mental strain, allowing Damien to focus on his own survival. He was lucky to have him.

Damien finished summoning the hell hound and brought up the other recent notifications for examination. Most of them were congratulating him on leveling up, but three of them were interesting.

A new trait is available! Choose wisely.
New building upgrades are available!
Summon Succubus Unlocked!

Ah, upgrades. The spice of gamer life. Where to begin?

The building could wait until he got home, that much was obvious. The summoning spell and the new trait could be checked here and now, since Bartholomew had already given Damien his dark blessing.

Summon Succubus: Mana: 500, Souls: 7 – You point at the ground, searing it with runes to open a portal to the demon world. After channeling for 10 seconds, the portal is opened and a succubus arrives on the mortal plane. The succubus will serve you until it dies or is dismissed. Succubi stats improve every five levels.

More than twice the soul cost of anything else he could summon? He was eager to test it out. At least he already had plenty of souls here. And having summoned ten imps and a hell hound, he had exactly enough Summon Limit available for this new minion.

No time like the present.

Damien pointed at the ground, wondering what form the runes would take this time. The grass under his finger withered and died as an eye burned into the earth. Upon completion, the pupil glowed white hot and a portal expanded out directly from its center, obscuring the runes entirely. The game designers had put a little more effort into this animation than they had for the minions that preceded it. This was going to be something special.

He wasn't wrong. The succubus surged upward through the opening, a twisting blur of red skin and pitch-black, thorny wings. The portal closed beneath her and she demurely touched down in the center of her sigil.

It happened too quickly for Damien to catch everything, but the wings were hard to miss. He now had two sets of flying minions. Off to a good start.

The succubus resembled a human, with a few notable exceptions. The most obvious was the blood-red skin she shared with the imps. Two ridged horns protruded from her forehead, curling round and jutting out in front. She had hooves instead of feet and her shins bent back. What Damien had assumed to be clothing was in fact thick black fur, covering her torso and waist as well as encircling her wrists and feet in a mimicry of bracers and boots. The fingers ended in long black claws.

She set her glowing red eyes on him. They blazed with fire, just like the eye in the sigil that had summoned her here, yet they were also cold and dead despite the unwholesome power they held.

The longer Damien looked at her, the less human she became. But while she looked fearsome, he was more concerned with what she had to offer strategically.

"Inspect."

Succubus
Stats:
Strength 15 - Agility 30 - Intelligence 50
Constitution 25 - Endurance 25 - Wisdom 50
Abilities: Chaotic Bolt, Bloodlust, Circle of Hell

She was a magic user! Excellent. Up to now, all his minions had been agility-based. An intelligence-based summon would provide a whole new dimension to his forces. Exactly what form that might take would have to wait, because Noigel had just landed on his shoulder.

"All done and ready for your inspection."

Damien closed the Stats page and turned around. Noigel had done exactly what he'd been told and it looked nothing like what

Damien had wanted. It actually looked a little bit better, albeit far less tasteful.

"Noigel. I don't remember asking you to spell out my name using the corpses."

"That's because you didn't, master."

"Then why did you do it?"

"Because you didn't tell me not to, master."

Damien looked it over. Noigel had used his gamer name, Daemien, as the core of the display. Krackle and Hammertime had indeed been given pride of place, joining forces in death as they had proven incapable of doing in life to form the first letter. Many of the other players had been contorted into silly poses to fulfill Noigel's artistic vision. The unfortunate players who'd been selected to form the 'e's looked particularly stupid. Hammertime's weapon had been placed heavy side down with the handle pointing at the sky to form the full stop of an exclamation mark. Those who hadn't made the cut for the literacy club were laid out around the outside in a circle. It should have been macabre, but actually it ended up being quite funny... in a 'Noigel' sort of way.

Damien glanced around before beginning his speech. As important as this was, he wanted to get it over and done with quickly. There was no telling when more people might show up.

He gave Noigel a nod and the imp flew into position, hovering above and looking down. Not everything Damien had taught himself yesterday was combat orientated. With a little bit of guidance from Noigel, he'd learned how to record videos from the perspective of summons under his control. Most players would use a Mana Wisp specifically for the task, as Aetherius had when they'd first met. Damien had plenty of his own summons already.

As Noigel came to a stop, Damien removed his cowl and looked directly up at his imp. A mini-window showing Noigel's perspective showed up in his HUD and a second red recording light appeared next to his own that was constantly on. The minion cam would only work at a short distance to prevent using it to scout ahead, but since that applied to other players as well it was no bad thing. He'd had a long time to think about what he wanted to say, running over it in his head every night while he struggled to sleep. Damien threw his hands out to either side and a smile crept unbidden to his lips.

"Good morning, and welcome to the first episode of 'Damien's Not Dead, But a Whole Lot of Other People Are'. Unfortunately, just like when he chickened out of fighting Toutatis, Aetherius couldn't make it today. Maybe next time."

Noigel dropped down until Damien filled the screen from the waist up. Damien took a deep breath. He had a lot of anger to vent at a large audience. The preparations had taken half a week. He was going to make the most of it.

"Since Aetherius was a no-show, I've secured one of his raid leaders to give us an interview. Just minutes ago, Krackle was conducting a daring raid into Godhammer's Twisted Forest with twenty Rising Tide players at his command. How do you think they fared? Let's ask the man himself!"

Damien crouched down over Krackle's body and put on his most deeply serious face.

"Hello, Krackle, thanks for joining us on the show. How are you holding up? That's fantastic. Listen. Remember when you fire-bombed four of your own party members to try and save your own skin? Learned that from Aetherius, did you? Betraying players who were relying on you for help? How did that go? Oh. I see. Thanks for your time!"

He stood up and looked directly at Noigel again. He put a finger to his ear.

"And this just in, we have a surprise guest! I'm proud to introduce the one and only Hammertime! Leader of Godhammer and self-appointed guardian of the Twisted Forest! I'm sure we could all use some words of wisdom from a man of his stature."

Damien crouched down and put his serious face back on. He hadn't planned on having a go at people who weren't part of Rising Tide, but Hammertime had pissed him off.

"Hello, Hammertime, and thanks for joining us at such short notice. How are you doing? Outstanding. Listen, you might not be part of Rising Tide, but I'm not sorry you died. I think I speak for all of Saga Online when I say that building your guild outpost right next to a popular dungeon, then denying everyone who isn't part of your guild access, is a dick move. It was me who sent those messages, by the way. Thanks for coming when I called, man. Couldn't have done it without you."

Damien rose and stared straight at Noigel, his eyes flickering briefly onto the minimized camera screen to make sure he was in the shot. This was the important part.

"I've got a message for Aetherius as well. I count... let's see... thirty-two members of Rising Tide dead by my hand, so far. That's right. Those disasters your guild has been having over the last few days? All me. All because you couldn't kill a single level 1 player. That's a shame. But I know you don't care. Your guild is just a shield for you to hide behind. So, here's something you will care about. I'm coming for you. I'm going t—"

Damien froze. He'd been so absorbed with his broadcast he hadn't noticed until now; until it was too late.

Behind Noigel, not even a stone's throw away, watching him as he made his big speech, was a player encased in golden plate mail from head to toe. The armor was clearly of the highest weight category, boasting huge shoulder pads that practically doubled their frame. The strength requirement had to be enormous. He was leaning up against a tree with his arms folded.

As Damien halted, the player made a circle in the air with his finger, beckoning him to continue. Damien scanned their basic details. It was a paladin. He was level 35. And above his class in thick red writing appeared the name of his guild: Rising Tide. Damien kept his eyes trained on him as he ordered the imps to disperse into the trees, the hell hound to guard Noigel's back and the succubus to his side. In the face of the sporadic activity, the player made absolutely no move to defend himself whatsoever. He smacked the top of his helmet with one hand, making the same motion as before with the other. 'Keep going'.

Damien wasn't sure what he was up to, but it was no longer safe to keep broadcasting. He looked at Noigel, who'd managed to keep his eyes on Damien but was looking extremely uncomfortable.

"If you want to see Aetherius put in his place, give me your vote in the competition and I'll do everything I can to make it happen, or die trying. Like and subscribe!"

He ended the feed and Noigel leapt onto his shoulder, hissing angrily. The paladin pushed off the tree and raised his hands. Damien was sure they'd burst into golden light at any moment, enveloping either him or his minions. Instead, he found himself on the receiving end of a slow clap.

A voice echoed from the helmet, making it sound tinny and light.

"So, you're Damien? You're shorter than I expected."

Damien held his ground. All he needed to do now was loot the bodies and get out of there. He'd be damned before a single player stopped him from taking his hard-earned loot.

"Don't come any closer or you'll be joining your friends."

It wasn't much of a bluff, what with most of his minions cowering in the trees. The paladin laughed and made some broad strokes in the air, operating their menu. After a few moments, the helm faded away and Damien saw their face.

It was a girl.

She had short blond hair, not even long enough to cover her ears, and a delicate face that seemed preposterously out of place above her heavy armor. Her blue eyes bored into him above a wry smile. He'd seen her from time to time when he watched Aetherius's broadcasts. She was the primary tank for Rising Tide and her name was Lillian. But that wasn't what people called her.

She had several nicknames she'd earned during the early days of Saga Online, when guild wars and player killing were rampant. Many of them were extremely rude, but as she led Rising Tide in wiping out their enemies the ruder names died on their lips and only one remained: The Immortal. There was one other pertinent detail.

She was Aetherius's girlfriend.

Together, they'd carved out territories across Arcadia and made Rising Tide one of the most prominent guilds. Some guilds were definitely more powerful, but few were more famous. 'The

Immortal' was a huge part of that. Now she was here, and Damien was standing on a mountain of her guild's corpses.

"They weren't my friends, and I won't be joining them either. Please don't attack me. I won't kill you unless it's necessary."

Damien clamped his jaw shut. Lillian had come to a stop on the edge of the circle of bodies, one hand on her hip as the other scratched her chin thoughtfully. She wasn't even looking at him. She was observing the bodies of the fallen. She lingered on Hammertime for a few moments before twisting her head to the end of the line, where the hammer was slowly digging into the dirt from sheer weight. Her eyes gleamed.

"So, here's what's going to happen. I'll be taking this hammer. You look a bit weedy for it anyway. Then you're going to scram before the rest of Rising Tide comes online. There's been a call to arms, they're gathering as we speak. You talk big, but I don't think you're ready to fight Aetherius just yet. Any objections?"

Damien stared at her, dumbstruck. The longer she spoke, the more confused he became. When he didn't answer, she strode toward the hammer and grabbed it in one hand before straining upward. Her feet sank into the earth, but the hammer didn't budge. Until then she had seemed demure and controlled. Now her brow furrowed, and her lips drew themselves into a tight thin line. She was taking it personally.

Damien had seen a character three levels higher than her using two hands to swing it around; he knew there was no shame in not being able to use it one-handed. He was about to suggest she use both hands when her body exploded into white light, consuming her entirely in a holy aura. She pulled again, and the hammer lifted into the air. Divine Might.

Damien didn't know the details of the skill, he only knew it was insane. Lillian took a couple of experimental swings with her new weapon, manipulating it as though it were no heavier than one of his daggers. Then it disappeared into her inventory.

"Right, it's time for you to go, but first here's some free advice. You'd be better off not posting that video you made. Andrew... Aetherius is vindictive. If he thinks you're a threat to his popularity he'll stop what he's doing and hunt you down. It's your call."

She went back to her tree and leaned against it again, folding her arms and regarding him evenly. Her eyes flickered for a few moments and the text above her head abruptly changed color, from red to green. She had manually set her hostility towards Damien back to neutral. Damien wasn't sure why she wasn't murdering him, but he wasn't going to let his guard down.

While the imps went about looting the bodies, the succubus, hell hound and Noigel stayed by his side, watching Lillian warily. Damien knew it was a bad idea to ask, yet he had to anyway. He wet his lips and addressed her with more confidence than he felt.

"Have I missed something? I just killed an entire Rising Tide raiding party and you're letting me go? Don't you want to avenge your guild?"

She smirked at him and shifted her weight on the tree, pushing it back slightly and causing it to creak. Her Divine Might was still active.

"How do you think I got here so quickly? I came to ambush the raid party, just like you, and I wouldn't have needed Godhammer to help me either. Still, I can't complain. The hammer is a nice trophy."

She'd come to attack her own guild? Wait, what? Lillian was turning on her own team?

She registered his surprise and her face lost its gaiety, hardening until she looked every bit like the face he recognized from the videos of Rising Tide stamping its authority on the game.

"Rising Tide is rotten. And Aetherius is the core. After everything I did..." Her lip wavered, just for a moment, before she regained her composure. "I have my own axe to grind."

Noigel tapped Damien on the shoulder. The loot bags had all been gathered up and his minions were waiting for their orders. It was time to go. Damien summoned a portal back to base and ordered his minions to throw the bags through. There were too many for them to carry in a single trip. Then he sent them in, one by one, hanging on the edge of the portal in case he needed to jump through himself. He tensed, waiting for the surprise attack from Lillian as his forces dwindled. It never came. She had been sincere. As the succubus stepped through, Damien gave the gaming titan a final wave.

"Thanks for not killing me, I guess. See you around?"

Lillian smirked and shook her head.

"I doubt it. Good luck with what you're doing. Try not to die."

Lost for words, Damien gave her a nod and stepped through, the portal closing behind him. The light of the forest was quickly replaced by the dimness of his home.

He was safe.

25

TINKER TAILOR SOLDIER DEMONS

That had been an interesting turn of events. *Busy day.* And it was still so early. The minions he'd left in his base had helped his combat force to gather the bags by his item chest, ready for inspection.

Damien had managed to take all the bags, but Lillian's arrival had prevented him from making the most of the souls gathered there to fill up his Soul Well with either souls or minions. It would have been unwise to stand around summoning more forces with a potential threat watching him from just a short distance away. It was only obvious now he'd left without incident that she was never going to attack. Bloody hindsight strikes again.

Having completed their duties, the imps had all crowded around the succubus and were ogling her, tongues wagging. The succubus folded her arms across her chest and snootily cast her head upward, swatting away any imps who got too close with a swift flick of her tail.

Damien examined her abilities in detail.

Chaotic Bolt: Mana: 50 – You channel a pulse of rift energy in your closed hand. After 3 seconds the energy can be launched, dealing damage to the first thing it hits. After 5 seconds the rift energy explodes, regardless of its current location. At higher intelligence thresholds this ability will be upgraded, dealing more damage but costing more mana.

Bloodlust: Mana: 100 – Non-player allies in the caster's vicinity have their attack and movement speeds increased by 20%. The effect lasts for 30 seconds, or until the caster is neutralized. At higher intelligence thresholds this ability will be upgraded, providing greater benefit but costing more mana.

Circle of Hell: Mana: 150 – A wide circle of flames is cast on the floor, inflicting damage over time and reducing the armor of any non-demons caught in the effect by 50%. Upon leaving the circle, the damage and armor reduction persist for a further 3 seconds. The circle lasts for 15 seconds, or until the caster is neutralized. At higher intelligence thresholds this ability will be upgraded, dealing more damage but costing more mana.

This was great! Having a minion that could provide Chaotic Bolt was a considerable improvement to his team's overall utility. It wasn't a Krackle-style fireball, but it would do a nice chunk of damage. If it hit. After magic damage reduction was applied. If it didn't explode in her hand. So, some variables, but at least Damien had an operable magic missile now.

He was more interested in the other two abilities. Bloodlust was straightforward. It would help immensely with his hit-and-run tactics, allowing minions to close in faster and get their hits in sooner. Circle of Hell was what Damien had been waiting for. For a long time, he'd lacked something that would work consistently against heavily armored targets.

He'd also lacked an AoE damage ability. Having neglected his intelligence stat, he'd worried that no such abilities would come, but the succubus was providing him with a soft fix to both of these shortcomings in one spell. She only had 50 wisdom, translating into 500 mana, so she wouldn't be able to churn out these spells indefinitely. She might get more mana if her wisdom increased as Damien leveled up, but until then he'd have to be conservative.

Damien closed the menu just in time to watch a bold imp step in front of his peers to present the succubus with a wilted bouquet of flowers. It had probably picked them up for her while they were still in the Twisted Forest. The succubus glared and swatted him in the face with the back of her hand before casting her gaze at the ceiling again.

"Sometimes I can't help feeling ashamed to be an imp, watching how the rest of them behave."

Damien looked at Noigel, who in turn was looking with disgust at the line of imps forming in front of the succubus.

"Good for you, Noigel. I'm glad you're not in line with the rest of them."

"Are you kidding? I'm only here because you still need my guidance. As soon as we're done, I'm going right to the back with the rest of the scrubs. But what kind of imp thinks a succubus wants flowers? He's a pox on our species."

Noigel had no sooner finished speaking than another imp trudged to the front of the line, holding a gelatinous, shapeless, dark brown blob. Damien recognized it from his early gaming experience. It was the coveted ruptured rat spleen. The succubus leaned in and popped it into her mouth, revealing rows of jagged teeth much the same as the imps that were courting her. Damien couldn't help but wince.

She chewed thoughtfully before smacking her lips on the imp's cheek. The rest of the imps immediately stampeded out of Damien's base into Bartholomew's dungeon, no doubt looking for more rat spleens to ply her with.

"Yeah! That's how you do it! Flowers are for sissies! Get that girl some iron! Know what I'm sayin'?"

Damien covered his face with his hands. He should have known better.

"What's the guidance you need to give me?"

Noigel resisted the urge to join his brothers in the great spleen hunt and reluctantly turned his attention back to his master.

"The recorded memories I took in the Twisted Forest are in your 'Media' tab. Do as you please with them. See you later!"

He ran out to join his brethren without looking back. Damien left him to it and navigated to the Media tab. He was still looking through the footage when the imps ran back into his dungeon, screaming in terror. They were soon followed by Bartholomew, who sounded sourer than ever.

"This is exactly why I didn't want you staying here. Can't you keep control of your demons? What gives you the right…"

His voice trailed off as he caught sight of the succubus. She glared back at him haughtily, looking at his empty hands before proceeding to shoo him away. This was a mistake. Bartholomew reared over her, his lips curling back over his fangs and his eyes widening until they were the size of fish bowls, hissing down into her face with the malice of a thousand angry cats.

She staggered backward and retreated into the furthest corner of Damien's base, swishing her hair behind her as if nothing had happened. The imps quietly followed her to continue their courtship.

"There, that's how you control minions. How did you manage to dominate a succubus so early in your training? Even if you've chosen to specialize in minions, you haven't invested a fraction of the time…"

His voice trailed off yet again. He was looking at Damien, taking in his level and stats in whatever way it was that his game-bound brain was designed to process such information.

Damien ignored him and kept editing the footage. He was just reviewing the final segment, asking people to vote for him in the competition, when Bartholomew found the exact words to express his sentiment.

"How the hell did you do that?"

'Your reputation with the Occultist faction has risen to Revered.'

Now it was Damien's turn to be smug. He saved the edited footage and closed the menu to look at Bartholomew. There was something about him he hadn't expected. His character was now powerful enough to see Bartholomew's level. His mentor was level 35.

"I killed a lot of Rising Tide members today, Bartholomew. Twenty people, plus some guests I invited on top. It was... wonderful."

"I see. Congratulations on your rapid rise to power. It appears you are close to making good on your promise."

Damien winced. He hadn't checked Aetherius's stats since he started playing, but the last he remembered was that his nemesis was on the verge of hitting level 40. He still had some catching up to do.

"Not just yet, but I'm making good progress. I'm hoping to hit another party before the end of the day, but first I need to check the haul from the last fight."

He thumbed toward the pile of loot in front of the chest and Bartholomew followed the gesture, sucking on his teeth as he took it in. It was several times larger than the one that preceded it, and that had been no small amount of gear.

"Would you mind if I join you in examining your well-gotten gains? I may be able to make you an offer of my own."

Damien shrugged ambivalently and beckoned Bartholomew to come along. He couldn't see any harm in having someone else to watch him unveil his new goodies. He started opening the bags one by one, putting items he was interested in for personal use on one side, trash and non-useful items on the other. It was soon clear which side was going to be the larger.

When all the bags were opened, the pile of useful items was extremely modest indeed. Worse yet, while the stats may have been better than his own gear on many of them, very few of them looked the part. Damien knew the importance of his appearance for the purpose of a streamer contest; running around wearing a frilly white archer's jerkin on the basis that it had a high agility stat would not win the respect of the gaming community. It would also make him an easier target to spot in those situations where he was sneaking. He sighed and narrowed his search still further, putting all the items in the discard pile except those that met his standards for both func-tion AND form. There were a few items that were easy choices, occupying gear slots he hadn't yet used.

Krackle's Ring of Foresight:
Stats: +30 Wisdom.

BlackKnight's Persevering Amulet:
Stats: +20 Endurance, +15 Constitution.

He equipped them and kept browsing, hoping something a little more impressive would soon appear to replace either of them. While there were other items of jewelry, they focused on stats or skills that provided him no real benefit. He threw them into the discard pile as well.

Soon there was only a discard pile.

It was a big disappointment. He'd been hoping for some major upgrades to his gear.

"Look at this," he vented. "I take down well over thirty people and all I get in return is crap. I wanted something I could use, not more scrap to melt down!"

Bartholomew tore his gaze from the items and focused on Damien with some difficulty.

"I can't say I'm surprised. You are quite possibly the only occultist hero in existence, and you're building a very particular skill set. I doubt there are many people out there wearing items that would suit your needs. Fortunately, I have a suggestion for you."

He casually swept an arm through the pile, pushing approximately half of it off to one side. Then, for good measure, he picked out some choice items from what was left and deposited them in the new pile as well.

"If you give me these items as tribute, I will provide you with an upgrade to your current gear. It will look identical, but the power it holds will be significantly improved."

Damien looked at the pile Bartholomew had allocated for himself. It was an enormous hoard, enough to fully equip at least five people. Damien wasn't having it.

"You're kidding, right? You want all that, just to upgrade something that you already gave me in the first place? There must be over a thousand gold's worth of items in there!"

Bartholomew fluttered his eyelashes, such as they were.

"Why don't you go sell them, then?"

A vein pulsed in Damien's temple. Of course he couldn't sell them. He couldn't sell them because Bartholomew had made him an occultist in the first place. He'd known playing an outcast would have its difficulties; he hadn't realized that Bartholomew would use his lack of access to 'civilized' society to turn a profit.

"You're a monster, you know that? Fine. Take the bloody items and give me the upgrades. And it better be good, for what I'm giving you!"

Damien had no sooner uttered the words than Bartholomew withdrew his infinite capacity bag from his robes and started sweeping the items into it as fast as he could, before Damien could change his mind.

"It will be good. And yes, I'm very much aware that I'm a monster, thank you for reminding me. You don't become leader of the occultists with your morals intact." He finished sweeping the items into the bag and stood up before extending a hand to Damien. "Your Occultist Apprentice Robes and your Sacrificial Dagger, if you would be so kind."

Damien glowered at him. So he was going to have to be naked as well. Joy. He equipped the rags he'd hoped never to use again and, memories of Aetherius pushing him flashing painfully in his mind, thrust out the equipment to Bartholomew. The vampire couldn't quite conceal a greedy grin as he delicately pried the items from Damien's fingers.

"It's a pleasure doing business with you. I shall return momentarily."

Damien scowled and turned his back, returning to his Media tab as Bartholomew showed himself out.

He ran the video through from the beginning, feeling a bit better as he reviewed the footage. It looked great. All that was left to do was create an account and post it. Creating the account was easy enough; the headset already had his account details and did most of the work for him. Damien clicked 'submit' and the video entered the public domain.

He added his footage from The Maw for good measure. It

wouldn't tell his enemies anything they didn't know already, so it was a pretty safe bet. It also backed up his claim that he was responsible for Rising Tide's recent woes.

He'd just finished uploading the second video when he realized something important; he had an unallocated trait. In all the excitement he'd completely forgotten. He rushed into his Abilities tab and found his list of traits, with a new glowing trait for level 20 waiting to be selected.

1. **Unstable Energy**: Chaotic Bolt afflicts a charge of 'Unstable Energy' on the target. Upon inflicting 3 charges on the target, it will explode for heavy damage.
2. **Purgatory**: Circle of Hell immobilizes enemies caught in its radius for 5 seconds and the damage of Circle of Hell increases over time.
3. **Rift Walker**: Killing blows that grant experience, performed by your character, reset the cooldown on Demon Gate.

Damien could see a clear choice. Demon Gate was his main survival tool. If he'd had this trait before he went to the Twisted Forest, he wouldn't have almost been killed in the tree. That was the clincher for him. Confident, he selected trait three: Rift Walker.

He already knew how to use the spell, and he certainly knew how to procure kills that granted experience. All he had to do was put the two together. Easy enough... right?

"Your upgraded items, Daemien."

Damien might have closed the level gap between them, but Bartholomew hadn't lost his ability to sneak up undetected. Damien grumpily put his hand out to one side to accept the items, not even wanting to look at the vampire who'd fleeced him. The items were placed in his hand and Damien took them into his inventory before examining them in his menu.

The Occultist Apprentice Robes were now Adept Robes. The level requirement had doubled from 10 to 20, and the stats the set gave had doubled as well. They now gave +30 to agility, constitution, endurance and wisdom. While it wasn't much of an improvement, it was better than nothing and it was certainly better than trying to cut a dashing figure in mismatched gear.

The Sacrificial Dagger had received the same treatment, the base damage doubling to 50 per strike while the agility increase had risen to 30. It was now evenly matched with the keepsake he'd looted from Shankyou.

The upgrades were still under-leveled for him and weren't worth anything like what he'd given in terms of market value. Even so, they were more useful than the raw materials he'd have got from breaking them down. It would have to do.

Between the new ring and the upgraded gear, Damien's wisdom had risen by a further 45 points. His Summon Limit rose to 25, but his Soul Reserve still remained stuck at 10. The Soul Reserve had probably hit the maximum.

That was a bit of a blow. Still, at least his minion count was still rising. That was what he really needed. And ten souls were still enough to upgrade his Soul Well each time he came back.

He smacked himself on the head. Of course! He hadn't looked at his building upgrades yet! He went into his Buildings tab and found the Soul Well was due another upgrade. That was no surprise. What did surprise him was that the Demon Forge icon was also highlighted in blue. He clicked it and checked the description.

Demon Forge: Advanced Smithing
Grants your Demon Forge the ability to craft weapons and armor for your minions.
Requirements: 10 iron bars, 5 steel bars.

Did Damien feel like using his limited resources to deck out his minions in armor and weaponry? Yes. Yes, he did.

He got to work, ordering the imps to smelt down the gear Bartholomew hadn't appropriated for himself. There had been more than a few warriors in the last run, so there was plenty of metal equipment to process. In fact, now he thought about it, most of the items Bartholomew had taken were cloth and leather: the very items Damien didn't need.

For a moment, he decided maybe Bart wasn't so bad. Then he remembered just how many items had been greedily stuffed into the bag. Still, he'd left Damien what he really needed, and that was good enough. After the smelting was complete, Damien had fifty-six iron bars, twenty-eight steel bars and even fifteen true-silver bars, courtesy of a truesilver breastplate that was almost certainly sorely missed by the original owner. A few items that Bartholomew had missed provided him with a modest amount of leather, as well.

Damien selected the upgrade and almost immediately a familiar high-pitched shriek from Noigel echoed around his base. The imps zoomed out of the corner they'd been nesting in and retrieved their work tools and the requisite materials from the item chest before setting to work.

Noigel appeared a few moments later with the succubus by his side, looking thoroughly pleased with himself. She leaned down and kissed him on the top of his head, a proper kiss rather than the playful peck she'd given to her earlier suitor.

The lecherous imp caught sight of Damien's incredulous expression and gave him a wink as he sauntered past.

"She's smart, but she can't speak humie. Rule one: Chicks dig foreign languages."

Torn between embarrassment and disgust, Damien took refuge in his menu.

He navigated to his old haunt: the Rising Tide raid schedule. It wasn't long before he found something to suit his needs. The next event taking place that day was a ten-man raid in just three hours' time, and it was yet another dungeon in Brociliande: The Malignant Crypt. That sounded suitable for an ambush. It was a slightly lower level than the Twisted Forest, the mobs anywhere between level 18 to 23.

It was closer to Damien's entry point than the Twisted Forest had been, so traveling there would be much easier. This was important, since he'd be traveling during the day.

He looked up the players who were registered for it, just to be on the safe side. As expected, their levels matched the dungeon they were targeting. This was a group he could deal with all by himself. He might not level up much, if at all, but it would be a perfect opportunity to twist the knife in Aetherius's pride.

Target selected, he closed his menu and inspected his Soul Well. It could support up to a minion count of thirty, yet there were only ten imps bound to it. He bound the ten imps still in his party to the Soul Well and they all scrambled to assist in upgrading the Demon Forge.

With twenty imps assigned to the task, the construction time plummeted to twenty-six minutes. Good. He'd be able to look over the options and get his minions decked out before the next skirmish.

"Noigel, tell the imps to hurry it up; I've found our next target." He rubbed his hands in anticipation. "It's going to be a slaughter."

26

WELCOME TO HELL

O nce again, Damien found himself navigating the plains of Tintagel from his base to the luscious forests of Brociliande. With the sun high in the sky, stealth was all but impossible.

Not that it mattered. He felt almost as safe as he did in his own base. There was a lot you could do with a 25 Soul Summon Limit.

Damien had tinkered with squad setups while the Demon Forge upgrade was under construction, eventually coming up with what he considered to be a solid line-up: one succubus, three hell hounds, eight imps and Noigel. He'd used 6 of the 10 soul energy in his Soul Reserve to summon two more hell hounds and the remaining 4 souls had gone into his Soul Well, bringing it up to 24/30 Soul Capacity.

It was a considerable force, especially taking into account their new gear: each imp now wielded a trident, providing them with an extra 5 damage and an armor-penetrating attack.

He'd decided not to armor them, since it reduced their movement speed and above all else he needed them mobile. He'd opted not to waste materials on armoring the hell hounds, since they'd either have hardened skin of their own or would waste his efforts and resources when they ignited. It was the succubus who had made the most of his new Demon Forge: she now represented the core of his forces, so he'd taken measures to keep her protected. He'd had just enough leather to craft her a set of light armor, covering her torso while still giving her wings freedom of movement.

It wasn't much but it would at least reduce the damage of any projectiles that came her way, which was what he anticipated as the main threat to her continued existence. Since she had wings, the succubus would be able to avoid melee attackers with relative ease. The armor wasn't very exciting, but he'd also commissioned a whip that was a unique option for her. It was a black lash, barbed with vicious shards of steel that glinted in the sunlight.

Despite their numbers, the thirteen-strong throng was keeping a relatively low profile. They had huddled together under Damien's instruction and kept a tight formation on him, copying his every move. If the need arose he could have them fan out at a moment's notice.

Noigel was on his shoulder, keeping his eyes peeled for any activity, but they avoided the road and the trip to the tunnel was uneventful. Just the way he liked it.

It was as he came out the other side into the forest that Damien's guard went up. He sent his succubus and the imps to fly above in the cover of the trees to watch for threats, keeping only his hell hounds and Noigel by his side for protection. He'd rather not be seen by too many people.

As it turned out, he didn't need to worry. It was just past 1pm. The population of Arcadia had steadily dwindled over the last hour as people logged off to eat, rest and, as it happened, watch his declaration of war against Aetherius.

The video was a success. Following a few choice links to his profile in the comments section of trending videos, it was already building considerable momentum. By the time he headed out, his profile had accumulated over ten thousand views.

Considering the content, it was only going to get better from there. Using tactics of this nature to garner attention were usually frowned upon by the community. However, this was a special case: all the trending videos from earlier that morning had revolved around the fight between Rising Tide, Godhammer and himself.

The main focus of these videos had been his demons. The comments sections were rife with conspiracy theories and conjecture as the Saga Online community bashed their collective heads together, trying to figure out how and why a coordinated party of hostile creatures – which clearly didn't belong in the forest – had crashed the biggest guild fight in months. Damien had merely provided the answer.

As he approached the Malignant Crypt, the trees started to thin out and the foliage above became patchy and thin. Their cover gone, he called the flying minions back to accompany him for the final leg of the trip.

This part of Brociliande was far removed from the luscious greenery that defined the rest of the zone. The closer he got to the crypt, the more the decay altered the landscape around him, blackening the earth and warping the trees into hollowed-out ashen husks. Even the sun was nullified as a thick sheet of lifeless gray cloud obscured it from view. A promise of what was to come.

The promise was fulfilled when the ground in front of him burst open, a full bloom of putrid flesh and ragged screams.

Ghouls. A score of them.

Good thing he'd come prepared.

"Bloodlust, now."

The succubus breathed a haze of glowing red mist into her cupped hands. Then she released it and blew it out with a smack of her lips. The mist sought out the other minions as if it had a life of its own, splitting into particles of crimson light that clustered around their heads like a swarm of mosquitoes.

Imps twitched under the effect, their permanent grins, already disturbing, becoming freakishly wide. His hounds were no less affected, their breathing quickening and their claws pawing at the dirt in excitement.

The ghouls finished unearthing themselves only to find that they were the ones under attack, each hound biting down with no regard for their oral hygiene while the imps flitted between enemies, driving tridents into their tender flesh from above.

Damien sat back to see how his demons would fare alone. His troops were outnumbered but their enemies were lower level than his normal targets and they fell pleasingly quickly. Victory, however, had not come without loss.

While the armor-plated hounds had managed to endure the flailing blows of their adversaries, three of his imps had fallen before the demons had gained the upper hand. Damien didn't mind. Not only did he now have a decent measure of his minions' battle strength without his own spells added to the mix, but thanks to the clouds overhead he could bolster his forces with a vital missing component.

The barely worthy enemies had only left half a soul each, but it was enough to summon a wraith. His work done, the demons formed up and they continued forward.

Before long, the trees disappeared entirely and a stone mausoleum loomed from out of a cloying, miserable mist.

It was only about the size of a house, hardly enough space to encompass an entire dungeon. Damien wondered why it was so small until he moved closer and found that what he'd assumed was the way inside was actually the way down. The dungeon lay under their feet, at the bottom of a broad, steep flight of steps. Set to one side were the ashes of a predictable cooking fire, still simmering.

He was right on time.

Damien sent the wraith in first before following after, his eyes adjusting to the darkness as the dim gray haze of the overworld faded to nothing behind them. The only sound he could hear was the echo of their footsteps as they descended. After about a minute the stairs opened out into an expansive hallway, lit by lanterns that pulsed with unnatural green light.

Two neat rows of sarcophagi lined either side of the hallway like the pews of a church for a very sleepy congregation. Or perhaps not so sleepy as they should be. At the end of the room was a massive set of stone doors, taking up almost the entire back wall. But they were closed. That was odd. There was no other way through here that he could see.

He forced himself to walk rather than run down the aisle, keeping an eye on the stone lids to make sure they were keeping their containers sealed. Undead mobs were nothing if not predictable. All was still quiet as he and his team gathered around the door. At his head height, in about the position you'd expect a keyhole to be, was an empty socket. Damien reached out to touch it and received a new notification.

"This door can only be unlocked after you complete the 'Curse of Morgan Le Fay' questline."

Wait, what? It was still locked? But he'd seen the campfire outside, so the party had definitely been here. He'd seen dungeons with similar mechanics in online streams; the doors were supposed to remain open until the raid was complete and everyone had withdrawn, allowing the dungeon to start resetting.

Rising Tide wasn't a noob guild. Damien sincerely doubted they'd organized a raid and then forgotten to bring anyone who'd completed the relevant quest chain.

He checked the time again, to no avail. It was fifteen minutes past the hour; they should have had plenty of time to get underway. He scratched his head. Hopelessly, he looked at Noigel perched on his shoulder. The imp looked every bit as confused as he was.

What the hell was going on? Why weren't they here? And if they weren't here, why was there a fire outsi—

Oh. Oh no.

He had to get out.

Damien ran for the exit, but it was too late. While he was busy examining the door, his hounds had already turned to snarl at the stairs. They needn't have bothered.

Clattering footsteps echoed down into the chamber, moving at pace. Damien had come to hunt, but it was they who were hunting him. He'd been trapped.

He pointed down at the ground to summon a portal back to his base, but the spell sputtered and died in his hands. A notification informed him that this spell was unavailable when enemies were nearby. He attempted to logout, thinking his minions could buy him the thirty seconds he needed while he waited to be removed from the game. Another notification informed him that option was unavailable in dungeons, as well.

Cursing, he looked around for somewhere, anywhere to hide. All he had was the stone tombs. He ducked behind the one closest to him, twisting his head at Noigel and hissing his instructions through his teeth.

"Hide them. All of them."

Noigel didn't ask for clarification. His claws dug into Damien's shoulder as he rose up to peer over the tomb's stone lid, pointing furiously with both hands and dictating his commands in uncharacteristically hushed tones.

There was a flurry of activity as the minions took their places. Damien peeked over the top of his own hiding place. He couldn't see any obvious sign of them. Noigel had done an excellent job.

The first set of feet appeared at the top of the stairs, rapidly followed by the second and the third. Damien waited until the first player had reached the bottom before he drew back his head, but he already had a good idea of what he was up against.

It confirmed his suspicions of being outplayed beyond any doubt: this wasn't the group he'd come here to fight. They were all in the low 30s, serious players who'd been on Saga Online for at least a month. They'd all have their third traits, making for a significant power gap.

And that wasn't even the worst part.

He'd only seen six of them before he pulled his head back, but the three at the front had all been paladins and were immediately followed by a pair of priests. This wasn't going to be a fight. It wouldn't even be a scuffle.

"Noigel, where's the wraith?"

His second in command pointed a claw straight up. Damien followed it and found the wraith hanging directly above them, right in the center of the ceiling. If Noigel wasn't so ugly, and if his situation hadn't been so dire, Damien could have kissed him then and there.

Instead, he tilted his head back and muttered, "Possession."

He opened the eyes and tilted the wraith's head back to absorb the situation in depth. There was his prone body, with Noigel staring up at his new vessel expectantly. The succubus was directly behind them, crouched down behind her own tomb. The rest of them were scattered around the tombs in Damien's vicinity, his mighty army reduced to hiding. Damien could see it had been the right choice.

Rising Tide had only sent ten players, but that was where the good news ended. The groups he'd fought before had been haphazardly put together and poorly coordinated by comparison, their levels and gear varying wildly from player to player.

This was different.

None of them had said a word since they entered. What's more, it looked like the group was specifically designed to hunt him down. The two priests were at the base of the stairs, standing behind two shield-bearing warrior tanks. The remaining three slots were a triple combo of ranged units: a gunslinger, a mage wreathed in lightning and a stealth-oriented ranger.

Five of them were heavily armored, two of them would keep everyone alive and the remaining three could kill him in a single hit. He couldn't have come up with a worse group of enemies to fight.

The party blocked the only exit. Damien wasn't going anywhere unless some of them moved away. He got his wish when the paladins gave each other a nod before carefully walking forward in tandem, checking behind each tomb with their weapons drawn.

While he'd been watching them, the gunslinger and the lightning mage had taken up positions on the two tombs nearest the exit, granting them line of sight over everything in front of them. The survival prospects of anything the paladins chased out of hiding were zero. The stealth-oriented ranger had done what stealth-oriented rangers do best: disappeared.

With every row the paladins cleared, the party behind them tensed a little more. There was only one minion that might be able to get a hit in; the one he'd possessed. With the healers protected at the back and the ranger in stealth, Damien's options were limited. The paladins had passed the fifth tomb. Now only one tomb separated them from the first line of Damien's group.

There was no time to think.

The front and back lines of the party were heavily armored, but the middle was exposed and their attention diverted.

Damien hurtled down the side of the wall, the blade on his arm outstretched. It took all of a second to line up behind the mage and plunge the blade into his lower back, as high as he could reach.

Even with the Sneak Attack totaling 300 damage, less than half the mage's health was removed. This player was built to survive Sneak Attacks, not just with stats but also with skills: before Damien could draw back his other arm to strike again, the lightning that had been arcing over the mage's body drew toward the wound and pulsed down the wraith's arm, paralyzing it.

Everyone turned to the sound of the electrical discharge and before the effect had dissipated, the priests were channeling healing spells and the gunslinger had leveled both barrels toward the attacker, firing at close range.

The possession was canceled, leaving Damien back where he started minus one wraith. He glanced over the top of his tombstone in time to see the mage's health return to full in a brilliant white flash, the wraith behind him disintegrating in a smoky black haze. That wasn't all that had happened, though.

Over the echo of gunfire, another sound had appeared: the grating of stone upon stone.

The gunslinger stumbled as his vantage point shifted beneath him, leaping clear of the stone lid as it crashed to the ground. From there it spread across the tombs like dominos, each falling stone tile preceding the fall of those next to it.

The first ghoul to emerge leapt out and clung to the wall, teeth chattering and head twisting. It was the same level as those Damien had faced outside, but that was where the similarity ended. These were elite dungeon mobs, designed to be taken down by multiple players working together.

The ghoul sighted the rogue reloading and leapt again, only to have a lightning bolt pierce through its chest. The mage had summoned a cloud and was riding it in the center of the room, avoiding the chaos playing out below. The ghoul screeched and fell short, twisting and writhing more in fury than pain. The mage was level 33, ten levels higher, and yet hadn't managed to kill it in one shot.

The paladins stopped advancing and instead moved to protect their party, each of them running back down their lanes. The one on the far left put his glowing mace straight through the convulsing ghoul's head, spattering mushy brains all over the wall. This respite was short-lived. As the first ghoul expired, three more leapt from their tombs to take its place.

For Damien, this was a mixed blessing. On the one hand, the people who had come to kill him were now distracted by dungeon mobs. On the other, they were perfectly capable of surviving this encounter. He was not. And his only way out was now blocked by two groups of enemies rather than one.

Crashing stone, followed by a feeble squawk, brought him back to his senses. One of the stone lids had fallen directly on top of an imp at the front of the group.

If Damien didn't act quickly, he'd have nothing left to fight with at all.

He crouched, desperately trying to remain hidden, and instructed his succubus to use Bloodlust. Before the spell finished casting, he gathered his minions around him and advanced down the far-right lane. The succubus remained at the back of the group.

He had no healing spells, no health potions, no sustainability.

Escape was the only option.

His previous combats had been carefully orchestrated, allowing him to engage only when he saw fit. This was pandemonium, and his troops suffered for it.

His second front-line imp was pinned down and savaged by a leaping ghoul before it could rally with his group. This was painful. Imps were the foundation of his Demon Gate and

Implosion abilities. Without them his chances of escape would be severely limited, but he couldn't risk standing still for ten seconds to summon more in the middle of combat. He pressed on, sending his hounds ahead, gathering the surviving four imps around him.

Most of the ghouls were setting their sights on the entrance, where the roar of combat was at its peak. Damien couldn't avoid combat entirely, though. A ghoul leapt from the wall at one of his hounds. It responded in kind, meeting with it in mid-air before the two of them landed heavily on the floor.

They exchanged hits, the hound sinking teeth into its neck as the ghoul flailed on top of it with extraordinary strength, its claws tearing through the natural armor plating like wrapping paper. A lightning bolt screamed through them both from the center of the room, ending the combat as abruptly and violently as it had started.

Damien stuck his back against a vacated tomb and peered over the edge. The mage was flying straight toward them, his staff projecting another arc of lightning. It missed Damien by inches, instead vaporizing an imp that had failed to find cover.

Panting in fear, Damien considered himself out of options. He was about to send his succubus to try and buy them time when the mage crashed into the wall above them, a ghoul straddling his chest. He'd drawn too much attention to himself.

The ghoul was quickly paralyzed by the lightning aura and the two of them fell to the ground at Damien's feet. He wasn't going to look a gift horse in the mouth. He and two hounds finished the pair off.

But even as Damien whooped in triumph, he saw the three paladins were once again advancing down the lanes on his position.

He had two hounds, three imps and a succubus remaining. Even at full force, fighting three paladins head-on would be suicide. Behind them, more ghouls were leaping from their tombs. Going back was not an option. He'd have to go through.

Now the mage was dead, the air was that much clearer.

Damien sent the succubus and all three imps up, instructing them to fly straight for the far right-hand corner ahead of them.

They flew over the advancing paladin and had almost made it unharmed when an arrow strummed into his succubus's side from the opposite corner of the room. The ranger had found a target worth breaking stealth for. The armor allowed her to survive the hit, but only just. She shrieked and crash-landed on the ground behind the last tomb, Noigel rushing to remove the arrow from her side.

Damien couldn't worry about that now. One of the paladins was bearing down on him, pausing a few feet away with his buckler and mace raised against the snarling hounds. To the side, a cluster of rampaging ghouls was keeping the other two paladins occupied. This one guy was just here to hold him in place.

Damien couldn't turn his back, but the howling of the ghouls was drawing ever nearer behind him. He waited as long as he dared before pointing at an imp who'd escaped the carnage and casting Demon Gate. Now he was at the front of the crypt.

The paladin stared at the imp dumbfounded, then turned to find Damien half the room away. Taking his eyes off the hounds was a mistake. Each of them grabbed him by one of his ankles, holding him in position as five elite ghouls set upon the lot of them indiscriminately. The imp and the hounds were quickly wiped out, then the ghouls turned their attention to the paladin. The other two paladins arrived too late to save him, and then they too found themselves locked in combat.

The hardest part was yet to come. Nothing Damien did mattered if he couldn't find a way around the tanks. And he only had two imps and a dying succubus left to do it with. Rising Tide's tanks were holding their position against three ghouls, which quickly became two when the gunslinger blasted one in the face from the stairs. Behind him, the two paladins were wounded but winning. Only two of the five ghouls remained.

By now the graves were empty. This was Damien's last chance.

He stared at Noigel and focused on what he wanted to

happen, the scenario playing out in his head for the imp to actu-
alize. Noigel's eyes widened, the freakish grin Bloodlust had
bestowed on him faltering.

For a moment, Damien thought Noigel was going to refuse.
Then he yelled a slew of demonic commands and rose into the
air, the other imp heading straight for the stairs. The succubus
leaned out of cover and cast Circle of Hell directly over the foot
of the staircase.

The floor his enemies stood on became as black as the void.
Then flames erupted, not from the ground, but from their own
bodies. The health of the ghouls was dropping, slowly but surely,
yet their attacks were no less ferocious. The tanks had high
health and suffered little from the damage over time, but their
armor had been reduced by 50%. Which meant they were
suddenly only half as good at not dying.

Previously, the ghouls had been inflicting only scrapes and dents
on their shields; now they were tearing through them like putty.
The priests' hands were constantly bursting into light as they tried
to keep up. Damien's succubus began charging her Chaotic Bolt
next to him. In a few moments, the cooldown on Damien's Demon
Gate would reset. They wouldn't have much longer than that.

The imps shot toward the bottom of the staircase, just as the
gunslinger let loose another pair of high velocity rounds, putting
another ghoul back to rest.

It was now or never.

Noigel pelted over the enflamed tanks while the remaining
imp took its place a few feet back from the ghoul. In perfect
unison, the succubus released her Chaotic Bolt at the foot of the
stairs and Damien drew his daggers, casting Demon Gate on the
only imp he could see.

The Chaotic Bolt was fast, but Demon Gate was instant.
There was Damien, stood front and center for all to see. Not half
a second later, the Chaotic Bolt screamed into the ghoul's flank.
It had already been whittled down by Circle of Hell and the
sustained pokes from the tanks, but this brought it right to the
edge of death. Damien darted forward while it was still stag-

gering and drove his daggers into either side of its head, receiving XP for a killing blow.

And then Rift Walker activated.

Damien could use Demon Gate again, and he was in the perfect position to see Noigel flying up the stairs as fast as his wings and the succubus's Bloodlust could carry him. It was also the perfect position to die horribly if he didn't move fast. The gunslinger had reloaded and was already raising his hand-cannons, the faintest look of confusion settling into his eyes as his body continued to burn and the hands of the healers flashed on either side of him. Damien pointed past him and cast Demon Gate on Noigel, stumbling onto his hands as he picked up where his imp had left off. In two seconds he'd gone from being trapped behind a wall of tanks and healers to halfway up the stairs to safety.

He turned to find the gunslinger swiveling round, training his guns up the stairs. Noigel was still in view. Damien Imploded him. The rogue fired his rounds into the ceiling as he was swept away, straight into the middle of the circle. Damien didn't stop to admire the maneuver. He kept running. It was only as he neared the top that he realized an armored outline was silhouetted against the exit.

Damien had nothing left. There was no way around this. No more tricks up his sleeves. All the fight drained out of him and he slowed to a crawl. He'd come so far, only to fail at the final hurdle.

It was yet another paladin.

What a bad joke.

They started running down the stairs toward him, clearly intending to use the bottle-neck to their advantage. Damien drew his daggers and screamed in defiance as he used the last of his stamina to rush them head-on. He was totally outmatched against a paladin in hand-to-hand combat, but he would go down fighting. Or so he thought.

As he swung his blades, running at full tilt, the paladin effortlessly sidestepped him and caught him by the scruff of his neck, using his momentum to fling him up the stairs where he landed heavily on his front.

Damien staggered quickly to his feet, expecting to be struck down at any moment. The paladin was still facing down the stairs, away from him. Now the half light was at his back, he could see who his opponent was. He'd seen that armor before. He'd seen that inhuman strength before as well. It was Lillian.

There was a hiss and a ting as an arrow that had been intended for him ricocheted off her shield instead.

"What are you doing? Get out of here!"

Damien couldn't believe what he was seeing. He could scarcely have been more surprised to be saved by Aetherius himself. Lillian was not impressed. She ran up the stairs and grabbed him again, forcibly dragging him out into the cold light.

"There, you're out, congratulations! Do your teleport thing or whatever and get lost! I can't hold them off forever!"

Damien hadn't thought this far ahead, but she was right. Now he was both out of the dungeon and out of combat, he'd be able to use his portal spell.

As the portal started to form, Lillian braced herself at the dungeon's entrance with her shield planted firmly in front of her. He watched her to make sure there was still time, but there was no one better suited to protecting people in the entire game.

She'd really saved him. He had so many questions, but they would have to wait until he was sa—

The dagger was driven with perfect precision, piercing straight through his back and coming out through his chest. His portal spell died and a heavy hand on his shoulder forced him to his knees. It had been a sneak critical, his favorite kind of hit. The hand moved to his forehead, forcing it back to expose his neck. The same blade that had run him through was now pressed against his throat.

Lillian heard his gasp and turned, running with all her might to save him. It was too late. The player behind him lowered his face and whispered into Damien's ear.

"This is for posting my death online and taking my dagger, bitch."

The dagger was drawn across his neck, another critical hit. The last thing he saw was the rage in Lillian's eyes as she ran toward him. Then everything went dark.

A message popped up on his screen, the only thing he could see.

You have been killed by 'Shankyou'. Your experience has been reset to the start of your current level and your body may be looted, at which point a random item of equipped gear will be forfeit.

Remember, it's only a game!

Death cooldown – 23 hours, 59 minutes and 54 seconds.

Thank you for playing Saga Online.

27

BAD ENDINGS

Damien stared at the timer, his breathing coming in short, sharp heaves. He could feel the bed underneath him, the plastic sheet clammy against the bare skin of his forearms. He clutched at his chest, then at his throat. Both were intact. He was out. The sensory nodes of the IMBA set had disengaged, easing him back into reality so he was provided with only visual input. It was an important feature.

Without ending the immersion gently, players were liable to go into shock. The measured release wasn't very helpful to Damien. His trauma wasn't limited to the physical.

He stared at the message that was being thrust so rudely into his face. An unequivocal, uncompromising, insensitive testimony to his failure. One sentence in particular he read over and over, the lightheartedness that should have been comforting serving only to unbalance him further: 'Remember, it's only a game!'

Only it wasn't just a game. His failure was going to have very real consequences.

At last, he couldn't stand it anymore. He pulled the headset off and dropped it on the bed without sitting up. The shock was still spilling over him, but it hadn't crested yet. It was only a matter of time.

For the moment, he was thirsty. He was hungry. He sat up

and extended a shaking hand toward the canister of sludge Freja had given him, his vision blurry as his pupils trembled against his will.

He forced himself to stare at the rim of the canister as he raised it to his lips, struggling to hold it steady. As he tried to tip it back, his throat sealed itself closed, forcing the liquid back out as he retched all over himself like a newborn child. While he'd been out on his ill-fated trip, his only food had gone rancid. Nutrient juice was usually bad, but there was a big difference between 'bad' and 'expired'. So now he had no food either.

He lashed out before he could even stop himself, throwing the canister into the side table. It spun upside down, the putrid dregs decorating his only safe space in a spiral of green bile.

He'd found a way to make a bad situation worse. The nutrient juice was a far cry from food, but the mess he'd made reminded him of a similar situation from not so long ago.

He picked up the pillow and held it over his face as he howled into it.

Eventually, he ran out of energy and his rage began to ebb away. Damien discarded the pillow and threw himself on the bed, not wanting to sleep but with no desire to do anything else either. It was only when his eyes settled on the wall that his shame provoked him to action.

Freja was one of the only people who had shown him any kindness since he left his home. This was no way to repay it. He only had tissues to clean up with, but at least there was hot water to help it along. The plastic cover on the bed had prevented most of the damage and was easy enough to deal with, but the stains on the ceiling gave him plenty of time to assess his situation.

He had three days left until the competition drew to an end, and now one of them was completely lost.

The retaliation had come far faster than he'd believed possible. And he'd called his channel 'Damien's Not Dead Yet'. That had aged about as well as the nutrient juice. The video of him being slaughtered was probably already doing the rounds online.

He'd look a fool. He was a fool.

In his short time playing as an occultist, his arrogance had got the better of him. He should have played it safe. He should have listened to Lillian.

He was still berating himself as he finished cleaning up his latest mess. The plastic sheets had been no problem, but no amount of rubbing would remove the faint green stain on the walls.

Maybe it was just his negativity taking over, but the faint scent of rotting plant matter seemed to be filling the space.

He'd only be able to start playing again in twenty-three and a half hours' time. And he didn't have the money to stay here more than a single extra day, even if he got a normal rate.

Grudgingly, he put the visor back on and confronted the irritating message.

"Menu."

The usual options were there, albeit with the inventory tab grayed out. He'd have to wait until he logged back in to find out what had been taken. Maybe he could ask Lillian? Assuming she hadn't died as well. Somehow, he found that unlikely.

Damien went to the Friends tab to see about adding her when he saw a name there he'd all but forgotten. Kevin. His name was grayed out, but the chat box was highlighted in blue. He opened it and found that Kevin had left him a message last night.

'Hello Damien, how's it going? I'm looking for some feedback on the headset, please call me when you can. K.'

Hmm. What was he supposed to do with this? He decided to keep it brief. He could do without Kevin grilling him about the headset. That was just about the least of his concerns at the moment.

'Hi Kevin. Sorry, busy week. Headset works great. I've been recording, so you'll see for yourself in a few days. Little busy at the moment. Talk soon.'

Damien had no idea if that was true or not. It probably was. Either CU would catch him and the headset would find its way back, or… well, there wasn't really a second option. His capture was just about guaranteed, sooner or later. The real question was whether it would happen before or after the competition ended. Not a question he felt like contemplating right now.

There was enough on his mind. His death was a hideous setback, without a doubt, but there had to be something useful he could do. What was he doing before he saw the message? Right. Adding Lillian.

He found the contacts request list and had started sounding out her name when the whole screen faded and a familiar window pressed itself into the forefront of his vision.

Voice Chat Invitation: Mobius46, Gamer I.D 000046, A/D

Seriously, Kevin? Right now?

Damien let it ring for a while. He couldn't decline without letting Kevin know he was there and had decided not to talk to him. Yet he really, really didn't want to talk to anyone right now. He'd just have to wait until Kevin gave up.

Only Kevin didn't give up. The call remained there for well over a minute as Damien resolutely stared it down, determined to be left in peace so he could try and salvage something from his ruined plans. Still it rang.

His eye started to twitch.

He couldn't stand it anymore. He had no choice but to answer the call.

"What?"

"Hey, Damien… how's it going?"

Damien's lip twitched. That innocuous question, casual yet so insincere, could not have come at a more inappropriate time.

"I'm actually busy at the moment, I'll call you back when—"

"Hey! Don't be like that! We haven't spoken since you got the headset! Surely you've got a few minutes for me?"

"Fine. What do you want?"

Kevin enthusiastically plowed ahead, the coldness of Damien's replies apparently going completely unnoticed.

"That's the spirit! You can tell me how the controls are, does the interface feel more responsive than before… oh, I know! When you were in the character creation page, how was the customization process? Did the facial scanners help? Yeah, let's start with that!"

"Sorry, Kevin, this really isn't a good time. We can talk later?"

Kevin's cheerfulness evaporated. There was a pause before his voice returned low and condescending. Damien's favorite form of address.

"Damien, I only want you to tell me about your gaming experience. That's the whole reason I sent the IMBA set to you."

Something inside Damien snapped. What part of 'not now' didn't he understand? Kevin wanted to know about his gaming experience? Fine.

"All right, Kevin, you win. Where should I start? You remember Cassandra, right? You should, you were talking to her for a good five minutes while I got the crap kicked out of me."

"Damien, I don't know where this is coming from, but I don't apprecia—"

"My mom has a heart condition," Damien continued over him loudly, "did you know that? Guess what happened after I disobeyed her to help you, Kevin? Can you guess?"

Kevin had gone silent again. That suited Damien just fine.

"She nearly died, Kevin. She's in hospital now, waiting for help that won't come. But that's not even the best part! You know where I am right now? I'm in a pod hotel. CU won't let me stay in my own home while my mother fights for her life…"

"Damien, you need to listen to me—"

He couldn't give a damn what Kevin thought he needed. Damien needed to vent.

"And now, after all that, you show up and ask how the headset is working out for me? I'll be honest, Kevin, it's not—"

Damien had been so focused on his rant he hadn't noticed; Kevin had already hung up.

One less problem to worry about.

Still fuming, Damien voiced out the letters of Lillian's name and searched for her ID. That was her name and profile on the screen all right, but he couldn't add her as a friend. Figures. She was internet famous. Probably had random admirers trying to add her on a daily basis.

There was a ping and Kevin's name lit up again. So, he'd resorted to sending messages by text when he couldn't get through to Damien verbally.

He opened the chat thread, bracing himself for the wave of judgment. What he read was worse than anything he could have possibly imagined.

'Damien, I'm so sorry. CU contacted me. They wanted me to call you so they could track your location.
'I didn't know why they wanted to find you. I didn't know about Cassandra. I'm so sorry.
'They'll be coming for you. You need to leave. Right now.'

Damien stared at the messages, his fury completely eclipsed. Kevin's name was already grayed out again, so he had no way of sending a reply. Was this a joke? Kevin's way of getting his own back? That was just cruel. Yeah, it was a joke. How would CU know to contact Kevin, anyway? Except for the video with Toutatis... yeah, that was pretty popular, even with people who didn't play Saga Online... and he'd just posted videos of himself playing again earlier that day... crap.

Damien's sense of urgency built up as he considered the facts. He started packing slowly, but by the time he'd finished his analysis he was throwing everything within reach into the bag.

After being killed in the game, he'd at least thought he'd have time to wash, eat and change his clothes. Just when he'd assumed things couldn't get worse, he'd been proven wrong again. In the span of an hour, he'd lost everything. Even the safe refuge he'd started to take for granted was gone. He felt every bit as tired as when he'd first arrived, yet now he had to go back onto the streets.

He took one last look at the pod, wincing at the stains he'd failed to wipe away. There was nothing he could do about that now. He clambered out to the ground and stepped through the curtain without stopping.

"Hey! Where do you think you're going?"

He swiveled on the spot and found Freja looking at him, her eyes narrowed in suspicion. The image of the canister she'd so kindly given him hitting the pod wall flooded into his mind. He'd left it in the room, along with the stains he'd created.

"Thanks for letting me stay. I've got to g—"

Freja advanced on him, an authoritative finger held up in front of her face.

"You're welcome, but I'm going to check the pod before you go. Gimme a minute."

She turned, glancing over her shoulder to keep an eye on him, before brushing the curtain aside and stepping through.

Damien ran.

Freja's shriek of anger followed him out into the street and he turned down the first alleyway he came across, still running.

A tram pulled up on the street ahead of him and hummed to a stop. A throng of people gathered around the front doors in a tight circle, pressing against each other to get on first. Damien couldn't run forever. At least the trams were free. He joined the back of the cluster and they shuffled their way on board as a single mass, the doors hissing closed behind them.

Every inch of space was occupied by somebody. Damien didn't even bother trying to move away from the front doors. There was nowhere to move to.

Damien stood there until they reached the next stop. The doors opened to a whole new throng of people who wanted nothing more than to join Damien in his purgatory, yet no one wanted to leave. It transpired that, with a great deal of pushing and shoving, it was scientifically possible to accommodate a further three people on board the tram. Damien's personal space was now a long-lost concept, a distant memory from happier times.

After three more stops they reached the central ring. Just when it seemed like it would go on forever, everyone started filing off en masse. Damien managed to find a seat. When at last he sat down, it was a struggle not to fold into his chair. As far as he could tell, he'd successfully gotten away.

The bigger problem was that he didn't know where he was going. He was drained. Tired, hungry and alone. It had already been a stressful day; he hadn't had much sleep because of the early morning raid and there'd been no rest since then.

Several stops later, and it was only Damien and a few stragglers left, everyone spaced out as evenly as possible among the empty seats. He furtively looked around to see if there were any cameras. There were none in his view, although there was a sign saying the tram had Wi-Fi. He'd only be browsing, not playing; that was as safe as he was going to get.

Damien pulled the IMBA set out of his bag and retreated to the window seat before putting it over his head, the visor half up so he would still be able to see if anyone came too close. A quick search of 'internet café no ID' was not helpful. It appeared pod hotels didn't advertise by whether or not they were illegal.

So, Damien was going to have to go on a long search again, except this time CU would be certain he was trying to find another pod hotel. It was a simple pattern. If they notified pod hotels that a fugitive minor might visit that afternoon, how many venues could Damien walk into before someone informed on him?

He looked over the search bar again and considered typing in his mom's name. Then he took the thought one step further. He could visit her. Say goodbye. If he went now, maybe he'd get to her before they came to pick him up. She'd still be unconscious, but at least he'd see her one last time.

There was only one flaw with this plan: his last memory of Cassandra would be sitting by her bedside, choosing to see her instead of save her. He'd have to live with that for the rest of his life. It would be better to fail doing the right thing than to succeed and regret his decision forever, wondering what might have been.

It was settled, then. He would wait until the tram reached the outskirts of town again, away from the high intensity monitoring of the inner city, and go find some food. Assuming he made it that far.

With nothing else to while away the time until he was out of the town center, Damien went back to his online profile.

He was getting more views, but that was no surprise. They'd all be coming online to look at the loser. To confirm that it was the real Damien who'd been taken out before he even got started.

His friend list was flashing. Probably more messages from Kevin. Damien opened the menu and got an unexpected notification.

User Mobius46 has deleted their account. To remove them, you can select the option from your friend management settings.

That was strange. Kevin was a Mobius employee. There was only one reason Damien could imagine why his account would have been deleted.

Kevin had been fired for aiding him. Mobius was making an example of him, likely to keep on CU's good side. They were taking it seriously.

Kevin had risked his job for Damien, and lost it. Damien felt a little sick. But there was a second notification.

You have received a chat invitation from Lillian.

He was sure he hadn't been able to send her a message. Lillian was messaging him of her own volition.

'Hey. So, uh, Shankyou looted your body after he killed you.'

What, was she trying to rub it in?

His eyes ran through the text and found the next sentence gave it a completely different meaning.

'I got your gear back. How do I return it to you? Do you have an in-game inbox? Pm me.'

He'd been looted, and she was trying to give it back to him. It sounded like Shankyou had met a second painful end.

'Hey, thank you, but I'm having some problems over here. No in-game inbox. Sorry. If you could hold on to it for me, just in case I manage to get back into the game, I'd be grateful. What did he take?'

That should cover it. Now he could go back to figuring out how the hell he'd get back into the game at all. The best idea he'd had so far was finding a public data center, but he'd still have nowhere to sleep and he'd need ID to enter. Which meant it wasn't a very good idea.

He was still mulling over his options, the tram approaching the edge of the inner city limits, when his headset rang a dialing tone for all his fellow passengers to hear. The webpages he'd been looking at were replaced with the calling box.

Voice Chat Invitation: Lillian, Gamer I.D 000864, A/D

When he'd received the call from Kevin, he was alone. This would attract unwanted attention. He couldn't reject the call, though, or else he might risk offending Lillian and not getting his stuff back.

He answered and the blare of the incoming call was replaced with the ring of Lillian's voice inside his head. She seemed plenty offended already.

"Hey! What's that supposed to mean? You know how hard it was for me to escape, with your item, and all I get is a lousy 'thank you'? And what's this rubbish about not getting back into the game? Wait, don't tell me; you're one of those delicate flowers who dies once and never wants to play again!"

Damien muttered into the headset so his voice wouldn't carry.

"It's a little more complicated than that. But I really am grateful you got my stuff. Thank you! But it might not matter. I don't think I'll make it back onto Saga Online. If I do, I'll—"

"I knew it! We got ourselves a snowflake, ladies and gentlemen. One death and he's out of the game for life! Should have figured after watching you make that announcement video. You seemed *so* confident you weren't going to die."

Damien wasn't sure what to make of this. She'd gone from angry one second to teasing the next. It was an improvement, kind of, but it was still touching a sore spot.

"You seemed pretty sure you'd saved me as well. I saw the look on your face when your guild mate got me. You weren't too happy."

There was a pause on the other end of the line, and then Lillian came back a little more somber.

"Yeah, sorry. If it makes you feel any better, I got him too. Almost immediately. If he'd escaped from combat before I got him, he wouldn't have dropped the item he just looted and it would be gone for good. You're welcome. So anyway, let's quit messing around. Where do you want me to leave it?"

"No, you're not listening. I can't get back into the game. I've been thrown out of my house."

The tone of her voice had no sooner turned silky than it hardened with flat pragmatism.

"Well, you better go get yourself unthrown out."

Despite himself, Damien felt a twinge of anger. *It always seems so easy to fix other people's problems, especially when you don't know anything about them.*

"I had a fight with my mom. She left the house. The next day, CU calls and says I can't stay there by myself. No way of contacting her and I've run out of money to stay in pod hotels. So when I tell you I might not make it back, I mean it."

It wasn't the whole truth, but Damien didn't feel like going into detail.

"That sounds… rough. Where are you, Zone 1?"

That wasn't much of a guess. Zone 1 was home to about 50% of the city's population.

"Yeah, so no shortage of street food. I'll be fine."

"And... how old are you?"

Damien frowned. That was an odd question. Unknown to him, Lillian had set him at ease. He'd already forgotten where he was. It had all faded away around him as he focused on the conversation.

"That seems like a very personal question!"

There was no reply. Reality began to creep back in around the edges as he waited in the silence. He wanted to hear her talk again.

"I'm sixteen," he relented. "There. You happy?"

There was still no reply. Damien's eyes flickered to the call box, checking she hadn't disconnected. No, she was still there. She was just keeping her thoughts to herself. He was about to speak again when Lillian got there first, the words tumbling out of her mouth as though it were an idea she didn't want to take back.

"Why don't you come crash at mine? Just for tonight. I'd been meaning to have a chat with you anyway, about taking down Aetherius."

Damien seized up. He'd been trying very hard not to be pitied, and he'd obviously failed in that regard. But this was a good offer. Better than anything he was likely to find.

"Are you sure? I'm literally a stranger to you, and I could be lying about my age."

"Oh, piss off, Damien. I've seen you on the streams. I'm confident you're sixteen. If you're not sixteen when you get here I'll lock you out. Does that make you feel better?"

"Um, yes?"

"Good. It should. I'll send you my address. You can show up anytime between now and 7pm, but no later! I'm making dinner. See you!"

And just like that, she hung up. A few moments later the chat box lit up again and Damien received her address. The clever headset was already showing routes and estimated times of arrival. He canceled out the ones using closely monitored transport and found the fastest time. He could be there in forty-five minutes. More than that, he could face using another tram to get there, because now he had something to look forward to.

He pulled the IMBA set off and crammed it into his bag, his route already safely stored in his head and the beginnings of a smile gaining ground on his face.

28

THE IMMORTAL

D amien took a deep breath, staring at the compound.

It wasn't too far from the city center, very well connected for a domestic facility. Probably one of the early domiciles. One of the few buildings that housed residents within the central ring, built before the mega-city rush in the forties.

If it were any older, it would've had speed bumps. There was a man sat in the antiquated sentry box, but the gate was wide open and people were coming and going as they pleased. They probably got a bit stiffer during the evening. It was a good thing he'd shown up before nightfall.

Damien walked in, keeping his head forward while his peripheral vision lingered on the man to see if there would be any response to his entry. There was none whatsoever. He kept his pace and checked the address on his visor.

A few minutes later, he'd found the correct quadrant and was standing awkwardly in the middle of a long corridor, directly outside the apartment he'd been sent to. Having got there in one piece, this was the moment he decided to have second thoughts.

Lillian was supposed to be Aetherius's girlfriend, right? What if this was another trick? A really sick, finely tuned piece of social engineering designed to humiliate him completely? The last prank had been in VR; if Damien fell into this one Aetherius would have got him in real life, too.

But it didn't seem likely.

Lillian could have killed Damien, or at least tried to kill him, when they first met. That would've been much easier. If she was only acting like she hated Rising Tide, it was a good act. Damien was sold. And it wasn't as if he had the luxury of choice. It was this or nothing.

Damien pushed the buzzer and a soothing chord echoed through the apartment. He had halfway retracted his hand when he noticed the second buzzer a few inches below it, a small black box emblazoned with the Mobius logo. A call-box. He pushed it and there was no sound, but a couple of seconds later the logo lit up and started speaking to him.

"Hello, who's this?"

Lillian's voice. Damien sighed with relief. One of the easiest things she could have done to screw him over was send him to the wrong address. He was much more vulnerable than he'd have liked.

"H-hey. It's Damien."

"Already? Gimme a minute. I'll log out."

The light dimmed, and Damien was left standing outside, waiting. A last chance to collect his thoughts in private. Assuming Lillian decided to let him stay. He looked down at himself and couldn't find any reason why she should.

The hours on the trams and the walking in between had taken their toll. Now he was a sweaty, stinky mess.

A bolt clunked. The door gently swung open, and Damien's eyes widened in surprise.

She was a perfect match for her avatar. Most players got stuck in the customization options for a long time, making their online representatives slightly more perfect than they were themselves. A little thinner. Slightly bigger eyes. Higher cheekbones and a more appealing smile. It had seemed obvious that Lillian's character had undergone the same treatment, with her delicate features. But it hadn't. That was just how she looked.

The only obvious difference was her hair. It was the same shining blond but longer, falling behind her back where he couldn't see. Her clothes were different too, unsurprisingly.

Strange to see the girl in the bulky golden armor down to just a slender pair of tracksuit bottoms and a black tank top.

The strangest part? Her Saga Online height was accurate. She was just shy of six feet tall, almost a head taller than Damien himself.

Lillian braced her back against the doorframe and folded her arms, exactly the same way she'd rested against the tree when they'd first met, looking him up and down.

"You look the same as your avatar! That makes things easier. Come on in."

Damien's feet carried him inside. He didn't know what to say in a situation like this. A 'thank you' might be a good start. He'd hardly opened his mouth before Lillian swept past him.

"You've got slippers here by the door, toilet's that way, bathroom on the opposite side," she said, pointing around the spacious apartment. "There's a blue towel there if you want to freshen up. Washing machine and drier, too. If you're hungry I can make you something. Is pizza OK?"

Damien nodded, his mouth still hanging slightly open as he took in his surroundings. This was an A-rank living space.

It was so big, and it seemed like she had it all to herself. There were no signs of a second housemate appearing from anywhere to give him an inspection. At last his mind stopped working for long enough to express himself.

"Thank you for having me. Pizza would be awesome. Can I go take a shower first?"

Lillian grinned.

"Good choice."

She stood there smiling as he awkwardly removed his shoes and jigged into the plastic slippers she'd left out for him, one arm still burdened by the IMBA set.

"There's a cabinet in there to put anything you don't want to get wet. I'll show you where you're sleeping afterward. You can put your stuff there and then we can get to know each other. All right?"

Oh. *Oh.* Conversation. Words. He should use those.

Damien's lips stammered his thanks, but his relieved eyes probably did far more to convey the depth of his gratitude.

"I'll be out in a few minutes."

"Take your time!"

He locked the door and checked it twice before he'd finished stowing away his headset and dumping all his clothes into the washing machine. Damien turned up the dial and warm water blasted out onto the nape of his neck, washing away all the grime he'd accumulated over the last couple of days.

A real shower. The water wasn't getting colder either, so no need to adjust the temperature dial upward. It just kept coming at the correct temperature, like it was supposed to. Amazing. So, this is what tier A living was like.

He finished quickly and grabbed the blue towel, but he hadn't thought ahead any further than that. His clothes were now all in the washing machine, which was diligently chugging away. A bathrobe hung on the back of the door.

Delicately, he reached out and touched it. It was much softer and lighter than any towel he'd ever encountered. He carefully wrapped the blue towel around his waist and tightened the robes with the convenient cord encircling the midriff before poking his head out the door.

Lillian was on the other side of the apartment with her back to him as she fed the food processor instructions.

"Lillian? Is it all right if I use this? I should have asked, but I put all my stuff in the washing machine without thinking and n—"

She turned as he was speaking and quickly raised her hands to cover her mouth, giggling into them. Damien's eyes flickered to her wrist, where a familiar device rested. It looked just like the guardian wristband his mother had been using to measure her heartbeat. Was Lillian sick? She seemed OK, but some things didn't show up on the surface. What could it be? Maybe she—

"No problem, it looks very cute on you."

Damien blinked and his eyes darted from Lillian's wrist to the crinkles of her nose. What had they been talking about? Ah, the dressing gown. Crap.

Try to say something normal.

"Err, thank you."

Goddammit.

Lillian's smirk widened as she turned back to the food processor, calling out so he could still hear.

"Your room's over there, second on the right. Dump your stuff and come back, pizza's almost done."

A whole room. He was going to get a whole room? He'd figured he'd be sleeping on the couch or something. He quickly gathered what few belongings he had left and followed Lillian's direction to his new safe space.

It was bigger than his own room at home, albeit with nothing to denote it belonged to anybody. But it had a made bed in it, with sockets carefully positioned at the top next to the pillows. Whoever set it up that way clearly had VR gaming in mind. All that mattered to Damien was that it was somewhere he could sleep. Existing was possible.

Now he could try getting everything else back on track, starting with food. He carefully sat on the sofa. Lillian came and sat down a seat away from him, the pizza placed on a plate between them.

It was masterfully made, each supplement added at the correct stage to decorate it with a variety of toppings. Food processors had won against the complexity of most food, but any pizza besides plain cheese was a difficult task. One Lillian had just accomplished effortlessly.

"That's a pretty outstanding processed pizza."

She flashed her teeth and put her arm across her waist to perform a mock bow, her guardian wristband now close enough for Damien to identify it beyond any doubt. It looked more intensive than the one his mother had. Maybe Lillian's condition was worse. Or maybe it was just designed to monitor different symptoms. She caught him looking.

"You're wondering about this thing, huh? You know what it is?"

Damien nodded, biting back asking what it was for.

Lillian wanted to share.

"I'm a med student. This is a device we're testing out for our hospital sponsor, an upgrade to the guardian wristband. With regular calibrations it not only reads my blood but my nervous system too, so it can tell if I'm under significant stress. If any abnormal readings are detected, I immediately get a call. If I twist my wrist like this—"

She twirled her wrist around in a full circle and raised it to her lips, continuing to speak evenly as if she'd only just started the sentence.

"Hi Becky, Lillian here. Am I still on duty all day tomorrow?"

"Yup, no change. Sorry, Lil', see you tomorrow."

She lowered her hand and the call ended.

"And if it's removed without warning or detects severe stress, the hospital contacts security in this building. They can get here in forty-five seconds. They've timed it."

Damien raised an eyebrow at the device. It was a significant upgrade on the one Cassandra had, that was for sure. Maybe it would've got her an earlier response team. That still didn't explain one thing.

"That's very cool, but why are you telling me?"

Lillian smiled wanly and leaned back on the sofa, resting her head in the crook of her arm.

"Because the device only works for my safety if everyone around me knows what it does. The more I tell you about it, the safer we get. You can take it easy, stay as long as you need, all you have to do is leave everything the way you found it. But don't do anything stupid. OK?"

Wow. That had taken a sudden turn. But it was understandable. He really was a complete stranger and until now they'd only ever spoken online. She was being honest. Showing her cards in return for him doing the same. Damien was raising his first slice of mystery pizza to his lips when Lillian sighed, pulling her bare feet up to rest underneath her on the sofa.

"You sound like you've had a rough week. Wanna talk about that?"

Damien took a bite of pizza and chewed thoughtfully. How much could he tell her? He'd already told Aetherius about his mother's sickness. Aetherius had been recording at the time, but he'd never shown that part. No surprises there.

The video wouldn't have been as funny if it showed Damien begging for his mother's life before he was kicked down the hole. *Thanks, Aetherius.*

He'd already told Lillian in the online chat that CU had kicked him out of his home, but he hadn't said they were chasing him; that was something she deserved to know if he was staying here.

Besides, she was the perfect audience; a medical student who played Saga Online! And he'd been through the last four days almost entirely alone. He wanted to be honest with her, to share his ordeal with another human being. So he decided to tell her everything.

Lillian had already seen the Toutatis fight, but she dutifully nodded along as Damien described the circumstances surrounding it. Right up until he described his mother's episode, at which point Lillian went entirely still.

Damien pushed on, looking at Lillian carefully as he told her how Aetherius had messaged him and offered a boost. How Damien had fallen apart and begged him for help. And how that plea had been answered. Lillian didn't change her pose, but her eyes widened at every step.

He felt a lot more comfortable sitting in her house after that. He proceeded to give Lillian a timeline of what he'd done in Saga Online, cross referencing it with his travels over the last few days. He was sure to mention the two CU agents that had been assigned to his case so Lillian would be aware.

It was an hour and a half since the pizza was completed, yet in all that time only a single bite of it had been eaten. Having finished his story, Damien gave Lillian a nod to indicate he'd fulfilled his part of the bargain and started to cram cold slices into his face. He hadn't eaten solid food in nearly twenty-four hours.

Lillian still hadn't moved, although she was gently shaking her head. Damien had almost finished his half of the pizza when she finally managed to speak.

"Wow."

"I know, right? Can I have one of your slices? Solid food is just great."

"Sure, have as much as you want. I'll be back in a couple of minutes."

She uncurled herself from the sofa and paced into the room next to Damien's, closing the door behind her. Hmm. Maybe he should have toned it down after all. Maybe having heard everything, she'd decided to contact CU for him. If that was so, there was nothing he could do about it now.

Even if he gathered up what he could and left immediately, it would be difficult to avoid the authorities wearing nothing but a blue towel and a white dressing gown.

He'd eaten his way down to the crust when Lillian came back, her cheerful smile replaced with an ashen-faced grimace and a gold VR headset in one hand.

"I wanted to let you settle in, get around to why I invited you here later, but now I've heard your side... grab your headset. I have something to show you."

By the time he'd been talked through the encryptions for the Wi-Fi, Lillian had already invited him into a chat session. Despite sitting next to each other, the two headsets together were a bit of a barrier to clear communication. Fortunately, they were also the solution.

"We'll just talk like this," hummed Lillian's voice into his ears, slightly too loudly, "I'll stream and you watch while we talk. It'll be faster that way."

Damien focused on lowering the volume a few points as Lillian navigated to a video. The sound on it was muted, but Damien recognized the show. He'd even watched it himself, on occasion, back when he hadn't known any better.

It was the real-life portion of Aetherius's stream.

Here he was Andrew, although the show still used his gamer name: 'Aetherius Offline'. It was dated a week ago.

The channel was a collection of different things, sometimes reviewing technology, sometimes talking about events happening in real life, but everyone's favorite were the prank compilations. This was one of those.

It started, as usual, with Andrew sat in his chair talking. He wasn't much different from his online avatar, although he lacked the emerald green eyes and consistently good hair days that he enjoyed as his mage. No elf ears, either. As his lips silently worked away, Lillian's voice was the one Damien heard.

"You remember when Saga Online just came out and everyone was fighting for their piece?"

He nodded, then remembered she couldn't see him.

"Yeah. Crazy time. I watched all the top guild streams. Rising Tide pushed hard for territory and even harder to defend it. And wherever the fighting was worst, that's where you and Aetherius would be."

"We made a good team. All I had to do was survive while he picked enemies off, one by one. I was his shield. We got a good foothold on the game and he became a serious contender for the streaming contest. Then the holiday ended and the fighting died down. Guilds started protecting what they had. I continued my apprenticeship in the hospital, so I played less and less. Meanwhile, Andrew here starts playing double time. Builds a big following and decides to go pro."

She sighed.

"Good for him, but suddenly he doesn't have time for me anymore. Cancels every plan, last minute. I suggested I come back on Saga and appear on one of his streams. I thought he'd like it, but he got really angry. Then, out of nowhere, this happens."

While they spoke, the video had cut from Andrew at his gaming rig to Andrew being wheeled into a hospital. It was a showstopper. Blood everywhere. His arm hanging off the trolley with gouges so deep you could see the muscles. It looked for all the world like he'd been in a fight with a car and lost. The only assurance it wasn't real were the words 'Ultimate Prank!' thrust in a banner across the top.

There was no such banner for the people in the video, though. It was good enough to fool a team of nurses, who quickly seized the trolley off the masked attendants and started running with it to the operating theatre.

Special attention was paid when a young woman, her long blond hair pulled into a tight bun, came running to the bedside as it was still in motion. Lillian had arrived on the show.

She moved to hold Andrew's hand and found it in tatters, recoiling and screaming in one swift second before the tears started to fall. At which point Andrew triumphantly stood up, laughing and pointing at her.

The nurses stopped running to look on, dazed and appalled. While most of the tattered body had been fake, Andrew's real body had been concealed within a hidden compartment beneath.

Only his head, heavily made up with bruises and scrapes, had been poking out from the grizzly fake cadaver's neck. It was truly a magnificent prank. The most ambitious and gory attempt at a phoenix metaphor ever devised by man.

It was masterfully executed. And to Lillian, completely devastating.

She was frozen in shock, her hands covering her mouth. Andrew stood in front of her defiantly, striking a pose as if he'd done something impressive. Lillian's eyes welled up and she quickly hurried back into the building. The moment she turned, Andrew pumped a fist into the air. Victory was his, apparently.

Then Lillian's voice cut through, quiet but angry.

"He knew that was my worst fear, that someone I care about might get wheeled in while I was on duty. He took it and used it to humiliate me. I had a panic attack, so I was placed on mandatory leave and had this thing strapped to my wrist."

"That's terrible," Damien whispered.

"But he didn't do it for fun; it was political. When I logged into Saga Online the next day to blow off some steam, I'd lost twenty-five thousand votes in the Streamer Competition overnight. Most of them swapped to Aetherius. He did it to win votes from sickos who enjoy this kind of thing. I never planned on winning the competition myself. I was just promoting Rising Tide, for Andrew. But for him to turn around and use me like that? After helping him become a full-time streamer, like he'd always dreamed?"

Her lip curled in contempt, marring her face as she spat out her final thought.

"What a waste."

Damien narrowed his eyes at the still image on the screen. It was hard to imagine how Aetherius could have been more unlikable, but this was a giant leap for douche-kind.

Damien couldn't stand looking at him anymore.

"I'm sorry he treated you so badly. You deserved better. Can we please get his face off the screen?"

Lillian fast-forwarded past the end commentary and the thoughts of the viewers at home. When she returned it to normal speed, the scene had become one Damien liked even less. It was him, from Aetherius's POV, standing at the entrance of The Downward Spiral with nothing but the rags he'd spawned in and a forced smile.

"But I'm not the only one he's treated badly, am I?"

Damien flinched as his character ticked the air and his rags disappeared, leaving him with only the loincloth. His underleveled, gearless, ridiculously helpless avatar at the mercy of the one he'd thought to call savior. He certainly didn't want to watch it with Lillian.

"Yeah, I was there for that one, thanks. I can live without seeing it again."

She closed the video as his naked character's smile faltered and a Saga Online profile page appeared in its place. His profile page.

Modest was a good descriptor, with little besides a hastily chosen profile picture and the two videos he'd posted. But despite the simplicity, it had been looked at often over the last few hours. The profile had over a hundred thousand views. The videos, a hundred and fifty thousand each.

Most amazingly of all, Damien had almost twenty thousand votes in the competition, displayed under his profile views next to the competition emblem.

He'd done it. He'd broken into the competition, and the

number of votes meant that he couldn't be ignored. A major milestone in his plan, and he'd been too busy to notice. Too preoccupied with thoughts of giving up and his situation being hopeless.

Lillian quickly put the numbers into perspective.

"Aetherius's account has been seen by pretty much everyone in the game, so about two million people. He's about to break two hundred thousand votes. But he's been around since the start. You just got here, and you got twenty thousand votes for doing almost nothing; you have a profile page with two videos on it. That's it. With no description, no bio, no theme, no playstyle description, no screenshots. Nothing. At. All."

Damien was delighted. All this time he'd been clutching at straws, the idea of winning the competition nothing but a pipe dream. But his hard work had paid off. It wasn't such a far-fetched plan anymore. He had twenty thousand little competition emblem icons that said so.

"Thank you," he started, "I worked very hard to get—"

"I'm not complimenting you, you idiot! Why is your page so empty? A hundred thousand people visited your profile today, and you netted twenty thousand of them. One in five. How much higher might that have been if they had something to look at?"

Damien's eyes widened as Lillian inflicted her perspective on him. Suddenly his page looked like a disaster. He could have had another twenty, forty, maybe even sixty thousand votes toward the competition, and he'd lost them for nothing more than an uninteresting profile.

"Wait! I thought you told me not to join the competition in the first place?"

"I was wrong!" She'd raised her voice, a perfect blend of defensiveness and frustration. "I didn't think you'd get these numbers! But you need to do something about this page."

She took a deep breath and then let it all out in one go, the views on Damien's profile climbing slightly higher in the background as she adjusted herself.

"I... I didn't just decide to have a bad profile page," Damien said. "I went to the raid, where you saw me again, and—and I died. And then I woke up and had to leave Freja's—the pod hotel. I just haven't had time. I'm sorry, okay?"

All of a sudden, the IMBA set was coming off his head. Lillian gently set it to one side before removing her own and looking down at him.

"Stand up."

What was she doing? Was she going to yell at him some more? Did she feel like she had to do it to his face?

Damien stood up, his arms folded in front of himself as he focused on the floor. Lillian stepped forward, lowered her head to rest on his shoulder and wrapped her arms around him, her headset clutched around the base of his back while her other hand held the back of his neck.

"I'm sorry, man. I'm sorry for what you're going through."

Damien's hands dropped to his sides, and then wrapped around her shoulders. It was a struggle not to cry. Lillian kept talking into his ear.

"I should have helped you from the beginning. But you're here now. And I can help you with your profile. I can help you win this competition. It's the reason I invited you here."

Damien released his hands and pulled back a little to look at her face. She was smiling sincerely, and it didn't sound like a joke.

"Why are you helping me?"

She let go as well, contemplating him.

"I might not care about the competition, but I do care about what Andrew did to me. I haven't been to work since. If he's willing to hurt me professionally for the sake of winning a gaming contest, I'm going to help you win instead. Sure, I'm pretty well known in SO, but I haven't played seriously in almost a month and Andrew's way past me now. I can't catch him in just a few days. But you? Showing up with a hidden class and taking on Rising Tide, by yourself, after only four days in the game? That got people's attention. All you need now is the right support. Here I am."

Lillian grabbed his headset and pushed it back into Damien's waiting hands.

"So, first things first: we're going to get on your profile and I'll talk you through what you should add. We can edit the footage you've got together and get your video count up. If we do it fast enough, we'll have your page ready before the evening rush. Then you'll have to make a statement about getting killed in the game. Let people know you're coming back, so they should still vote for you. Andrew hasn't posted your death yet; we need your profile ready for that. Hustle, man, hustle!"

Lillian pushed his headset forward and Damien fell onto the sofa heavily, staring at her in awe as she grabbed her own headset and sat down by his side. It sounded like she knew what she was doing.

"You think this will work? That we can do this?"

She pulled the headset halfway down and gave him a last smirk before she disappeared into it.

"Yeah, man. Get votes, win the competition. That was always the plan, right? Nothing's changed. I'm just on your team now."

Damien was quick to transfer his video files and the two of them got to work, editing the footage to keep it as fast-paced as possible. Damien focused on cutting out anything with Bartholomew in it to keep his base's location secret, as well as removing uneventful travel time. Then he'd pass it to Lillian, who wrestled it into shape for viewing. She was incredibly skilled, both with the headset and the software it housed.

Before the rush hour started, Damien had four videos ready for commentary, starting with his first raid on the low-level Rising Tide outpost and ending with his recent skirmish in the Malignant Crypt. There was a lot of content there. Lillian guided him through narrating an episode, making sure he knew what his audience would want to hear.

"No rambling!" She'd been very clear about that. "You focus on what's going on in the video right at that second and explain what you're doing and why. If you don't have time, rewind it and play it through again slowly. Pause it if you have to. But no longer than twenty-three minutes! It's as easy as that."

She'd listened in on the first one, stopping him occasionally when he over-explained simple mechanics like soul energy, or under-explained complicated class skills like Shadow Walker. It took about an hour to get through the whole twenty-two minute segment.

They put it up on his profile and moved to the next, Lillian showing outward signs of frustration as the afternoon blended seamlessly into evening. But Damien was a quick, highly motivated learner. He narrated most of the next video on his first try and finished a twenty-one-minute commentary in thirty-five.

Lillian left him to do the third one on his own while she looked for good screenshots to decorate the page. Images of his demons were arranged into folders so they could be easily browsed, along with video clips of their flashier moments. By 19:30, Damien's profile page was almost unrecognizable. It lacked the adverts and the sponsor badges to look like a pro account, but it had just the right amount of everything else. He was playing in the big leagues.

"You'll have to do the video talking about your death pretty soon, but that one can wait. Rising Tide still hasn't said anything about it on the streams. We'll wait for them to go first, then respond directly. That way they'll give us free publicity."

Damien was investigating the folder entitled 'Imps'. He'd gotten to the stage where he could pick out Noigel from the rest of them at a glance. What would the imp have to say about his death? Probably that he was surprised it hadn't come sooner.

At least thanks to Lillian, Damien's afterlife was being well spent. Finding a safe place to play Saga Online was his primary concern above all else, but the professional touch Lillian applied to his profile had proven almost as valuable as not being caught by CU. He hadn't understood just how terrible it looked until she was done fixing it.

By giving him a place to sleep and upgrading his presentation, Lillian had shunted his dreams one step closer to becoming reality. But first, it was time for Damien to let his reality become dreams.

He'd been awake since the crack of dawn to ambush Rising

Tide and Godhammer at the Twisted Forest. Truth be told, he hadn't slept much at all recently. With a safe place to rest, a belly full of congealed pizza and a death timer on his account, there was nothing stopping him from finally getting a good night's rest.

He yawned deeply and loudly, prompting Lillian to remove her headset and look at him sympathetically.

"You must be wiped out. Why don't you go to bed? If you like, you can give me administrative access to your account first so I can polish it up a bit while you get some rest. I won't be able to do it tomorrow; I'm finally going back to work. I won't see you until evening, so while I'm out you can finish commentating the other videos by yourself. All good?"

Damien nodded at her and put the headset back on. She talked him through setting her as an administrator on his account, granting her access to all his headset's recordings and full editorial permissions on his account. She'd already proven it was far more valuable in her hands. It was a real relief to have found someone he could trust. When they were finished, they both took off their headsets at the same time and he gave her a nervous smile.

"Thanks again for letting me stay. You have a great place."

"It's all good. Much nicer around here with something to do, anyway. I'll see you tomorrow. Have a good sleep."

She gave him another hug, not all that tight but longer than he might have expected, before pushing her hair out of her eyes and returning to the sofa. She already had her headset back on by the time he passed by, but that didn't stop her from sounding out a final, crucial instruction.

"Throw the dressing gown in the washing machine when you're done with it!"

He hummed his assent, closing the bedroom door behind him. The bed looked a damn sight more inviting than those of the pod hotels from the nights before. Damien clambered under the sheets and immediately felt relaxed. The shower and the home-made food had made him feel human again, and the work he'd done with Lillian had made him hopeful.

His last thoughts before he drifted off were of home, but for once they weren't grounded in remorse. He was in the competition. He was doing it. He could still put everything back the way it was before. Cocooned by ignorance and optimism in equal measure, Damien closed his eyes and drifted away.

29

KEEPING UP APPEARANCES

D amien woke up on a large, comfortable bed, with absolutely no idea where he was. He lay there for all of six seconds before enough memories had connected to form the outline of his life.

He threw the covers off and lurched toward the door. It was the only reference point he had, courtesy of the light leaking in from the hallway. He opened it, but it only opened a crack before it collided with something heavy on the floor. Poking his head around, Damien found his clothes, cleaned, dried and neatly folded in a basket.

There was a piece of paper on top with his name chicken-scratched onto it. A note. He'd only ever received notes from his mother before, and even that had stopped years ago. Nobody had time to write these days.

In his eagerness to seize it, he was about to step out when he realized he was still completely naked. Lillian was almost certainly gone already, but better safe than sorry. Damien arched his hand round the door and dragged the basket through the gap, quickly closing the door and putting on underwear. Then he turned on the light and took a seat on the bed to read the paper.

Back at 17:30. Food processor still has some juice, eat whatever you want. They didn't announce your death yet. Keep an eye out!

Lillian.

Still no death announcement? Strange. When it first happened, Damien had thought it would go viral almost immediately. Now it was coming up to twenty-four hours and... what time was it? He quickly dressed and went into the living room to find out.

Lillian was a gem. Not only had she sorted out his clothes, she'd put his headset on charge overnight, leaving her own headset next to it. There was no mystery as to who owned the charger: it was the same glitzy gold as her offline headset, her online armor and her hair.

Damien unplugged his own headset and placed Lillian's on charge in its place, putting it over his head to check the internal display. It was just past midday.

Damien powered up the industrial-sized food processor, several times larger than the one he was used to, and the display blinked at him. Damien blinked back. He'd thought he'd be getting the leftovers of Lillian's breakfast. In fact, the gargantuan machine was completely full of almost every option he could think of.

He'd never seen a full food processor before.

His mom had only ever filled their own enough for whatever they were making. If the readings were right, this thing was well stocked enough to feed a family for a week.

After five minutes of browsing, Damien settled on steak and potatoes. The processor was faster than he was used to as well. In just five minutes it was ready, and he wolfed the food down in three. Utterly delicious. Whatever brand of processor paste Lillian used, it blew anything he'd ever made for himself out of the water.

Full and focused, Damien dumped his cutlery in the washing cabinet and went to work on the last three videos. First up was the footage of his three-way battle with Rising Tide and Godhammer. There was an awful lot of explaining to do, not least of all why he'd decided fighting two guilds would be easier than fighting one. Having almost died in the process, Damien wasn't even sure he knew himself.

After an hour-long struggle, he finished with it and went to his profile to upload – and was stunned. He'd gone to bed last night before peak gaming time, too early to see if his and Lillian's efforts had paid off.

Now, his profile had almost half a million views. His votes hadn't increased quite as dramatically, but it was still huge to him. Somewhere, out in the world, forty-two thousand people wanted him to succeed. The word was out. He was internet famous. Again.

He loaded up Saga Online and was met with the same page as when he'd just died, with the notable exception that there were only seven minutes to go before he could log back in. *Finally*. Damien took his last chance at a bathroom break and then retired to his room. He lay back on the bed in time to watch the last few seconds drag past and at zero, the annoying message was finally replaced with the first notification window of his second life.

Choose your respawn location:
1: Camelot
2: Base
3: Zone Entrance

Phew. At least there was a choice. Then again, it made sense. Mobius Enterprises wouldn't have made many friends by ending a twenty-four-hour timer with a long walk of shame. Or in Damien's case, if they'd plonked him in the middle of Camelot, another twenty-four-hour timer.

He quickly selected his base and the loading animation appeared, re-integrating him with the game. The screen aligned with his vision, the weight of the headset faded, and everything went dark.

He blinked, staring up at the domed ceiling of his base. At least he hadn't been dropped on his backside this time. He turned his head and realized where he was: lying upon the altar of the Soul Well.

Damien propped himself up on his elbows, flinching when a surprised squawk rang through his ears. Garbled screeching of pure euphoria followed. The remnants of Damien's forces came running from every corner, whooping with excitement and prostrating themselves before him.

One of them offered him a ruptured spleen, which he politely declined while still appreciating the sentiment. Then he swiveled his legs around to sit on the edge of the altar and they fell silent, their eyes boggling. The imp at the front of the group cracked first, snorting back a laugh. That was all it took.

Suddenly, all of them were rolling around, slapping their knees and braying. Damien folded his arms and looked down to where they were pointing. *Oh.* It was like that dream he used to have: he wasn't wearing any pants. While the robes hung low enough to cover his modesty, his bare legs made it seem more like a skirt than an assassin's garb. It seemed he was destined to spend his life periodically finding himself in a state of undress with an audience nearby.

Why weren't his leggings equipped? He opened his menu, looking to see if they'd somehow escaped to his inventory, before the realization hit him like a poorly calibrated driverless truck.

Shankyou had taken them. And without them, Damien would be missing his stat bonus for wearing the whole set.

He yelled with frustration before sheepishly cutting it short, remembering Lillian had retrieved them for him. He'd have them back by the evening.

Damien shooed his laughing imps away. They scattered to the outskirts of his base, resuming their dissonant chatter.

"Welcome back to the land of the living."

Damien's heart leapt in his chest before easing itself loose. His tolerance to Bartholomew's sneak attacks had gone down, thanks to his absence.

"I hope your death doesn't dishearten you too much. I've

died plenty of times and just look at me! I'm the picture of health."

Damien could think of no one, dead or alive, who looked less the picture of health than Bart. He looked more like the picture of advanced necrosis coupled with severe leprosy. But at least he was being supportive.

"Don't worry, Bart. I still got this."

Bartholomew's fetid forehead furrowed.

"I should hope so. I'd hate to have tolerated your base here for nothing. I see you've lost my lovingly crafted Occultist Leggings, as well. This generation has no respect, no respect at all!"

"Actually, I've got a friend who picked them up for me. She's coming later."

Bartholomew scoffed and shot him a scathing sneer. Damien thought he was about to be mocked for claiming to know a girl, but Bart was way ahead of him.

"A friend? You? Made a friend? I'll believe it when I see it. In any case, I've been waiting for you. I have the item you commissioned."

His hand retreated into his robes and returned holding a golden disc with a golden chain fastened to it. In the center there was a gap, where a glowing green stone hovered as if held there by magnets. The color jogged Damien's memory. This was the artifact he'd paid Bartholomew to craft out of the rare boss drop more than two days ago. Damien inspected the trinket, hoping against hope for something truly incredible.

Unrelenting Talisman
Charges: 1/1
Unique effect: Upon using a charge, the next spell you cast will have its casting time reduced to 0.1 seconds for ten seconds.

Damien frowned. A single use item? That was a shame. He'd rather have had an increase to his stats, a new spell he could use or a permanent passive ability. The random number gods had not smiled on him this day.

The artifact would've been more valuable in the hands of a caster with high intelligence and heavy hitting spells that had long cast times but no cooldowns. With an ability like Chaotic Bolt, you could fire off dozens in the time it would normally take to cast one. It wouldn't really benefit spells like Demon Gate or Implosion, since they already had instant casting times but cooldowns of over 10 seconds. He put it away in his inventory, trying not to show his disappointment.

"Thank you for reminding me, Bart. I'll try and put it to good use."

"It was my pleasure. Try not to die again."

Bartholomew gave his standard curt nod and seamlessly floated out the door. Damien was at last allowed to sit and think about what he should do next. At least one thing came to mind. He dismissed two of the base's imps, granting himself a single soul. Then he pointed at the floor and resummoned Noigel.

The imp dropped through and landed at his feet before taking in his surroundings. Then he looked up at Damien, his usual sardonic grin giving way to a surprised 'O' as he took in Damien's empty gear slot and the bare legs below the hem of his robes. With Noigel resummoned there were exactly ten imps in the base, granting him Forbidden Knowledge. He knew what the missing gear meant, and he didn't find it funny at all. He raised his eyes to meet Damien's own, his face twisting in agony.

"What happened? Were there more outside?"

Damien nodded slowly. That pretty much covered it. Noigel wrung his hands around the top of his hairless head, venting his frustration in a piercing screech that made the other imps stop and stare.

"Don't worry. Even if I died, something good came out of it. Give me a few minutes to figure out what we're doing today. I'll call you when I need you."

Noigel saluted, his lingering anger clear from his narrowed eyes and clenched fists, then stomped behind the Gateway to pout in private. The other imps might not have been as clever as he was, but they knew well enough to cut him a wide berth.

Damien rose to his feet. It was good to be back. It wasn't the coziest place in the world, but he'd spent more time here over the last few days than anywhere else. It might not have catered to his physical needs, but it was the place he was most familiar with and had control over.

It felt like home. Almost.

Damien checked his item chest, seeing if he had anything to cover his bare legs with. He only had the rags. Still, just like when he'd started, they were better than nothing. He selected them and they appeared over his legs, a little scratchy but otherwise tolerable. It was a shame he'd either traded all his back-up gear for an upgrade or broken it down for parts. The rags would have to do.

He opened his Stat page and inspected the Soul Well simultaneously, comprehensively reviewing his situation. It was a bit of a mess. Ten imps was not much of a fighting force. He'd have to replenish his minions if he was going to be of any use. His Soul Well was still 6 souls shy of full capacity as well, at 24/30. Last, but not least, the missing leggings of his Occultist Adept set had cut his endurance, agility, constitution and wisdom by eighteen points each, thanks largely to losing the set bonus. The worst part of this for Damien was that his Soul Summon Limit had gone down from 25 to 23. He still had five hours before Lillian returned. That would be enough time to replenish his Soul Summon Limit, gather souls to max out his Soul Well and fill his base with minions while he was at it. He certainly wasn't going to spend five hours sitting around here doing nothing.

Damien bound all ten imps to himself and picked his way through the traps littering The Downward Spiral, the imps avoiding the gauntlet by simply flying up through the open space in the middle.

What had once seemed like a dangerous journey was now a simple trip. Damien's route away from the road, coupled with his familiarity of the mountain passage between Tintagel and Brociliande, allowed him to arrive at the next zone in less than twenty minutes. He was now the same level as his old avatar, Scorpius, and he knew a good Player vs Environment zone deep in the forest with reasonably straightforward enemies. He'd have to keep an eye out for players, but he'd be able to harvest soul energy there in relative safety.

Soon he came to a barrier of trees and stepped through them, halting at the edge of the meadow within to observe. It was an open space, full of wild boar clumped together in groups of three. They were level 26, high enough to be worthy enemies but not high enough to pose a significant threat. Ideal for farming soul energy, even if it would take a little longer than dealing with more dangerous foes. Thankfully, there were no other players in sight. Grinding was not a popular way to level up.

Damien pointed at the nearest group and his imps charged out of cover, swarming over the boars like ants and attacking them in a rain of claws. He made a mental note to re-equip his imps with tridents when he got back, as long as he had the materials to do so. The reduced damage from their lack of equipment resulted in each boar impaling an imp on their tusks before being overwhelmed. But each boar dropped a soul on death. A net gain of zero imps. Damien looted the bodies, then summoned a hell hound instead and withdrew his Sacrificial Dagger to join the fray. That should speed things up.

With the hound occupying an enemy, Damien only lost two imps to the next group. So he summoned another hell hound, converting his utility-focused imps to close combat troops by degrees. Once he had three hounds, it became possible to take down the enemies consistently without too many casualties.

Damien was now glad he'd decided to campaign against Rising Tide early in his leveling. He'd forgotten just how long it had taken him to get Scorpius to level 28, and why. Players granted far more XP than he'd get from normal mobs, thanks to his Soul Harvest ability. They also awarded souls more consistently, and their unpredictability could be negated by luring them into traps and taking them by surprise. Unless they had the same idea, as he'd so recently discovered to his cost.

It was a high risk, high reward playstyle, and he'd experienced both sides of that balancing act. Playing an occultist in the manner of a regular class, doing quests and killing mobs, would be a rather arduous process at lower levels with only imps and wraiths as servants. Even those damned rats had caused him grief early on.

All in all, it was a longer process farming souls this way. Still, it was a safe, if time consuming, system for replenishing his army.

He'd refilled his minion count and had just finished filling his Soul Reserve when a blue chat box popped up, along with a dialing tone. It was Lillian.

Thinking he'd lost track of time during the battles, he checked the clock. It was only 14:30. That was odd. She wasn't due back for another three hours. Damien called his minions in to protect him while he was occupied.

"Hey, what's going on?"

"I got home a few minutes ago, now I'm standing outside your base. Come here. We're going on a little trip."

She hung up. Whatever was going on, it had to be serious if she'd left work early. Damien activated a new portal back to the base and sent all his minions through before following after them. He looked over his forces briefly.

Fourteen imps and three hell hounds. The beginnings of a new army. He gratefully dumped 6 souls into his Soul Well, finally bringing it to 30/30. Then he led his party back up the stairs of The Downward Spiral again.

They broke the surface and Damien picked his way through the trees, coming to the edge of the shadowy veil nearest the road. He poked his head through and was met with a gorgeous sight.

On his way up, he'd been wondering how Lillian could have got there so quickly. The enormous brown warhorse she sat on was more than answer enough. She stirred and gave Damien a grin, tossing him a bundle of fabric with her free hand.

"I believe these are yours. Put 'em on and let's get going."

Damien looked at the bundle. His lost leggings. He equipped them and they phased out of his hands back to where they belonged. He was complete again. He gave himself a quick inspection before stepping out of the forest and into full view of the outside world.

His horde of demons followed him out, eyeing Lillian suspiciously but remaining docile at his instruction. Lillian's mouth dropped open. For a moment Damien thought she was impressed, then she started rapidly shaking her head.

"Can't take them with you, man. There are too many and we need to keep a low profile. Unsummon them for now."

Damien stared at her incredulously. She might as well have asked him to throw away his daggers because the pointy bits were dangerous. He opened his mouth to say as much, but Lillian wasn't in the mood for debate.

"Did I forget to mention we're in a hurry? No? So hurry! Get rid of them, now!"

Damien gave up. Lillian wasn't going to listen. Whatever had brought her back so early had her agitated. If she wasn't going to let him have his minions, he should at least have a full Soul Reserve. He thought about it and dismissed the three hell hounds first, getting 4.5 soul energy refunded. Then he dismissed three imps to get the last 1.5 souls he needed to bring his Soul Reserve to max. When he cast a portal to send what was left through, he realized he'd miscalculated again: the portal had cost another soul to open.

Muttering darkly under his breath so that Lillian wouldn't hear, he dismissed a final two imps before ordering the pitiful remnants of his afternoon's labors back to the base. A mere nine imps. It was one less than he'd started with, but at least his Soul Well and his Soul Reserve were both full. It was well concealed, but he had in fact made progress.

Noigel was the last to pass through, but before he could go Damien beckoned him back to his side. If Noigel was bound to his base, he wouldn't be able to resummon him wherever they were going. He might be needed. Lillian eyeballed the offending imp pointedly, her impatience palpable. Damien responded by ordering Noigel to take refuge under his cloak and eyeballing her back. He'd already sacrificed half his army on her say-so, he wasn't going to compromise on this.

"Where are we going?"

Lillian glared at him for a few moments longer, then relented, smacking her hand on the saddle behind her. Damien didn't ask again. He leapt on, helped up by Lillian's gauntleted hand.

As they set off, Noigel poked his head out from the folds of Damien's cloak and gave him an imploring, drawn-out stare. He couldn't speak without any other imps fueling his 'We Are Many' ability, but Damien knew why he was so spooked.

He hadn't gotten around to telling Noigel that Lillian was on their side. He'd have explained it if there wasn't a more immediate problem coming up. Having spent the last three days painstakingly avoiding the road, Lillian was ploughing them straight onto it in broad daylight.

"Uh, Lillian, can we be a bit more subtle? I'm not a big fan of traveling where—"

He was cut off by a text window that popped into his peripheral vision. He focused and drew it to the center.

Lillian has invited you to join her party. Accept/Decline.

He accepted just as they pulled onto the road itself. A new health bar appeared above his own and Noigel's, with a whopping 1500 health in it. Lillian immediately raised the tempo, spurring her steed into a full gallop.

"As long as you're in my party, it won't be a problem. I've been doing quests for the Empire for two months and my reputation with them is Exalted. As long as I'm party leader and you keep your mouth shut, we'll be fine."

She sounded pretty sure of herself, but Damien couldn't help worrying. It was totally ingrained in him to avoid attention on the move by now, on and offline. What she had to say next increased his anxiety tenfold.

"We're going to Rising Tide's waiting room."

Damien stared at the back of her head listlessly. All the big guilds had settlements connected to each other with portals. The biggest guilds would also build a compound, accessible to select players from the portal stone network.

These specialized settlements served as clubhouses, areas for the high-level guild members to relax until enough people came online to form a party. Damien raised his voice to be heard over the sound of Noigel's gibbering.

"I'm not sure that's a good idea," he said, more calmly than he felt. "I've only just got back, I'm not ready for an all out fight."

"That's OK, neither are they. Right now, Aetherius has all his best players on a giant forty-man raid with him for a special stream tonight. All his strongest are knee-deep in monsters. The waiting room's almost empty. It's the last place they'll expect to be attacked and it's the perfect time to do it."

Damien mulled it over. The reasoning was sound; the target, not so much.

"Why do we have to hit the most dangerous available option? Can't we do something safer? Like, I dunno… cover ourselves in cooking oil and fight a dragon?"

Lillian abruptly pulled on the reins and the horse drew to a stop, right next to a pair of guardsmen on horseback. Damien quickly concealed Noigel under his cloak, but he needn't have bothered. The NPCs gave her a cheerful wave and Lillian waved back as the two of them rode past. Damien may as well not have existed. She turned in the saddle to look at him directly, her eyes boring into his skull.

"Look. You've done well over the last few days. Really. I don't think anyone's ever leveled so fast. But it's not enough. You may have hurt Rising Tide, but you haven't even touched Aetherius. I was waiting for him to post your death and it never came. Then it hit me. He doesn't want to acknowledge you as an enemy. He's only got to ride out the competition for a couple more days and he'll win by a landslide. We have to bring the fight to him."

Damien returned her stare. Noigel had stopped gibbering and was listening with interest. Damien remained unconvinced.

"I already died once. Just turn this horse around and let me—"

Her closed fist whacked into his shoulder. She'd pulled the punch and Damien's pain settings were low, but it still hurt like hell. 56 points of damage in a single unarmed attack. Good grief. She made Bartholomew look like a wuss.

"There *is no time*! For some reason, they haven't kicked me out of the guild yet. They ignore me, and they've removed all my privileges, but I can still see the notifications. They're going into lockdown this weekend, then they'll sit in their fortified positions and hold their defenses until the competition ends."

She muttered under her breath and pointed at Damien. He was filled with warmth at the core of his body and then it all flowed into his shoulder, healing his wound. Damien had never been healed by another person before. It felt every bit as soothing as watching his hit points rise. Lillian patted him on the same shoulder, some of the intensity fading from her stare. She was remorseful but undeterred.

"I've been thinking about this all day. We need to do something big to boost your campaign. This is that thing. But you're going to have to follow my lead and do exactly as I say. Can you do that, or should we find you some cooking oil?"

Noigel was poking Damien in the chest. His color had returned, his eyes set and unflinching. Without looking away from Damien, he pointed at Lillian and nodded vigorously. Great. So now Noigel was in Lillian's camp as well. Everybody was in a rush to die today.

"Fine. Let's get on with it. The sooner we die, the sooner we respawn tomorrow."

He expected an angry retort. Instead, Lillian smiled broadly and tousled his hair.

"Awwww, dat's da spiwit!"

Noigel brayed laughter for all of half a second until Damien shot him a glance that would have made Toutatis flinch. The imp hurriedly turned and stared straight at Lillian's back, his hands clamped over his mouth.

"Sorry, Damien," Lillian said, barely holding back a laugh. "This is really important. I'd do it alone, but you're the one who needs exposure here. You'll be disabling their base while I whittle down their numbers, and then you'll deal the coup de grace: we're going to record you killing Aetherius's pride and joy."

Damien raised an eyebrow.

"Kill? It's just an outpost. It's not alive."

She shot him a grin that had no place on a paladin's face.

"No, that's not what I meant. Aetherius's pride and joy is *inside* the base. And you're going to kill it."

Without waiting for his reply, Lillian dug her heels in and the horse surged ahead. Damien almost fell off, his arms wrapping around the only thing he could see to hold on to: Lillian's waist. It was covered in plate mail and she would barely have felt a thing, but beneath his headset, Damien went a deep shade of Noigel red.

"So, are you listening? Here's the plan…"

30

ASSAULT

I t didn't take long for Lillian to explain the plan of attack. They were just entering Brociliande by the time she finished, passing through the Empire's guard post with no more resistance than smiles and waves.

After all his reservations Damien hated to admit it, but it was a good plan. On paper. Whether everything would go as smoothly as Lillian described was another matter entirely. But now he knew what the real target was, he could see why she was so excited. He was getting fired up himself just thinking about it. There was just one, teeny, tiny problem.

"You know I can't resummon minions from my base, right? I can only summon new ones to help us. My portal only works one way."

Lillian turned so violently in the saddle that the horse almost veered off the road.

"Are you serious? Why didn't you say so? Is that going to be a problem?"

Damien thought about it. He still had 10 soul energy with which to summon new units. For Lillian's plan, he could.... yes, that should work. He still couldn't help being a little annoyed.

"I was trying to! If you remember, you were pretty adamant I needed to get rid of them. It should be fine, if things go as you said. Not ideal, you know? Just... fine."

Lillian groaned and set her eyes ahead again, shaking her head.

"I'm sorry your class is weird, all right? We only ran through your combat abilities yesterday, I didn't know it worked like that. I just assumed it.... ah, screw it. It doesn't make any difference, it would have taken too long to avoid the guard posts if we brought your demons along. We'll just have to do our best."

The road curved left, but rather than following it Lillian led them straight into the trees. They reached the mountain range at the edge of the zone and drew to a stop. Damien jumped clear as Lillian wheeled the horse round to set on her way again.

"Follow the wall and you'll find it. Stay in the trees until I give you the signal."

She didn't wait for a reply before spurring her horse back to the road. Damien set off ahead, keeping the rock face on his right as Noigel perched on his shoulder. After a few minutes' jog, Damien started to pick out spots of gray in between the trees ahead of them.

Despite the abundance of resources the forest provided, this outpost had been built from stone. The craftsmanship was well thought through: the wall slanted forward ever so slightly and was a smooth surface with no gaps in the mortar, making it almost impossible to scale by conventional means. Rising Tide had really pushed the boat out on this one, although they'd saved on time and resources by incorporating the mountain range into the back wall.

A circular parapet overhanging the wall provided excellent line of sight up and down the length of the barrier. It would be a perfect platform for ranged heroes to shoot down anyone foolish enough to attempt the climb. If there had been anyone stationed there, at least.

Damien needed to get higher. Fortunately, this was a trick he already knew. He sent Noigel up to find a decent vantage point, waiting for the thumbs up. Then he Demon Gated, his hand instinctively tightening around the top of the trunk Noigel had been holding a moment earlier.

He was still a long way from the outer wall, much too far to jump, but the tree was high enough for him to see into the base. While Noigel returned to his side, he scouted out the hidden compound in front of him.

Lillian's intel had been good. Only a single level 33 ranger stood on the parapet overlooking the main gate. An inner wall divided the waiting room into two sections. The front was built less like the military outpost Damien had envisioned and more like a funfair with vendors and stalls, full of NPCs easily recognizable by their green names. They were idling away at each other in the absence of anyone to buy their wares.

In the center was a huge open courtyard offering a variety of activities: there were fighting rings for duels, training dummies to test your damage with, target practice ranges and even a racing track. Damien could see why players would spend time here. The customized shops were a luxury feature and the courtyard offered plenty of good training and fun rolled into one.

Right now, there were only two players using the facilities: a level 32 mage testing his spell rotation on a training dummy and a level 30 assassin backstabbing the one in the next lane, surreptitiously looking over to see whose damage numbers were higher while feigning disinterest.

Damien was jolted back into the moment when he spotted Lillian riding out of the trees toward the main gate. He lost sight of her behind the wall, but the ranger stood up and moved to the edge of his parapet.

Damien couldn't hear what they were saying from this distance, but the ranger was shaking his head and waving her away. That hadn't been the plan. Lillian was supposed to ride inside and cause a scene so Damien could do his part uninterrupted. This was not going well.

The argument continued for a full minute before the ranger pantomimed her crying, flipped a swift finger over the wall and turned his back on her. So, they weren't even inside yet and already Lillian's plan was fraying around the edges.

At least she'd been right about the lack of defenses. As long as nobody else showed up while he was working, Damien could do his part first and worry about Lillian's later.

He tore his eyes away from the front gate and twisted his head past the inner wall all the way to the back, where Lillian had said the core buildings would be. The Guild House was a fortified bunker, set in the middle of the back wall at the safest point in the base. The Gathering Hub was out in front of it, a circular ring of floating stones with a portal stone resting in the middle. That was his first objective.

Damien pointed at it and Noigel flew straight from the branch, maintaining his height until he was over the wall and then swooping down towards the Gathering Hub. Damien was keeping an eye on his surroundings, making sure nobody else happened to show up and spot him, when a resounding crash from the entrance turned all eyes in that direction.

The main gate was wood reinforced with iron, but the right-hand panel had caved inward and the timber bar holding it closed splintered. The ranger ran to the edge of his parapet, looking down just in time to witness the creation of a matching dent on the other side of the gate. He drew his bow, loosed an arrow downward and was nocking the next when another blow tore the doors apart. The wooden beam lay in two pieces, the cracked doorframe showering the alcove with splinters.

The mage and rogue had stopped what they were doing, moving toward the intrusion. They paused when Lillian stepped through, her Divine Might active and Hammertime's war hammer twirling between her fingers. It seemed she'd had some practice with it since she acquired it from Damien. The players hesitated for a moment when she stepped through the breach. Then the assassin ran in, daggers drawn, and the mage started channeling mana.

Damien shook himself. Lillian had managed to cause the distraction after all. Now he was on the clock.

He looked to Noigel and found him hiding behind the portal stone – with good reason. Two more players, a dual-wielding warrior and a priest, had come running out of the Guild House on their way to defend the front gate.

Damien hesitated.

Five against one was a little much for someone to handle in a straightforward fight, even for a paladin. If Lillian died, Damien wouldn't be able to handle them by himself without the element of surprise. He looked back to the battle and saw it had already taken a turn for the worse.

The assassin had vanished into thin air and Lillian had returned to using her sword and shield, the latter of which she was trapped behind as the mage cast a churning beam of raw red energy at her. In the instant Damien looked, the assassin reappeared in her blind spot, running at full tilt.

She'd locked herself up guarding against the Arcane Beam and left herself exposed to the assassin's attack. Why had she done that? What was she thinking? They all found out together seconds later.

As the assassin committed, her shield started to glow brightly. Then it pulsed and a broad beam of red mana, a perfect reflection of the one cast against her only twice as strong, blasted back toward the mage. 'Repent'. A trait granting Paladins a spell reflection skill with a full minute cooldown, usually passed over in preference of something more useful for PvE. Yet it had contributed a great deal to Lillian earning her nickname. Engulfed in a stream of his own empowered, vaporizing energy, the mage obligingly disintegrated.

The assassin was still in mid-leap, his daggers raised high to penetrate Lillian's heavy armor, when the rim of her newly available shield whirled around and struck him directly in the throat. His body stretched out under its surface, his arms helplessly pinioned over his head, as Lillian delivered a knee to the base of his spine that folded him in half. His body bounced on the ground, then was pinned to it by her sword, which she drove through his leather jerkin, into the earth, down to the hilt.

The entire maneuver had taken three seconds from start to finish.

Two players were dead. It was surgical.

Damien reconsidered Lillian's need for assistance.

Yeah. She's probably fine.

The remaining guards had rounded the inner wall and reached the courtyard. Damien Demon Gated into the ring of stones marking out the teleportation zone and immediately pointed at the ground to summon a succubus. A new player could arrive at any moment and he was completely defenseless. Ten seconds had never seemed so long.

The succubus leapt from her portal and picked up Damien's intention immediately, landing at the base of the portal stone and raking her claws through the runes covering its surface.

A health bar appeared showing the structural damage being inflicted. The Gathering Hub had 1000 durability points, but the succubus was only inflicting 14 damage with each rune she scratched out.

Noigel returned to help her as Damien used his last 3 soul energy to summon a hell hound. The spell was almost complete when a luminescent blue sphere cracked into existence within the ring of stones and a player started to materialize inside it.

This wasn't going to be pretty.

They'd be fully formed in just a few moments and the sphere would render them immune to all damage before then. Damien immediately had his succubus turn to face them and start casting her Chaotic Bolt. Rather than adopting a combat stance, Noigel crouched behind the port sphere on his hands and knees.

The summoned hound and the player arrived simultaneously, a level 33 heavily armored warrior with a two-handed war-axe strapped to his back. Not a good opponent to have at close quarters.

He looked curiously between Damien and the succubus, his hands reaching out to conjure his weapon into his grasp, before the Chaotic Bolt pelted into his face at point blank range. The warrior stumbled backward and tripped over Noigel.

Damien took no chances.

As the hound moved in to engage, his succubus cast Circle of Hell under the warrior. Damien neatly stepped out of the area of effect as it formed, just in time for Noigel, the hound and the succubus to gang up on him as his armor was reduced and the damage over time took effect. Noigel leapt onto his face while the succubus slotted her claws into gaps in the prone player's plate mail, mitigating the damage reduction it provided even further. The hound latched onto his arm and wrestled it to the floor, igniting to inflict extra damage.

The heavily armored warrior was stuck on his back like a turtle, Noigel was preventing him from guarding against the succubus with his free arm by sitting on his face, the hound savaging his other arm prevented him from equipping his two-handed weapon, he was on fire of both the regular and infernal variety and his armor value had been cut in half. By the time he wrenched Noigel off with his free hand, inflicting more damage on himself in the process, he was already well on his way to the big Gathering Hub in the sky. He resorted to repeatedly punching the hell hound in the head, fracturing the armored plates and inflicting severe damage despite the awful circumstances, but didn't manage to take it down before he finally, mercifully, succumbed to his wounds. It was a bad way to go.

Had he been able to equip his weapon things might have turned out differently, but Damien didn't feel like giving his enemies a sporting chance; he was fighting on their turf. This was a war. He'd promised it, now he was delivering.

With the warrior vanquished, the demons returned to the task of destroying the portal stone. The Circle of Hell had done minor structural damage as well, an unexpected bonus. Damien had received a good chunk of experience and 3 soul energy for the warrior's grisly death, which he turned into imps as fast as he could.

By the time he'd finished summoning the second imp, the portal stone still had over 234 left of its durability. He needed to destroy this thing before Aetherius and his party left the dungeon.

If they were properly organized, they'd have already heard about the attack and would be hightailing it to the dungeon entrance so they could teleport back. The fastest of them would be here in, what, three minutes?

This wasn't going fast enough.

Damien summoned the third imp and the succubus used up most of her remaining mana to cast Bloodlust, speeding up the group further. Damien joined in too, scratching through the symbols with the tips of his blades. His daggers weren't designed for this kind of target, but he could repair them at his demon forge when he got home.

After a lot of excruciating work, the Gathering Hub was reduced to a state of utter entropy, where it would be as easy to start rebuilding it from scratch as it would to repair the damage done. It had zero durability.

Damien got a good chunk of experience for disabling a high-level enemy structure. His XP bar had returned to zero following his death, but after an afternoon of grinding, killing a higher-level player and now an act of sabotage, it was starting to look well fed again. It had risen back to 18482/28000.

Better yet, he'd bought them valuable time.

The nearest Rising Tide outpost to this one was a ten-minute ride away. If he helped Lillian finish off the last players, they'd have officially taken control of the settlement.

Damien ran around the inner wall and into the courtyard, his minions fanning out behind him. Lillian was in a standoff against the warrior, deflecting the wide sweeps of his dual axes with her sword while the ranger peppered her with arrows from the parapet above. Her Divine Might had run out and a nearby priest was keeping Lillian's adversary at full health and stamina, allowing him to make dangerous lunges without worrying about the consequences.

Damien allocated his targets. He sent the succubus to distract the ranger, along with two of the imps. The hound and another imp went to help Lillian with her warrior problem. Noigel he sent out last, diverting him around the outside to land lightly behind the priest.

Damien Demon Gated and performed a textbook dual dagger execution: one dagger through the heart via the back and the other drawn across the throat. At least Shankyou had taught him something. His damage was more than high enough for the double sneak critical combination to translate into instant death.

All eyes fell on him as the priest's life signs vanished. The ranger had already dealt with his succubus from a distance and was taking aim at the imps as the priest fell. Now he turned and fired a rapid volley of three twisting, armor-penetrating arrows toward the new threat – ignoring the two imps closing in on his position.

Damien's kill had activated Rift Walker: resetting the cooldown on Demon Gate.

He used it again, swapping positions and momentum with the imp that had been closest to his target. Unfortunately, in his haste to avoid the arrows, he hadn't entirely thought this maneuver through: the imp had been flying through the air, straight towards his enemy. The ranger turned his head at the sound of Damien's scream, his intense concentration replaced with utter bewilderment. The bow was swiveling round when the two collided, the ranger hitting the parapet hard and skidding across it on his back with Damien on top.

Damien was only slightly more prepared for the collision than his foe. The extra half second was crucial. He jumped up and stuck his knee on the ranger's chest, holding him still and pinning his off-hand to the floor as he squirmed. He'd withdrawn the Striking Dagger from his enemy's chest for the second time when the ranger's right hand lunged upwards, holding a dagger of his own. He'd kept it out of sight by his side while he swapped weapons, using the time to find a critical point: an open section at Damien's core which his Leather Bindings did not quite cover.

The dagger plunged into it, up and under Damien's ribcage. Then, to his mounting horror, the ranger twisted it and drove it still deeper. The damage was much higher than it should have been. It wasn't just a regular attack, it was a melee ability. Damien dropped his weapons and grabbed the ranger's wrist with both hands before he could do any more damage. His foe still had half his health after the collision and two hits, Damien had been reduced to less than 30% by the frightening technique. The wound was bleeding and his health was still dropping. Even with both hands against one, it was a struggle to stop his enemy from withdrawing the blade to strike again. Damien had brought his wisdom stat to a knife fight.

He was still locked in the losing stalemate when his wisdom

stat paid off. The second imp crashed into the ranger's forearm head first, mouth open wide, and bit down. Hard. In the distance, drawing closer very quickly, Noigel was having what could only be described as a rage-fit. The other two imps were closer and arrived first. They clamped down with their teeth, clawing frantically and screaming shrilly, even with their mouths full. Damien clung to the ranger's dagger hand, trying to hold it steady as his foe kicked and yelled. Noigel finally arrived at maximum volume before doing his best hell hound impersonation: biting down on the ranger's throat.

The ranger finally stopped yelling and his hand went limp. Damien tossed it away. With the XP from the priest and ranger, Damien rose to level 29 and his health was blissfully restored.

It had been a close-run thing. Wings on the imps had proven invaluable on multiple occasions. Without numbers and the element of surprise, occultists might be the squishiest melee class in history.

Below him, Lillian had dealt with the warrior. Without his healer, he couldn't handle her alone. The hound lay dead, unfortunately, a clear axe wound through its head. The NPC vendors had already boarded up their shops to wait for the situation to pass.

For now, at least, the outpost was theirs.

"You took your time," grumbled Lillian as she looted the warrior. "Did you finish destroying the Hub?"

Damien decided it would be better not to share just how close to death he'd come. Lillian was under enough stress already. So was he. He played it cool.

"Sorry it took so long," he shouted down from the parapet. "I can't stab structures in the back."

He looted the ranger, an act of revenge for mocking Lillian and giving him such a scare, before Demon Gating back to the ground so he could gather the souls littered there. "Destroying buildings is more your scene. Glad you're making use of the hammer!"

"I told you it would be better in my hands. Let's go get what we came for."

Without waiting for a reply, Lillian headed straight to the back of the courtyard. She moved fast, despite her heavy armor. Damien ran behind her, the four imps flying out in front of him. Their destination was the stable lining the inner wall.

Stables were a valuable resource in Saga Online, much like parking spaces back in the real world. Also, like parking spaces, they weren't much use unless you had something worth putting in them. And according to Lillian, Aetherius had a sweet ride.

"He showed it off on his stream when he got it," she said over her shoulder. "He's planning to ride it in a victory parade when he wins the competition. If we take it out, nobody can deny we've hurt him."

It was a generic stable, full of straw and stalls in a high-roofed barn. The compartment on the end was separated from the rest of them and significantly bigger, large enough for what-ever was inside to run around in. That was where Lillian was headed. She reached it and Damien drew up beside her to look inside.

"Are you serious?"

"Yup. Isn't she a beauty?"

Standing casually, looking brooding and majestic all at once, was a pegasus. A mythical mount. It wasn't quite as big as Lillian's warhorse in frame, but it was far more beautiful. Radiant white fur gave way to sleek white feathers on the wings, which were folded neatly against its sides.

"Can't we just steal it?"

"Nope. We're making a statement; stealing it looks like we did it for the money. Besides, it won't let anyone ride it except Aetherius. You're going to have to kill it."

"But it's so pretty!"

"I know. That's why it's going to hurt Aetherius. Just get on with it!"

She turned and headed back across the ground toward the broken gate.

"Hey, aren't you going to help me?"

"Nope. My part is to watch out for enemies, your part is to kill the pretty horse and take a trophy. Suck it up!"

She was halfway across the courtyard before Damien could reply, leaving him alone. Great. He knew the pegasus wasn't a real animal, but killing it felt wrong. Assassinating players was one thing; they'd signed up for it. Killing monsters offered no moral quandary; it was either him or them. This was somehow different.

The pegasus was just owned by the wrong person. It had to be done, though. They'd come too far not to do what they'd come here to do. And it was just a collection of pixels for crying out loud.

Damien climbed into the enclosure, out of the sun, and summoned two wraiths. If he had to kill it, he could at least do it quickly. The pegasus was looking at him now, the wording of 'Aetherius's Pegasus' changing from green to orange as it extended its wings. It wasn't hostile yet, but it was debating whether or not Damien was a threat. The two wraiths blended into the shadows and came around it on either side. By the time they were at their positions, thirty seconds had passed. The pegasus had tired of Damien's presence. The text changed from orange to red. It was now hostile. In addition, a level popped up next to it. Level 30. Higher than Damien had expected.

It lowered its head and prepared to charge, making Damien's next orders that much easier. As one, the undetected wraiths dropped the scythes on their arms through its neck.

Damien sighed as it toppled over sideways. What a waste. He was still mourning the loss of the rarest mount he'd ever seen when his experience bar surged upward. What the pegasus lacked in durability, it made up for with rarity. The slaughter of the mythical creature had given him 11,500 experience points, far in excess of what he'd received for destroying the Hub. He was lucky the creature hadn't been expecting an attack. For such a considerable reward, it likely would have packed enough of a punch to have him for lunch.

In one kill he'd got a third of the way to level 30. It had left 3 soul energy behind as well, replenishing Damien's Soul Reserve to 9 points.

Previously, he'd felt conflicted about the deed. Now he was

just sorry Aetherius didn't have more pegasi he could work through. He went into his chat box and messaged Lillian.

'Finished, got it all recorded. Great exp. Do we have time for the last part?'

He placed his hands on the horse and inspected the loot. All it had to offer him was the severed head. How ironic. Aetherius had wanted to mount it in his parade, now Damien was going to mount it on his wall. He selected the head and willed it into his inventory, but it wouldn't budge. His inventory was too small. He got the four imps to carry it between them instead and headed outside.

Lillian was already running past the stables, toward the Guild House.

"Hurry it up! They're almost here!"

Damien sprinted after her, his laden imps and sun-kissed wraiths lagging behind. Lillian re-activated Divine Might and stormed into the building, hammer in hand. Moments later, there was a huge crash and a durability bar with 3000 points appeared above the entire building as she started to wreck shop. They'd already taken the settlement but had no way of holding it. Destroying the Guild House wasn't as personal as depriving Aetherius of his mount, but it would net a good chunk of XP and represented an undeniable victory over Rising Tide.

Damien had the imps drop the trophy next to him and they headed inside to help Lillian out. The wraiths limped in behind them, restoring their forms as they entered the shade. Damien summoned a new succubus and sent her in to cast Bloodlust while he remained outside, watching out for any players that might appear. Within five minutes, the building was nearing half health. The interior had been completely destroyed. Damien used one of his remaining two souls to cast a portal back to his base. Once this was done, they'd want to be out of here in a hurry.

It was halfway summoned when Lillian's hammer tore a hole through the outer wall, spewing out swirling blocks of granite.

She had started work on the infrastructure. Damien called his minions back. This was beyond what they could do, and he wanted them clear so she didn't end up killing them by mistake. They crossed the threshold as a second explosion tore through the building a little further along the wall. The Guild House groaned and then, in the wake of a third explosion, caved inward.

The durability bar disappeared as the building it pertained to crossed the line between ruins and rubble. It hadn't put up much of a fight, but it had been as sturdy as any boss.

Damien received another 9775 experience points for his assistance in destroying the core of the Rising Tide settlement. It wasn't nearly as much as he'd received on his raids against large parties, but between the players, the Hub, the mythical mount and now this, he'd managed to accumulate a level and a half.

He was torturously close to level 30. Lillian punched her way out of the debris and started running toward him, looking deeply serious.

Damien knew it wasn't part of the plan, but he couldn't help trying his luck.

"Nice job! Do we have time for another building? I'm just about to hi—"

She reached him, grabbed him by the scruff of his neck and casually dragged him behind her with her sword hand, thrusting her shield into the space he'd been occupying. It rang loudly as the arcane missiles intended for Damien exploded across its surface.

Rising Tide's raid party was back. They were trying to cut off their escape, the ranged units running along the walls and hurling projectiles as the melee units tore across the open ground. Lillian had blocked the arcane missiles well and sustained little damage, but they were under heavy fire now.

Lillian kept her shield raised in one hand and Damien clutched firmly in the other, her shield glowing white as she redirected a fireball into the first wave. Damien's attention was elsewhere. His portal was flickering at the edges and had started to contract. They'd entered combat. It was closing.

"Lillian! Portal!"

It might not have been the skill she knew best, but her instincts were finely tuned. She looked between the shrinking portal and the pegasus head laying tauntingly in front of it. She had no hands available to pick it up, but when there's a will, there's a way. Lillian was not short on real willpower.

She drew back her leg and punted the head through the portal, screaming obscenities at no one in particular, before dragging Damien bodily through it. The portal closed, leaving what was left of his minions behind.

He'd not even had time to order them through in the chaos, but they were a small price to pay for what had been accomplished. He'd have to apologize to Noigel later. Lillian stood up and extended a hand to him, which he took and pulled on until they were face to face. For the first time since they'd reconvened, she was smiling again.

"There. I'd like to see him ignore that."

31

EARNING YOUR NAME

L illian set the newest video in pride of place at the top of Damien's profile and removed her headset, grinning broadly.

"I don't think that could've gone much better. Shame I had to give away the pegasus head, though."

"Are you kidding? If that's all Bart wants, let him have it. Trust me."

"I believe you. He's a weird one, isn't he? My reputation with the occultists is 'tolerated'; I didn't know that reputation level even existed."

That was something Damien hadn't thought of. Bartholomew hadn't been pleased to discover Damien's new 'friend' was a paladin, exalted with the Empire. At least, not until Lillian quit her guild on the spot and offered the head of Aetherius's mount as proof of disloyalty. Following some uncomfortable sniffing and an all too familiar round of condescending questions, to which Lillian had responded with gusto, he'd taken an instant liking to her. They hadn't mingled with the vampire much longer before logging off.

Lillian wanted to edit the footage as quickly as possible, ideally making it public before Aetherius's forty-man raid stream was out. It was a lot of work, but she'd stitched Damien's footage together with her own to create a single video showing what each of them had been doing. The two of them voiced it together, credited it as a collaborative effort and it went out at 17:55, five minutes before Aetherius's raid stream was due.

Damien stretched into the sofa, groaning with relief. He hadn't had a moment's rest since Lillian called him to action three and a half hours ago.

"So, what do we do now?"

"Now? We wait. Keep an eye on the streams. We need to see how people react."

Damien nodded and reluctantly put his headset back on, waiting for Aetherius's raid footage to show up. In fact, their attack yielded an unexpected bonus: Aetherius's raid stream, eagerly anticipated by every Saga Online fan with a pulse, had been delayed by an hour.

This gave everyone plenty of time to browse their way to Damien's new video and figure out why for themselves. Lillian linked the footage in all the right places to get it maximum exposure. When the forty-man raid was finally uploaded, the comments section was full of people asking how his pegasus was.

Lillian placed a new link in the comments section of Aetherius's video itself, where it accumulated five thousand clicks before it was picked up on and deleted. It was far too late by then. Bit by bit, everyone was learning of that afternoon's events.

The hype was real. It was as real as when Damien had fought Toutatis, granting him his unscheduled fifteen minutes of fame. He'd hoped to make something of that, to take advantage of the publicity to get support in the competition. Despite Aetherius taking that away from him, he was still here. More than that, Damien had made himself a threat.

Together, he and Lillian had heaped humiliation upon Aetherius, just as he had heaped humiliation upon them. His entire competition campaign had been reduced to a cautionary tale, living proof that you made your own demons. It was the big news of the day, and the timing of it, just as the competition was entering its final phase, couldn't have been better: Daemien's profile was raking in views.

Even better, the votes on Aetherius's profile were decreasing. In the wake of this embarrassment, people were rescinding their votes and re-allocating them elsewhere. While the competition leader was still far ahead, the gap between them was diminishing.

Normally it was advisable not to check the comments, but Damien took a deep breath and plunged into the comments section on his pegasus video.

Mr.Rheeeeeeeeeeeee: Is that a blink? Can this guy blink?!?
WomboCombo: Not exactly, but it's close. He switches places with the imps. Go check his profile, he's got some videos about it.
BrawndusTheEverythingMutilator: here ya go 'Daemien v Rising Tide v Godhammer'.
RonFlawedSpamBlam: I don't get it. Why does he get so much experience for the horse?
FullThottle: S'not a horse. It's a Pegasus. Uber rare creature, level was lowered after training but you still get big rewards for killing them. Aetherius should have kept it safer.
CactusLover: Yeeeee! Scorpius, mah boyyyy! Lillian has the tank, you have the spank! Put Aetherius over your knee and teach him some manners! (⏝) <(^o^<)
Shankyou: Whatever. Daemien's nothing special. Killed him myself yesterday XD So easy. Put it on my channel just now, check it out if you don't believe me: 'Revenge! Suck it, Daemien!'

Oooooie. Get a load of Shankyou. Still sore about your dagger, no doubt.

Given the inconvenience and misery he'd caused, not to mention the gloating as he performed the killing blow, Damien couldn't care less. But now he was ripping on Damien on his own video, using it to publicize his death. So, Rising Tide had finally got around to making the announcement Lillian was waiting for. Not that it meant as much now Damien had hurt them so badly. Still, it warranted a decent response.

Damien raised the visor on his IMBA set to speak with Lillian.

"Hey, do you remember Shankyou? That guy who killed me outside the Malignant Crypt? You got him just after, right? Were you recording?"

"Yup. Kept that one for if they posted your death. Why? Did they?"

Damien nodded and Lillian immediately slipped on her headset, clicking the link to Shankyou's profile that Damien had provided. He started watching the video at the same time as she did. It was strange watching the scene play out from Shankyou's perspective. He wasn't kidding. It really had been all too easy. The video conveniently omitted the part where Lillian had got involved. Lillian sent the footage Damien yearned for to his chat box. It was short, a mere ten-second clip. He opened it and watched. Then he sputtered. He involuntarily closed his eyes for the last five seconds and had to watch again from the beginning, grimacing in a bizarre mix of horror and satisfaction.

Oh yeah. Shankyou's revenge had been short lived.

"Do you mind if I post this publicly?"

"Go for it! Tag me, you and Shankyou in it. That way people can connect the dots and get the whole picture. More exposure for us!"

Damien named the video, tagged all three of them and added a thoughtful little message.

Daemien: That was a great kill. Might want to work on your exits: 'Revenge! Suck it, Daemien! Continued, part 2 of 2'. Thanks for the dagger by the way. It's a winner. P.S, Lillian's shield apologizes for moving too fast. It should have at least bought you dinner.

He posted the comment and held his breath. A few seconds later, Lillian was giggling into her headset. She pulled it off and grinned over at him, her cheeks flushed red.

"Nice! We want the publicity focused on you, though, so I'll pledge my support for you officially on my channel. That way, hopefully, some of my fans will vote for you instead."

Damien was touched. He knew pledging to him made sense if they wanted to put him in contention with Aetherius, but it was still a huge gesture. She was pinning all her hopes on him. He didn't want to let her down. She had the headset back on, so he pulled down his visor and voice called her instead.

"I'm sorry I wasn't too happy about the plan today, it just came so... anyway, it was an awesome plan. I don't know how I can ever repay you for this."

"Hey, don't get all mushy on me. It's not all good news. Over on Aetherius's channel he's pitching this like I've betrayed him out of nowhere. As if he didn't pull that prank in the hospital, or have everyone in the guild treat me like dirt. What a scab!"

Damien diplomatically decided not to point out that since Rising Tide would've already known she murdered Shankyou in cold blood by then, keeping her out of the waiting room had been a sensible decision.

"Andrew wanted me to turn. I bet it's why they never kicked me out of the guild. He wanted it to look like I'd turned traitor publicly, a little controlled drama to liven up the last days of the competition and leech my votes away."

The food processor hissed and pinged, loud enough to be heard even through the headsets. Lillian hung up the call and tapped on Damien's visor as she went to fetch plates.

"Anyway, long story short, Aetherius and you will split most of my votes. I'll guide them in your direction as best I can. We'll keep putting everything in place tonight and see where we are tomorrow. Lasagna?"

Damien hummed his agreement and went back to his profile. He worked on it for the next hour, taking short, frequent breaks to cram lasagna through the gap in the IMBA set. When he finally let himself stop at 8pm, they settled in to see how the voting would go.

As expected, the majority of Lillian's voters migrated in the wake of her actions. She'd had 21,000 votes that morning; by evening's end it was down to just 8,000. Aetherius might have got a chunk of them, but it wasn't enough to balance out the rain of blows he was suffering across Saga Online's media. At the cusp of hitting a record 200,000 votes, his score had plummeted.

By the time it started to balance, Aetherius's account had dropped to 165,000 votes. A serious blow.

Damien's own rise eclipsed Aetherius's meagre fall. His votes had been steadily accumulating throughout the day, sitting at a cool 50k by the time they had logged out of the game.

A short time after their raid stream had been posted, it was already having a visible effect. The extra videos and his reply to Shankyou stoked the fervor even further, unhalted even when Shankyou removed his original comment. Once the stream commentators got their hands on it and confirmed he was the player who'd fought Toutatis, the entire community was beset with Daemien fever.

People were making parody videos of him arguing about killing the pegasus, cosplaying as him online, and as had happened with Scorpius, all variations on his in-game name were swiftly taken. By the time the dust settled and the voting was slowing down at 10pm, he'd amassed 125,000 votes. His target was in sight.

The only complaint he was getting, besides those leveled at him by Aetherius's supporters, was that nobody knew how he'd obtained the occultist class. Damien had sensibly remained silent on that score. He couldn't tell them how to do it without half the world descending on The Downward Spiral, at which point he'd have to find a new base. That would have to wait until after Bartholomew threw him out, and by then his mother's fate would already have been decided.

It was a lot to take in.

So, at 22:30, with Saturday morning looming large and the online community waning, he told Lillian he was heading to bed. She didn't remove her headset but paused whatever she was doing to address him directly.

"I can't come home early tomorrow. I've had the whole week

off after what Aetherius did, then today I cried off as well. Don't die while I'm gone. Got it?"

"I won't do anything stupid. Cross my heart. See you tomorrow evening."

She nodded, her lips pursing as she tried to look serious, then it broke and she beamed at him earnestly.

"You're poised to win this thing now. We'll have some work to do tomorrow evening: I'll take you on a little tour, we'll meet some of your fans in the game, you'll kiss some babies and sign some autographs, then we'll see where we are. Sleep well!"

She gave him a blind wave, which Damien returned before wondering why as he headed back to his room. At least now he had clean clothes to sleep in. It had been a relatively short day, but it had been busy, and tomorrow was going to be important. Every day until the competition ended was important.

Only the weekend was left. He'd made huge strides toward accomplishing his goal, but he was still tens of thousands of votes away from realizing his objective. That was a problem for tomorrow.

32

DRAGONSLAYER

He woke up feeling much fresher than usual. It was the first time that week he'd gone to bed without needing to catch up on sleep. He put on some fresh clothes and headed into the open plan living room. Lillian was already there, dashing around with a piece of toast in her mouth as she gathered her things to leave.

"Hey, you're up," she said, mumbling through the bread.

Damien stood in the doorway, feeling a bit awkward for interrupting her morning routine.

"There's another piece of toast going if you want it?"

Damien wasn't hungry just yet, but he didn't want to be a bad guest. He plucked up the second piece of toast and took a seat while she continued her preparations. After a few more minutes running back and forth in what looked like a frequent key-card finding ritual, she retrieved it from the bathroom and was ready to go.

She slung the kit bag over her back and patted down her pockets before her eyes finally unglazed and focused on him.

"I was thinking. You said your mom's waiting on a new heart, right? If you like, I can do a little digging, find out how she is. Do you know which hospital she's at?"

Damien might not have been sleep deprived anymore, but he

certainly wasn't awake enough to deal with this revelation. She could do that?

He'd abandoned all hope of checking up on his mom right after the CU agents had come for him, so much so that he'd had a med student right in front of him for the last two days and hadn't even thought to ask.

"Yes! She's at St. Mary's. Do you really think you can find her?"

Lillian shouldered her bag and checked her wristband.

"I don't know for sure, but I'll do my best. See you tonight. Oh, and *don't die!*"

She regarded him severely for a few moments before popping the last corner of toast into her mouth and making for the door.

Damien retrieved his headset from the table where it had been charging and logged into his profile page to behold it in all its glory. It was beautiful. He'd scrolled through many a cool SO profile but never had he assumed that one day he'd have an equally polished profile of his own. It had only been there for a couple of days, but there was enough content to make him seem like a full-blown veteran.

His votes had increased ever so slightly since he logged off, another two thousand on top of his 125k windfall. But worryingly, Aetherius's vote count was recovering, pushing back up to 170k.

The gap between them was widening as the furor surrounding the waiting room attack died down. On top of that, people were voicing their appreciation of the forty-man raid he and his guild had provided.

Damien opened the video and settled in to watch the two and a half hour long event.

The raid had been recorded from the perspective of a mana wisp, which Aetherius had set to hover behind him at a distance. This was one of the reasons his broadcasts were so popular: the perspective this tactic offered was far clearer than viewing directly from his eyes, reminiscent of the camera angles employed in the third-person video games many of his viewers enjoyed.

On the downside, it meant his HUD didn't show, hiding his health, stamina and mana bars.

While most streamers were open about their stat allocations, explaining how many points they'd put where and why, Aetherius kept his build secret. There was a lot of debate about what he'd done with his stats, but everyone agreed a lot of it had gone into intelligence. Even considering the stats on his gear, his damage was outrageous. However, he also must have pumped a lot into wisdom as he had a seemingly unlimited mana pool. He had never been seen running out of mana in any of his streams.

While a ten-strong wall of tanks kept the enemy mobs at bay, he joined his ranged units in raining death upon the clustered hordes. In Aetherius's case, that consisted of wave upon wave of Arcane Missiles. The damage numbers were hidden as well, preventing anyone from mathing out his stat allocation, but the power was undeniable.

It was efficient experience points for everyone involved. No wonder his guild remained so loyal. He could throw a bag of puppies in a wood chipper and they'd still rush to defend him, as long as he got them through elite dungeons with minimum fuss.

Damien skipped his way to the final boss fight.

He watched in awe as it swooped down from the ceiling and crashed to the floor, his heart pounding as if he were in the room with them. It was a dragon. A *dragon*. A giant, golden, living and breathing, killing and flaming dragon. A dragon.

He'd only been joking when he told Lillian they could find one; he hadn't even known they existed in the game. Yet here one was, and Rising Tide had already killed it. Knowing the outcome didn't make it any less exciting.

Damien found himself rooting for Rising Tide and had to pause the video for a few seconds so he could focus on being disgusted with himself.

He could only imagine how angry Aetherius must be to have accomplished such a feat, only to lose 30,000 votes and create an arch-rival immediately after. Nevertheless, his votes were recovering. The dragon video had been eclipsed by Lillian's superb timing, but it was too big to be completely erased.

Unlike the dragon itself, apparently.

Damien's train of thought was interrupted twenty minutes into the epic boss fight when the dragon twisted its neck round and unhinged its maw, pointing directly at Aetherius. The final phase of boss fights was always more intense, and this was no exception. The mana wisp was in just the right position to peer down the open gullet as dragonfire gathered, getting brighter and brighter. It was akin to standing at the mouth of a tunnel with a freight train roaring toward you, the survival prospects of being hit by either identical.

All the players around Aetherius, from the tankiest tank to the squishiest squishy, threw discipline to the wind and ran headlong for cover. Aetherius remained exactly where he was, his arms folded and his foot tapping against the stone. Even from behind, his body language was crystal clear: boredom.

The dragon declined to track the moving targets, remaining trained on the arrogant individual who'd decided not to run. More likely than not, Saga Online had assessed the party's damage and designated him as the primary target. A scorching, churning, white-hot orb lodged itself at the furthest point in the dragon's throat and spun there as it accumulated power.

For a moment, Damien thought he understood why Aetherius hadn't moved. Mages had a powerful short-range tele-portation spell, available as a trait at level 20. Blink. Aetherius was showboating, waiting for the dragon to release the payload before narrowly escaping the danger. The recording's viewpoint transferred to a Rising Tide player off to one side. They had a great view of the scene in front of them, the beam of white fire searing a trench into the floor all the way up to Aetherius and beyond. It hit the wall and dug a sizzling hole into the bedrock before finally dissipating. When the beam faded, there was a clear view of absolutely nothing where Rising Tide's guild leader had stood just moments ago.

Damien's lips parted. If Aetherius had blinked he would've shown up wherever he'd blinked to immediately, yet there was no sign of him anywhere. Had he died? Really? Just standing there, tapping his foot like an idiot?

The camera panned sideways as the player looked from where Aetherius had been to the dragon's head. It was resetting its dislocated jaw, leaving it vulnerable to attack, but no one was in position to take advantage.

Except... now the camera was focused on the dragon, Damien could make out someone standing underneath it. They were in the safest and yet the most dangerous place imaginable: directly under the dragon's head, tenuously obscured from its line of sight.

It was Aetherius. Still looking bored.

He raised his hands while the dragon reorganized its bone structure, the grating clicks and clacks loud enough to reverberate off the walls as the jaw rotated from side to side. The absurdly overpowered attack was accompanied by an absurdly long recovery period.

Aetherius responded in kind. His hands glowed red and pulsed, forcing the beast's head upward on a roiling wave of energy. It was the spell Lillian had been subjected to during the attack on the waiting room: a channeled Arcane Beam. At least, Damien assumed it was. It was the same deep shade of red and it behaved the same way. That's where the similarity ended. This thing was immense. Lillian's 'Repent' skill had doubled the power and dimensions of her foe's spell before reflecting it back at them. This was still bigger.

The dragon's jaw was knocked loose before it could reset. There was a crunch and a roar as bones cracked and ligaments severed. Aetherius stopped channeling and Blinked away, just as the car-sized head crashed back to the floor where he'd been standing. The mighty enemy had been reduced to a broken creature, splayed out on the floor with its jaw hanging loosely off to one side.

Damien had seen enough. He paused the video and scrolled into the comments, hoping to find out what spell Aetherius had used to avoid being incinerated. It couldn't be a Blink. The range was too short to have covered the distance to the dragon's head in one jump. Even if that wasn't the case, it had a cooldown. If Aetherius had Blinked in, he wouldn't have been able to Blink away. Unfortunately, everyone in the comments section was equally adrift.

Vegetus: 2:17:46 Huh? What did he do? ELI5 pls.

MadMarx: The dragon was very angry. Then he hit it with his sleep ray and it went beddie bye-bye.

Vegetus: Ha-ha, I mean how did he get from way out in front of it to right underneath it so fast?

Kira-ai: *deleted*

Vegetus: It's not blink. Blink Read the skill description.

Kira-ai: *deleted*

Vegetus: Read. The. Skill. Description.

RedDeadPrevention: I knew it! It's a two-man job! There's another player who looks just like Aetherius, and the real Aetherius stays invisible until the first one dies! That's how he keeps doing these last second saves!

OccumsAxe: Ha. Hahaha. Haha, HAHAHAHA! No.

RedDeadPrevention: Do you have a better idea?

I-CC-U: That just doesn't work. There's a list of all forty people in the raid. None are Aetherius look-alikes. Sorry to disappoint you.

Walrusface: BUSTED!

Ice-T: Wish he'd show us the level 40 traits. Maybe there's an improved blink? That might explain what he did during the fight.

Vegetus: Okay, maybe there's an improved Blink at level 40. MAYBE. But he's been pulling stuff like this for weeks and he only hit level 40 a few days ago. IT'S NOT BLINK PEOPLE, LET'S MOVE ON.

Jannaaaaaa: Y'all are super excited about his trick, but everyone's missing the BIG question: what's going on with his mana? That video was two and a half hours long and Aetherius didn't pop a mana potion once. How much mana does he have?!?

Ohmnipotent: Noooooooooobody knows. Current consensus is it's infinite. Here's a link to the discussion board.

BlackArrow: Why don't you get your friend Ohmniscient to help out? We'll have the answer in no time.

Ohmniscient: I'm focusing on easier problems, like world peace.

Damien minimized the window to check Aetherius's profile. While he'd been watching, Aetherius had received almost 2000 more competition votes. Almost one vote every second, and it wasn't even peak streaming time.

If it continued like this, Lillian's hard work would be undone. Damien couldn't sit there waiting for her to return; it would be too late by then. Something needed to be done now.

He re-opened the window to the comments section. Rising Tide's members had put plenty of criticism on his videos, even if they'd been largely ignored.

Shankyou's comment was the only one that had taken off, and that had backfired dramatically. Damien felt he could do better.

> **Daemien**: Aetherius, hi! How's it going? Listen, since we've both killed mythical creatures now, I was thinking we could get together and trade notes. If you like, when we meet, you can take off your gear and I'll give you a boost. Or you can keep it on, I'm good either way. In return, you can share your stats and skills with everyone instead of being a big edgelord and keeping it to yourself. How about it?

He'd linked Aetherius's name in so he'd get the notification and posted it. It went straight to the bottom of the list, where it would have no visibility. Damien had learned a thing or two from Lillian over the last couple of days. This was an easy fix. He took a screenshot of the comment and saved it on his own profile for posterity. Then he made a new comment and pinned it to the top of his very first video.

> **Daemien**: Hi everyone, thanks for your interest in my videos! Sorry I haven't been replying, the last few days were very busy. I've just sent Aetherius a message asking him to share his stats and skills! Exciting! If you'd like him to share his build, please head over and let him know.

He let out a long breath as the second message was sent. All he could do now was wait to see how it was received. The messages had been short, but tinkering with them had taken the better part of an hour.

He minimized the window and pondered what to do next. Inspiration struck almost immediately. Some of the comments on Aetherius's video had contained links to player-made databases comprising the known skills of Saga Online. Damien had been surprised by the more outlandish abilities he'd seen over the last few days. It could only help to brush up on his knowledge.

Damien worked his way through the lists, swapping between different databases if the one he was using had gaps. Whenever his attention span waned, he'd watch a stream hosted by whichever class he was currently examining to see the skills put into practice.

He was so invested he didn't move from his place on the sofa until the door slammed shut. Damien snapped the visor upward and brought his eyes back into focus on Lillian as she wrenched off her bag.

"Hey," Damien greeted her. "How wa—"

Lillian bolted the door and set her back to it, hands covering her face. Something was wrong. Damien took off the headset and stood up, but Lillian still didn't move. She was just standing there, her chest rising and falling as one deep breath rolled into another.

He had no idea what to do in this situation. He was stepping around the table when Lillian looked up from her hands. Damien stopped, his lips parting. She was harrowed. Her wristband was producing a blip every few seconds.

"Lillian, what's going on? Are you OK?"

She nodded weakly, then finally turned to face him.

"Those CU agents you told me about. The ones that were chasing you. What did they look like again?"

Now Damien was starting to get the picture. He stammered out what he could remember.

"There was a big guy. Bald and maybe middle-aged? He was

wearing sports clothes last time I saw him. Then there was another one, smaller, still bigger than me though. He seemed a bit older, and he had a bea—"

"—a beard, a pair of V-Tec glasses and a cheap suit? Yeah. They had a chat with me at the front gate."

Damien swallowed. Welp. That was the end of that. It had been real nice while it lasted. He went straight into his room and started throwing clothes into his bag.

"What are you doing?" Lillian asked from the doorway.

"I'm leaving. Thank you for letting me stay, I was really happy here. I'll try to get online somewhere, I don't know, and I'll let you know if—I'll let you know when I find a place. We'll have to talk over the voice chat, but we've got the profile set up already so at lea—"

Lillian had walked up beside him as he spoke. She gently grasped the top of the bag, holding it closed so he couldn't put any more clothes in. Firmly and pointedly, she tipped it upside down on the bed, shaking it out to make sure it was completely empty. Then she dropped it and looked him dead in the eye.

Some of the Lillian he knew was starting to make a comeback. Anger, mostly.

"As if I would let you do that. Idiot. Go and sit down."

"Lillian, if they're here, I need to leave quickly. I don't wan—"

"Go and sit down. Please."

She held his gaze. Damien hadn't counted on resistance. He couldn't leave without causing more drama, and that was the last thing he wanted. Lillian's wristband punctuated the silence with another jarring blip. If he made a scene, she might lose her cool completely and inadvertently summon the building security. She was his savior, but in this scenario she was also his captor.

Damien walked back into the living room and sat down on the sofa. Lillian followed him out, closing the door to his room behind her.

"They know you're here. And if you leave, you'll be caught. Instantly."

Damien put his head in his hands. Everything had been going

so well. Why had this happened? How had they found him? Then he remembered.

"You checked up on my mother today."

Lillian leaned on the door and nodded. Her wristband had stopped bleeping, but her expression was grim.

"Yeah. She's still there. Currently twenty-fifth in line for a new heart. Woop-tee-do. I put a call in to the hospital and asked if they had a Cassandra waiting for heart surgery. They asked me for my name. I didn't think anything of it, but now.... I'm sorry, Damien, I should've been more careful."

Damien cast his eyes down at the floor. No. It was his fault. He should've told Lillian not to check on his mom in the first place. He'd just wanted to know so badly, and it had seemed so safe. And now here he was. Waiting for the inevitable.

"You may as well let me leave. If I go now, I can pretend I was staying somewhere else. It beats them letting themselves in while we're asleep."

Lillian blew a fat raspberry between her lips.

"If they force their way in here without a warrant, they'll lose their jobs. They look so dodgy they couldn't even make it past the front gate. The sentry was watching us talk, and when we were finished I told him I didn't know either of them and they were not to bother me under any circumstances. Frankly, I hope they try to come in and security shoots them. Assholes."

It was nice to see Lillian regaining her composure. She seemed pretty confident, although Damien had his doubts.

"How long does it take to get a warrant?"

"I dunno. Do I look like a CU official to you? Probably a while. It's not like you're a dangerous criminal, right?"

Damien shook his head. He supposed not, although the way he'd been hounded certainly made him feel like one. Lillian didn't allow him to linger on the thought.

"I think we'll be fine for tonight. We might want to hurry things up a little, though. You know, just in case. Especially after what Aetherius had to say to you today."

Damien's thoughts crashed into each other and he was left

dumbly staring up into Lillian's face. She registered his surprise and her jaw dropped.

"You don't know? Seriously? Get on your profile, now!"

Damien pulled the headset back on and reopened the window that had sat, minimized and forgotten, while he was studying Saga abilities. His profile was not how he'd left it. He was up to 176,000 competition votes. Ordinarily he'd be ecstatic, but Lillian had him on edge. With good reason. He opened the Twisted Forest video with his comments pinned to the top. Set underneath them was the reply Damien had never thought he'd receive.

> **Aetherius**: Daemien. You seem confused. I don't know if it's because you're so new to the game or because you landed on your head, but let's clear things up: I killed the dragon because it was fun. Hundreds of thousands of people agree. I kicked you down a hole because it was funny. Hundreds of thousands of people agree. You've got a chip on your shoulder about it, which is not clever. An ant doesn't hold a grudge against a boot.
>
> You also seem to think you've accomplished something notable. I'll put it into perspective. It took an hour to repair the damage you and Lillian did (Hello, you traitor. I'll deal with you soon enough). My new pegasus is already here and ready for my victory parade. You've accomplished nothing. Oh, and calling me an edgelord because I, a competitive player, am unwilling to share the subtleties of my build, when you, a min-maxing nobody, won't even share how you got your class, is laughable. Go crawl back under whatever rock it is you call home.

As Damien read, he forgot about the CU agents. He had to go over it several times to process the full depth and breadth of his anger.

"Yeah, that might not have been such a good idea." Lillian took a seat on the sofa next to him and patted him on the back consolingly. "He brought you down to his level, now he's beating you with experience. Don't troll a troll."

Damien wasn't listening. He was already formulating

responses in his head, but none of them were generating traction. The rug had been well and truly swept out from under his feet. It was a very tidy little comment.

He selected Aetherius's name and looked at his profile. He'd broken 200,000 votes. It was 17:30; peak streaming time was minutes away. Damien needed a response, or the gap would only continue to widen.

"I know we're running out of time," Lillian said, "but before you respond we need a plan. Otherwise you'll end up playing into his hands again. We can't hit his outposts anymore; everyone will be online and ready to port to anywhere that's under attack. If we go outside and get spotted – and we will, playing on the weekend of the competition finale – they'll quickly show up in force and try to murder us. So, what are we going to do?"

Damien was starting to calm down. He'd found the responses to two out of three of Aetherius's jibes. He was stuck on the last one. Calling Aetherius out for not sharing his build had seemed like such a good idea, given how everyone online had complained bitterly about it. He hadn't thought of how it would reflect on himself. And now he was trapped.

The moment he shared how to become an occultist, Rising Tide would come running to the... they'd come to The Downward Spiral and... wait a second.

"Lillian, log on with me. Right now."

He landed on his feet back inside the game. There was a crackle of static in his ear and then Lillian's voice came through, loud and clear.

"—espond to the message first. If the first thing people see when they come online is Aetherius's reply—"

"Lillian." Damien cut through her. He'd been filled with glorious purpose. "I am going to respond, before six, but first I need you to come here. I have a plan."

He marched out of his base, ignoring the imps that were waving at him, and headed into Bartholomew's domain. He stood in the center of the dungeon floor and looked up at the entry point high overhead, his eyes following the winding pathway running around the outside that he'd negotiated so many times before. Lillian appeared at his shoulder, holding a torch over her head to see by.

"I want to trick Rising Tide into coming here, then ambush and kill them all. What are your thoughts?"

"You're not serious?"

"I am. Look at this place! A narrow path all the way around the outside with no cover, forcing them to travel one by one. Leading to open platforms, where they'll be clustered together and we can fence them in on either side. Traps all along the route that we can add to with traps of our own. And my base is here, so I'll have twice as many minions to throw at them. Not to mention Bartholomew himself. They might have beaten him already, but he's not exactly a pushover. This is a strong position!"

Lillian narrowed her eyes at him.

"You make it sound so easy, but we're talking about fighting an entire guild! They killed a dragon yesterday. Do you think you'll do better?"

"We're not going to fight fair. I can't win this competition without a fight, not after I promised I'd kill Aetherius or die trying, and I'd much rather fight them here than on their turf. This is the best plan I have, and we need to agree on it now, before I send the message. Will you do this with me?"

Lillian pursed her lips and gently shook her head. Damien was crestfallen until she cracked the barest hint of a smile.

"Are you the same person who said attacking the waiting room was suicide? Fine. What do you want me to do?"

Damien opened his profile and started typing Aetherius a reply. He'd taken a long time to type out the first two messages; he'd have to work fast to get this out before six.

Daemien: Aetherius, so nice of you to join us. I thought you'd never stop deleting my messages. Lillian informs me you're planning on hiding in your base until the competition is over. Are you doing that for fun as well? No, I think it's for the same reason you wouldn't fight Toutatis: you're a coward. The leader of Rising Tide, trapped in his own base by an ant. I understand why you're scared. I've lost count of how many of your people I've killed by now. Not that you seemed concerned about their deaths in your reply – you were more concerned with your club house and your magic pony.

I'm not like you, though. I didn't do it for fun. I did it to show the world what a spineless, useless, self-absorbed guild leader you are. As for the class, I'm announcing how to get it this weekend. A gift, for everyone who plays Saga Online. What have you got to offer? You have fun riding around in your second-rate, second place parade. Keep an eye out for me, though. That last pegasus was great exp, but I'd rather spare the mount and kill the moron on top of it. Hundreds of thousands of people agree.

He sent it to Lillian first for approval, and waited for a few minutes as she considered it. She looked up at him and nodded. He posted it just after 18:00. Upvotes accumulated almost immediately. There was no going back now.

"Alright. Aetherius or bust. Let's get to work!"

33

PREPARATIONS

D amien showed Lillian around the base, taking her all the way up while he pointed out traps. On the way back down, the two of them discussed possible battle plans. There was a lot of back and forth, a little searching online to figure out some of the game mechanics and plenty of arguing, but eventually they settled on a strategy for each of the six platforms on the way to the final floor as well as the narrow causeways that linked them together. Once that was done, Damien returned to his base and set his imps to work.

In addition to the new weapons they'd need, Damien had come up with an idea for a particularly diabolical set of traps. He scrolled through the Demon Forge options and found something that fit the bill perfectly: buckshot. Ammunition for guns. It was cheap, only taking one iron bar to make a hundred pellets.

By degrees, Lillian started to become more optimistic. She was especially optimistic when she checked Daemien's profile. He'd crested 190,000 votes. Aetherius was ahead by 20,000 and his votes were still rising, but Damien was gaining on him, bit by bit. Better yet, after an hour Aetherius still hadn't replied. Nobody could stop talking about the competition beef, except for those people who were more excited to play as an occultist. Competition votes were flooding in.

That evening, he and Lillian set out into the forest under

cover of darkness. Soon enough they found a large cluster of sturdy dryad mobs which offered decent experience and soul energy - one and a half soul energy for each fallen dryad. It was much easier to get Damien's Soul Reserve back up now that Lillian was tanking the mobs for him.

After fifty minutes of killing dryads, Damien had fully replenished his stores of minions, for him and his Soul Well. He hadn't been at full strength since the Malignant Crypt. It was a good feeling. His summons by his side, Lillian played defensively and let him do all the damage, allowing him to get the majority of the experience.

It was a long grind. An hour in and hundreds of mobs dead, Damien was wishing he'd slept earlier. He found something new: the IMBA set could detect his mental exhaustion. It started popping up with warnings and advice, which Damien steadfastly turned down: No, it wasn't just a game. Yes, he had eaten that day. Errr, how could a fifteen-minute break help at half past two in the morning?

At last, at 03:47, on the dawn of the penultimate day of the competition, Damien thrust his dagger through a dryad's back and a flurry of notifications popped up on his screen.

Level Up!
Summon Incubus Unlocked!
A new trait is available for selection. Choose wisely.
Building Upgrades Unlocked!

Damien smiled weakly. He'd done it. It hadn't all been glamorous, but he'd got to level 30 in less than a week. Lillian came forward and shook him roughly by the shoulder, her face split into a grin.

"Congratulations. Did you get traits?"

Damien nodded and summoned a portal. They'd been here long enough. He could check the traits in the comfort of his own home. His army filed through, with he and Lillian going through last, together. His base was rammed. Thirty souls of minions attached to his Soul Well, another twenty-six attached to himself, plus a vampire and a paladin. He reviewed his new traits.

1. **Unhallowed Ground**: Circle of Hell heals demonic minions in its area of effect.
2. **Coven Leader**: Succubi calculate their spell damage based on your intelligence.
3. **9/10 of the Lore**: The stats of possessed minions are doubled.

Oof. A triple whammy of minion-based traits. On closer inspection, he realized the first two weren't much good to him. They relied on intelligence. He didn't know if the succubi Circle of Hell counted for the first trait, which was important since he hadn't even accumulated enough intelligence to get the spell himself. It wasn't the best pick anyway. The last trait was the best for him. He selected it and was filled with an overwhelming wave of satisfaction.

Then he opened his stat sheet, promptly piling the final five unassigned points into wisdom.

Account Name: Damien Arkwright
Class: Occultist
Level: 30
Health: 840/840
Stamina: 890/890
Mana: 2440/2440
Stats:
Strength 39 - Agility 129 - Intelligence 39
Constitution 84 - Endurance 89 - Wisdom 244
Stat points: 0
Experience: 55/30000
Soul Summon Limit: 27/27 - **Soul Reserve:** 10/10 (+1/1)

Damien wanted to keep going, maybe even summon the incubus, but he was just too damn tired. Lillian, usually the more persistent of the pair, had hit her limit as well.

They logged off and pulled off their headsets, each examining the dark rings under the eyes of the other.

"What time are we waking up?"

"I… think whenever it happens. Let's try for midday; we need to be awake if we're going to do this right. Come get me if you wake up first. I'll do the same."

Damien yawned. 4am. It had taken a long time, but it was worth the effort for the trait and the minions.

Lillian headed for the bathroom, looking over her shoulder.

"Damien… whatever happens tomorrow… today… I'm really glad I met you. I'm only sorry I couldn't help you more."

"What are you talking about? Without you, I'd still have two videos and a profile picture up on my account. You're the brains of this outfit. I'm just the pretty face."

She laughed at that. Damien couldn't help but smile.

"We'll give Aetherius a hard time tomorrow. Today. Dammit, I need to go to bed. Sleep well, man."

He gave her a thumbs up and lumbered into his room. They'd done a lot of prep. He was ready. As ready as he could be. All he needed now was sleep.

The morning came all too soon, and not soon enough. Damien stirred as the knocks reverberated off the door, immediately followed by a chirpy Lillian.

"Morning, sleepyhead! Get up, I made you breakfast!"

Damien wandered into the lounge to find bacon and eggs steaming on a plate on the table. Lillian was on the sofa, her headset already on.

"Oh wow," Lillian said, waving at him to hurry. "You have to see this."

He scoffed his breakfast down as quickly as possible, eager to join her. Two minutes later and with his mouth still full, he wiped the egg yolk from his lips and sat down beside her, jamming his own headset over his head.

She wasn't kidding. With the competition coming to a head, the votes were starting to polarize. People wanted to use their votes somewhere they'd count. Right now that meant either Aetherius, or Daemien.

Aetherius's lead was unchanged, but the two of them had so many votes that it hardly seemed like a big gap at all: Aetherius had 318,000 votes. Damien was at 290,000. He felt light-headed and had to pull the visor up, lying back until the world stopped spinning.

"And I haven't even given them the class yet," Damien whispered. "Let's do this!"

"You go first," Lillian said. "I'll clean up and join you in a sec."

He gave her a nod before pulling his visor down to log in.

Landing on his feet near his Soul Well, he willed Noigel to his side. It was easier than trying to find him, the way his base was now. His oldest minion picked his way through the hordes and snapped to attention in front of him.

"Noigel, gimme a minion count."

"Twenty-one imps, a wraith and two hell hounds bound to the Soul-Well. Three imps, a wraith, two hell hounds and two succubi bound to you."

Not as bad as Damien had expected, given the state he'd been in when he made those choices. He had a difficult choice to make now, though. He had to decide whether or not to make room for an incubus, without knowing its stats.

"Noigel, what can you tell me about the incubus?"

"It likes walking in the rain, long sunsets and grinding enemies into fine powder, master."

"A little less snark and a little more information, O forbidden knowledge one."

"It's a strength-based summon. Expensive but sturdy. And that part about grinding enemies into powder? That was purely informative, master."

All right, it was worth a look. Damien checked up on the skill in his menu. He confirmed one part of Noigel's analysis immediately: it was the most expensive minion he had, costing 10 soul energy to summon and 10 slots to field. His entire Soul Reserve.

The mana cost was prohibitively expensive as well: 1000

mana. It could've made Damien wary, but in fact he only became more curious to see. First, he'd have to make room. He took a long, hard look at his summons, trying to decide what he could afford to lose. He wanted the two succubi. This was likely to be a prolonged fight, and one alone might not have enough mana.

He could definitely use the wraiths. That left hell hounds and imps. He already had an unallocated Soul Summon slot from putting points in wisdom yesterday, so he dismissed six imps and a hell hound to free up the required ten slots. Their refunded soul energy was drawn toward him as he emptied his Soul Reserve to summon his newest asset.

The sigil burning into the floor was a pair of huge horns, protruding from either side of a head that looked to be about 60% teeth and 100% malice. The ring of fire was twice the diameter of his other summoning spells. It was necessary. The portal opened in the floor and a huge hand, about the size of Damien's torso, thumped down on the edge. Damien took a step back as the incubus raised itself out of the pit.

It was... big. Big enough to make Hammertime look like a gnome. If Damien stood in front of it on his tiptoes, he'd just about come up to its midriff. If he stretched his arms out and tried to embrace it, he might just about reach from one side of it to the other. Not that he felt like doing either of those things. A long, powerful tail stretched out behind it, equal parts reptilian and demonic: while it had no scales, there were sharp ridges along the top of it that continued all the way down to the tip.

The incubus looked around and all the other minions retreated a few steps, except for the two succubi. They were smitten.

Noigel's window of opportunity for extra-curricular activities had passed.

Having cowed the majority of his forces, the demon abruptly looked down at Damien and shot him a hideous grin, the lips curling back further and further until it was all smiles and halitosis. Damien grinned back. This seemed like a very fitting reward for hitting level 30. He inspected it, hoping the stats would be as impressive as its appearance.

Incubus
Stats:
Strength 75 - Agility 10 - Intelligence 5
Constitution 100 - Stamina 75 - Wisdom 5
Abilities: Charge, Enrage.

Look at that. A proper tank. It was about damn time.

"Oh boy, looks like I've got competition, huh?"

Well, that wasn't entirely fair. Lillian strolled past him and around the incubus, taking it in. Its head swiveled around to track her motion and a deep rumble echoed from the center of its chest, bothering her not one iota. She courteously stepped over its tail, finished her lap and leaned on Damien's shoulder.

"What are you going to do with this thing? It's a big target. I don't see it lasting long in a full-blown raid."

Damien saw the size in a different context now. That was a good point. But in addition to the unique role the incubus filled, it had an advantage none of the other minions possessed: Rising Tide didn't know he had one. He could use that.

"I have some ideas in mind. Come on, let's go sort this out."

Damien led the way out of his base, Lillian following swiftly after. He focused on Noigel and the imp swooped through the alcove before landing on his shoulder.

"Noigel, in case you haven't been paying attention, we're about to host a big party for Rising Tide. Get all the minions out here and line them up for inspection."

Lillian snorted into her gauntlet. Damien had shared much with her, but it was only now he realized she'd never heard Noigel speak. The imp might've dropped a few intelligence points following the dismissal of six imps, but even if his eloquence had diminished, his pride and quick wit were unaffected.

"Sure thing, master. Does that include the paladin, or can you direct her yourself?"

The snorting was quickly replaced with a sharp intake of breath and a long, surly stare. Damien stared at the floor for a few moments, trying to compose himself.

"She can take care of herself. She'll take care of you too, if you're not careful. Get those minions out here."

Noigel saluted again and flew back into the base. His screaming as he asserted himself over Damien's horde was loud enough to wake the dead.

It did.

Bartholomew shimmered into view next to Damien, just in time to watch the incubus squeeze its way through the alcove onto the dungeon floor. The rest of the minions followed in its wake, pouring out of his base like blood from an open wound. Bartholomew's attention was firmly fixed on the incubus at the far end of the line.

"It pains me to admit it, but when you suggested your aim was to kill Aetherius in a week I was... skeptical. Even more so when you declined to invest in the many Maleficium spells my gift bestowed upon you. I am not often pleased to be proven wrong. Well done."

"Thank you. If it makes you feel any better, I wasn't all that happy when you forced me to become an occultist. I was much more wrong than you."

The corners of Bartholomew's mouth turned up ever so slightly. It was funny to think how much they'd despised each other during his apprenticeship. His character's level and his reputation with the Occultist faction had both risen phenomenally in a short space of time, and the tone of their conversations had adapted accordingly. A hint of the old Bartholomew came back as he leaned forward to murmur in Damien's ear.

"While I admire your aptitude, I don't appreciate my dungeon being designated as a battleground without my permission. Nor do I appreciate being treated as a tool in your plans. It's just as well we both desire the same thing. Next time, keep me in the loop."

Bartholomew turned on the spot, floated a few paces away and faded out of existence. If nothing else, he certainly appreciated having the last word. Damien hadn't factored Bartholomew's willingness to participate into his plans. Having played a multitude of games unburdened by AI, it was easy to forget how adaptable Saga Online's non-player characters were. And nosy.

Noigel landed on Damien's shoulder and coughed pointedly to get his attention. The minions had organized themselves into a long line. Now he could visualize what he was working with.

Damien used up all the resources he had left bit by bit, building armor and weapons for all the minions until most of the metal and all the leather was gone. He debated using what was left to equip his imps with tridents and decided against it, converting the last three blocks of iron into buckshot instead. Then he looked through his item chest to see what else was available. He'd accumulated a lot of useless items from trash mobs on his journey: boar tusks, bone splinters, rock fragments and several hundred petrified twigs from the dryads. Usually they'd be ingredients. Damien had other ideas. He gathered them into his backpack, giving what he couldn't carry to Lillian, and kept looking.

The only remaining item of note was the Unrelenting Amulet Bartholomew had crafted for him. He took it out and stared at it. He'd disregarded it before, preferring the slight boost to health and stamina BlackKnight's Persevering Amulet gave him. This seemed like an occasion worthy of thinking a little harder. If Damien could find a use for sticks, stones and bones, surely he could find a decent use for this.

He went into his spell list, checking the artifact against every spell in turn. He lingered the longest on those with no cooldown and long casting times. It would've been fantastic with Chaotic Bolt or Corruption if he'd built his character the way Bartholomew had suggested. It was useless with Implosion and Demon Gate. The only spells left were his summoning spells. They fit the bill, in theory: they all had long casting times and no cooldown. The problem was they had a different limitation: the soul cost. With his Soul Reserve capped at 10, he'd only be able to summon 10 souls' worth of minions. Unless he managed to stand near a big pile of Soul Energy before he used it....

If he could kill enough Rising Tide members in one go, the amulet might just come in handy after all. He could engineer the circumstances required to make it shine, then resummon his entire Soul Summon Limit in one go! Well, not quite.

The special ability would only reduce the casting time of the first spell he used after activation. So, he'd have to fill his Soul Summon Limit with the same minion rather than creating a balanced army. While it would require a complicated set-up, the potential benefit was too great to be ignored. He equipped it and tucked the chain under his robes where it couldn't be seen.

Finally, the preparations were complete. Damien took his forces and distributed them around Bartholomew's dungeon. Then he strategically placed the detritus from his bag where he felt it would have the desired effect. They were all set. All that was left now was to trigger the trap. Lillian stood by, fidgeting with her hands, as Damien drafted a message.

Daemien: Hello, everyone. Today is the day of the occultist. Please watch the video if you want to learn how to make an occultist hero for yourself! Only level 1 heroes who haven't picked a class yet, please. Have a great weekend!

He sent it to Lillian's chat box and she looked it over.

"Nice touch with the requirements list. We should still be careful of other people visiting, but if we can't handle them we'll never deal with Rising Tide. Where are you putting it?"

"I've got that recording we didn't use from just after Aetherius kicked me in here, right before I met Bartholomew. We've already edited out the CU call at the end; I'll post it as it is. I was still learning the class, so it's pretty self-explanatory... if not a little embarrassing."

Lillian nodded and Damien uploaded the first recording he'd ever made onto his profile, entitled 'Thanks for the Boost'. In about five minutes the first people watching would know how it was done. After that, it showed his torturous learning experiences with the rats.

While he wasn't as keen on that part, he'd managed, so no big deal. Then it showed Bartholomew conceding to him building his base there, following his pledge to kill Aetherius in a week. That would come very close to the end.

He posted it and put it at the top of his profile. Lillian was still watching it herself, leaving Damien to link it on his other videos, when the views started to climb. In ten minutes the footage gained 1000 views. In fifteen minutes, it had 10,000. Twenty minutes later, it was well and truly out of control.

The video already had more views than his profile had votes, and his votes were rising as well. It seemed everyone online had stopped what they were doing to watch him fight rats.

Damien closed his browser page and ran up the spiral, rechecking his troop positions. They were all exactly where he'd left them. Five minutes after that, he did another sweep. He couldn't sit still. The wait was agonizing. He was in the middle of performing his third sweep when his chat box blipped. It was Lillian.

'Bartholomew wants you, come quick.'

Damien moved to the edge of the platform and looked down at the imp in the center of the floor. He Demon Gated to it and moved toward his two allies. Lillian had closed her menu and had her hammer at the ready. Bartholomew was stood next to her, staring up at the entrance with his hands clasped behind his back. He spoke to Damien without looking away.

"We have visitors. A large number of heroes are entering my domain."

"What's a large number?"

"Fifty... sixty... seventy... seventy-seven people. Aetherius is among them."

It had worked. Aetherius had taken the bait. Everything he'd been through, everything he'd suffered, had come to this.

34

THE SIX PLATFORMS OF HELL

T he decisive battle against Rising Tide had come to them.

Damien looked to his comrades; a tenacious, temperamental paragon of a paladin and a snooty, sadistic vampire. It had been a strange week.

"Stay safe, you two. Lillian, you know what to do."

Lillian turned to him, her shoulders set. She was in gaming mode. All traces of nervousness had disappeared. In fact, she was smiling.

"Your votes are rising fast. If we beat him here, we've won."

Damien turned and Demon Gated to the fourth platform. He held his nerve as the first imp died, placed halfway to the first platform as an early warning system.

They were coming, and he didn't want to be a bad host. He ordered a wraith to his side and it was there in seconds, climbing the walls faster than a person could fall to the bottom. He would know.

"Possession."

He opened the wraith's eyes and continued upward, circling the walls directly under the narrow walkway to remain in complete darkness. He paused above the second platform, where he had another imp sitting, and waited.

The wraith's night vision was even better than his own,

granting him a clear view of the pathway leading from above. He'd use the opportunity to spy on the army as it approached.

So he was surprised when a dagger appeared in the middle of the imp's chest and an assassin materialized on the other end of it. The imp faded away, burning to dust, as the assassin crouched and disappeared again. So that's how they were playing it. Fair enough. Damien would repay them in kind.

He eased the wraith down the wall onto the platform and pushed it forward onto the stairs. Shadow Beast allowed him to remain near invisible in the darkness. A player came into full view ahead of him. It was the stealth ranger he'd run into at the Malignant Crypt.

He silently floated forward until he was directly behind them, more silhouettes appearing as Damien reduced the gap. He counted five, traveling in single file. A little team of covert operatives, all specializing in stealth. Good. They'd have less armor and lower hit points.

Damien was so close to the ranger now he could hear him breathing. All five of them were looking straight ahead as they crept forward, totally unaware they'd been compromised.

He could have decapitated the ranger easily, but that would be noisy. There was a simpler solution. He drew up alongside, observing the ranger's stern face to make sure he was still focused on the path ahead of him.

And shoved him over the edge.

The ranger, bless his soul, was so focused on being quiet that he didn't start screaming until he was already falling past the next floor. As one, the players in front darted to the edge to look down. Damien hadn't inflicted any damage with his little shove. They had no idea it was their own party member who was screaming.

Damien briskly moved forward and shoved the next player in line to join his friend. This one screamed a little sooner. Damien didn't quite make it to the third player before their head twisted to the right, eyes wide.

It was Shankyou. *Oh, glorious day!*

Damien cocked his left arm and drove the attached blade through Shankyou's back, punching him between his shoulder blades. Then he pulled him in and drew his right arm across Shankyou's throat. He didn't have time to savor the karma before an arrow thunked into the assassin's chest.

The element of surprise was gone.

Damien floated sideways over the edge, releasing his human shield to ragdoll into the abyss as the shadowy tendrils of the wraith's tail clung to the walkway and spun him round to put him underneath it, hanging upside down.

From exposed and vulnerable to safe and sound in two seconds flat. This was his house. The Downward Spiral was built for demons to thrive.

Damien shot forward upside down, speeding up the walkway on the underside to repeat the process on the last two players. They had aborted the mission, abandoning stealth to flee to the exit at full speed. Their full speed couldn't make up for the wraith's wall-walking.

Damien dropped down the wall onto the walkway and guided the wraith up it like a homing missile, arms outstretched. He caught up with the first and pulled his arms sideways through their retreating back. Another mess for Bartholomew to clean up.

The lone survivor made it to the first platform, where there was too much exposure to light for him to be worth following. He'd get to tell the rest of them what happened without having to message through the chat box.

Damien faced the center of the room and tilted forward, passing through the walkways until he arrived at the bottom floor. Lillian was standing over the ranger's headless body. Damien wasn't a forensic scientist, but Lillian's blood-coated hammer-head offered some clue as to where the player's head had gone: everywhere.

Damien scraped his arm-blade on the floor, unable to signal to her vocally and not wanting to be mistaken for an enemy. She immediately activated Divine Might and spun toward the noise, hammer raised. The wraith's skin hissed in the glow and Damien gave her a little wave. The ability was swiftly deactivated.

"This one had the Air Jump trait– he arrived down here with full health. Be careful with your body. If they land near you alive, it's game over."

Damien nodded, gave her a thumbs up and started his ascent. He placed the wraith back above the second-highest platform, hanging under the walkway again.

Rising Tide was taking things a little more seriously this time. It was a party of ten, and they'd been paying attention. Warrior tank at the front. Paladin tank in the back. Extremely jittery squishies in between. All of them were hugging the wall, standing as far away from the edge as possible.

Some of them were using torches, and there were two mana wisps from two different mages that circled the group. The light they cast wasn't enough to reach the wraith at the moment, but he wasn't going to be able to get the jump on them.

Time for phase two.

Damien canceled the possession and instructed the wraith to move down and hang over the third-highest platform instead. The platforms gradually got bigger the further down you went. This was the first one large enough to host the entire party.

The light may have prevented him from engaging with the wraith but it made the group incredibly easy to track, even from below. Damien pulled two imps toward him, keeping them on standby. He opened his chat box to Lillian.

"Get ready."

When the trail of light breached the third platform, Damien sent the imps out into the dark to fly underneath. Then he instructed his wraith to scrape its arm-blades against each other. There were murmurs, and a mana wisp flew upward to investigate the noise. The moment the wraith was illuminated, hissing sinisterly in the blue light, Damien made his move. While the party responded with absurd force, obliterating his decoy in a hail of shrapnel, arrows and magical power, one of the two imps flew up and over the edge, hovering at head height.

All eyes were set on what was left of the wraith. Not a single player was looking out for an attack from the center of the room. Damien was already pointing at his imp across the divide. It was in position for less than a second before he triggered it.

"Implosion."

The piercing crack was followed by ten piercing screams. The whole party was pulled toward the void. One of the mages was fast enough to Blink back onto the platform and the warrior tank was left hanging off the edge, clinging on for dear life. The rest of them were not so lucky. Most of them fell to the bottom, their screams turning to strangled yelps if they survived or silence if they didn't. One of them collided with the edge of the platform Damien was standing on, arms impotently outstretched to grab it, catching it with his head instead. He was a quiet one.

There were more screams as Lillian set about finishing off the survivors before they had time to recover.

Above Damien, the mage was struggling to pull the warrior back onto the platform, his low strength making him ill-suited to the task. Damien still had the spare imp waiting under the platform, just in case the first one was spotted and killed before he could trigger it. There was a perfectly good use for it now, though. Damien flew it around and above the mage then Demon Gated, putting his full weight behind the daggers as he dropped down and plunged them between the mage's shoulder blades. The mage toppled forward into the warrior's face, dislodging him on the way down. *Two for one. Everything must go.*

Damien peered over the edge. Lillian and his second wraith had dealt with two of the players, another two of them had landed poorly and not survived, but four more were struggling to their feet. Damien set the three hell hounds on them to buy Lillian time and prepared for the next wave.

He was halfway through summoning a new wraith when a war cry rang into the dungeon from top to bottom. It was quickly followed by the clomp of footsteps, the clatter of armor and a trail of bright lights rushing down the walkway.

Aetherius had had enough. He was sending the rest.

Damien finished summoning and sent the new wraith down

to the dungeon floor. It would be more useful there. Then he ran down the steps, carefully picking his way around the highlighted paving stones where Bartholomew's more conventional traps lay. He reached the fourth platform and looked up. The lights had already reached the second level and showed no signs of slowing, even when punctuated by the shriek of metal as Bartholomew's traps were triggered again and again.

The flickering flames were soon accompanied by bursts of white and gold as the healers attempted to save their comrades from themselves. The damage they were sustaining must have been considerable, but the sudden rush was leaving Damien with little time to prepare.

This next bit was going to be tricky. He had a leather-armored, whip-equipped succubus and ten imps with him on this level, eleven if you counted Noigel. The ultimate interference team. They needed to play for time while the hell hounds positioned themselves for stage three.

He focused on Noigel.

"Send the hell hounds, now!"

Noigel was over the edge and diving straight down before Damien had even finished the order. He touched down on the dungeon floor just as the first of Rising Tide's members reached the third level.

Damien sent an imp flying straight toward it, hoping to repeat his Implosion strategy without the need for a wraith. The imp got halfway across the room before an arrow struck it out of the sky. Rising Tide had been smart enough to position a spotter with night vision, turning the empty space of the dungeon into a no-man's land.

Lillian had said this might happen.

Damien had devised counter-measures.

He focused on the succubus and it cast Bloodlust, the red mist seeping into his imps' heads via their ears. Then he sent three of them out into the danger zone: one circling round from the left, one on the right and the last zig-zagging straight down the middle. The erratic movement of the central imp drew the spotter's attention first, but the increased movement speed bought it some time. It evaded the first two shots before the spotter successfully predicted its movement and brought it down. The spotter pipped the imp traveling on the right on their first try, just as the third and final imp reached the now well-illuminated third platform.

Damien Imploded it and a host of players spiraled through the air, many of them already damaged from the traps they'd bulldozed through on the way. It wasn't the solid group of ten he'd caught previously, but it was well worth three imps.

He'd dealt with the front-runners, but there were already more coming to take their place. With such a long cooldown on Implosion he wasn't going to have the luxury of using another one before they reached him. There was nothing for it. He stepped back until he was against the wall, at the most poorly lit part of the platform, and gave his imps their orders before pointing at the succubus.

"Possession."

He opened his new eyes and gripped the whip as the six remaining imps positioned themselves around him. Then he willed himself straight up, heading for the underside of the spotter's platform to remain out of line of sight. The imps flew out and orbited him effortlessly with their increased movement speed, providing him with a swirling meat shield.

Damien charged Chaotic Bolt with his left hand. The doubled stats his trait enhanced Possession provided had proven especially useful with the succubus. Not only did her spells now hit twice as hard while she was under Damien's thrall, she had twice as much mana to cast them with. It was a truly excellent trait. By the time he drew level with the third platform, the Chaotic Bolt was charged and whining.

Rising Tide were already there in force, pausing their descent to recover from the traps. There were too many players to count, with yet more spilling in behind them. Damien didn't have time to think. He continued upwards as he pitched his prepared spell at the most obvious target, a group of five damaged players huddled under a priest's Dome of Healing. While the Chaotic Bolt traveled, Damien pointed his already extended left hand and cast Circle of Hell directly in the center of the platform, covering it almost entirely.

Both spells arrived simultaneously, eclipsing the dome's soft light in a maelstrom of fire and rift energy. The players had been looking for trouble from below or the middle; they hadn't expected it from the darkness above.

It took a moment or two for them to realize what was happening and run back the way they had come, still burning. The five players under the dome were the hardest hit, and in the least position to do anything about it. The two weakest died on Chaotic Bolt's impact while the other three dithered, not knowing if they should exit the flames and thus the dome as well.

A warrior with a sliver of health left opted to run, then died moments later as the burning persisted but the healing did not. The priest was left frantically casting healing spells between the remaining two, racing the flames to keep them alive. His healing was more potent than the Succubi's damage, but Damien had successfully stopped the front runners in their tracks.

While the priest played out every healer's worst fear, Damien crested the rim of the second-highest platform. He wanted to deal with the spotter and free up his movement in the dungeon's core.

He found himself directly in her sights. An imp stopped orbiting as it took an arrow straight through the abdomen for him. It hadn't even finished disintegrating before the spotter nocked another arrow, charging for a moment before releasing.

Damien pulled back his whip arm and swung it forward as a piercing arrow went straight through another imp and sunk into the succubi's leather armor. The armor, the imp and the increased health from Possession all worked to keep the succubus alive, although she lost a third of her health in the process.

The quick-thinking ranger hadn't quite nocked a third arrow

when the whip lashed around her waist. Damien tightened his grip and yanked her over the edge. She tried to Air Jump, straining against the whip and taking even more damage, before falling past him and spinning at the end of the rope like a yo-yo. The cruel serrated blades sliced through her before coming free, leaving her to spiral to the bottom of the dungeon five floors below. Somehow, Damien didn't think Lillian would have to finish her off.

The platform the ranger had fallen from burst into light as a mana wisp pulsed, catching Damien at the rim of the effect. He was exposed and in full view, but at least he could see what he was facing as well. It was not a pretty sight.

All of Rising Tide had entered the dungeon now, and those who weren't on the lower platform or heading toward it had gathered here to wait while the cannon fodder triggered traps. These players were much stronger than those leading the charge. Not a single one was lower than level 35. A full party of the twenty best Rising Tide had to offer. The most leveled was a level 42 mage standing amidst a tight defensive cluster.

It was only the second time Damien had seen Aetherius in-game. How time flies.

The group turned to face Damien and the more quick-witted among them started raising weapons and channeling spells. The gunslinger at the front was the fastest to attack, firing his musket straight from the hip.

The imp who'd volunteered to take the hit was blown apart, preventing the shrapnel from hitting Damien's succubus at its core. The succubus's arms and legs, however, were shredded.

Damien was knocked back and rolled with the hit, twisting round and diving down. The other players fired into the space he'd vacated, one of his imps not moving fast enough to avoid annihilation.

His little foray into Rising Tide's back line had been fruitful, but the succubus was too weak to survive another hit and he only had three imps left with him. He needed the succubus alive, as well as at least one imp for his next Implosion. Worse still, while he'd been absorbing hits, the front-runners had rallied and were already halfway to the next platform, where Damien's defenseless body lay.

Damien repositioned the succubus in the blind spot and canceled Possession, leaving her far up over his head in the darkness. He called the imps back, just as Noigel arrived with his order of hell hounds.

The three imps dropped onto their mounts and took their positions at the back of the platform as Damien ran for the next flight of stairs. He just made it to the exit as the first Rising Tide tanks stepped onto his level, the players behind raising torches over their heads to illuminate the circle.

The hell hounds crouched against the back wall, waiting. Damien hunkered down below the rim of the steps, sending Noigel to the platform below so he could make a quick escape if necessary. For a moment it looked like he'd need it.

Rising Tide was getting the measure of the dungeon now. With tanks at the front, the players behind them had taken minimal damage. Rather than pausing for breath on the trap-free level, as Damien had hoped, they were making a beeline for the next exit. For him.

Damien sent a hell rider sprinting forward through the torchlight, gunning for a priest who'd been left exposed by their fast advance. The hound caught the player around the throat and the three of them went sailing over the edge.

Damien resisted the urge to Implode the imp riding on its back. He and Lillian had agreed they couldn't risk relying on fall damage from the lower floors. It was too risky. If too many players landed well, she'd be overwhelmed. Which is why Damien had allocated his most dangerous set-ups to the fourth level and below.

Now the threat had been established, Damien ran the second hell rider into the light. He needed the players to stop advancing and stay on the platform. The players at the front ran forward to engage, only for the dog to skirt around them as it went for the center of the group. When they turned to follow its movement, Damien sent the third one running in behind it.

The ranged players in the back opened fire, some of them

hitting their own team in the process. A few of them did manage to find their target, though. The hell hound took two arrows and a round of buckshot in the face before toppling over, the imp rider propelling itself forward and weaving between players as it tried to reach the platform's center.

Damien ordered the succubus overhead to cast Circle of Hell and pointed at the imp, but it was slain by a well-timed Arcane Bolt before it could be Imploded. The last hell hound, already burning from a paladin's Smite, jumped over his predecessor's body as the Circle of Hell formed over all of them. It was just shy of the target destination before it crumbled, the last imp leaping forward off its back.

Damien cast Implosion.

The closest players were almost completely unaffected, but those on the edge of his Circle of Hell were swiftly drawn in. Now all the players were suffering damage over time. More importantly, they also had their armor reduced by half.

The players weren't the only thing being pulled into the center of the platform. Damien had spent a great deal of time and energy fastidiously lining the walls with half the junk he hadn't found any use for: boar tusks, splintered bones and, best of all, hundreds of rounds of buckshot. They were right on the edge of the Implosion – the exact place they needed to be to achieve maximum velocity.

The roar of ricocheting projectiles echoed around the dungeon.

By the time it passed, there was very little left of them to loot. Every last item had been weaponized, producing the kind of firepower you'd expect to see from a Gatling gun. Except a Gatling gun is considerate enough to put the bullets out one at a time. This was instantaneous and nearly 360 degrees.

In a fraction of a second, seventeen players were reduced to cautionary tales. Precious few survived the onslaught; none who were on the platform when Damien had triggered the ability outlasted the succubus's Circle of Hell. From where he was crouched, Damien could see the stragglers gathering at the foot of the stairs, saved by their tardiness.

They looked suitably horrified. Even so, he didn't want to hang around now that his trap had been used up. He crept to the edge and reached out for an imp, Demon Gating to the dungeon floor.

In the wake of the many casualties he'd inflicted, Damien had only leveled up three times. Many of the players he'd killed had been too low level to grant XP. That was fine. This was not a leveling exercise. He didn't care as long as they were dead. The mana he'd restored on leveling up was reward enough.

This was the perfect opportunity to replenish his forces with the Unrelenting Talisman. He'd painstakingly gathered souls on the dungeon floor with his earlier Implosions to prepare and his minion count was now low enough to justify its use.

He got there and looked around, mystified. There were no souls anywhere. The bodies hadn't faded away yet, and plenty of the players he'd knocked down had been high level. It made no sense. He looked to Lillian, hoping for some sort of explanation, and was met with an even more confusing sight.

She was standing over the body of the recently departed priest, having a heated discussion with... Bartholomew? But it couldn't be.

Damien moved a little closer and the vampire's head abruptly turned, the jet-black eyes pinpointing him effortlessly in the darkness. If not for them, he was hardly recognizable. His face, once little more than a skull, had reformed into quite the aristocratic visage.

He had hair now, long, black and curled, framing gaunt cheeks and a haughty, thin-lipped sneer. It was Bartholomew, all right. Even his tattered robe had changed, glowing with regal purple light to display myriad occultist symbols. Damien marched toward him, his fists clenched. He was starting to get an idea about where his hard-earned soul energy had gone.

"Bartholomew, why are there no souls here?"

"Come now, Damien. Surely you didn't think you'd reap all the rewards for yourself? Think of it as a hosting fee."

This had not been the plan. Including his base minions, he was already down to just thirty-four souls' worth of minions.

There was a screech from above as his battle-scarred succubus was spotted and destroyed, bringing the number down to twenty-seven. Low enough to control with just his own Soul Summon Limit. It wasn't going to be enough.

"That's great, Bartholomew. Really, I'm so happy you gave yourself a little makeover, but I needed those souls! How am I supposed to hold them off now?"

"I shouldn't worry. I can make far better use of them than you. Besides which, you have more than enough souls to make use of in your base. There's no need to be selfish."

"What are you talking about? There are no souls in my base! The souls I needed were right here!"

Bartholomew tutted and slowly shook his head.

"I thought I taught you better."

Damien was about to lose it when Lillian butted in, her eyebrow twitching as she stepped between them to grab him by the shoulders.

"Sorry to interrupt, but in case you forgot, we're under attack! Bartholomew says another fifty players have shown up! We need to get into position!"

Damien gritted his teeth. Reinforcements. As if he didn't have enough problems already. He shot Bartholomew a final angry glance before turning his attention to Lillian.

"Let's go. I'll see you up there."

He checked to make sure his destination was unlit before beckoning Noigel to the edge and Demon Gating to the fifth platform. *Man, this skill is useful in here.* It was becoming less useful as he lost control of more of the dungeon, though. Rising Tide was already more than halfway through. He'd softened them up with his 'imp-rovised' trap. On this floor, he intended to hurt them the most.

The incubus and his second succubus had been waiting stoically for Damien's arrival. These two units were where he'd invested the vast majority of his pilfered metal. He usually opted for leather armor on his succubi so as not to limit their movement, but this one would be right in the thick of things. She was wearing steel armor from head to hoof, along with the whip Damien had become familiar with.

The incubus was something else entirely. While the succubus was sleek and refined, Damien had not equipped the incubus with subtlety in mind. It was a brutal war machine. Every last scrap of iron that hadn't been commissioned for buckshot was now wrapped around its considerable frame, right down to the tip of its tail.

The weapon choice had been difficult. There were so many options in the Demon Forge he wanted to try, but he'd lacked the materials to experiment with. In the end he'd gone with a weapon he'd never heard of before. It was called a macuahuitl.

While he didn't have the foggiest idea how to say it, he'd been encouraged by the description: 'A hefty, flat wooden paddle with blades affixed around the rim. The flat side can be used for stunning blows and blocking while the jagged edge is capable of decapitating a horse.' Damien had decapitated a horse already, so this struck a chord with him. He'd poured his scarce true-silver into this weapon to increase the damage as much as possible.

There was a clang as Bartholomew's spiked door trap smashed into the side of the player shield wall, followed by a choked scream. The group was continuing their descent and soon the last of Rising Tide's expendable forces breached his floor.

They were terrified. At the back were a couple of the elites that had previously been part of Aetherius's honor guard: the wretched gunslinger from the Malignant Crypt and one of the paladin tanks. A good sign. Damien had scared them enough that the big players were stepping in to babysit.

Damien had an incubus, a succubus, two wraiths and four imps to repel them. He picked out his targets and ordered the succubus to set her Circle of Hell when the gunslinger pointed his gun into the darkness and fired. It was a flare. It pinged off the wall over Damien's head and landed right at his feet. *Oh, goody*. So much for directing the battle from the shadows.

After that, everything happened very quickly.

The Circle of Hell opened in the middle of the enemy ranks

as everyone in the group turned toward Damien and opened fire. Damien gave his orders and threw himself behind the incubus, the majority of the arrows and shrapnel pinging off its iron armor. His resources had been well invested.

But the mages were already channeling their spells and melee units were closing in. The incubus's armor would be much less helpful against their assault. Fortunately, they were very close to the bottom of the dungeon by now.

The wraiths ascended from the underside of the platform and commenced their butchery on the unarmored, distracted back line. An imp flew over their heads and landed in the middle of the succubus's circle, all but ignored in the frenetic activity of the last three seconds. Damien Imploded it and the party members that weren't already being torn apart by his wraiths were pulled in, capturing all but the fastest-acting of the melee units heading for him. They'd be on him in moments. Damien had no choice. He ordered his succubus to cast Bloodlust as he possessed the incubus.

The enormous size was a drawback against missiles, but it had at least one identifiable advantage: long reach. As an assassin leapt for his throat, Damien drew back the macuahuitl with both hands and cleaved the air ahead of him at chest height. The weapon was light for its size yet still had enough heft to build up considerable force. Possession granted his new vessel 150 strength, his attack speed was Bloodlust-buffed and the assassin had the lingering effects of the Circle of Hell's armor debuff. Damien's first weapon test was a roaring success.

He looked up to find the other players fleeing back towards the Circle of Hell, preferring to burn rather than face this monstrosity. The Rising Tide party was getting a handle on the situation. The paladin tank had Smote one of his wraiths. The remaining wraith was still stabbing anything within reach, but it had lost the element of surprise and was quickly put away by a shot from the gunslinger.

Damien's window of opportunity was closing. Once the party was out of the burning effect he'd be outmatched. He couldn't take advantage of their disarray without leaving his true body behind, exposed in the light of the flare. Damien gritted the incubus's savage maw and expelled a sigh that rattled in his throat like a lion's roar. This was going to be messy. He scooped up his own body in his left hand, clutching it close to his chest like a gargantuan child holding a stuffed toy. He faced the center of the Circle of Hell, lowered his head so that his targets were directly between his horns, and charged.

Ground trembling under his feet, Damien leapt forward, his macuahuitl stretched out behind him with his real body pressed firmly against his chest. Noigel's assessment of the incubus hadn't been entirely accurate. His enemies were too watery for the incubus to grind them into powder. 'Mush' would have been a more fitting term.

Damien landed double-footed on the center of the dogpile, his feet sinking into the struggling mass as if it were a sentient pile of mashed potato, and swept his jagged baton in a single-armed sweep that took full advantage of the demon's enormous reach. He cut through the fleeing debuffed enemies without even the slightest trace of resistance.

The gunslinger and the paladin tank had avoided the carnage, making full use of the guild's cannon fodder. Now the former was taking careful aim at the vacant body clutched against his chest, and Damien could do nothing to stop it.

Damien barely had time to throw his hand out to the side before the trigger was pulled and an explosive shell detonated over his breastplate, cratering a hole in the iron and cutting a 450 chunk out of his health points.

The paladin stepped forward and clenched his fist. The incubus burst into white flames as the Smite took hold, inflicting little damage since the paladin was built to tank but illuminating Damien clearly. Then the bombardment from above started. Aetherius's group had taken their positions on the trap floor.

Even from a distance, the burning incubus was a very obvious target. As a line of red energy streaked its way toward him, Damien's warrior instincts kicked in. He spun the macuahuitl round and covered his torso with the flat of the paddle.

The macuahuitl cracked under the brunt of the attack, the beam forcing it against his chest and knocking him back. His fall carried his shoulder into the beam's path for the last second of the spell. His armor offered no protection against the overwhelming power of Aetherius's assault, cooking him alive. Braised shoulder of not-lamb.

The beam subsided and Damien tried to push himself up, but his right arm refused to move. He'd barely assessed the damage before a fully charged fireball lazily plummeted down from on high, lighting up the dungeon as bright as day. He pulled his occultist body back against his chest, rolling onto his front to protect his empty vessel from what was to come.

The ground around him glowed as the fireball screeched closer and closer, threatening to end the campaign in a single hit.

Lillian had been standing at the top of the stairs, waiting for the Circle of Hell to dissipate before she made her move. This unfortunate turn of events had changed her plans. She ran up the incubus's back and leapt toward the fireball, her brow furrowed in her trademark combination of zen calm and righteous fury.

Damien lifted his head to watch helplessly. Lillian must be sacrificing herself for him.

Nope. She drew her shield across her body as it glowed a brilliant white, then slammed it into the fireball with carefully calculated malice. The white of her Repent skill leaked into the spell, encasing it in holy energy and expanding it to the size of a wrecking ball. At the end of her swing, it screamed away in the direction she'd chosen: toward the two high-tier players who'd avoided the carnage. The Repent-buffed fireball landed in their midst and expanded to consume them, scorching the dumb surprise off their faces.

The floor was clear. Lillian touched down on the edge of the platform, her armor black and charred from stepping into the Circle of Hell. There was a brief pause as everyone processed what just happened before Aetherius's party expressed their disdain the best way they knew how: by carpet bombing the now ally-free platform.

The incubus was no longer lit up by Smite, but it was still well illuminated in the glow of the fireball's aftermath. Damien put it back on its feet and was about to cancel the possession when a ranger on the floor above obliged him, loosing three silvery arrows toward it in rapid succession.

The first two missed their mark, but the third went cleanly through the hole in the armor over its dark heart. Damien was dropped and repossessed his own body while still falling and under heavy fire. He dove behind the incubus as it started to disintegrate, leaving only the empty armor and irreparably damaged macuahuitl behind. Now that he was in contact with the floor, he was taking damage from his own Circle of Hell. At least the black flames weren't illuminating him, but that wasn't much of a consolation.

Damien only had the succubus and three imps left. A string of arcane missiles from Aetherius put an end to the former, the steel armor Damien had equipped her with counting for nothing. Without the advantage of striking from the darkness his minions were little more than sitting ducks.

Lillian's armor was weakened from the Circle of Hell debuff, arrows sinking into her normally impenetrable plate. She gave up on standing her ground and started zig-zagging back, heading for the lower levels. The black flames finally left her, but she'd already taken heavy damage and her armor was too heavy to use this tactic effectively for long.

Damien crawled under his incubus's back plate while Rising Tide were still focused on Lillian, calling all three imps up so he could try and Demon Gate out. Rising Tide saw it coming. The moment they crested the platform's edge, all attention turned to the imps instead. Had Damien Demon Gated to them, he'd have been obliterated.

Noigel survived the longest, darting and looping in every direction to draw fire, but a fresh round of Arcane Missiles put his heroic efforts to a miserable end.

Damien had nothing left. He was stuck in the middle of the floor. The only thing saving him was his Shadow Walker skill, preventing his opponents from seeing where he'd gone. If he moved from cover and into the light of the flames, he was as good as finished. But he had to try.

He was counting down from three when the clatter of arrows and hum of missiles were drowned out by whoops and cheers from above. The Rising Tide reinforcements had arrived on Aetherius's floor. The last nail in his plan's coffin. It was only going to get worse from here.

He had to move, and he had to move now.

Damien crawled out from under the sheet of iron and started running after Lillian as fast as he could, expecting to be dropped by a spell at any second. Only the barrage had stopped. Stranger still, Lillian wasn't moving, instead gawking at the platform above with her shield hanging loosely by her side. Damien turned to follow her gaze and then drew to a stop halfway across the floor to stare with her.

Rising Tide was under attack.

The whole platform had been illuminated by a pulsing mana wisp while the battle raged beneath. Rising Tide had turned around, concentrating their power at the stairs leading down to their level, but despite their efforts the horde of players was still surging through.

They all looked exactly alike. They wore the same armor, wielded the same swords, played the same class and shared the same face. A fifty-strong party of warriors. All with variations on one name. Scorpius.

It was a spectacle. They were all low level, but what they lacked in stats they made up for with gusto and numbers. As Damien watched, one of the Scorpius clones managed to break through to a ranger on the edge, plunging his broadsword through their body before the two of them went tumbling over.

The ranger cried out with dismay but 'Scorpenis' was ecstatic, trotting out an evidently pre-rehearsed line with much merriment in the face of his imminent death.

"MY MOM'S EXPECTING ME FOR DINNER IN TE—"

They plummeted past the platform and the rest of it was lost to gravity.

Scorpenis had done better than most. Very few of the players were breaking through and those who did were being swiftly cut down now the element of surprise was lost.

Damien was still watching when Lillian grabbed him by the arm and dragged him away down the stairs, the one-sided yet relentless skirmish still raging above them. The Scorpius crew looked like they were doing it for fun, yet they'd helped him and Lillian traverse the thin line between life and death. Better yet, they weren't Rising Tide. Suddenly the battle seemed far more winnable.

Lillian ushered him past the sixth level before the yelling started to diminish, but the damage had been done. Their silly sacrifice had bought valuable time. Lillian channeled a heal at Damien, hissing between her teeth.

"Hurry up! They're coming! Summon something!"

Damien shook himself and re-summoned Noigel first. He didn't have the largest health bar, so it didn't take long for Lillian to bring his hit points back to full. Then she began healing herself. That would take a bit longer.

Damien rushed below the sixth platform to summon two wraiths. If he used them right, they'd last longer than anything else he could summon. In the face of properly leveled players, his only realistic option would be stealth and ambushes.

The sounds of battle above had perished, the Scorpius clones likely perishing with them. Aetherius's party would be on the move. He could already hear his enemies approaching from above as he moved to summon three more imps, draining the last of his soul energy.

His heart sank as he realized it was too late to trigger the second Implosion-based shrapnel trap he'd set on the sixth level. Somehow, he and Lillian would have to deal with well over a dozen fresh, high-level Rising Tide enemies by themselves.

Lillian was already in position protecting the alcove leading to Damien's base, waiting in the darkness. Damien dispersed his two wraiths and three imps to the far edges of the dungeon floor just as Aetherius's group arrived.

The first of them had no sooner reached the bottom than a portal opened in the middle of the floor, clear for all to see, and the reborn Bartholomew strode out of it with his hands clasped behind his back. Where once he'd favored stealth, he was now standing in plain sight, the demonic sigils adorning his cloak glowing in the darkness.

"Welcome back to the final level, Aetherius and friends. I trust you're enjoying your stay?"

35

BARTHOLOMEW'S REVENGE

R ising Tide stopped advancing and stared, taken aback. Bartholomew's question hung in the air until a mage fumbled with his staff and pointed it at their revived foe, the tip crackling with luminescent blue electricity.

Bartholomew leapt back into his portal with surprising speed and it snapped shut, the jagged thunderbolt streaking through empty space. A new portal opened right next to it and Bartholomew nonchalantly appeared in its frame, tutting loudly and smiling broadly.

"Same old Rising Tide, I see, fighting first and trading niceties never. Since you're so eager—"

His hands blurred round in a circle, index fingers extended and glowing. Five portals hummed into existence on the outer walls of the dungeon floor, much larger than those Damien used and imbued with the same regal purple tinge as Bartholomew himself.

"—let us begin."

Bartholomew withdrew and the portal closed around him. As he departed, the group started murmuring among themselves anxiously. They'd come here to kill a single player, not to tangle with an elite dungeon boss. How many of them had accompanied Aetherius here when he'd vanquished Bart the first time? From the looks of it, not enough to reduce their fears.

Aetherius was, of course, the exception. He looked absolutely livid. He stepped behind a paladin and smacked him across the back of his armor-encased head.

"Don't just stand there! Go do your job!"

The paladin crossed himself and lit up with the silvery light of his own Sanctification before trotting reluctantly into the darkness ahead. The party edged forward behind him, their heads swiveling between the five ominously humming portals.

Damien couldn't know if Bartholomew had done it on purpose, but none of the portals had appeared too close to him, Lillian or his minions. If it had turned out otherwise they might have had their positions revealed by the glow.

As the players moved in, Aetherius subtly merged back into the center of the group, out of harm's way. Damien had his eye on him. If he could drop Aetherius, this would all be over.

The paladin hadn't quite made it to the center of the arena when one of the portals flashed around the rim and Bartholomew tore out of it, floating above the ground with his hands folded across his chest, a towering line of roaring red flames in his wake. He was heading for one of the two portals on the opposite side.

Aetherius chose that moment to start screaming at his colleagues.

"Don't let him make a pattern! If he goes through the portals five times he'll get stronger! Fire! FIRE!"

Bartholomew uncrossed his hands, each of them holding a Chaotic Bolt, before flinging them one after the other toward the group without changing course. The designated tank darted sideways to intercept, shield raised. The two projectiles broke against it one after the other, the resulting explosions pushing him back but inflicting minimal damage.

Damien was disappointed. He'd expected something more impressive given Bartholomew's earlier showmanship. One of the priests channeled a heal as the rest of the group spread out to get line of sight.

Bartholomew was faster, launching another Chaotic Bolt at the paladin, the barest flicker of a contemptuous smile flickering over his features. The paladin confidently raised his shield.

"Dodge it, dodge it you moron!" Aetherius screamed.

The paladin did not dodge it. He took it squarely on his shield again. A prominent symbol lit up over his head, indicating the successful application of a dangerous stacking ability. This one was called 'Unstable Energy' and it had three charges out of three. The paladin looked down, his pride turning to alarm, just in time to watch himself explode.

He seamlessly switched roles from party tank to party decor, spreading himself across the front line of their horror-stricken forces in dashing shades of red. Bartholomew himself floated through the portal on the opposite side of the arena, humming with disconcerting glee.

The only signs he'd been there were the towering wall of flames cutting a trail from one portal to the other and the paladin's thoroughly redistributed remains. The flame wall had separated Damien's base from the rest of the party, which would have been wonderful if not for the fact Lillian had been stranded on the other side as well.

Bart emerged from another portal, Chaotic Bolts charging in his hands. The Rising Tide party was directly in his path. They scattered every which way out of their tight-knit bundle, each determined to evade the instant death magic being pelted at them.

Aetherius remained exactly where he was. His hands glowed red for the span of a second before the Arcane Beam seared out of them toward his foe. It was a direct hit, but he did not maintain the beam for long. While Bartholomew reeled, Aetherius blinked to the larger portion of the dungeon and turned, folding his arms and tapping his foot at the other players. They hurried to join him before Bartholomew could recover.

There were still thirteen members of Rising Tide fighting the good fight. Bartholomew was a beast, that much was certain, but he was only level 35. Elite boss mob aside, all the players were higher level than him, more than capable of dealing with him if they worked as a team, and they had all the components required: two priests and a paladin with dedicated healing, a paladin and two warriors as tanks, a warrior, an assassin and two rangers for physical damage, and three mages, including Aetherius himself.

As Bartholomew resumed his advance, the ranged units unloaded into his back, with the exception of Aetherius who was too busy tapping his foot to participate.

By the time Bartholomew cleared the floor, gnashing his teeth with every impact, he'd been reduced to 18,000 hit points out of 30,000. Aetherius abruptly stopped foot tapping and started barking orders, jabbing his fingers around him authoritatively. The paladin tank stayed by his side, operating as his personal bodyguard.

"The boss has a pattern. It'll come out of the first portal it escaped through, going into this one behind us. You two tanks block its path. Everyone else spread out. Priests, DISPEL first, help Judgementday heal when you're done, and don't let it through! If you see Daemien, shout. I'll kill him myself."

Damien edged a little further away from the portal Bartholomew was apparently going to pass through next and which Aetherius had sent the two tanks to guard. They'd almost reached it when Bartholomew burst forth from the opposite side of the dungeon and started hurling Chaotic Bolts. The entire party was ready and waiting, descending on him in full force.

Damien's imps were flying in over the walls of flame. Bartholomew couldn't handle this by himself. Damien was going to have to do something drastic. He knew his target priority. It couldn't have been more obvious from the instructions Aetherius had been so kind to deliver at full volume.

The first imp arrived behind a priest in the middle of channeling Dispel. Damien Demon Gated and was stabbing him before his feet even touched the ground. A sneak critical and three more strikes brought him to a swift end. His Rift Walker trait triggered, resetting the cooldown on Demon Gate. As long as Damien targeted people he could bring down quickly, his mobility would remain almost limitless.

The assassin heard the priest's death rattle and turned to watch Damien withdraw his daggers.

"It's Daemien! He's over th—"

He'd taken his eyes off the imp, who was now swooping in behind him. Damien Demon Gated before the imp was in position, hurtling through the air as he and his winged ally swapped momentum. Where once this had been a disadvantage, now he was prepared. He extended his Sacrificial Dagger in front of him and his body weight drove it through the back of the assassin's neck, literally cutting off his yell.

Damien didn't withdraw the dagger this time, holding his enemy in place on the ground as he thrust Shankyou's infamous weapon into his back again and again. The assassin died soon enough, but he'd alerted Aetherius to his location. Aetherius turned from Bartholomew, his hands switching from blue to red.

Damien teleported across the dungeon just in time, the Arcane Beam searing through the assassin's body and destroying the imp that had taken Damien's place. Only two imps left, plus the two wraiths.

Yet his moment of surprise was gone. The party knew he was in there with them. Before Damien could drop into stealth and move away, they picked him out in the light of Bart's portal. *Whoops.*

The mages were the fastest to react, turning the Lightning Bolt and Arcane Beam they'd been preparing to hit Bartholomew with onto him. Damien ran with Noigel flying out in front of him, feeling the heat of the spells scorch past and then the flames of Bartholomew's deadly trail behind as his mentor passed through the same portal that had exposed him. Thanks to Damien's distraction, the latest wall of flames had split Aetherius's forces in half, but that still left Damien with five angry players to avoid.

He came to the next flame wall and skidded to a halt, not rating his chances of passing through without being burned to a crisp. Demon Gate was still on cooldown and the damage-dealing warrior was rapidly closing in, not giving him time to wait. That only left one way out.

He sent Noigel to hover above the flame wall, took three steps back and used the last of his stamina to leap up as high as he could. As Damien entered the very edge of the effect radius, he Imploded Noigel.

He'd never been subjected to one of his own Implosions before. It was every bit as unpleasant as it looked. It grabbed him by the shoulders and sent him spiraling through the air head first, cartwheeling him over the hungry flames to land in an undignified heap on the other side. The fall hurt a little, but he was alive. Damien lay down on the floor, panting as his stamina replenished, thinking the danger past.

He thought wrong. There was a yell from the other side of the flames and the warrior tore straight through, looking around to find Damien close by and well illuminated by his own burning body. He charged in to finish him off with no regard for his own rapidly diminishing health, yelling in triumph as he raised his claymore to bring it down on his drained, defenseless foe.

He never saw Lillian coming.

While his sword was still scything down, she collided with him at full tilt, her shield braced in front of her. It smashed into his torso and punted him back through the flames from which he'd emerged. Lillian seized Damien by the scruff of his neck and dragged him away from the flame wall.

Damien didn't understand. Lillian shouldn't have been there; they were still separated from his base entrance by the first wall of flames. When she released him, he turned to look at her and his eyes widened. Her health was at barely a third and her armor was black and charred. She'd walked through the hellfire to stand at his side.

Ignoring her own wounds, she started channeling her heal on him, only to be interrupted when a bolt of jagged lightning scorched her back. The lightning mage had left the rest of the group to pursue Damien, riding his nimbus high above.

The mage was channeling another spell when a Chaotic Bolt from Bart slammed into his back. Blasted off his cloud, the mage tumbled head over heels toward his targets. Lillian was quick to capitalize, Divine Might activating as her hammer materialized in her grasp. The mage landed at her feet and her hammer blurred through his head, cratering the ground beneath it with a low boom that fittingly sounded like distant thunder.

Damien resummoned Noigel and immediately sent the imp upward, out of the flames and into the dark, before directing him toward the sixth platform across from them. He needed to get out of here. Lillian was healing herself, but she wasn't specced for it and her health was dangerously low. Defending him had brought her to her limit.

She was still at less than half health when someone Blinked through the flames and set his haughty gaze upon them, his face contorting with glee. His Mana Wisp floated over the wall and came to rest behind his shoulder.

Aetherius had come to finish them off personally.

His hands glowed red and Lillian leapt in front of Damien, her shield hastily equipped and glowing to repel the attack. Aetherius threw his hands out to his sides, canceling the beam before it had even begun, and then brought them together again. This time they glowed blue. His smile twisted further as he savored his victory, before he leveled his full power to fire off Arcane Bolts that spiraled towards them from every direction. They did not travel in a straight line. He was trying to hit Damien directly.

Lillian would not have it. Confronted by the man who'd caused her so much grief, her thin veil of calm, tenuous at the best of times, completely evaporated. Damien couldn't see her face from behind, but the scream of rage alone was enough to chill him to the bone.

She planted her feet, Divine Might coursing through her veins, and her sword arm became the conduit for all her expertise, willpower and hate. Damien couldn't even follow her movements. All he could see were the explosions as she sliced the tip of her blade through one projectile after the other at arm's length, a string of unending blows so fast and accurate it would bring shame to the mightiest of warriors.

It looked like she was going to win. Until her sword snapped in half and the tip clattered to the floor, unable to sustain the stress of her unorthodox methods any longer.

There wasn't enough time to recalibrate. She swept the broken blade short of the next two missiles and missed both, taking the hits on either side of her body before she could raise her shield. The rest of them pounded into it, inflicting grievous wounds despite being blocked.

At last, with her health at less than 100, the barrage ceased. Aetherius was out of mana. He looked distressed for just a moment, his chest heaving up and down, but he quickly drew himself up and feigned a confident grin. As if he'd always been certain that this would be the outcome.

"You should've known better than to use your sword like that. Only a noob would make such a rookie mistake. Give up."

And then his face took on that bored air as he folded his arms and tapped his foot against the stone.

Lillian was a mess. Her face was battered and bruised, her armor was charred and dented, and both her shield and her sword had become useless hunks of twisted metal. Even so, she remained defiant until the end. She turned sidelong to Damien and spoke to him out of the corner of her mouth.

"It's up to you now. I'll cover your escape. Kill this asshole."

She put the shield and sword away and started running toward Aetherius, the hammer materializing in her grasp. Damien tore his eyes away and focused on the sixth platform where Noigel had just arrived. He Demon Gated and turned in one swift motion to look out over the dungeon floor.

Lillian leapt into the air, the ground cracking under the force of her anger, and swept her hammer around and behind her with a blood-curdling scream that made everyone freeze.

Aetherius was still tapping his foot, not even looking at her. At the peak of Lillian's jump, he blurred around the edges and phased out of existence. A fraction of a second later he reappeared off to one side, his hands glowing red. The same ability combination he'd used to cripple the dragon. He caught her perfectly with the Arcane Beam. Lillian the Immortal was dead before she hit the wall.

Damien had never felt so alone. Or so powerless. If it had just been Lillian against Aetherius, he had no doubt who would have won. Instead, she'd put all her faith in him, wasted all her efforts on keeping him alive, and he'd been able to do absolutely nothing to help.

This was all wrong. He didn't deserve to be saved.

His self-pity was brought to an abrupt end as Aetherius let out an enraged scream of his own, stamping his feet. He'd realized Damien had escaped. Even Noigel had been left with enough time to make his getaway, landing on Damien's shoulder without incident.

Aetherius held a hand out to the side and a half-drunk mana potion materialized within it, which he drained in a few seconds before returning to his impotent tantrum. Damien's jaw dropped. Aetherius was using mana potions to support his abilities. His mana was far from limitless. And the mana potion he'd been drinking had only been half full.

Damien put the pieces together. Whatever illusionary trick Aetherius used, he did it to drink mana potions without being seen. Lillian's attack had forced him to break the illusion to strike her in the air before she destroyed his copy. That explained why he was always folding his arms and tapping his feet in combat; it was a fake, just like him. He'd been using consumable items to supplement his skills. He had low wisdom. He was a min-maxer.

Still, that didn't explain everything. The forums online had often stated that Aetherius couldn't be using mana potions, on or off camera. The reason was simple: he had no backpack, no inventory from which to draw consumable items. Yet Damien had just watched him drink a mana potion right in front of his eyes. He had to have an inventory somewhere. Was it invisible? Did he have an ability to conjure potions out of thin air?

There was a low rumble, followed by a long, heinous laugh that turned Damien's attention away. Bartholomew had passed through the last of his five portals. The fires on the ground had seemed like a typical boss fight hazard, but from his vantage point Damien suddenly realized it was a much more intricate set-up.

The five lines of flames on the ground had turned Bartholomew's dungeon floor into an enormous pentagram. It looked just like the sigil Damien used to summon imps, only many times bigger. A new portal appeared at the center and Bartholomew floated out of it with almost 3000 health remaining, badly wounded but still very much undead. His hands swept above his head and pulsed with the deepest, darkest magic.

Damien's mentor was protected by the towering flames on all sides. There was no one to stop him. He smashed his open palms against the floor and was engulfed in black flames. The pentagram diminished to nothing and suddenly the floor was open again, allowing the surviving party members to regroup while Bartholomew underwent a terrible transformation.

Great, twisting ridged horns erupted from his head. A pair of hideous, taloned wings sprouted from his back, snapping and creaking as he stretched them out to either side. His robes tore away and his body expanded, rippling with muscles. The purple sigils that had adorned his robes emblazoned themselves on his pale white skin, glowing in the darkness. The black flames extinguished as his transformation came to an end. He was comfortably twice as large as the incubus had been. As boss mechanics went, Bartholomew had just enraged.

Only six of Aetherius's party were left and Bart was stronger than ever. This was now an entirely different fight.

Bartholomew swept his wings against the ground and went straight for the nearest tank, the warrior. For something so large, the vampire was incredibly fast. The warrior had no time to raise his shield, but it wouldn't have made any difference. Bart's closed fist was larger than the warrior himself. He was blown to smithereens. The rest of the group opened fire and Bartholomew's wings folded over himself for protection, absorbing the brunt of the attacks. He was going down, but slowly considering the power being leveled at him. He needed help.

Damien still had his two wraiths. He sent one into the fray, preying on the priest at the fringe of the party. It did some serious damage before Judgementday turned his Smite from Bart onto the wraith instead. The paladin's high intelligence stat coupled with the innate light of the spell killed it instantly.

While they were distracted by the wraith on one side and Bart on the other, Damien directed his second-to-last imp over the holy magic wielding players, hovering it in the sweet spot before he Imploded it. It caught both the priest and the offending paladin in its grip. They collided in mid-air, and then Bartholomew's huge palms whirled around from either side. They were pulverized in the middle with an earsplitting clap, as if they'd been no more than mosquitoes. Only three Rising Tide players remained.

Their final tank, Aetherius's paladin bodyguard, performed about as well as his predecessor. Bartholomew raised his foot and leaned in to put all his weight behind it, then brought it crashing down with full force. Two to go.

Damien held his breath, waiting for Bart to engage Aetherius. If Aetherius Blinked away when he attacked, Damien could track his movement and intercept while Blink was on cooldown. A fine plan, with one small flaw. Aetherius's foot was tapping, and he looked bored.

Aetherius blurred at the edges and faded away. Reappearing directly underneath Bart's body, he pressed his pulsing red hands together and fired on Damien's master at point blank range. The beam carved a hole through the occultist leader and out the other side. With a last gasp, Bartholomew fell to the ground and disintegrated, leaving no trace except for a huge loot bag. The fight was over.

The surviving priest cheered and Aetherius spun round, warning him not to let his guard down. Too late. Damien's remaining wraith forced an arm-blade through the priest's chest, the second blade stabbing again and again. Aetherius decided he was a lost cause, put his hands together and expended the rest of his mana to destroy friend and foe alike.

Only Aetherius and Damien now remained.

36

THE FINAL BATTLE

A etherius stood in the middle of his slaughtered raid group and drank another mana potion, glancing around to make sure nothing was coming for him. His wariness was telling: he didn't know that with the exception of Noigel, all Damien's forces had been depleted.

Damien's mind raced. How was he going to replenish his minion count now? All the soul energy from the raid had been soaked up by Bart, leaving Damien with nothing.

Aetherius yelled furiously into the dungeon, the slightest tremor of fear ringing his words.

"Where are you, Damien? You chickenshit!"

He fired off a single bolt of energy, tracing the blue light all the way to the wall where it exploded in a glowing sphere. An interesting use of the aesthetic properties of his spell. It was crude, but he wasn't leaving himself open by sending the mana wisp away. He whirled, firing off three more in a spiral. It was certainly creative. They illuminated the space around him for a good five seconds in expanding circles before they exploded in the air. This would be a problem.

"What, did you run? Having second thoughts after what happened to Lillian? She was a lot better than you, and she didn't stand a chance!"

Damien seethed silently. He needed a plan and doubted he'd be able to kill Aetherius with just Noigel to help.

Five more Arcane Bolts were fired, this time in straight lines. One of them burst on the wall next to Damien's base entrance, illuminating it clearly. Yet another problem. Aetherius had been looking the other way, but if he kept doing this he'd find Damien's base before too long.

Aetherius would definitely trash his base before he left. A pyrrhic victory, but a victory nevertheless. The first thing to go would be the core of his base, the Soul Well, since he'd put it right—

Damien's eyes widened as the full weight of his stupidity fell onto his shoulders. Hadn't Bartholomew specifically said there were plenty of souls in his base? The clue was in the goddamn name.

They were in the Soul Well.

He'd been accumulating souls in that thing since day one! There were thirty in there. Taking all of them and using the amulet Bartholomew had created for him, Damien could replenish his entire personal minion count. *Oh, Bartholomew, you cryptic Socratic bastard, why couldn't you have just said so?*

He communicated his orders to Noigel, the imp flying overhead toward his base as fast as he could. Damien waited until another set of spiraling bolts collided with the wall before prompting Noigel to drop deftly into the alcove. He Demon Gated and swiftly stepped inside his base.

He ran up to the altar and brought up the information window. In the top right corner sat the red cross that would allow him to destroy the Soul Well: the same option he'd disregarded, back when it had been no more than a shabby pile of rocks.

'**Destroy the Soul Well?** Yes/No?'

Damien nodded and there was a piercing crack as the metal sacrificial table snapped in half and toppled over on either side, revealing the stone foundation below. The rocky dome crumbled and the souls within seeped out on all sides, covering the ground around it in a thick silver mist. Ten souls' worth flooded into his hands and the rest of it pooled around his feet.

An Arcane Beam passed an arm's length from where he stood and burnt itself into the back wall. Apparently, the acoustics were pretty good in here. Aetherius had heard the demolition from the dungeon floor. Just what he needed.

Damien clutched the amulet in his right hand, the surface of the metal turning hot as it activated. He couldn't use this thing to summon a balanced team. The amulet would only remove the casting time of the first spell he chose. There was only one sensible choice Damien could see.

He pointed at the ground and summoned an imp. This time, the sigil appeared fully formed and the portal came instantly, the imp dropping out soon after. Damien dragged his finger around himself in a circle and sigil after sigil seared into the floor, over-lapping each other in a long line as one imp after the next fell out of the portals in perfect synchronization. As he spun, the soul energy on the floor flowed into his free hand in a constant stream.

Soon, he'd hit his full Soul Summon Limit and have twenty-seven imps. They were gathering in front of him when Aetherius lit up the doorway, his silhouette appearing within the frame until the mana wisp jetted forward over his head. The ring of light it provided exposed the horde of imps at Damien's feet.

"What the f—"

The imps screamed hysterically and launched into the air, swarming in every direction like a flock of manic bats. Damien ran for cover, sprinting to the side and throwing himself behind his Gateway.

Aetherius opened fire. Each imp attempted to dodge and weave through the stream of Arcane Missiles. There were so many of them and the space was so enclosed that Aetherius could hardly fail to hit, but their numbers meant they couldn't all be repelled.

He'd fired about six bolts before the first imp attached itself to his leg and bit into his calf. Aetherius looked down and flailed his foot, trying to kick it loose, only for another one to wrap itself around his head before clawing at his face. Then the rest of them came flooding in, covering the mage from head to toe in a rippling wave of wailing red rage.

Aetherius screamed and his hands stopped glowing as he tried to rip them off, to no avail. They weren't good at much, but they certainly liked clinging onto things. Still completely coated in minions, Aetherius turned with difficulty and Blinked out of Damien's base, the imps collapsing to the ground in his absence.

Damien darted forward and leapt over them through the doorway, wanting to press his advantage. The imps quickly rose and followed, spreading out when they reached the wider space of the dungeon floor.

Aetherius was only a short distance out in front, his back turned, but he was tapping his foot. Damien sent a single imp on the attack, swooping it in to attach itself to the back of Aetherius's head. It arrived there at full pace, claws extended, only to pass straight through the illusion and land on the floor in a squealing heap.

The mana wisp started flying away to the left wall, to where Aetherius must really be. Damien chased after it, looking ahead for Aetherius with his night vision but seeing nothing. The wisp arrived at the empty wall, then promptly turned around and hovered high over Damien's own head, illuminating him as though he were on stage. Aetherius wasn't there.

Damien whirled around and picked him out on the opposite side of the dungeon with his night vision. Aetherius had gotten the better of him. He was back at full health, too; apparently he'd stocked up on healing potions as well. And his hands were glowing red.

Damien pointed at the first imp he saw, Demon Gating into the air a fraction of a second before the Arcane Beam ripped through his minion in a severe case of overkill. The mana wisp whizzed after him, the patch of light searching for Damien's new location. He sent an imp upward to dispose of it before it could track him down, the claws slashing through it with ease.

Aetherius summoned a new wisp and sent it up high above

himself, keeping his surroundings well-lit before firing a stream of Arcane Missiles in a wide spread. Damien fled out of their path, scattering his imps to avoid the magic, then crouched at the edge of the wall to direct them properly. He had to end this, fast.

As far as Damien could tell, Aetherius had a near endless supply of potions. Damien had made his last big play already. He wouldn't get a second chance.

The imps were closing in on either side, but with so many of them the beats of their wings were easy to hear. The mana wisp pulsed, suddenly increasing the range of the light, and Aetherius began firing again. Damien's summon limit was already at eighteen; it wouldn't be long before he had too few imps to make an impact.

He switched tactics. Instead of flying the imps aggressively toward Aetherius, he fanned them out in a wide circle and instructed them to stay at range and focus on dodging. With the extra distance, the imps did a much better job of avoiding the spells than he'd expected. They bobbed and weaved away from missiles in unison like a shoal of fish, although their incessant yelling gave them more in common with geese.

With the imps dodging, Damien would preserve more of his forces while Aetherius would still be using up his mana. When he paused to drink a potion, that was when Damien would send them in.

Noigel landed on his shoulder, causing Damien to start. He hadn't given Noigel instructions since he Demon Gated into his base, preoccupied first with using the amulet and then dueling Aetherius. It was a good thing Noigel had his own prerogative.

"Master, this isn't going to work. His bag is—"

Aetherius cast a last pair of Arcane Missiles, both of which were dodged by the imps at the edge of his mana wisp's circle of light, then crossed his arms and started tapping his foot. This was it. Damien was about to attack with everything he had when Noigel hissed in his ear, disrupting his focus.

"Master, you have eighteen imps left. I won't have Forbidden

Knowledge once you've got less than ten. Now would be a very good time to listen."

Damien just managed to hold back a yell of frustration. Noigel had interrupted his focus at the crucial moment. Now he'd have to wait until Aetherius was out of mana again. More annoyingly still, his enemy was showing no sign of running out of potions, despite his lack of backpack. He wasn't playing conservatively enough for Damien to suspect there was any end in sight.

Damien pulled his imps back out of the light and eyeballed Noigel. Whatever he wanted to say, it had better be pretty damn important. Noigel ignored his angry glare and pointed at Aetherius's foot-tapping form.

"Do you see that bag, the one attached to his belt?"

Damien focused and found it. It was no surprise he hadn't noticed it before. It was barely larger than a closed fist.

"That's the same type of bag Bartholomew uses," Noigel said. "It doesn't contain items; it has a portal inside connecting to another inventory, probably in his home base. He'll never run out of potions."

This was much worse than Damien had imagined. Aetherius could chug all day long and never have to worry about running out.

If his wisdom was as low as Damien suspected, without that bag his build would be worthless. It was why the coward wouldn't fight Toutatis – because the fight had been on a test server and the bag probably wouldn't function prope—

Wait. That's it.

It was a long shot, but if Damien could pull it off, victory would be certain. Lillian would not have died in vain.

Aetherius was on the offensive now, moving out into the dungeon with his hands raised and the mana wisp scouting out ahead of him.

Damien stared Noigel dead in the face and thought out very clearly what he wanted him to do. Noigel stared back, then out at Aetherius, then at Damien again.

"Are you sure?"

"Just do it. You're the only one I trust to get it done. I'll give you the opening. I'm counting on you."

Noigel puffed out his chest and saluted, then lifted off into the air to wait for his moment from high above. Damien ordered his imps to maintain distance at the edge of the mana wisp's light as he moved around the outside, watching Aetherius closely. As long as his presence was concealed he could still try to resolve this the old fashioned way; with a dagger in the back. It would certainly be a simpler task than the one he'd entrusted to Noigel.

He'd almost made it when Aetherius's hands glowed blue and swept around him, firing off another two swirling bolts of energy to guard against this very tactic. Damien picked out the first imp he could see and Demon Gated.

His feet hit the ground, the sound giving him away. Aetherius's mana wisp shot toward the noise, thrumming directly over Damien's head and staying there.

Damien had no Demon Gate and was fully illuminated. He ordered all his imps to close in as Aetherius split his hands, launching both straight-firing and circling bolts to attack and defend simultaneously.

The only choice left was to run. It was about as much fun as dodging traffic. Imps dove to block shots that would otherwise kill him, whittling their numbers down further.

It was pandemonium. Imps were exploding all over the dungeon as they flew headlong into the circling bolts, buying Damien valuable seconds of life. The straight fired bolts forced him to keep running forward, the circling bolts that his imps couldn't reach had to be dodged left and right. Only six imps remained. He threw a glance back at Aetherius and his adversary's lips immediately curled into a contemptuous sneer.

In that moment of lost focus, Damien failed to dodge a bolt soaring in from the front. There were no imps in range left to intercept it. It smashed into his stomach and blew him off his feet. The knockback of the first carried him back into the second, one of the straight shots that Aetherius had been tracing his movement with. It knocked him to the ground as the next volley arced over his head. They hit hard. It was the weakest spell in the mage arsenal, yet each hit had done over two-hundred damage. Aetherius had upgraded it plenty. Damien was down to a quarter of his health.

Having stopped his target's movement, Aetherius's hands cupped and turned from blue to red, preparing to finish Damien with a single, powerful blow.

Behind Aetherius, a single imp had finally managed to get within range. Damien twisted on the floor, pointed, and used Implosion just before the Beam activated. Aetherius was interrupted by the pull of the spell. He skidded across the floor, yelling with surprise and anger as Noigel seized his long-awaited opportunity. He plummeted down from above, landing double-footed on Aetherius's stomach as he went to work on his waist. The remaining three imps arrived moments later, attaching themselves to Aetherius's hands and face.

After a few seconds of flailing, he resorted to his tried and tested method of imp removal. Noigel disengaged just before Aetherius Blinked away, the slower three imps falling to the ground. Aetherius turned back the way he'd come and fired a burst of Arcane Bolts in a tight spread, killing all three in one go.

Noigel, the only minion left, was flying back to Damien's side as fast as his wings could carry him. Damien looked at the damage Aetherius had sustained. He had some scratches on his usually pristine face and the back of his hands but his health points hadn't taken much of a hit. The mana wisp was still over Damien's head, allowing Aetherius to see how badly wounded Damien had been by just two of his multitudinous projectiles. It was clear which of them had come out worse.

Aetherius put a hand on his hip and dropped the other one to his side for a new mana potion, his derisive laughter echoing off the walls. Damien stared unflinchingly into his eyes as Aetherius attempted to rub salt into his wounds.

"Is that it? Some imps? I expected more after everything you promised your fanboys! 'Kill Aetherius or die trying', was it? I bet you wish—"

He abruptly stopped talking and looked at his hand. It was

quite bereft of mana potion. He focused on it and flexed his fingers, achieving nothing. He looked back at Damien just in time to watch Noigel land on his shoulder and drop a small bundle into his open palm. Damien kept his eyes locked on Aetherius's as he mimicked his stance, holding his empty hand out to one side. A high-grade health potion appeared within. He continued looking at Aetherius as he raised it to his lips and chugged it down. Slowly. Savoring this perfect moment.

Aetherius stared listlessly at the potion, then turned his attention to the bundle Noigel had delivered. He gagged, his eyeballs widening until it seemed they might drop out of his skull. His hands fell to his waist and groped all along his belt. His Bag of Holding wasn't there. Of course it wasn't. Damien had it.

Damien wiped his lips with his sleeve, not breaking eye contact for even a second, and passed his verdict.

"You are so screwed."

Aetherius goggled at him, his lips flapping without making any sound. Then his face abruptly became a mask of calm. He folded his arms and started to tap his foot. The illusion had never been less convincing.

Noigel leapt off Damien's shoulder and flew straight through the image, leaving a smeared haze in his wake. The moment Noigel dispelled the copy, Aetherius reappeared running toward the wall, panting heavily and looking over his shoulder. Damien didn't move.

There was no need. He was running the wrong way.

Aetherius found this out to his cost when he hit the wall, falling over backward and yelling in literal blind panic. The mana wisp abruptly left Damien and traversed the dungeon toward him. Noigel intercepted it and slashed it through, plunging the chamber into total darkness.

Aetherius bellowed in fear and staggered to his feet, fumbling his way along the wall with his hands – still going in the wrong direction.

The outbursts gave way to a series of uncontrolled whines, much like you'd expect to hear from a dog who wants to be let outside. Damien decided it was time to put him out of his misery.

He walked toward him, making sure not to cover the sound of his approach at all. The yelling came back again.

"Don't–No. No! It's my bag, give it back! You cheated!"

Damien pulled out his daggers and twirled them around in his hands, whistling a tune that was punctuated by his purpose-fully loud footsteps. Aetherius cowered against the wall. Totally defenseless.

Damien stood over him, feeling both elated and exhausted. He struck once.

"That's for my mom."

Struck twice.

"That's for Lillian."

Three times.

"That's for calling me a min-maxer, you filthy hypocrite."

He raised his daggers for a final, twin blow.

"And this one is for the fans. I can't wait for them to see who you really are."

Locking eyes with Aetherius's blind, terror stricken gaze, he brought his daggers dow—

His entire field of vision became searing white light, accom-panied by a piercing shriek that felt like it would split his head apart. He couldn't feel his body, he couldn't hear anything except for the high-pitched whine ringing through him. It was agony. As it took hold and increased tenfold, his thoughts were scat-tered by the pain until he was left with only one. The one that had haunted him the longest and had finally come to pass.

He had failed.

37

PICKING UP THE PIECES

Damien's world was darkness. Slowly, he blinked, and lines formed a matrix above. It was a pattern, black lines forming white diamonds. Or squares. He focused on them, still too disorientated to realize he'd regained the ability to focus, and more details started to emerge. Light and dark patches, flecks of wear and tear... it was a paneled ceiling.

Each new discovery gave way to another. He was on his back, lying on a bed and looking up. So far, so good. He tried to rise, and his head pounded with the effort. It felt like he'd been on the wrong end of Lillian's hammer.

He moved his hands up to cradle his head, but only one of them arrived. Something sharp was digging into his wrist. He gently turned to look, suppressing a wave of nausea, and found the cause. His hand was cuffed to a metal rail at the bedside. The nausea was supplanted by panic, which increased as his eyes alighted on the sophisticated machine up against the wall.

Wires from it trailed along the bed, to his head. He yanked at his manacled wrist, the jangle of the chain overlaying the hum of the device he was hooked to.

"Hey, shh, shh, it's okay."

A reassuring hand touched his forehead. Looking left, he found Lillian, her hair tied back and her blue hospital overalls equipped. Worn. Whatever, that wasn't his primary concern. Her eyes were brimming with tears. It looked like relief.

"Lillian, what's going on? Where am I? What did—"

Then he remembered. He'd been a single blow away from killing Aetherius, but he'd been robbed of his victory. Someone had pulled off his IMBA set. He knew it wasn't Lillian who'd done it. Which could only mean one thing. Before he could form it into a sentence, Lillian obliged him.

"You're in Jefferson Hospital, the one I work at. I, uh, I lost my temper after Aetherius finished me off. My guardian wristband activated and security was notified. I told them nothing was wrong and sent them away, but ten minutes later they showed up again, with those two."

Her eyes narrowed as she thumbed at the door behind her. Standing to one side of it, well within earshot but staring steadfastly ahead, was the goateed henchman Damien had spent the last week avoiding. Only the arm of the other appeared inside the frame, but it had to belong to his well-built co-worker.

"Turns out they were tracking my guardian wristband through the hospital as well. They used it going off as an excuse to invite themselves in. Told compound security they suspected a 'dangerous criminal' was squatting in my house and they were 'concerned for my safety'."

The CU lackey took a deep breath, but his tech-enhanced glasses remained fixed on the corridor wall across from him.

"So, they insist I open up, still flanked by security, and see you on the sofa. Minding your own business with your headset on. Ask who you are and I tell them you're a friend who's staying with me for a few days. Not good enough for that BEARDY DOUCHEBAG over there."

The aforementioned beardy douchebag reacted to that one, rotating his shoulders one after the other. Lillian was in full flow.

"He DEMANDS that I remove the headset so he can identify you, and I tell him you're logged into an online game. If he just waits outside for a few minutes I'll put my headset on and send you a message so you can log out safely. Then the IDIOT—" she yelled at full volume, now facing the doorway and pointing at the idiot vindictively, "—runs over and rips the damn thing off your head, and when he's done you have a goddamn seizure! CU's finest, ladies and gentlemen."

Damien had noticed by now that Lillian was no longer wearing her wristband, but he was pretty sure that if she had been it would've gone off. The chastised CU agent had come to stand at the foot of Damien's bed.

"May I remind you, the individual in question evaded authorities for a week. If he'd simply co-operated from the beginning, none of this would have happened. I was not about to let—"

"The 'individual in question' is sixteen years old!" Lillian snapped. "You chased him out of his home onto the streets, then when he was finally safe with me you nearly killed him with gross negligence. I'll have your badge. You sure as—"

The agent was nearly as red in the face as Lillian herself. Her voice had carried into the corridor, prompting people to try and look inside while the larger agent on the door waved them past, glancing behind with concern. The smaller, redder, older of the two paced out the door.

"Stupid civs."

There was the click of a key as he locked the two of them inside. Lillian trounced up to the door and drew the bolt, then banged her palm on the observation window.

"Enjoying your power trip now? Pube-face!"

Damien was still feeling a little woozy, but watching this exchange made him feel quite a lot better. After kicking the door for good measure, Lillian busied herself by filling a paper cup with water and returning to Damien's side. Her voice trembled a little, but the volume had gone back to normal.

"There, now we have some privacy. Drink this. You were on a drip earlier but it can't hurt."

The cuffs clanked again before he took it with his unimpeded hand and drank it down greedily. He gave it back to Lillian, who promptly went to refill it as Damien's questions formed one by one.

"How long was I out?"

"Not long. About three and a half hours." She handed him the next cup and sat by his side as he drained it. "Anyone with a headset knows you're not supposed to pull the damn thing off without logging out first, but…" She glared at the door again, confirming it was closed, before lowering her voice even further. "Have you ever had seizures before? Does anyone in your family have them?"

Damien shook his head. His mom had the heart condition, but never seizures. He didn't know his father very well, but he'd never heard anything like that about him either.

"Don't tell our bearded friend, but the reaction to being forcibly logged out is never as bad as what you had. Lots of documented cases of headaches, fatigue, brief synesthesia, never seizures though. You said your headset is a prototype. Didn't you?"

Damien didn't answer. He was staring off into space. So, the headset he'd been strapping himself into all week wasn't entirely perfect. 'Warning: may cause seizures' was probably not the glowing endorsement Mobius had been looking for when they asked him to test it. At least now he'd be able to give Kevin some useful feedba—oh, wait, never mind.

Lillian interpreted his silence as a yes.

"Right. I'm going to recommend we keep you under observation overnight. I'll be back in a while, after I've talked with Thing One and Thing Two about my recommendation and confirmed it with my supervisors. In the meantime, I brought you this."

She leaned down and pulled out her bag from under the bed, then dipped her hand in and brought it back out holding the IMBA set. Damien stared at it, lost for words. She didn't plan on him using it again, did she? She saw the look on his face and interjected.

"Browsing isn't a risk. It'll be fine, so long as you don't log in to play. And, um…" She bit her lip. "You didn't quite manage to kill Aetherius, either. There's been lots of talk about it online. You should catch up."

She patted him on the chest, gave him another smile and made for the other side of the bed, printing off a page of results from the machine he was plugged into before pulling the nodes off his head and heading for the door. Damien stared at her as she worked, the IMBA set clasped in his free hand. She was putting on a brave face for him. There was no way she could really be that happy.

He hadn't killed Aetherius. After all that, when he was right on the verge of winning, his victory had been snatched away. Forlornly, he called to her as she waited for the agents to unlock the door on their side.

"I'm sorry Lillian, it's all my fault. I should've killed him faster. I ruined all our hard work."

Lillian looked over at him, her mouth dropping. Then she walked back to the bed and embraced him in a full hug, marred only by the manacled hand Damien couldn't pull free. Behind her, the bigger agent opened the door and poked his head into the room, only to find Lillian had returned to the bedside. Lillian completely ignored his polite cough as she pulled back to look Damien in the eye. She tousled his hair and heartened him with a few carelessly chosen words.

"Stop blaming yourself. You always take responsibility for everything, even when it's beyond your control. You're not perfect and you never will be. But you are amazing."

She leaned forward and planted a kiss on the center of his forehead, prompting a louder throat-clearing from behind her. She ignored that as well, pulling back to grin at her shell-shocked patient with a sudden vindictive flash of teeth.

"Besides, I never said you didn't get our revenge. You *did* kill Aetherius. In a manner of speaking."

She waggled her eyebrows. Damien was completely thrown. Before he could ask any more questions she'd already headed out the door.

Damien saw her brandishing the results sheet at the older agent through the gap, employing a long string of exquisitely complicated medical terms that may as well have been delivered in a foreign language. Some of it probably was. The words 'hypersynchronized posterior cortical neurons' floated through the gap before the door gently clicked shut and was locked again.

He'd had reservations about putting the headset on again, but Lillian had become even more cryptic than Bartholomew. He had to see for himself.

Dragging the set onto his head awkwardly with one hand, he navigated to his Saga Online profile page. He had over 700,000 votes. A golden '1' in the center of a royal blue shield next to the vote number indicated his position in the competition.

He was in first place!

With that many votes, he'd be surprised if anyone was even close to him. He was going to win the competition. He'd be able to pay for his mom's surgery.

What was going on? He'd missed out on completing his objective at the last hurdle. Had grievously injuring his nemesis before being forcibly logged out been enough to satisfy the voters?

He navigated to Saga Online's homepage and found his answer in bold writing that took up the entire screen:

AETHERIUS, EX-COMPETITION LEADER, IS SLAIN BY SCOREPEEUS63, WITH A GENEROUS ASSIST FROM DAEMIEN.

Damien stared at the link, blinking. It took five seconds for the words to sink in. He read it again three times, his grin widening with each pass. Then he started howling with laughter. He pulled back his visor to wipe the tears of mirth out of his eyes before snapping it shut again with a long, happy sigh.

He selected the link. This was going to be the best thing he'd seen in his entire life. He was laughing again the moment he heard Scorepeeus63's voice. He sounded like he was about six years old. Then he realized the clue was in the name. Scorepeeus63 was actually nine.

"Guys, it's really scary down here, are you sure this is the right way?"

He leaned over the edge of the platform he was standing on, holding the torch over the edge. He was in The Downward Spiral. The light his feeble torch cast barely breached the darkness at all. All of a sudden, a whirlwind of Arcane Missiles erupted from the bottom floor, accompanied by a long stream of them that chased a dark hooded figure around in a circle.

Damien was watching the final leg of his fight with Aetherius through Scorpeeus63's eyes. The two of them had been so preoccupied they hadn't even noticed the torchlight of this late arrival.

Scorepeeus63 hurriedly paced back from the edge, his torch held out in front of him as if it would keep the danger away. Like pulling the blanket over your head to protect yourself from imaginary monsters.

"I don't wanna go down there! They're too OP!"

There was a babble of barely discernible voices as the crowd of people talking into his headset all vied to be heard at once. Their sentiment was easy enough to pick out. They expected him to go down there.

"Alright, STFU noobs, you're the ones who died. I'll go. I ain't scared!"

He ran down the final flight of stairs, huddling up against the wall, and screamed when one of Aetherius's spiraling projectiles exploded some twenty feet out in front of him. The voices laughed and urged him forward again, imploring him to get involved. Some of them sounded urgent, but most were laughing as they fed him contradictory instructions.

Damien realized who they were. It was the rest of the Scorpius fan club, the crazy people who'd thrown themselves at Aetherius's back line and given him and Lillian time to regroup. One of the muffled comments was seized upon by the boy.

"I'm not scared. I'm a real Scorpius. I'm low level, but I can help!"

It was only then that Damien spotted his level in the HUD. It was a perfect match for his age. A straggler who'd been left behind by the main party, most likely. Now the rest of them were dead, they'd resorted to peer pressuring this guy down.

They must have known they were sending him to his certain death. Yet the title of the video told a completely different story. Damien chuckled into his headset as the clamor of voices rose to a peak, all of them goading him on.

"Fine! I'm going! One… two… three!"

He ran down the last of the stairs, still clutching his torch in both hands instead of equipping a weapon as he ran screaming onto the dungeon floor. When he neither immediately died nor found himself on the receiving end of an Arcane Bolt, he hurriedly ended the scream in a whisper, prompting a fresh peal of laughter from the people watching and talking to him on their channel.

"Guys, where are they? Come on, guys, help me out he—"

There was a louder, wimpier scream from the other side of the dungeon. Aetherius had already been rendered bagless. Damien couldn't see himself in the dim light the torch provided, but it was a recent memory. He was already moving in to finish him off. The shocking thing for him was that this guy had been right behind him and he'd had absolutely no idea. The chat group started yelling at their charge to get the hell in there.

Huffing and puffing, from fear rather than exertion, Scorepeeus63 moved to obey. He was in the center when Damien heard the words he recognized bouncing off the walls.

"That's for my mom."

A piercing scream followed. Scorepeeus63 stopped running and took a step back, immediately prompting the chat to yell at him hysterically. He whined a little before reluctantly trotting forward.

"That's for Lillian."

Another scream, but to his credit Scorepeeus63 didn't stop moving toward the noise this time.

"That's for calling me a min-maxer, you filthy hypocrite."

Scorepeeus63 kept the pace, his shoulders hunched and his feet dragging forward. At last he was close enough for the torch to catch Damien's back in the light. The tiny fraction of health points that were left of Aetherius knelt at his feet, his hands held up in front of him as he tried to drown Damien out with his screams.

"And this is for the fans. I can't wait for them to see who you really are."

Damien raised his hands to either side, froze, and abruptly faded out of existence.

Aetherius continued screaming for a good five seconds, now fully illuminated in Damien's absence. He was a broken man, his eyes squeezed tightly shut and his robes tattered where the daggers had struck.

There was a pause over the chat as everyone else absorbed what was going on and saw Aetherius in his full disgrace. Then there was the most incredible wave of noise as every single one of them hollered with all their being for Scorepeeus63 to finish him off. He was just standing there, paralyzed with fear against the competition leader... who was also paralyzed with fear.

At last, Aetherius stopped screaming and blinked against the torchlight. A sword appeared in Scorepeeus63's off hand. Aetherius saw him and looked aghast. Being a Scorpius clone, the young player had imitated Damien's own face. Aetherius babbled, pushing his hands together to create nothing but a dull gray light where the Arcane Missile should've been.

Scorepeeus63 stumbled forward, his sword held out clumsily in front of him as the least imposing battle cry of all time rang out through the dungeon in a broken falsetto chime.

"Yaaaaaaaaaaaaaaah!"

The clumsy strike inflicted 36 points of damage. It was enough. Aetherius finally stopped whimpering and collapsed to the ground. Dead.

The objective of Damien's week of efforts and planning, brought to fruition by a scared, solitary, level 9 Scorpius clone. There was total silence, then, as though from afar, came cheers, laughter, screaming and delirious wailing over the chat.

Aetherius had been brought down by a nine-year-old boy.

"What the hell are you doing? Stop that! What's wrong with you now, you idiot boy?"

Damien was laughing hysterically himself. He raised the visor, tears streaming down his face and still very much in the middle of his fit, to find the two CU agents looming over and staring at him in alarm. He tried to mouth the words, but he just couldn't do it.

"It's Aefffff— it's Atherahaha!"

The older CU agent's eyes narrowed bitterly as his companion's widened. Then the big man leaned down to murmur in his ear.

"Maybe we should get a doctor?"

His superior threw up his hand irritably and turned to leave. Damien garbled out his thanks.

"Th-thank you so much for pu-pulling off my headset! That's the funniest thing ah-aaaaah-aaaaaAAAHAHAHAHA-HAAHAHA—"

Looking extremely grumpy, the agent stomped out of the door, leaving his subordinate to hurry after him. Damien removed the headset so he could laugh properly, loud and hard, and was just about recovering when Lillian strode into the room. She caught his eye and returned his borderline manic grin.

"You saw it, then? Congratulations! I uploaded our footage to your profile myself, but this one's a bit more popular. I guess you can see why."

Damien might have been lying in a hospital bed, but he'd never felt better in his entire life. He managed to rein in his smile and fixed Lillian with the most serious gaze he was capable of producing. Which was not even half as serious as he felt the situation merited.

"I couldn't have done it without you. Thank you so much, for everything."

"You're more than welcome. By the way, you'll be staying under observation here until tomorrow. I'll bill the agents outside for your stay. By midnight tonight, you'll officially be the competition winner. Try not to get into any more trouble before then, huh?"

Damien jangled the handcuffs against the rail.

"I'll try not to."

Lillian smirked, poured a fresh cup of water and set it at his bedside.

"I have to get back to work. You have any problems, hit the buzzer and I'll be there."

She headed out and Damien turned off his headset and put it

on the bedside table before lying back to beam at the ceiling. He closed his eyes, and it wasn't long before he was deeply and peacefully asleep.

It was dark when he woke up. He blinked as the IMBA set rang out a calling tone at his bedside. He fumbled it with his free hand, jammed it on backward in the dark, then laboriously removed it while muttering angrily.

The calling tone rang on throughout without pause. By the time he'd got the headset on, he was awake enough to appreciate the seriousness of the caller ID.

Voice Chat Invitation: Mobius_Adler. Gamer I.D: 0000001 A/D

Oh. He checked the time in his HUD. It was 00:02. The competition was over. He hadn't known what to expect. Maybe a polite email, or a visit and a handshake from a Mobius representative some time later in the week. He certainly wasn't prepared to take a call from the CEO of Mobius Enterprises. He couldn't exactly reject it, either. The time ticked over to 00:03. Keeping him waiting any longer would be a bad idea. He accepted the call.

"Hello?"

"Congratulations on winning the competition, Damien Arkwright."

The man's tone was light and airy, as if he were calling simply to chat about the weather, but his voice was deep and self-assured. Damien swallowed, he hoped not audibly, and tried to remain as polite as possible.

"Thank you very much, sir. It wasn't easy."

Adler chuckled at that, something between a hum and a laugh.

"No. It most certainly was not. I must admit, I've been watching your exploits with great interest. I'm a big fan of yours!"

Damien had no idea if this was true or simply rehearsed, but it was a nice thing to say either way.

"Thank you, sir. Coming from you, that means a lot."

There was a loud clap and Adler continued a little faster.

"So, on to business! As the competition winner, I am pleased to inform you that you're the winner of the 100,000-credit prize. I would also like to extend to you the opportunity to become an official streamer for Saga Online. Your victory over Aetherius was remarkable, but it has left us with…. something of a vacuum to be filled in the advertising department. I would be very grateful if you were to take on this role. Especially since you are directly responsible for the vacuum in question."

"I'd be very happy to become a streamer for Mobius Enterprises."

There was another loud clap over the line.

"Excellent! I shall have an employee come and visit you with a copy of the contract in the morning. Please take your time to read the details and make sure you are satisfied before you sign. As you are technically a minor, it will require the signature of an adult custodian along with your own. Will that be a problem?"

Damien considered his position carefully. Although he didn't want to be rude, there were a number of problems he still had and this was a unique opportunity to solve them.

"About that, sir, there are a couple of things I should tell you about my current circumstances. I'd be very grateful if you could help me."

"By all means. I shall assist if I am able. What circumstances are you speaking of?"

Damien paused. He knew Adler was more than able of assisting him with his problems. Whether he would follow through with his word was another matter entirely. He took a couple of breaths to steady himself. Then he made his gambit.

"My mother is currently in hospital, waiting for a new heart. I would like the prize money to go directly into paying for her operation, including a bionic heart, as soon as possible."

He'd been worried, but there was another loud clap. Adler was doing a startlingly good impression of a magic genie.

"Done. I will put my aide onto it immediately. He will send an email asking for the details and you can hash it out between you. What prize money is not used to fund the operation will be sent to you at a later date. We can wait with the contract until your mother has recovered for her to countersign on your behalf. Is there something else?"

Adler had responded immediately. He probably already knew about the situation and had the solutions lined up. Damien made his second request more tentatively.

"Thank you, sir. In fact, there is. I am also in hospital. I had a seizure after someone removed the IMBA set your employee, Kevin, sent me for testing." There was a pause this time. Adler did not seem inclined to fill the gap. Damien waited as long as he dared before rambling on, explaining everything about CU and how they had presumably pressured Kevin in some manner, ending his story with the IMBA set being torn off his head.

When he finished, there was another silence, but this one had a different quality. There was a palpable tension over the line. When Adler's voice came back, it was stiffer than before.

"I am very sorry to hear that. I will of course have the headset returned to the R and D department, where they will face severe repercussions for their poor judgment. What is your request?"

Of all the people who'd suffered in the wake of Damien's actions, there was one who had suffered more than the rest. He'd never have an opportunity to make amends like this again.

"I would like Kevin to continue his role as my handler with Mobius Enterprises."

The silence was deafening. The blood rose in Damien's ears, but he held his nerve. The time ticked over from 00:15 to 00:16, yet still neither of them spoke.

Finally, Adler gave his answer.

"Kevin has already been dismissed following his interaction with CU. If what you tell me is true, his dismissal was based on false pretenses. To the best of my knowledge, CU came to my HR department stating that Kevin was aligned with dangerous criminal elements."

Damien was gobsmacked. So that's why Kevin had been fired. Lillian had been right: 'beardy douchebag' fit the bill perfectly. His temper was already rising when Adler's voice came back calm and crystal clear.

"However, given the 'criminal' in question was a homeless sixteen-year-old boy, I believe their accusations of aiding and abetting were overblown. Kevin should not have been fired for such a minor infraction. I'll see to it he is brought back to the company and that the matter is fully investigated on our end. Whoever oversaw retrieving you clearly had a swollen sense of importance. An official complaint against CU will be lodged by Mobius; that should be enough for them to back down. I doubt they want to risk a protracted legal battle."

Damien realized he'd started crying, an escape of his nerves and fears in the face of Adler's overwhelming support and generosity. He was going the extra mile on this for sure.

"Thank you. I really can't thank you enough."

"I'm only doing what's right, Mr. Arkwright. Besides, I can't have our new top streamer embroiled in a trumped-up case with CU. Rest assured, the matter will soon be behind you."

Damien sighed with relief.

"In return," Adler suddenly continued, "I am going to insert a non-disclosure agreement into your streamer contract, asking you not to mention the unfortunate experience you had testing our headset. Your valuable insight has prevented a catastrophic PR disaster for Mobius Enterprises. I would prefer to avoid any bad publicity stemming from this incident, especially since you'll be working with us in the near future."

Damien could see that this was a very shrewd decision, but he didn't hesitate to give his reply.

"Of course, sir. Thank you again."

"You are a very interesting young man," Adler said. "I shall watch your career with great interest. My aide will message you shortly. Until next time, Mr. Arkwright."

The call ended. Damien pulled off his IMBA set and sat in the darkness, breathing heavily. He'd done it.

Aetherius had been dethroned. Damien had won the contest.

Kevin would return to Mobius. His mother would be taken into surgery as soon as possible. The money he'd won would pay for the best doctors and the best new heart. Still, there was always a risk with these things. But it was now out of his hands.

He'd done all he could, and though slightly nervous, Damien closed his eyes and drifted back to sleep. For the first time in a week, he wasn't worried about tomorrow.

EPILOGUE

Days later, Damien stood outside another hospital room door, his mouth dry.

"She's still exhausted from the operation," a young doctor said. "But you can go in."

Lillian gave him a small nudge. "Go on."

Damien swallowed the lump in his throat then opened the door. There she was, lying on the bed, her head elevated by a mound of pillows. Damien ran to grab her hand. She looked so frail; little more than a shade. Yet the moment she set her eyes on him, color entered her cheeks and she gave him a huge, brave grin.

"Hello, Damien."

It was hopeless. The tears spilled down his cheeks, all his fear and longing expelling itself in an unstoppable flood. He pulled up her hand and set it against his cheek, the tears spilling over them. She stroked his face as she started to cry as well. They remained like that for a few minutes, none of the doctors daring to interrupt.

It was Cassandra who spoke first.

"How did you manage this? You didn't ask your father for money, did you?"

Damien shook his head, then choked out a single laugh. If only it had been that simple.

"No, I didn't, but... well, it's a long story."

Cassandra arched an eyebrow. "It's not like I've got much else to do."

She looked at him expectantly, but it was clearly a struggle to stay awake. She was halfway through stifling a yawn when her eyes widened again.

"Have you been able to study?" she added in a very motherly hurry. "You know the exams are coming up."

Damien's eyes widened. Now? She wanted to do this now? Despite himself, he blew out a sigh of relief. She was definitely on the mend.

"Not exactly, but there's a good bit of money on the horizon for me. You don't need to worry. Rest for now, I'll tell you all about it when you get home."

"That's... that's so... wonderful." She yawned deeply, eyelids fluttering to fight back sleep.

A gentle hand fell on Damien's shoulder.

"Let's come back later," Lillian said.

Damien nodded and gave his mother a final smile. "I love you."

"I love you too," she said. Her eyes closed, her chest rising and falling gently.

Damien rose and left with Lillian. A great weight, one that had been resting on his shoulders from that fateful moment in the kitchen, finally fell away.

He felt like he was in a dream, wafting through the hospital corridors on the way back to the waiting room.

Somehow, everything was going to be OK. All because he had never given up and was good at doing the thing he loved.

Playing Saga Online.

AFTERWORD

Hello again from the Portal Books Team,

On behalf of Oli, we'd like to thank you so much for reading *Occultist: Saga Online*. This book was a headache at times but one we've all poured blood sweat and tears into, Oli most of all. For a debut writer we are simply blown away by him.

Oli currently lives out in China and so his connection to regular social media channels can be patchy but he'd love to hear from anyone who has enjoyed his book. It would mean the world to him.

One way to reach out is over Facebook and if you join the Portal Books Facebook group you'll be able to find him in there:

www.facebook.com/groups/LitRPGPortal/

Like many out there, Oli's dream is to one day write full time. Another way you can help him out is by reviewing a review on Amazon and/or Goodreads.

Reviews really do make all the difference to a book's success on

Amazon. A brief two minutes of your time can help an author in immeasurable ways.

Finally, if you'd like to sample FREE content from our other incredible authors you can do so by signing up to the Portal Books mailing list. Doing so right now will grant access to the Story Bundle with over 45,000 words of LitRPG content, including the prequel story to Occultist - *Rising Tide*. Read how Aetherius turned from hero to villain.

Sign up at the link below:

https://portal-books.com/sign-up

By signing up you'll also be the first to hear about all our titles such as:

Bone Dungeon by Jonathan Smidt
God of Gnomes by L. M. Hughes
Mastermind: Titan Online by Steven Kelliher
Battle Spire (A Crafting LitRPG Book) by Michael R. Miller
The Nova Online Series by Alex Knight
Aether Frontier by Scott McCoskey
Dungeons of Strata by Graeme Penman
Cryoknight by Tim Johnson
Aztec Arcane by Peter Hackshaw
Empires Online by Anthony Wright

For more general discussions about the genre, these groups may be useful to you.

www.facebook.com/groups/LitRPGsociety/

www.facebook.com/groups/LitRPG.books/

www.facebook.com/groups/LitRPGGroup/

Best wishes,
The Portal Books Team
www.portal-books.com

MORE LITRPG FROM PORTAL BOOKS

Portal Books will release many new titles this year - it's going to be a big one. But out right now is our first Dungeon Core, *Bone Dungeon*!

"Reborn as a dark dungeon, Ryan was happy defeating adventurers with undead minions. Then a necromancer arrived, and un-life got a whole lot harder..."

It's available on Kindle Unlimited and Audio will follow soon from Soundbooth Theater!

Also out now is *Battle Spire: A Crafting LitRPG Book.* Battle Spire is a meeting of *World of Warcraft* and *Die Hard*, using crunchy LitRPG mechanics with a heavy focus on crafting.

It's available on Kindle Unlimited and Audio will follow soon from Soundbooth Theater!

We also have the sci-fi themed LitRPG, Nova Online Series: *"Imprisoned for a murder he didn't commit, Kaiden's only hope of early release is in serving as a Warden in the game-world of Nova Online.*
   Book 2 is now out!
   It's available on Kindle Unlimited and on Audio.

Printed in Great Britain
by Amazon